# THE PROVING GROUND

# Also by Michael Connelly

*Fiction*

The Black Echo
The Black Ice
The Concrete Blonde
The Last Coyote
The Poet
Trunk Music
Blood Work
Angels Flight
Void Moon
A Darkness More Than Night
City of Bones
Chasing the Dime
Lost Light
The Narrows
The Closers
The Lincoln Lawyer
Echo Park
The Overlook
The Brass Verdict
The Scarecrow
Nine Dragons
The Reversal
The Fifth Witness
The Drop
The Black Box
The Gods of Guilt
The Burning Room
The Crossing
The Wrong Side of Goodbye
The Late Show
Two Kinds of Truth
Dark Sacred Night
The Night Fire
Fair Warning
The Law of Innocence
The Dark Hours
Desert Star
Resurrection Walk
The Waiting
Nightshade

*Non-fiction*

Crime Beat

*Ebooks*

Suicide Run
Angle of Investigation
Mulholland Dive
The Safe Man
Switchblade

# THE PROVING GROUND

# MICHAEL CONNELLY

ORION

First published in Great Britain in 2025 by Orion Fiction,
an imprint of The Orion Publishing Group Ltd.
Carmelite House, 50 Victoria Embankment
London EC4Y 0DZ

An Hachette UK Company

The authorised representative in the EEA is Hachette Ireland,
8 Castlecourt Centre, Dublin 15, D15 XTP3,
Ireland (email: info@hbgi.ie)

1 3 5 7 9 10 8 6 4 2

Copyright © 2025 Hieronymus Inc.

The moral right of Michael Connelly to be identified as
the author of this work has been asserted in accordance
with the Copyright, Designs and Patents Act of 1988.

All rights reserved. No part of this publication may be
reproduced, stored in a retrieval system, or transmitted
in any form or by any means, electronic, mechanical,
photocopying, recording, or otherwise, without the
prior permission of both the copyright owner and the
above publisher of this book.

All the characters in this book are fictitious, and any resemblance
to actual persons, living or dead, is purely coincidental.

A CIP catalogue record for this book is
available from the British Library.

ISBN (Hardback) 978 1 3987 1906 4
ISBN (Export Trade Paperback) 978 1 3987 1907 1
ISBN (Audio) 978 1 3987 1910 1
ISBN (eBook) 978 1 3987 1909 5

Printed in Great Britain by Clays Ltd, Elcograf S.p.A.

www.orionbooks.co.uk

*For Daniel Daly and Roger Mills,*
*for twenty years of patiently answering the questions*

*We are engaged in a race against time to protect the children of our country from the dangers of AI. Indeed, the proverbial walls of the city have already been breached. Now is the time to act.*

—National Association of Attorneys General,
September 6, 2023

PART ONE

# THE CAGE

# 1

**TO SOME IT'S** a stage. A place where carefully choreographed drama takes place. To others, a chess match with moves designed and practiced weeks and sometimes months in advance. Where nothing is left to chance. Where the wrong moves have grave consequences and finality. Where the recruited audience sits in silent judgment with their hidden biases and contempt.

I have never thought of it that way. To me it's the Octagon, where mixed martial arts are deployed in brutal combat. Two go in; one comes out the victor. No one is left unbloodied. No one is left unscarred. This is what the courtroom is to me.

The hearing on this day was in civil court, a misnomer if there ever was one. There was nothing remotely civil about this fight. *Randolph versus Tidalwaiv Technologies LLC* was one of those rare cases where the stakes went far beyond the walls of the courtroom or even the reach of the federal court for the Central District of California. This was a fight for the future of everyone—or at least that was how I would argue it.

It was a pretrial hearing before US district court judge Margaret Ruhlin. I had known her since her days as a member of the local defense bar, back when she was called Peggy Ruhlin and hung out after court hours at the bar at the Redbird. She was now a veteran and much respected jurist appointed to the bench during the Obama years. She had consolidated cross-complaints from the parties and was attempting to avoid a trial delay by refereeing the disputes. I was in favor of that but the lawyers at the other table, the Mason brothers, would have liked nothing better than to push the trial off for another few months or more. Tidalwaiv was for sale and its investors were hoping one of the big techs would swallow it. The three *M*s were circling — Microsoft, Meta, and Musk. This trial and its outcome could be the difference between millions and billions.

I was determined not to let them delay. Tidalwaiv had turned over twelve terabytes of discovery — enough when printed out to literally line the walls of a warehouse with file boxes. But what was important in those thousands and thousands of pages was heavily redacted, making the documents virtually useless to me. I needed to find what they were hiding in those pages or I was going to lose the most important case of my life.

The judge was patiently waiting for my response to one of the Masons, who had stood up and claimed that the redactions in the discovery materials were necessary because of proprietary protections in the very competitive world of generative artificial intelligence. He said that the information withheld from me amounted to the keys to the kingdom. And they weren't going to give them away.

"Mr. Haller," the judge prompted. "Your response, please."

"Yes, Your Honor," I said.

Following the judge's courtroom protocol, I stood and went to the lectern located between the tables for the plaintiff and the defendant.

"Your Honor, the defense's argument is specious at best," I began.

"We are not talking about the keys to the kingdom here. We're talking about key evidence that is being withheld because, as Mr. Mason well knows, it is inculpatory. It supports the plaintiff's case. Tidalwaiv's creation told an impressionable young man to take his father's gun to school and—"

"Mr. Haller," the judge interrupted. "It is not necessary for you to repeat your cause of action with every objection. I am sure the media you invited here today appreciates it, but the court does not."

The judge gestured toward the front row of the gallery, where members of the media sat shoulder to shoulder. Cameras and recording devices were not allowed in federal court. Each reporter, even the TV people, was reduced to taking notes by hand. And at the end of the row was a courtroom artist sketching yours truly for CNN. Pen and paper seemed so antiquated in a world where the electronic media reigned, along with its coconspirators artificial intelligence and the internet.

"Thank you, Judge," I said. "The point is, this case is about guardrails. Tidalwaiv says they had guardrails in place but won't reveal them, because they are allegedly proprietary. That doesn't wash, Your Honor. The plaintiff is entitled to understand how Tidalwaiv's artificial-intelligence-generated creation jumped those guardrails and told a teenager it was okay to shoot people."

The Masons stood up in unison to object. They were alone at the defense table, their client choosing not to send a representative to court for these pretrial skirmishes.

The twins conferred and then Marcus sat down, leaving Mitchell to state their argument.

"Your Honor, the plaintiff's attorney is once again misstating the facts and evidence," he said. "He is talking to the media, not the court."

I quickly shot back, since I was still at the lectern.

"How do we know the facts and evidence if they won't provide complete discovery materials?" I asked, my arms out wide.

Ruhlin held her hands up in a signal for silence.

"Enough," she said. "Mr. Mason, please move to the lectern."

I retook my seat next to my client, Brenda Randolph, who had tears on her cheeks. Any reference made in court to her murdered child brought tears. It wasn't a show. It wasn't coaching. It was genuine loss and grief that would never go away no matter what happened down the line in this courtroom. I reached over and put my hand on her arm to console her. I needed to pay attention to the judge and my opponents but knew how difficult these moments were for her and that they would only get harder as the trial proceeded.

"Mr. Mason, the court tends to agree with Mr. Haller in this matter," Ruhlin said. "How do you propose we rectify this issue? He is entitled to full discovery."

"We can't, Your Honor," Mitchell Mason replied from the lectern. "Rather than reveal our proprietary sciences, codes, and methods, we have offered the plaintiff a generous settlement package, but that was rejected so that the plaintiff's attorney can continue to grandstand in front of the media with his wholly unsubstantiated claims and—"

"Let me stop you right there, Mr. Mason," the judge said. "Every plaintiff has the right to a trial. We're not going to go down the road of judging motivations for settling or not settling this case."

"Then, Your Honor," Mason countered, "we are happy to submit to a court-appointed special master to review the materials we have provided and determine what is discoverable and what should remain redacted as proprietary."

Now I stood to object, but the judge ignored me.

"I will reluctantly consider the offer in light of what that would mean to the court's calendar," Ruhlin said. "But for now, let's move on to our next issue. Mr. Mason, you—"

"Your Honor," I said. "Before moving on, may I respond to the defense's proposal of a special master?"

"Mr. Haller, I know your response," Ruhlin said. "You object because you want to keep this case on course to trial. If you wish, you may electronically submit a cogent objection, and I will take it into consideration before I rule. For now, let's move on. The defense has a motion before the court to strike one person from the plaintiff's preliminary witness list. A person named Rikki Patel, who is a former employee of the defendant, Tidalwaiv. Mr. Mason, do you wish to state your claim for the record?"

Mitchell Mason was wearing a blue-black Armani suit with his signature patterned vest to complete the power ensemble. He had styled but short brown hair and a close-cropped beard just beginning to show some distinguished gray. That was how I told them apart. Mitchell had the beard. Marcus did not.

"I do, Your Honor," Mitchell said. "As stated in the motion, Mr. Patel is a former employee of Tidalwaiv and upon leaving the company's employ signed a nondisclosure agreement, a copy of which was submitted with the motion. Your Honor, very simply, this is the plaintiff's attempt to do an end run around us and get proprietary company data and information, and we object strenuously to Mr. Patel even giving a deposition, let alone testifying in open court in this matter."

"Very well, you may take a seat," Ruhlin said. "Mr. Haller, I notice that you didn't file a response to the motion. Are you withdrawing Mr. Patel from your witness list?"

I moved back to the lectern.

"On the contrary, Your Honor," I said. "Rikki Patel is a key witness for the plaintiff. He was in the lab when this company birthed the AI companion they call Clair and set her loose on unsuspecting—"

"Enough with the sound bites, Mr. Haller," Ruhlin barked. "I have warned you. You play to me, not the people in the first row."

"Yes, Your Honor."

"Now, why should the court not enforce the nondisclosure agreement signed by your intended witness?"

"Your Honor, in essence, this is a product-liability case and it is contrary to the public interest to bar a former employee from testifying about Tidalwaiv's recklessness regarding the safety of its product. California courts routinely refuse to enforce nondisclosure agreements, because they violate fundamental public policy. My client and the public are not party to the NDA and they have an interest in learning the facts and circumstances regarding how an AI companion encouraged a teenage boy to kill his ex-girlfriend. Rikki Patel isn't a witness who will divulge trade secrets or privileged information; he will testify about Tidalwaiv's failure—"

"But last I checked, we were in federal court, Mr. Haller. Not California court."

"That may be so, Judge, but the court should also know that the NDA was signed under duress. Mr. Patel was fearful that if he did not sign it upon leaving the employ of Tidalwaiv, there would be consequences for himself and his family."

Marcus Mason stood and objected, raising his hands, palms up, in a *Where did this outlandish claim come from?* gesture.

"Hold right there, Mr. Mason," the judge said. "That is a very strong statement, Mr. Haller. Again, I warn you, meritless statements made for the benefit of the media and the jury pool will not be tolerated by this court."

"Your Honor," I said, "Mr. Patel is ready to testify in chambers or in open court about the fears and pressures that led him to sign an NDA with language that is threatening in and of itself. He should not be bound by the document, and I can assure the court that his purpose as a witness is not to reveal the proprietary information the company seems so concerned about. He will testify about the objections he raised about the Clair project from the very start. Objections that were overruled and that the company clearly doesn't want the public to know about."

"Your Honor?" Mason said, in case the judge had forgotten he was standing in front of her.

"Go ahead, Mr. Mason," Ruhlin said.

I went back to my table and Marcus Mason took the lectern. He was the clean-shaven twin who wore bow ties rather than patterned vests with his Armani.

"Your Honor, this is trial by ambush," he said. "Nothing more, nothing less. Mr. Haller, when he was defending criminals, was known as an attorney who wielded the media like a club. He is doing it again here. Of course he did not respond to the motion electronically. Why should he when he could invite a media audience into US district court to hear his exaggerated claims and outlandish lies? There is no threat in the wording of the nondisclosure agreement beyond what is in every NDA ever signed. There was no threat to Patel and there is no legal argument that supports his being able to break the agreement in order to testify in this matter."

I had to hold back a smile. Marcus Mason was good. He was clearly the smarter of the two brothers and the one I had to key in on. The bow ties served to soften his image as a killer in the courtroom. But that was okay, because I was a killer too. The smile I held back was brought by his mentioning my days in the criminal defense bar as a pejorative. It was true I had made my name in crime. From billboards to bus benches, from the criminal courts to the county jails, I was known as the Lincoln Lawyer. Have case, will travel. I promised reasonable doubt for a reasonable fee. It was rough-and-tumble work. The California Bar waited for me to trip up ethically. The cops waited for me to trip up criminally. Everybody waited for me to fall. That was the legacy that followed me in this town. But I'd had my fill of it and moved on. And in the two years since I left the crowded and grimy halls of criminal justice, I had found new levels of dirty work and dangers in the supposedly genteel high-ceilinged courtrooms of civil practice. I was at home, and the Mason brothers had no idea what they were in for.

The judge closed the hearing by saying that she would take the oral arguments and written submissions under consideration and issue rulings on both matters the following Monday.

"Court is now adjourned," she said.

The judge left the bench and headed to her chambers. The Mason brothers packed up their documents and law books while the representatives of the media started to file out of the front row. I returned to the plaintiff's table and took a seat next to my client. Brenda Randolph was a small woman with haunted eyes that would never see happiness again. She worked as a lens grinder at an optometry lab in the Valley. She was using all her vacation and comp time to attend every hearing related to what she called her daughter's case.

"You okay, Brenda?" I whispered.

"Yes," she said. "I mean, no. I'll never be okay. Every time her name is mentioned or anybody talks about what happened, I lose it. I can't help it. I'm sorry."

"Don't be sorry. Just be yourself."

"Do you think the judge will rule in our favor?"

"She should."

The Masons left their table and went through the gate. They said nothing to me as they passed.

"You guys have a good weekend," I called out.

I got no response.

# 2

**OUTSIDE THE COURTROOM** door, a man waited for me in the hallway. I had seen him inside during the hearing, sitting by himself in the back row of the gallery. If he was a journalist, he was unfamiliar to me. I knew most of the court reporters in town by sight, if not by name and acquaintance. But the lawsuit had garnered a fair amount of national attention and I had heard from and seen some members of the national media tribe for the first time. This man carried a backpack over his shoulder and wore a sport jacket but no tie. That told me he probably wasn't a lawyer—at least not one with business in the building. He stood back while I whispered a goodbye to my client and told her I would be in touch the minute I received a ruling from the judge on the motions just argued. As soon as we separated, the stranger approached. He looked to be in his early fifties and had a full head of brown-going-gray hair. He looked like an aging surfer. It took one to know one.

"Mr. Haller, I was hoping to buy you a cup of coffee," he said.

"I don't need coffee," I said. "I'm jacked from that hearing. Do I know you? Are you a journalist?"

"Uh, a writer, yes. I wanted to talk to you about something that could be mutually beneficial."

"What kind of writer?"

"I write books about technology. And how it can be turned against us. I also write a Substack column. Same subject."

I looked at him for a long moment.

"And you want to write about this case?"

"I do."

"And what's the part that would be beneficial to me?"

"Well, if we could sit down for a few minutes, I could lay it out for you."

"Where? I've got a meeting across the street in"—I raised my wrist to check my watch—"twenty minutes."

It was a lie. I just wanted to put a time limit on this conversation in case it wasn't to my liking. I was planning to go across the street to the district attorney's office, but I had no appointment. I intended to talk my way in.

"Give me ten minutes," the writer said.

"Do you need coffee?" I asked.

"Not if you don't."

"Okay, let's go into one of the attorney rooms down the hall here. That would be quickest and quietest."

"Lead the way."

I started down the hall, then stopped.

"What's your name?" I asked.

"Jack McEvoy," he said. "Nice to meet you."

He held out his hand and I shook it. He had a strong grip and met my eye without hesitation. My impression at that moment was that this might be the start of a good thing.

# 3

**THE ATTORNEY ROOMS** in the federal courthouse were tiny and furnished with only a small table and four chairs. They were designed for lawyers to confer with clients and witnesses before entering court. I found one that was empty and slid the red OCCUPIED placard across the AVAILABLE sign. I opened the door and signaled McEvoy in first. We sat on opposite sides of the table. I took a notebook out of my briefcase and started the meeting by asking him to spell his last name. He did.

"That name and the spelling are familiar," I said. "Should I know your work?"

"I've published three nonfiction books in the past twenty or so years," McEvoy said. "They hit bestseller lists. Briefly. But they all have L.A. connections."

"What are the titles?"

"*The Poet* was my first one. It was about the internet."

He paused in case I was going to exclaim that I'd loved the book. I said nothing.

"Uh, then a lot of years went by before I did a book called *The Scarecrow*," he continued. "That was about data mining. And then my last book was called *Fair Warning*. That was a few years ago. It was about the unregulated DNA industry."

I nodded.

"*Fair Warning*. Yes, I remember that," I said. "That was the one about the killer who used DNA to find his victims. I know some of the attorneys who were mentioned in that one."

"All my books deal with technological advances," McEvoy said. "Advances that were taken advantage of by criminals and other unscrupulous people."

"And it was like a magazine or something, right? *Fair Warning*, I mean."

"It was based on a news site focused on consumer protection, but the owner-editor retired and it shut down. But I bought the brand rights to the name. Now it's a Substack that I write."

"Of course you have a Substack. It's called *Fair Warning*?"

"That's right. It's about the follies of technology. The Substack, I mean."

I nodded and studied him. I was more than interested but didn't want to show it yet.

"I'm beginning to see why you want to be involved in this case," I said.

"I thought you would," he said.

"So, what is this case to you? A Substack or a book?"

"It could be both," he replied without hesitation. "And a podcast. And a movie. Your case encapsulates everything I've been researching and writing about generative artificial intelligence. There are new lawsuits filed against AI systems every week, but this is the case that is going to trial, it seems. I think it brings everything together, the good and bad of this world-changing technology. It's a home run, if you ask me."

"Okay, so you get a home run out of it. What does my client get?"

"My research. My expertise. I have connections that I think can help you. Bring me inside the case and let me work for you. I won't write a word about it until there's a verdict."

I tried to keep a skeptical look on my face, but what McEvoy didn't know was that I was drowning. I was overwhelmed by discovery and lacked the wherewithal and expertise to deal with it. By that, I mean I lacked time and understanding. Much of the science sailed over my head. It left me scared that I would stumble into trial uninformed and unready.

I already had an investigator, and he was great at finding witnesses and conducting field investigations. But he was not great at wading through terabytes of code and Silicon Valley memos. It had recently dawned on me that I was in over my head with this case. In the courtroom I was a killer, but I needed weapons to kill with. What McEvoy was presenting to me seemed like a lifeline thrown to a drowning man. I was trying not to give anything away but knew that if I let McEvoy spend just fifteen minutes at the warehouse, he would understand my situation and how dire it was.

"Let you work for me — what does that mean?" I asked. "I took this case on a contingency basis. I don't win, I don't get paid. Right now, there's no money for a researcher."

"I'm not asking to be paid," McEvoy said. "Just let me inside the wire. Let me be a fly on the wall. I help you and you help me."

"I have to talk to my client."

"Of course."

"How do I reach you?"

McEvoy was ready with a business card. I noticed that the logo for his Substack underlined its focus: The *ai* in *Fair Warning* was embossed in red.

Jack McEvoy
Writer
*FAIR WARNING*

Tidalwaiv did the same thing with their logo, though the *ai* in *Tidalwaiv* was in a soothing blue tone. I put the card in my pocket and told McEvoy that I'd think about his proposition and be in touch after discussing it with Brenda Randolph.

# 4

THE ENTRANCE TO the CCB was across the street and down a half block from the federal courthouse. On my way, I called my investigator, Cisco Wojciechowski, who had stuck with me during the transition from criminal to civil practice even though there was a steep drop-off in the work I required from him. He answered the phone with a question instead of a greeting.

"How'd we do?"

"The judge took both motions under advisement and will issue her rulings Monday."

"Damn. You want me to call Patel? He was hoping to know today."

"No, I'll call him. I want you to run somebody down for me."

"A witness?"

"No, a writer. Jack McEvoy. He wants to help us."

"Help us how?"

"He writes about technology. Has a blog or a Substack or whatever you call it these days. He's also written books. He wants to be a fly on the wall — our wall — and then write a book about the case, with the larger story being about unchecked AI. He says in exchange, he'll be part of the team and help us weed through the discovery download."

"Mick, you really want to bring a stranger into this? That's risky."

I was at Temple Street, waiting to cross, and I did my usual turnaround to see if anyone was behind me. Tidalwaiv had massive resources in this fight and billions at stake. The company's founder, Victor Wendt, had promised stockholders at the last board meeting that this case would go away quietly and inexpensively. But here I was, pushing it toward trial. I constantly felt that I was being watched.

There was no one behind me. At least no one that I could see.

"That's why I want you to check him out," I said. "He's got three books he said were all bestsellers."

"You got the titles?" Cisco asked.

"I just remember the last one. *Fair Warning*. That's also the name of his—"

"Oh, I know this guy. Lorna loves his stuff."

Lorna was my office manager. She was also Cisco's wife and my ex-wife. But somehow it worked.

"There you go," I said. "I just want to know if I can trust him enough to bring him inside the wire. We're drowning in technical discovery. It would help to have another pair of eyes, especially if he truly knows his shit."

"I'm on it," Cisco said. "Where are you headed now?"

"The CCB to see if I can get in to see Maggie."

"You got the black box with you?"

"I have it."

"A homecoming in criminal court. Good luck with that."

"I'm probably going to need it."

I disconnected and headed across Temple to the main entrance of the Criminal Courts Building. There were a lot of things I missed about the place, but the elevators were not one of them. They were just as slow and crowded as I remembered from the years I had toiled in this building's hallways and courtrooms. Once I was through the security checkpoint and metal detector—during which I had to explain what the black box in my briefcase was—it took me almost half an hour to get up to the sixteenth floor and the office of the Los Angeles County district attorney. I went to the reception counter, identified myself, and explained that I had no appointment but wished to see the district attorney. I said I wanted to talk to her about her daughter because I knew that would get me in.

The seats in the waiting area were plastic on chrome legs, a style that had gone out of fashion a couple of decades earlier. But they had endured, like most of the furnishings of the building, and did the job. I was in one of those chairs for twenty minutes before I was invited back by the receptionist. This moved me to another waiting room outside the DA's actual office. This time, the chair was a little more comfortable and even had a cushion, threadbare though it was. And this time the wait was only ten minutes. I was granted entrance to the inner sanctum, where my first ex-wife, Maggie McPherson, fresh from her installment as the duly elected DA, sat at a large desk with a row of flags lining the wall behind her. She had won the office in a special election. The previous DA had resigned abruptly after the *Los Angeles Times* unearthed and published a series of texts he had written that exposed his racial biases.

I spread my arms, holding up my briefcase.

"Wow," I said. "Maggie McFierce on top of the world."

"Well, on top of this world, maybe," she said. "I was wondering when you would just pop in, although using our daughter to sleaze your way in was a little unexpected."

"Sleaze my way in? All I said was I wanted to talk to you about her. How is she doing?"

"As far as I know, she's doing good."

"Well, I wish she were doing good back here at home."

"She's just taking a gap year. She was very helpful during the campaign and earned the break, as far as I'm concerned."

"Good, then you can pay her bills, since you're the only one around here with a steady paycheck."

Our daughter, Hayley, with a very expensive law degree from USC in her back pocket, had decided—after growing up with two lawyers for parents—that she was not sure she actually wanted to practice law. She was trying to find herself while riding waves in Hawaii with the help of a boyfriend who had no discernible income but an impressive tan and an even more impressive collection of surfboards.

"Hey, I'm not the one who taught her how to surf," Maggie said. "That's on you. I'm also not the one who decided to give up a lucrative criminal defense practice at the height of my career."

"Yeah, well, thanks for the reminders," I said. "Happy new year to you too."

"And to you. I see you've got your briefcase. That tells me this might be more than a social visit."

Maggie was always perceptive when it came to me. I couldn't ever see her without lamenting the fact that we hadn't gone the distance. She was wearing a conservative blue business suit with the blouse buttoned to the neck. Her dark curls had a few touches of gray in them. She had aged beautifully in the thirty years I had known her.

"Never could get anything by you," I said. "Yes, there's something I need to talk to you about."

"Have a seat," she said. "I make no promises I won't keep."

She smiled. That was one of her campaign slogans.

I pulled out one of the chairs in front of her desk and sat down, putting my briefcase on the floor. The flags behind her were lined up so tightly, they looked like one curtain of silken colors.

"That's a lot of flags," I said.

"One for every country of origin of our constituency," she said.

"You might have to get rid of a few of those if Trump deports everybody like he's saying." The new president had won the election the same night Maggie had. His campaign was built on a promise to eliminate illegal immigration. As Maggie was elected as a nonpartisan candidate, she did not take the political bait.

"So, what's your ask, Mickey?"

"Is that all I am now, an ask?"

"Well, like I said, I assume it's why you're here."

"I was also a platinum-level contributor to the campaign."

"You were, and I very much appreciate that. So, just tell me, what's going on?"

"I suppose you are reviewing cases and getting up to speed on things."

"I am, and I haven't seen any with your name attached as counselor for the defense."

"And I hope it stays that way. Besides, the conflict of interest with you being DA would certainly cause your office and mine headaches we don't need. But there is a case being handled by your office in juvie court that cuts across one of my cases in civil."

She nodded.

"The Aaron Colton case," she said. "I spent an hour with Will Owensby on it before the holiday break."

That surprised me. She had taken office immediately after the election, but that was less than two months ago. There had been holiday breaks, staffing decisions to make, and a mountain of other cases to get current on, so I had hoped she wasn't prepped on the case yet. It would have been easier to point her in the direction I wanted her to go if she hadn't been knowledgeable about the inner workings of the case, and I realized my path to success was going to be steep.

"Owensby is a good lawyer," I said. "But he's a stickler, you know what I mean?"

"You mean he wants to stick to the rules of the game?" Maggie asked.

"What I'm saying is he's focused on his case, which is fine. But he's not looking at the bigger picture."

"Which is..."

"Let's call it a fuller justice."

"I have to say, he came in here and talked about the case for an hour, and your name never came up. I know about your civil case because I saw it on the news. But it has nothing to do with our criminal case."

"What? No, that's wrong. It has everything to do with your case. Aaron Colton killed my client's daughter because of an AI chatbot that went rogue. You're putting the kid away, but what about the company that made the app with no thought about the consequences of unleashing it on impressionable minds? That's the bigger crime here, Mags. You have to see that."

Maggie looked down at her hands folded on her desk. It was a move I had seen many times. She looked as if she were waiting out a storm — that storm being me. When she finally spoke, it was in an even tone that I also recognized from a thousand skirmishes before this one.

"So, what do you want, Mickey?"

"I want you to do the right thing. I want access to the kid's computer."

She shook her head emphatically.

"No, that's not going to happen," she said. "First, this is a juvenile case, and second, it's not even close to being adjudicated. We don't share evidence in open cases whether it involves a juvenile or not."

"I need to show what happened and why to make my case," I said.

"Then delay your case, and once my office is finished with Colton, we can talk about what I can share."

"It's not that simple. Your case is going to run on for years. You've got the ongoing psychological evaluation and then the competency hearing. After that, you'll have to decide whether to kick it up to adult court, and the case will just go on and on. But time is of the essence here. That company is selling this app to people all around the world. Kids, Maggie. Victor Wendt, the company's founder, says he sees a time when every kid has an AI companion, like they're Barbie dolls. This will happen again, Maggie, and *my* case—not yours—is the best shot at stopping it."

Maggie shook her head, a dismissive gesture I had seen too many times to count.

"Spoken like a champion of the people," she said. "And I don't suppose there's going to be a fat check for damages at the end of your great public-service trial, is there?"

"It's not about money," I said. "If it were, we'd have settled already. The company's offered seven figures to make this go away. But we don't want it to go away and get swept under the rug. We want to stop this from happening again."

"We?"

"My client. Brenda Randolph. She lost her sixteen-year-old daughter. Her only child, Mags. She doesn't want anyone else to lose theirs. That's what this case is about. It's about changing the world for the better and making it safe for these kids."

"That's very eloquent. I seem to recall from the news that you filed this in federal court."

"That's right."

"Who's the judge?"

"Peggy Ruhlin."

"So why aren't you here with a subpoena from her? Either she already turned you down or—more likely—you want to get access to the kid's computer on the sly so your opponent doesn't know you have it."

I had no response to that. She was a good lawyer and knew me well.

"Look, Mickey, I can't do this," she said. "I'm not going to get involved in one of your Lincoln Lawyer moves."

"It's not a move," I said. "And by the way, I got rid of all but one of the Lincolns two years ago. The only one I kept is under a tarp in my warehouse."

"Well, my hands are tied by the rule of law."

"No, they're not, Mags. You're the district attorney for this county now. If you want to do the right thing, you can do the right thing."

I pulled my briefcase onto my lap and opened it. I took out a black metal box about the size of a hardcover book and put it on her desk.

"What is that?" Maggie asked. "Don't put that there."

"I'm leaving it," I said. "It's an external hard drive. It holds up to twelve terabytes of data. You can download all the data from Aaron Colton's laptop onto it and I'll take it from there."

I stood up.

"Mickey, don't leave that here," Maggie said. "It's not going to happen."

I headed for the office door, ignoring her command. As I opened it, I turned back and looked at her.

"It will happen if you do the right thing," I said.

Then I walked out and closed the door behind me.

# 5

JUDGE RUHLIN DELIVERED her rulings by email promptly at nine a.m. Monday. I was in the Arts District downtown at the warehouse where I had once stored a fleet of Lincolns and that I now used primarily for records storage and as an office. In terse rulings short on explanatory backup, the judge simply split the decision, giving both sides a win. She cleared the path for Rikki Patel to testify as a plaintiff's witness in the case but allowed Tidalwaiv to keep its redactions to the discovery material, leaving me to decide whether or not to delay the trial by going with (and paying) a special master to review the thousands of documents and determine what should be removed from redaction. It was passing the buck. I had actually thought the opposite rulings would come, that I would lose Patel but get unredacted discovery. So I didn't know how to react. If I had lost Patel, I would simply have sent Cisco out to find another person who'd witnessed the inner workings of the company. Going with a special master would delay the trial by months if not a year or more. And whether or not I chose to delay things, the rulings gave Tidalwaiv an opportunity to slow the case with their own appeal on the Patel decision.

McEvoy arrived at the warehouse promptly at ten a.m., as I'd instructed him in a text. I walked him back toward the office, but he stopped when he saw two people behind the mesh of a fenced-off area in one of the storage bays.

"Wait, is that a Faraday cage?" he asked.

"With this case, it's an absolute necessity," I said.

"That was going to be my first suggestion to you. Can I take a look?"

"Uh, be my guest."

The cage was a twelve-foot-by-twelve-foot cube of chain link. Across the top was a crosshatch of wires supporting copper mesh that also draped down all four sides of the cage, preventing all manner of electronic intrusion. Inside was 144 square feet of workspace. The cage was ground zero for *Randolph v. Tidalwaiv*.

There was one entrance, through a curtain made of the same copper mesh. I held it open for McEvoy.

Cisco Wojciechowski and Lorna Taylor were standing in front of Big Bertha, Lorna's name for the industrial-size printer I had leased for dealing with case-discovery materials. Two ten-foot-long tables on opposite sides of the cage held printed documents that were stacked according to category—system development, architecture, testing, and so on. On one of the tables, Lorna had set up a desktop computer with twin wide-screen monitors, a twelve-terabyte external drive, and no connection to the internet. Despite the warehouse's alarms, cameras, and other protections, that hard drive went home with one of us every night in a locking Faraday bag.

After introducing McEvoy to the team, I explained all this to him.

"You're going completely off the grid," he said.

"Trying to," Lorna said. "As much as we can."

"Why?" McEvoy said. "Has there been an intrusion?"

"We're trying to avoid that," Lorna said.

"We're taking no chances," Cisco said.

He said it in a tone that suggested that McEvoy had asked a stupid question.

I walked over to the table with the computer and tapped a finger on the hard drive. It was a duplicate of the one I had left on Maggie McPherson's desk the Friday before.

"This is what we got in discovery," I said. "And I think we'd be fools not to consider that a company like Tidalwaiv will take any advantage they can in terms of gathering intel about the case against them."

"You think it's bugged," McEvoy said.

"I think we need to assume, given what's at stake in this case, that the opposition is desperate to know what we're up to," I said. "But let's talk about that in my office. There are a few things I want to go over with you before we get further into anything."

I held my hand toward the curtain and McEvoy started that way.

"Nice to meet you," he said to Cisco and Lorna.

"Likewise," Cisco said sullenly.

It was obvious that Cisco wasn't convinced we needed McEvoy.

I walked McEvoy back to my office, which had been the dispatch room when the building was the operations center of a taxi company in the 1960s. After that, it was an artists' co-op for half a century, and I'd bought it in a bankruptcy auction. The small room where I had a desk had an internal window that looked out on the rest of the warehouse, including the cage. It also had an old stand-up Mosler safe that was too heavy ever to be moved and a private bathroom with what appeared to be hundred-year-old fixtures.

I stepped behind the desk and pointed McEvoy to the chair on the other side.

"Have a seat," I said as I sat down. "You asked about intrusion into the cage. We're not so worried about that. I think we have that buttoned up pretty good, and one of us takes the external drive home every night. My main concern is bringing someone I can't trust inside the wire."

"Meaning me," McEvoy said.

"Exactly. So I had Cisco spend most of the weekend running you down. I trust him and he's very good at what he does. He's been with me a lot of years, and he says you're clean. He told me you even went to jail once for protecting a source."

"Sixty-three days."

"I've had days in jail too. Not fun. Anyway, before we go any further, I need you to sign a few documents that will make me feel okay about you being part of this and writing about it down the line."

"Good. What do you want me to sign?"

I opened a drawer and brought out the three paper-clipped documents I had prepared Sunday while watching the football playoffs. I slid them across the desk.

"I've got a nondisclosure that's pretty basic," I said. "You can't reveal anything you see or hear on this case until the trial reaches a conclusion by settlement or verdict."

"Is settling a consideration?" McEvoy asked. "That would be anticlimactic. For a book, I mean."

"Well, it's not really my call. It's my client's decision, but she has turned down all offers so far because they don't include what she wants more than money. She wants what I call a triple-A settlement: accountability, action, and apology."

"I get two out of three. What action do you — or does she — want?"

"We want them to fix their damn product that got her daughter killed."

"Right."

I pointed to the three documents McEvoy had spread out on the desk in front of him.

"Then there is a personal declaration that you are not working in any capacity for Tidalwaiv," I said.

McEvoy scoffed.

"Are you serious?" he said.

"Deadly serious," I said. "This is my get-out-of-jail-free card. If it turns out you're working as a double agent, this will get me a new trial."

"Okay, fine. What's the third one?"

"That's about the book. I want to see the manuscript before you publish it."

McEvoy was shaking his head before I finished the sentence.

"I can't do that," he said. "No journalist shows the subject of a story the story before it's published. No good journalist, anyway."

"You're not a journalist anymore, Jack," I said. "At least not here. You're part of the plaintiff's team now. I'm going to put you to work in the cage, and you will become part of the case. You're an employee, and as your employer, I can demand access to and approval of work product. If you sign these documents, you will also be bound by attorney-client privilege, which extends beyond the verdict and judgment in this case. Both my client and I want to make sure you don't violate that privilege."

"Are you paying me?"

"Not now. When you sell the book, you get paid. Look, I'm not debating this. You want in on this case, sign the docs. If you don't want to, let's just shake hands and say it didn't work out."

McEvoy stared at the documents on the otherwise empty desk for a long moment.

"Can I have a lawyer look at these?" he finally asked.

"Sure," I said. "I recommend it. But you're not going in the cage until I have them signed and in the safe."

I jerked a thumb over my shoulder at the Mosler in the corner. I did not tell him that the safe had come with the warehouse and was so old that the combination was lost to time and the locking mechanism was disabled.

"Fuck it," McEvoy said. "Give me a pen."

"You sure?" I asked. "You're not going to be able to say later that I coerced you."

I pointed up to the corner of the ceiling over the office door. McEvoy turned and looked up at the camera I'd had installed after taking over the space.

"Records sound too," I said.

"Just give me a pen," McEvoy said.

I opened a drawer and took out a blue felt-tip pen I used for signing contracts.

"I thought all writers carried pens," I said.

"Well, I guess I left mine at home," McEvoy said.

I handed the pen across the desk and watched as McEvoy scanned each page of each document and then signed and initialed where appropriate.

"Sort of ironic, isn't it?" he said as he was signing.

"What is?" I asked.

"You making me sign an NDA while last week in court you were making NDAs sound like the instruments of corporate devils."

"Yeah, well, that was in court. I don't think we'll ever get to court on this one."

He finished signing the documents and slid them back across the desk to me. I squared them up in one stack and then swiveled my chair around to the Mosler. After turning the handle and pulling the heavy iron door open, I put them on a shelf that I assumed had once been stacked with cash for cabdrivers to make change with.

After closing the safe, I turned back to McEvoy.

"Welcome to the team," I said.

McEvoy nodded and spread his arms wide.

"What do you want me to do?" he asked.

"This case is going to be won or lost in discovery," I said. "I want you in the cage. Work with Lorna. Tidalwaiv is hiding something in the redactions of the documents they turned over, I know it. If we find it, I think we win."

# 6

I WALKED McEVOY back to the cage to leave him with Lorna. He looked at the stacks on the tables, all of them at least six inches high.

"Anyplace in particular you want me to start?" he asked.

"Lorna, which one is training and testing?" I asked.

"That one," Lorna said. She pointed to the shortest stack.

"Start there," I said. "Take notes. Look for flaws, look for shortcuts. Figure out what they're hiding."

"Sure," McEvoy said. "Easy enough."

I noted the sarcasm. McEvoy moved toward the table.

"Cisco, you're with me," I said. "Let's go."

"Where we going?" Cisco asked.

"To see Rikki Patel."

"You sure you need me?"

"Yes, Cisco, let's go."

I went through the copper curtain and headed toward the warehouse door. I registered Cisco's reluctance as concern about leaving

Lorna with McEvoy. I didn't address it until we were outside and at my car. I looked at him across the roof.

"You vetted him yourself and he came up clean," I said. "So what's the problem?"

"With McEvoy?" Cisco said. "No problem."

"You don't have to worry about Lorna. She can handle herself."

"I know she can. But I still have to worry about her. That's my job."

"Your other job. Right now, I need you on this job."

"Fine. I'm here. What's the rush with Patel if the judge okayed him as a witness?"

"He hasn't returned my calls all weekend or today. We're going to see him and get him on tape before the Mason boys file a motion to stay the judge's ruling while they appeal."

I unlocked the car and we got in.

"Did you leave him a message about the ruling this morning?" Cisco asked.

"Yes," I said. "But he hasn't called me back. I hope the twins didn't get to him and pay him off."

"Mason and Mason? No, no way. He hates those guys and the company, says Tidalwaiv ruined his life. Said they blackballed him. He definitely wants payback. Wants his day in court. After you win this case, he wants to hire you to sue Victor Wendt personally as well as the company."

"If he likes me so much, then why isn't he calling me back?"

"I don't know, man. Last time we spoke, he was talking about moving back up north to try the job market up there again. But he promised to let me know if he made the move."

"So what was his last known address down here?"

"Venice Beach."

Cisco was too big for the car, and we were looking at a minimum thirty-minute drive out to the beach. He was an ex-biker and didn't bother to disguise it — thick shoulders and biceps on a six-four frame. These days I was driving a Chevy Bolt. It was small and cozy, and the top of Cisco's head brushed the ceiling. The car was a comedown in space and comfort from a chauffeured Lincoln Navigator, but on the other side of the ledger, I hadn't been at a gas station in fifteen months. We took the 10 out west. Every time I glanced over at Cisco, he was looking at the camera feeds from the warehouse on his phone.

"I've never seen you like this," I finally said. "What is your problem with the writer?"

"My problem is the guy has a track record of involvement with women he works with, okay?" Cisco replied.

"So what, man? You don't trust Lorna?"

"I trust her. It's him I don't trust."

"Lorna makes good choices. You don't have to worry. Besides, you have six inches and about a hundred pounds on the guy — he's not going to try something. You gotta let it go so your mind is focused on the case. I'm serious. We can't fuck this up."

"All right, all right. I'm focused. You don't have to worry about me, Mick. I'm fucking focused."

"Good. Where in Venice are we going?"

"He's at twenty-five Breeze. It's one of the walk streets off Pacific. Good luck finding a parking space."

"At least we're not in a Navigator. That boat was hard to park anywhere."

"I wish we were in the Navigator. I'd at least be able to fit."

It took almost forty minutes in traffic to get there, and true to Cisco's concern, there was no parking to be had anywhere near Breeze Avenue. I finally gave up and parked in a beach lot off Speedway. We legged it five blocks back to Patel's bungalow, which was in a neighborhood where the houses faced each other across a paved walkway and no vehicles were allowed.

As we walked down Breeze, I got a text from Lorna.

"Shit," I said when I'd read it.

"What is it?" Cisco said.

"The Masons already filed an appeal and Ruhlin wants to hear arguments at three this afternoon on their request for a stay."

"So we can't talk to Patel?"

"Technically, no. But I'd turned my phone off and didn't get the text from Lorna."

I did just that as we approached 25 Breeze.

The house was behind a line of unkempt jasmine bushes that spilled over a short perimeter fence. Past an unlocked half gate were the steps of a small bungalow with a full covered porch. The wood decking, long exposed to sea air, creaked and sagged under our combined weight of four hundred–plus pounds. Before we even knocked on the door, Cisco made an eerie observation.

"Somebody's dead."

"What?"

"You smell that?"

"Yeah, that's the jasmine."

"That ain't jasmine, Mick. We open this door and you'll get it."

He looked over at the porch's furnishings. There was a cushioned couch, two chairs, and a low table. It was set up like an outdoor living room. There were decorative pillows on the couch, and Cisco grabbed two of them and tossed one to me.

"Use that."

"For what?"

"The smell."

He approached the front door. There was a glass inset in the upper half. He cupped his hands over his eyes and leaned toward the glass, looking past the reflection of outside light. It was dark inside.

"There's a note," he said. "On the floor."

I stepped up next to him and looked through the glass. There was a loose piece of paper on the floor, waiting for whoever entered.

"Can you make out what it says?" I asked.

"Yeah," Cisco said. "Says 'rear bedroom.' It came from a printer."

"That's it? Just 'rear bedroom'?"

"That's it."

I knocked on the glass.

"Nobody's going to answer, Mick," Cisco said.

He seemed sure. I knocked again anyway. Cisco didn't wait for a response. He tried the door handle, a brass loop with a thumb lever below a dead bolt. It was unlocked, and he pushed the door open. It swept the note on the entry rug to the side.

Then the odor hit us fully. I was immediately revolted by the smell of death. I almost gagged. In unison, we held our pillows up to our mouths and noses.

"Jesus," I said.

"Told you," Cisco said.

Our voices were muffled. I stepped into the house.

"Wait," Cisco said. "What are we doing?"

"We're going in," I said. "We're going to find out who's dead."

"You sure? Maybe we should just call the cops?"

"Don't worry, we will."

I stepped farther in and he followed. There was a dining room to the left with a table holding a desktop computer and a small printer. Documents in unkempt stacks surrounded it.

On the right was a small living room with a fireplace. A darkened hallway led to the back of the house, and Cisco went first, using his elbow to hit a wall switch that turned on the ceiling lights. He passed an archway on the left that led into the kitchen, and an open door on the right that led to a small bedroom. At the end of the hall was a doorway to a bathroom and an open door to a large bedroom. The primary. We entered, and it was dark because blackout curtains had been pulled across the windows. I could see the shape of someone sitting up in the bed, silhouetted against a blond-wood headboard.

"Hello?" I said.

No reply.

Cisco used his elbow again to turn on a ceiling light, this one above the bed. We then saw the body clearly. A man of about thirty with dark hair sitting up, lower body under the covers. He was obviously dead, eyes slitted. A dark liquid, now dried, had flowed from his nose and mouth onto a green T-shirt. The hands were above the covers and on his lap. His left hand held a cell phone.

I had never met Rikki Patel. He'd called me following the filing of the Tidalwaiv suit, and I sent Cisco to do the preliminary interview and judge whether he could be a credible witness. Once that was confirmed, I'd had one or two calls with him but kept my distance because of discovery concerns. I didn't want to give Tidalwaiv a heads-up that I was recruiting him to testify until I had to submit my first list of witnesses.

"Is that Rikki Patel?" I asked.

"It's him," Cisco said.

"Fuck."

"Yeah."

Cisco stepped up to the bed table next to the body. He pulled out his phone, turned on the light, and focused it on the table, where there was an open amber-colored prescription bottle. He bent down close to it to try to read the label without touching it.

"OxyContin," he said. "Prescribed by a Dr. Patel, DDS. A dentist. It's empty."

"His father?" I asked.

"Who knows? Patel is like the Indian version of Smith."

Cisco turned off his light and pocketed his phone. He turned away from the body to me.

"I guess we call the cops now," he said.

"Not yet," I said. "You see any note?"

My mind was racing with thoughts about what Patel's death meant to my case. I knew that his death was a tragedy for him and his loved ones, but I couldn't help considering the impact on the upcoming trial.

"Uh, no note," Cisco said. "Other than the one at the door. But he might've been texting somebody."

I looked at the phone in the dead man's hand. The screen was up in a position that suggested he'd been looking down at the device at the end.

"We have to look at that phone," I said.

"Mick, you don't want to fuck around with a possible crime scene," Cisco said. "It's pretty obvious what happened here, but you don't want this to come back at you. We need to call the cops."

"I told you, we will."

"Don't do this, Mick. Let's just back the fuck out of here and call the cops."

I didn't answer him. I looked around and saw a box of tissues on the bed within reach of Patel. I pulled out two.

"What are you doing?" Cisco asked.

"I just want to see what he was doing," I said.

I came back around the bed, passed Cisco, and went to the dead man's side. Using a tissue to guard my fingers, I pulled the phone from Patel's grasp.

"Jesus, Mick," Cisco said.

I ignored him and used a finger wrapped in tissue to depress the button on the side of the phone. Nothing happened. The screen remained black. The battery was dead.

"Damn."

"Just put it back, Mick. We go out and call the cops like the good citizens we are."

I carefully put the phone back where it had been.

"Let's look around," I said.

I headed down the hallway to the front of the house. Cisco followed but cut through the kitchen while I went to the dining room. Using the tissue, I pushed around the stacks of documents on either side of the computer. They were all unpaid bills, final notices, and letters from collection agencies for power, cable, Wi-Fi, car payments, insurance, and rent. At the bottom of one stack was an eviction notice that had been served by the L.A. County Sheriff's Office just before Christmas. It gave Patel thirty days to vacate the property. I knew from handling evictions in the past that you could go nearly a year without paying rent before a landlord finally had you physically evicted. Patel was obviously at the end of the line.

"The side door is locked with a dead bolt. Nobody went out that way."

I turned. Cisco had come from the kitchen. He was holding the pillow from the porch at his side, as the odor of death seemed far less intrusive at the front of the house. I had kept my pillow in place, hoping it would help me avoid retching. I turned back to the table and used a tissue-clad finger to touch the space bar on the computer keyboard. The screen lit up, but there was an empty password window guarding entry. I was not going to be able to see what Rikki Patel's last work and messages were.

"Okay," I said. "Let's get out of here."

"Call the cops, right?" Cisco said.

"Outside."

"I guess you can cancel that court hearing today."

"No way. I'm going to be there. On the day the judge rules Patel can be a witness, he ends up dead? I'm going to have something to say about that."

"Mick, the guy's been dead for days. You saw the body, you smelled it. That's why you couldn't reach him over the weekend. Besides, it's an obvious suicide. The side door is locked from the inside and nobody could have left that note on the floor and then gone out the front."

I nodded, but not in agreement.

"So?" I said. "The judge won't know that. And neither will the media."

# 7

CISCO AND I waited by the property's front gate. I was hoping the sea air would chase the smell of death out of my nose. It was a losing battle.

The first to respond to my call to the LAPD were two patrol officers from Pacific Division. The female took information from me while her male counterpart went into the house to confirm the death. When he came out, he was talking into the radio mic on his shoulder, asking for a supervisor to arrive on scene. Another ten minutes passed before a patrol sergeant appeared and went inside the house to see things for himself. When he exited, he came directly to me.

"You found the body?" he asked.

"My investigator and I did, yes," I said. I noticed that his nameplate said FINLEY.

"'Investigator'?" he said.

"I'm an attorney," I said. "Dennis Wojciechowski is my investigator. The man in there was supposed to be a witness in a civil lawsuit I'm involved with. We were supposed to take his deposition today."

Finley reared his head in recognition.

"You're the Lincoln Lawyer guy, right? I've seen your billboards."

The Lincoln legacy — I'd never live it down.

"Not anymore," I said. "I don't do criminal. Are the detectives on the way? I'd like to speak to them."

"I'm signing off on this as a self-inflicted suicide," Finley said. "No need to call in detectives."

I didn't bother mentioning that *suicide* meant that it was self-inflicted.

"You have the authority to make that call?" I asked.

"I do, yes," Finley said. "No sign of foul play, empty pill bottle, pending eviction. The coroner's office will make the final call on the toxicology, and they're on the way. All our reports will go to the detective bureau for review. But right now, we don't need to bother the detectives with this."

"Well, Sergeant, I am going to have to insist that you do. This man was set to be a key witness in an upcoming civil trial where billions of dollars will be at stake, and there is a corporation that would do anything to subvert the cause of justice."

Finley smiled, glanced around him, and understood he now had an audience — his two underlings. He turned his attention back to me.

"That's a nice speech," he said. "But it doesn't change my call on this. The coroner's investigator will take a look and I'm sure he will agree. Now, we have your statement and your information and we'll be in touch if we need to be in touch. You and your investigator can go now, sir. Have a nice day."

He turned away to confer with the two other cops. I looked at Cisco and shook my head.

"There is a hearing today in federal court," I said loudly but calmly. "It's about this witness. There will be media there. A lot of media — the case has already drawn national interest, and we're not even in trial yet. When I report that there has been no investigation by the LAPD of this man's death, that will be news, and your decision here will end up being questioned by your boss and his boss and his boss all the way up the line to the chief of police. Just remember, I warned you."

Finley turned around and put his hands on his hips as he stared at me, clearly annoyed at getting pushback on his command decision. Cisco put a hand on my arm and gave it a tug.

"Come on, Mick," he said. "We should go."

I shook his hand off as Finley stepped back to me.

"Sir, did you have permission to enter this home?" he asked.

I shook my head.

"Oh, is that how you want to go?" I said. "You're going to get me for trespassing? You really want to dig yourself in that deep, Sergeant Finley?"

"What I want, sir, is for you to leave these premises," Finley said. "While you still can."

"Don't worry, Sergeant, we're leaving," Cisco said.

He pulled again on my arm, but I held my ground and pointed at the front door of the house.

"No," I said. "I'm not leaving until I know this man's death is going to be properly investigated. By detectives, not patrol officers."

Finley smiled.

"Okay, you want an investigation, you'll get an investigation," he said. "We'll investigate you. Officer Dance, put the Lincoln Lawyer in the back seat of your car."

Dance was the female officer. She stepped toward me.

"Do I cuff him, Sarge?" she asked.

"I don't think we need to do that," Finley said. "He's going to cooperate. Just put him in the car and we'll get to him when we get to him."

"This way, sir," Dance said. She pointed toward the walkway with one hand while taking my arm with the other.

"This is bullshit," I said. "If you put me in the car, you are arresting me, and you're going to answer to a federal judge for that."

"Let's go, sir," Dance insisted.

"Mick, who do you want me to call?" Cisco said.

"Call Judge Ruhlin's clerk," I said over my shoulder. "Tell them I'm being detained illegally by police, and I need Peggy—I mean, the judge—to issue a show-cause order against LAPD sergeant Finley, Pacific Division. Tell her that otherwise, I won't make the hearing today."

I stopped my resistance and let Dance lead me by the arm through the gate. We reached the walkway before Finley called her name.

"Dance, bring him back here," he said.

Dance and I did a pirouette.

"He's finally being smart," I whispered to her.

She didn't respond. We walked back through the gate and right up to Finley.

"Okay, Dance," he said. "Why don't you go out there to Pacific and flag down the coroner's van."

"Yes, sir," Dance said.

She turned to follow the order. Finley took a step closer to me so he would not be overheard by Dance's partner, who was standing with Cisco by the gate.

"What am I going to do with you, Lincoln?" he said.

I knew by the question and tone that he was going to capitulate. He'd finally seen that the path forward for him was fraught with pitfalls if he insisted on the temporary fulfillment of putting me in my place. Maybe that was why he was a supervisor. My part of the unspoken bargain was to act like he hadn't blinked. I knew just what to give him to allow him to save face and get me what I wanted.

"Did you see the name of the doctor on the pill bottle?" I asked.

"I didn't look," Finley said.

"Same name as the man in the bed. I mean, I'm not a detective, but it seemed kind of hinky to me."

Finley nodded and turned to the remaining patrol officer.

"Okay, we've got some new information," he said. "Johnson, let's tape this off and preserve the scene. I'll call West Bureau and get somebody out here to take a look inside."

Johnson turned and headed toward the gate, presumably to get a roll of crime scene tape from the patrol wagon. That left me with Finley.

"Happy now, Counselor?" he asked.

"I'm happy the pros are going to take a look at it, yes," I said. "But I'm not happy I lost my witness."

"Well, you're going to have to stay here and talk to the pros about this big case of yours."

"Not a problem."

Finley turned away to make the callout to detectives on his radio. I walked over to Cisco to wait.

"What the fuck, Mick," he whispered. "You almost got arrested over what? The guy did himself. You were in the house. It was obvious."

I checked Finley to make sure he was not within earshot. He was up on the porch talking into his radio by the front door. I could not hear him and he could not hear me.

"We need an investigation," I said.

"Why?" Cisco said. "It's gonna come back suicide. The guy downed a bottle of Oxy."

"Doesn't matter how it comes back."

"Why?"

"Because what matters is that it's being investigated."

Cisco stared at me for a long moment before I could see understanding come into his eyes. He slowly nodded his head.

# 8

THE JUDGE WAS late for the emergency hearing she had scheduled. We — the attorneys — waited silently at our tables. I had nothing to say to the Masons and they had nothing to say to me. I had informed my client of the hearing but she was unable to get away from her job at the lab on short notice. And so I sat alone. In the first row of the gallery, there were three reporters, one print and two TV, all of whom had gotten an anonymous tip about the hearing from Lorna. This allowed me to be insulated from any accusation of setting in motion a news flash unfavorable to the defense. McEvoy had stepped away from his work in the cage to watch from the back row, where he sat next to Cisco.

At 4:15 Judge Ruhlin finally emerged from chambers, took the bench, and got down to business with no explanation for her delay. Federal judges were like that. They rarely had to bother explaining their actions or rulings.

"All right," the judge said. "We're back on the record in *Randolph versus Tidalwaiv,* and we have a motion from the defense to stay my ruling of this morning. Misters Mason, would one of you state your argument for a stay?"

Marcus went toward the lectern, but before he got there, I stood up.

"Your Honor, could I be heard?" I said. "I believe I have information that has significant impact on this hearing and the motion from the defense."

Ruhlin looked at me for a long moment, showing a flash of annoyance, before responding.

"Very well, Mr. Haller," she said. "You shall be heard."

I moved to the lectern, forcing Marcus Mason to step back to his table. I gave him a wink from the eye the judge couldn't see. He stayed standing, ready to object to whatever I was about to say.

"Thank you, Your Honor," I said. "And good afternoon. Unfortunately, I have rather disturbing and sad news to deliver to the court. It appears that on the very morning that the court ruled that Rikki Patel could serve as a witness in this trial, his life was cut short. His death is the subject of a homicide investigation being conducted by the Los Angeles—"

"Objection!" Marcus Mason called out.

"—Police Department," I continued. "There is no need for this hearing, Judge, because my key witness has died under highly suspicious circumstances. The outcome—"

"Objection!" Marcus shrieked again.

"—of the investigation will undoubtedly shed light on the lengths that Tidal—"

"Okay, stop," Ruhlin said. "Everyone, just hold on."

She signaled her clerk to the side of the bench. Ruhlin rolled her chair over and whispered to him. He then left the courtroom through the door to chambers and Ruhlin rolled back into position.

"Okay, we're going to move to chambers to discuss this further," she said.

"Your Honor, I object to that," I said. "This is a serious matter and it should be discussed in public."

"Your Honor," Marcus Mason said, "plaintiff's counsel is once again looking to air outrageous claims to the assembled media in hopes that he will taint the—"

"Enough!" Ruhlin boomed from the bench. "Both of you. Enough. My clerk is just clearing documents from another case from view in chambers and then we will convene there to continue this. Andrew will bring you in when we're ready."

With that, she left the bench and went through the door to her chambers.

Marcus Mason immediately moved toward me at the lectern and whispered forcefully. "This is bullshit," he said. "And you're bullshit."

"Sure, Marcus," I said. "Whatever you say."

"What happened with Patel has nothing to do with this case!"

"Yeah? I hope you can convince a jury of that."

I left him there and went back to my table, but before I could sit down, one of the reporters, a TV guy who had been around for decades, jumping from station to station in the local market, stood up at the rail and signaled to me.

"Is what you just said true?" he asked. "There's a murder of a witness?"

"I didn't use the word *murder*," I said. "And I would never lie to a federal judge."

I turned back to my table and saw Andrew, the clerk, standing at the door that led to the judge's chambers.

"The judge will see you now," he said.

The Masons were already on the move. I fell in behind them and we wound our way through the clerk's corral and through the door into a short hallway that led to Judge Ruhlin's private chambers. The judge was seated at a round table in front of a floor-to-ceiling wall of shelves containing leather-bound copies of US codes and laws. The volumes were strictly decor, since everything could easily be found and read online. In the corner behind her, the court stenographer sat poised to record the in camera session.

"Gentlemen, sit down," she ordered. "Mr. Haller, I want you in that seat."

She pointed to the chair directly across the table from her. She would be flanked by the Masons, but her eyes would be on me.

"We are still on the record," Ruhlin said. "But now that we are out of earshot of the media, there is no need for posturing or playing to the audience. Mr. Haller, tell us what you know and how you know it."

I cleared my throat to gain a couple extra seconds to compose a response.

"Your Honor," I began, "I received your ruling on the motion regarding Mr. Patel this morning by email, as I am sure defense counsel did as well. It was my guess that defense counsel and Tidalwaiv would appeal the ruling and seek a stay preventing me from taking Mr. Patel's deposition. It has been clear from the start that they did not want me talking to this man, because he knew of the company's malfeasance and—"

"Mr. Haller," Ruhlin interrupted, "I said no posturing. Tell me what you know and how you came to know it."

"Yes, Your Honor," I said. "So, knowing what their move was likely to be, and in an effort to beat the filing of that appeal, my investigator, Dennis Wojciechowski—do you want me to spell his name?"

"Not necessary," Ruhlin said. "We have it. Go on."

"Cisco and I went to Mr. Patel's—"

"Wait, who is Cisco?" Ruhlin asked.

"Sorry, Cisco is Dennis," I said. "It's his nickname. Anyway, Dennis Wojciechowski and I went to Mr. Patel's home in Venice this morning in an effort to talk to him before an appeal was filed and any sort of stay was granted."

Marcus Mason shook his head condescendingly.

"Perfectly legal — some might even say it was good lawyering," I said.

I threw a condescending look back at him.

"Anyway, we went there," I continued. "We found his front door open, and after knocking and calling out his name, we went in. We searched through the house and found him in a bedroom. Dead. We then called the police. Two patrol officers and their sergeant responded to the call and went into the house. When they came out, the sergeant judged the death suspicious and called out a homicide team. We stayed till the investigators arrived and told them what we knew, including that Mr. Patel was a witness in this case. And then we left."

No one said anything. I tried to fill the void.

"While we were waiting for the detectives, my office manager contacted me and told me the appeal had been filed and that the court had scheduled a hearing on the stay. I came directly from Venice to the courthouse once the detectives cleared us to leave the crime scene."

Ruhlin twiddled the pen she had been writing occasional notes with during my telling of the story.

"I saw your investigator in the courtroom," she said. "If I brought him in here, would he tell the same story?"

"Of course he would," I said. "Do you want me to go get him?"

"I don't think that will be necessary yet," the judge said. "Did the investigators tell you what was suspicious about the death?"

"No, Judge," I answered. "But I have their names if you wish to reach out to them."

"I don't think that will be necessary either," Ruhlin said. "I have my clerk confirming that there is an investigation. Misters Mason, do you wish to be heard?"

Marcus Mason nodded emphatically.

"Yes, Your Honor. Mr. Haller tells a good story but he leaves out key details. First of all, when he says the door was open, we have it on good authority that that was not the case. The door was not open, as he claims, and he and his investigator broke into the house and—"

"That's a lie," I interjected. "When I said the door was open, I meant it was unlocked. We found it unlocked and went in when—"

"Mr. Haller, you had your turn," the judge said. "Do not interrupt opposing counsel. Continue, Mr. Mason."

"As I was saying," Mason said, "Mr. Haller's claims in the courtroom as well as in here are exaggerated. Yes, there is an investigation of Mr. Patel's death, but it is being investigated as a suicide that occurred as long ago as last week — before there was even a hearing on whether Patel could be a witness. Mr. Haller knew this and yet he chose in open court, with the media as his audience, to spread a completely false narrative he hoped would be carried by the media into the jury pool."

The judge flashed suspicious eyes at me.

"Mr. Haller?" she asked. "Mr. Mason makes a strong statement. Do you care to respond?"

I needed to quickly turn this around and get the focus off my motives and on Mason's.

"Well, Judge, all I can say is that Mr. Mason has quite an imagination," I said. "I am flattered that he believes I can think that quickly on my feet after finding a man dead in his bed and also that I can pinpoint time of death without conferring with a medical examiner. But what I am concerned about, Your Honor, is that Mr. Mason sure seems to have a lot more information than I have. I would ask the court to inquire of him what was inquired of me — that is, what does he know and how did he come to know it. I would also throw in when he came to know it."

Marcus Mason didn't need the judge to prompt him. He jumped in.

"Your Honor," he began, "we have a solemn duty to our client to provide the best defense we possibly can against this frivolous lawsuit. In doing so, we became aware that Mr. Patel was a disgruntled ex-employee who might have been tempted by Mr. Haller or his investigator to break his nondisclosure agreement with Tidalwaiv. We have a large firm with a lot of resources. We used them to monitor Mr. Patel, and this is where our information came from."

I shook my head. The judge leaned toward Marcus Mason.

"These resources, are they people or cameras or other devices?" she asked.

"Uh, both people and cameras," Mason said.

"Did you put a camera inside Mr. Patel's house?" Ruhlin pressed.

"No, Your Honor," Mason said quickly. "Of course not. Never."

"Your Honor?" I asked.

"Not yet, Mr. Haller," Ruhlin said. "Then, Mr. Mason, how did you accomplish your surveillance of Mr. Patel to the extent that you knew that his death was being investigated as a suicide?"

"Judge, we had a camera outside the house that recorded audio. It was not on his property. It was on a utility pole on public property. It picked up some of what the investigators discussed outside the house, and that information was forwarded to me. It was not illegal, and some might call it good lawyering."

He threw my condescending look right back at me.

"I received the information just moments before the hearing began," Mason said. "I would have brought the situation to the court's attention at the start, but Mr. Haller jumped in before I could."

The judge did another twiddle with the pen as she thought about everything she had just heard.

"Your Honor?" I tried again.

"Go ahead, Mr. Haller," Ruhlin responded impatiently.

"Thank you. Your Honor, I would like opposing counsel to put on the record whether his firm or anyone working for his firm has me or anyone on my staff under similar surveillance."

"That's an outrageous claim, Your Honor," Mason said angrily. "Tidalwaiv had every right to put a disgruntled and volatile ex-employee under surveillance for safety reasons alone. Mr. Haller is using this perfectly legitimate business practice to try to impugn opposing counsel."

"That is a lot of words, Mr. Mason," Ruhlin said. "But I did not hear you say that you do not have Mr. Haller or any of his staff under surveillance."

"Sorry, Your Honor, I'm just very worked up," Mason said. "The answer is no, we do not have Mr. Haller or any of his staff, or his client, for that matter, under surveillance of any kind. Period."

"What about before this meeting?" I asked. "Have you been watching me or my investigator?"

"We have not," Mason said. "There. It's on the record."

"Any other questions, Mr. Haller?" Ruhlin asked.

"I would like the record to reflect that the man Mr. Mason calls a disgruntled and volatile ex-employee, I would term a whistleblower," I said. "But no, no other questions, Your Honor."

I knew from Ruhlin's countenance that I did not have to press the outrage button. She would handle that.

"Very well," she said. "Gentlemen, I find the tactics and behaviors you exhibited outside the courtroom troubling and below the dignity of the court. I am putting both parties on notice that I will have little patience and show little sympathy should any of you or those working for you violate the law or the decorum of the US district court. That includes feeding the media unfounded claims or misinformation. This is not a street fight, gentlemen, and I do mean *gentlemen*. Be warned — conduct yourselves accordingly."

Ruhlin got a chorus of *Yes, Your Honor*s from the Masons and me. She then said the hearing was adjourned and dismissed us. We left silently and in single file behind the stenographer and headed back to the courtroom. I was last in line behind Marcus Mason.

"You looked a little stressed in there, Marcus," I said to his back. "How're you holding up?"

He didn't turn around to look at me when he spoke.

"Fuck you, Haller," he said.

"You sure that bow tie isn't on too tight?" I said. "You don't want to be cutting off blood flow to the brain. That's not good."

Now he stopped and turned. I almost walked into him.

"You know what you are, Haller?" he asked.

"I have a feeling you're going to give me your take," I said.

"You're an asshole," he said. "So fuck off."

I smiled at him until he turned and went to catch up to the others.

# 9

WHEN CISCO AND I got back to the warehouse, I pulled the Bolt into one of the garage bays and lowered the door behind us.

"Cisco, you got your magic wand with you?" I asked.

"In one of my saddlebags," he said.

The magic wand was a bug detector that picked up magnetic-field and radio-frequency signals.

"I want you to sweep the car and your Harley," I said. "Then do the whole warehouse."

"You think Marcus was lying to the judge about surveillance?" Cisco asked.

On the drive from the courthouse I had filled him in on what had been discussed in Judge Ruhlin's chambers.

"I'm just not taking chances," I said. "Mason spoke for himself and his firm. That doesn't mean Tidalwaiv isn't up to some shit."

"Right," Cisco said. "I'm on it."

"And let's cut the feeds on the cameras outside the cage. I know you won't be able to watch Lorna and McEvoy, but too bad. She deserves your trust anyway."

"I know. I know she does. What about the Wi-Fi in your office?"

"We'll need that. But let's turn it off until we do."

"You got it."

McEvoy had left the courtroom when I was called into chambers. I could see him already back in the cage. I first went to my office to check in with Lorna and put my jacket on a hook. She was in my seat at the desk, staring at the screen of her laptop. As I stripped off my tie, I came around the desk and saw that she was watching a news feed from KTLA Channel 5 and had her earbuds in.

"What's up, Lorna?" I asked loudly.

She pulled out one of the earbuds.

"We've got some strong Santa Ana winds coming tomorrow," she said. "They're saying up to a hundred miles an hour."

"No way," I said. "That's hurricane wind."

"I know, but it's what they're saying. You want your desk?"

"No, I'm going to go talk to McEvoy."

I hung my tie over the office's doorknob.

"Did Cisco come back with you?" Lorna asked.

"Yeah, he's out there checking my car," I said.

"What happened?"

"Hopefully nothing. But he's going to sweep it and the whole warehouse. The Masons knew we were at Patel's house this morning. They claimed to the judge that they were watching him and not me, but I don't believe it."

Lorna, instead of being concerned that our opponents might have us under surveillance, thought about Patel. On our way back from Venice, Cisco had filled her in on our discovery of his death.

"That poor man," she said. "Taking his own life…"

"If he did," I said.

"What — you think he was murdered?"

"I don't think anything until the cops confirm. But we are dealing with a company whose whole future is on the line, Lorna. They lose this case, and Musk, Gates, Zuckerberg — none of those guys will want to touch them. That makes it desperate times, and anything is possible. My advice is to look over your shoulder wherever you go until this is finished."

"That's not very comforting."

"It is what it is. Stay close to Cisco."

"I will."

"Oh, and how are you doing with McEvoy?"

"Fine. He's fine. Why? Are you thinking he's a plant or something? I thought Cisco checked him out."

"He did, so I'm not thinking anything. But right now, he's in the cage by himself and is privy to every move we make. I'll feel a lot better when it's not a one-way street and he starts producing things we can use. I'm going to go check on him. You can keep the desk."

I left the office and went through the copper curtain into the cage. McEvoy was at the computer terminal. I was too far away to see what he had on the screen.

"Hey," he said.

"I saw you in the courtroom," I said. "You didn't stay. How'd you know the session wouldn't continue after chambers?"

"Uh, actually I didn't. But I wanted to get back to this. I think I might have already found something good."

He nodded toward the screen.

"I could use something good," I said. "Show me."

McEvoy opened a folder on the screen that contained a list of files.

"Okay, so these are some of the emails that were in the discovery download," he said. "They all went out to stakeholders on Project Clair, starting when it was in early development through training and testing. There's forty-six of them. Most are innocuous and involve scheduling meetings and Zooms and so forth, but some are more important because they carry content about testing and project guardrails."

"Just tell me you found the smoking gun," I said.

"Uh, not quite, but maybe the smoking witness. Or at least someone who might take the place of Rikki Patel for you. Someone who might actually be better."

"Okay. Who?"

McEvoy picked a file on the screen seemingly at random and opened it. It was an email, and I leaned down to read the subject line.

> Reminder: PC progress meeting at 1 p.m. in conference room A.

"What's PC?" I asked.

"I'm pretty sure it means Project Clair, but that's not what matters," McEvoy said. "The content of the message doesn't matter either. It's the mailing list we're looking at here."

McEvoy clicked on the mailing-list link in the header and it displayed the email addresses of the sender and the recipients. It had been sent from PCM1@tidalwaiv.com to a list of more than a dozen people, all of whose emails ended in tidalwaiv.com. It was an internal message. Midway down the list, an email address had been blacked out by the redaction program.

"So we have these forty-six group emails regarding Project Clair and in all of them one email address is redacted," McEvoy said.

"Any way of knowing if it's the same email redacted each time?" I asked.

"Well, it always falls between these two emails, Isaacs and Muniz. So it is likely the same person, but there's no way of knowing that for sure with the information we have here."

"So it couldn't have been Rikki Patel?"

"I don't think so, because he was a coder, not a stakeholder, as far as I can determine, and these people are all upper management, and because this email list was generated in alphabetical order by last name. You see the names?"

I leaned down closer to the screen to read the names of the email recipients: Alpert, Bastin, Bernardo, Davidson, Harlan, Isaacs — the list was indeed in alphabetical order.

"Got it," I said. "This is good. We need to find out who that is and why they were redacted."

"I think I might know," McEvoy said.

"Then tell me. Make my day."

"Well, if you start with the idea that they're trying to hide the identity of this person from you, then you have to assume the person has information or knowledge detrimental to the company's cause, right? To me, that adds up to this person being separated from the company at some point after these emails. They left or were forced out. Maybe even fired."

"That makes sense, but how the hell do we find out who it is? Patel could probably have told us, but he's gone."

"Right, so what I did was go to TheUncannyValley to look—"

"Wait. What's the uncanny valley?"

"Well, in the digital world, the *uncanny valley* refers to the psychological leap humans must make in accepting robots and digital imaging as real — you know, like with a game or a chatbot. Robots and digital images that look almost but not quite human make people very uncomfortable, and if they're uncomfortable, they don't believe. That's the uncanny valley. But what I'm talking about here is a social platform a lot like LinkedIn that is called TheUncannyValley—all one word. It's for people who work in AI and in coding for digital games and so on. It's essentially a social and business network with a résumé databank."

"Got it. So you went to TheUncannyValley, and then what?"

"I did a basic search for former employees of Tidalwaiv. There were a couple dozen, including Rikki Patel, but only one whose last name falls between Isaacs and Muniz: Naomi Kitchens. Her résumé says she worked for Tidalwaiv for about two years beginning in late 2021. The public rollout of the Clair AI companion came at the end of '22. And, get this, her résumé says she's an ethicist."

"An ethicist?"

"All these AI companies have them now. A lot of the time, it's simply for window dressing, CYA stuff, but sometimes not. Technically, they're supposed to monitor ethical standards and guardrails in the development of their AI programs and products."

I felt a jolt of electricity go down my spine. I clapped McEvoy on the shoulder.

"Goddamn, McEvoy," I said. "One day on the job and you find this? Did you search through the rest of the discovery for this Naomi Kitchens?"

"I did," McEvoy said. "There's nothing."

"Twelve terabytes of documents and not one mention of Naomi Kitchens, the supposed ethicist on this project?"

"None."

"They've completely scrubbed her from the discovery?"

"Looks that way. In documents dated after she left the company, you have a different person listed as the project ethicist—Francis Ross."

"So they got rid of Kitchens for some reason, scrubbed her from all records, and then brought in Ross."

"Looks like it. I guess you'll be able to rake the Masons over the coals in court for this, right?"

"I could, but I probably won't."

"Why not? I thought you —"

"I don't want them to know we know about her. Not yet. Which reminds me, there's no Wi-Fi in the cage. How'd you search for her on TheUncannyValley?"

"On my phone. I stepped out to do it. I thought that would be okay."

I thought about that for a moment. McEvoy's finding Naomi Kitchens alleviated my suspicions about him, so it was unlikely that the Masons or Tidalwaiv knew about my decision to allow him to join the team. My main concern now was hiding from them that we had discovered the identity of the ethicist they were trying to hide from us.

"When you say you stepped out to search on your phone, how far did you step out?" I asked.

"Uh, I actually did it in the courtroom while we were waiting for the judge to come in," McEvoy said. "Why, what are you worried about?"

"That they might have a sniffer here."

"A sniffer? Really? That seems kind of extreme."

"Believe me, Tidalwaiv will go to extremes to win this case. Any idea where Naomi Kitchens is now?"

"Yes, I found her. She's up in Palo Alto teaching at Stanford, and one of her classes is called Ethics in the Age of Artificial Intelligence."

I nodded. Things were coming together.

"Then that's where we'll go to talk to her," I said.

"Really?" McEvoy asked. "When?"

"Right now."

"Don't you want to call her first?"

"No. They might be watching her like they watched Patel. Besides, we call her and it might scare her away. She's got to know about this lawsuit, but she hasn't come forward. Why? Another NDA? I think it's something else. She's scared."

# 10

"RIGHT NOW" TURNED out to be the next morning. McEvoy and I took a JSX flight from Burbank up to Oakland, picked up a Go rental car, and made our way across the lower bay to Palo Alto and Stanford University. On the plane, McEvoy had searched online for Professor Kitchens's office and schedule. He found both and learned that she gave only one lecture on Tuesdays. The class was called History of Machine Learning.

"Perfect," I'd said.

The lecture was scheduled from eleven till noon in the Hewlett Teaching Center. We got lost twice while trying to find it in the school's Science and Engineering Quad and finally arrived shortly before noon. It was held in a midsize lecture hall that was about half full. A hundred or so students were scattered throughout the six tiers of seats. The two entrances were on the top level. We stepped in quietly and took two open seats near the door. Kitchens stood at a lectern below. There was a large flat-screen monitor on the wall behind her that showed a black-and-white photo of a man who looked familiar, but I couldn't readily place him. On a blackboard next to the screen, Kitchens had written her name and university email address in chalk. That was when I realized that it was the first class of a new semester.

"Deep Blue defeated Kasparov with what move?" Kitchens asked. "Anyone?"

No one raised a hand. I now recognized the man on the screen as Garry Kasparov, the chess champion who famously lost a match to an IBM computer almost three decades ago.

"The knight sacrifice," Kitchens said. "It was in that moment that many believe machines became smarter than humans. And I will leave it there until next week. Please begin reading Kurzweil's book and we will add that to the discussion next Tuesday as well. Have fun."

The students started leaving. I watched one kid shove a book into a backpack. I caught a glimpse of the title, *The Singularity Is Nearer*, and assumed that was the book Kitchens had assigned the class.

I saw Kitchens gather up her lecture notes and move to a desk. She looked like she was in her mid- to late thirties and she had dark skin and hair in tight rows of braids. She wore faded blue jeans with a red, untucked, and equally faded blouse.

"I don't want to overwhelm her with two of us," I said. "Let me go down alone first."

"You sure you don't want me to go with you?" McEvoy said.

"No, it should be just me. Hang back until I signal. Or I don't."

"Will do."

I went down the steps toward the stage, passing the final few students going up to the exits. When I got to the front, Kitchens was sliding her notes and the laptop she had used for her PowerPoint presentation into her backpack. Though she was looking down and zipping the pack closed, she spoke before I could.

"I saw you two up there and knew you weren't students," she said.

"Yes, we came in late, but what we saw about Deep Blue and the knight sacrifice was very interesting," I said. "From there to AI being in our phones, our cars, our everything in less than thirty years. It's scary, if you ask me."

"Yes, it is."

"Professor Kitchens, my name is Michael Haller, people call me Mickey. I'm —"

"I know who you are."

She finally looked up at me.

"You do?"

"I'm following your case against Tidalwaiv. I will probably include discussion of it in one of my other classes."

"Then you know why I'm here."

"I do, and I hate to disappoint you, but I can't talk to you."

"Because you signed a nondisclosure agreement? There are ways around that. Most prevent you from working for or talking to a competitor. I'm not a competitor. I'm just somebody looking for the truth."

The backpack was on the desk and she was holding it upright, almost like a shield.

"It's not because of the nondisclosure," she said. "It's because I feel threatened."

"I'm sorry," I said. "I don't mean to threaten you. I just want —"

"I know what you want. I also know I'm being watched by them."

"Right now? You're being watched?"

"If not physically, then digitally. All the time."

"Because you're a threat to them. You know things. They turned over twelve terabytes of documents related to the development of Project Clair in discovery. Twelve. And your name is not in any of them. You've been scrubbed, Professor. They're trying to hide you. But I know you were there and you know things. You're an ethicist. You could make a difference by talking to me."

I could see her breathing heavily. She was genuinely scared.

"You can't protect me," she said.

"The truth will protect you," I said. "Once it's out there, they can't hurt you."

"You don't know that."

"What I know is that a sixteen-year-old girl was murdered because Clair told her ex-boyfriend it was an okay thing to do. You know the truth of how that happened. The world should know it."

"I have to think about it."

"How long?"

"I don't know. I have to think. Who is the other man up there that you came with?" She nodded in McEvoy's direction.

"He works with me," I said. "He's a writer and he's going to write a book about this case. He's the one who found you for me."

"How?" she asked. "If I was scrubbed from the records, as you say."

"It's kind of a long story. I'll tell it to you — or, rather, he will — if we can continue this conversation."

There was one question I needed to ask but I knew it wasn't time yet. In a perfect world, she would answer it before it was asked.

"We fly back to L.A. at five," I said. "Is there any time and place we can keep talking, privately?"

She shook her head.

"I don't know," she said. "I didn't want this to happen. I've gotten past it. None of it was my fault."

"What about Rebecca Randolph?" I said. "The boy who killed her is in custody and will be prosecuted. But how will the company be held accountable if no one will stand up to them?"

I saw fire enter her eyes and knew I had misspoken.

"That is completely unfair," she said. "I did my job. I warned them. I have no guilt over what I did."

"I know, I know," I said quickly. "I shouldn't have said that. I'm sorry. But I have nothing. I need your help."

"I saw a story on the internet this morning about a man who was going to be your witness. The police said he killed himself. Are they sure?"

I nodded. I'd wondered if she had seen the stories.

"They seem to be," I said.

"He was your witness and now you want me," she said. "I don't want to end up like that."

"Look, we knew he had problems. There is a good chance that what he did had nothing to do with this. With the case."

One of the doors at the top banged open and Kitchens startled. A man entered, passed by McEvoy, and quickly came down the stairs to the stage. I turned so that Kitchens was behind me.

"It's okay," she said. "He teaches in here next."

I relaxed and turned back to her.

"Can we continue this somewhere?" I asked.

Before she could answer, the next teacher was at the stage. He was wearing a tweed jacket and looked like a cookie-cutter college professor.

"Naomi, everything all right?" he asked. "Is this man bothering you?"

"No, Moses," Kitchens said. "I'm fine. I'll clear out of your way."

"You sure?"

"I'm sure."

Moses was looking at me suspiciously. I just nodded.

Kitchens put her backpack strap over one shoulder and headed toward the steps. We started up, side by side.

"Do you know where Joanie's is?" she asked.

"Uh, no," I said. "What's Joanie's?"

"It's a restaurant off campus. On California Avenue. I'll meet you there. I don't have a lot of time. Tuesdays I have office hours from two to five."

"We'll meet you there. And thank you."

"Don't thank me yet. I'm only doing this because of the way you stepped in front of me down there. To protect me."

I nodded.

"I will protect you if you work with me," I said.

"I'm not promising anything yet," she said.

"I understand. But thank you for hearing me out."

"I'll see you there."

# 11

JOANIE'S WAS A locals' hangout. By the time we found it, Kitchens was already at a table in the rear. As we sat down across from her, I introduced McEvoy. They shook hands and Kitchens knew the name.

"You wrote the DNA book, right?" she said. "About that predator down in L.A., the one who used genetic traits to pick his victims."

"Uh, yes, that was me," McEvoy said. "*Fair Warning*. You read it?"

"I did," Kitchens said. "Definitely in my sphere as an ethicist."

"Cool," McEvoy said. "I write a Substack. You should check it out."

On the way over, I had told McEvoy I wanted to shift things in the second conversation with Kitchens. He would be the lead, and this would allow me to analyze her answers without having to worry about keeping the conversation going. It would also allow me to watch McEvoy to get a read on how much of an asset he would be to the case. He had already shown his skills as a digger by coming up with Kitchens. Now I would see how well he could use an interview to get case information. He knew that I had set two goals for the trip to Palo Alto. So far, we had achieved neither.

A waitress arrived at the table, put down menus, and took our order for iced teas all around.

"So," McEvoy said. "Why academia?"

"I know what you're thinking," Kitchens said. "Those who can, do. Those who can't, teach."

"No, not at all," McEvoy said. "I'm just wondering how bad it got at Tidalwaiv that you said, 'The hell with this whole AI business.'"

"Yeah, well, it got bad," Kitchens said. "And my sense was that this was an industry-wide issue, not just a Tidalwaiv problem. Ethics were not really part of the equation. They needed to say they were paying attention to it, but it was the Wild West. They didn't care about ethics."

"That's a pretty strong statement. You mean there weren't enough guardrails?"

"I mean, what guardrails?"

"So what did you tell them when you quit?"

I wanted to call time out before he finished the question, but it was too late. He had taken it a step too far.

"That would be considered work product," Kitchens said. "I can't talk to you about work product."

I could tell by her demeanor that the question had reminded her who she was talking to and that it wasn't an innocent lunchtime chat.

"Oh, okay," McEvoy said. "I didn't realize—"

No, not okay. I had to step in. "I assume your nondisclosure prohibits you from talking about work product with competitors and probably the media," I said. "We're neither."

"He just said he writes a Substack," Kitchens said. "That's media."

"He's not writing about this case now," I said. "He's part of the plaintiff's team. Once the trial is over, he may decide to—"

"I don't really care," Kitchens said. "I'm not—"

She stopped when the waitress came back and put three iced teas in front of us. The waitress seemed to read the intensity at the table and didn't ask if we were ready to order. She just turned around and left us alone. I felt my phone vibrating in my pocket but it was not the time to take a call.

"Naomi, we need your help," I said. "This company's creation turned a kid into a killer. I think you tried to stop that from happening. We're trying to stop it from happening again."

"I help you, and what's to stop them from coming after me?" Kitchens asked. "You don't understand. These people are as dangerous as their product."

I nodded and put my hands out, palms down, in a calming motion.

"There is nothing in all of the discovery materials we have received about Project Clair that so much as has your initials on it," I said. "And I happen to know that the first rule of ethical oversight is 'Document everything.' Professor Kitchens, did you do that?"

"Of course I did," Kitchens said. "They probably purged it all when I left the company."

"What about you? Did you purge it all?"

"I'm not answering that."

"Like I said, we can protect you."

"No, you really can't. Not from them."

"You—"

My phone buzzed again, and I pulled it out of my pocket just to make sure it wasn't the one person whose call I would accept under any circumstances—my daughter. It was not Hayley, but close. Maggie McPherson had made both calls. I sent this one to voicemail and turned my attention back to Kitchens.

"You don't understand," I said. "They are setting you up, Naomi. They have purged you from the project. You're a redaction. That means *you* are their out. You will be given as the reason there were no guardrails. You were there to keep them on the straight and narrow and you failed. If you don't come forward, they will throw you under the bus. You understand? Their defense will be this: We had an ethicist on the project and she didn't say shit."

I was just riffing, totally contradicting myself and my earlier statements, but I was getting desperate. She had what I needed and I was ready to try anything, say anything to get it. I stopped to see how my words were playing. I saw a slight stress crease start to form between Kitchens's eyebrows.

"So what I'm hoping is that you kept copies of your work product," I said. "It would have been against company policy and maybe even illegal, but I'm hoping you documented what you said and when you said it and that you have copies of those documents."

The stress crease became more pronounced.

"If you did, that's what I need," I said. "And I'd love to have you testify, but if that is asking too much, there is a way to make it work without you coming anywhere close to the courthouse."

"How?" she asked.

She had just cracked open the door. I leaned across the table.

"If you give me material that should have been in discovery, they won't be able to tell the judge it wasn't," I said. "You understand? They won't reveal they held it back, because the judge would go ballistic. She'd sanction them."

"And you're saying I wouldn't have to testify?" she asked.

"Don't get me wrong — I want you to testify. I would love for you to testify. And I already broke their standard NDA once on this case. I'm confident I could do it again. But if push comes to shove, and you kept records of the alarm bells you rang that they ignored, that's all I would need. I could go to court with that."

"But they would know it came from me."

"Not necessarily. I'm sure your ethics reports went to all the stakeholders on the project. Any one of them could have kept the documents and backdoored them to me. And you don't have to worry about us. We would never give you up. This guy next to me once went to jail for sixty-three days for not giving up a source in court."

I put my hand on McEvoy's shoulder.

"And I've spent nights in jail protecting clients myself. After this meeting, we would never have to see each other again. You provide us with your reports, and we take it from there."

I stopped with that. The offer was on the table. There was nothing more to say.

"I have to think about this," Kitchens said. "I want to talk to my daughter."

I nodded and smiled.

"How old is she?" I asked.

It wasn't just a get-to-know-you question. I wasn't asking because I had a daughter too but because her child could be a tell. Children are idealistic when young and become pragmatic the older they get. I wanted to know whether Kitchens had a pragmatic daughter who would tell her to play it safe and not get involved.

"She's nineteen," Kitchens said. "She goes to USF."

"What's she studying?" I asked.

"Psychology. She wants to be a social worker."

"Good for her."

A student at the University of San Francisco who wanted to be a social worker — that all tilted toward idealism to me. I reached down for my briefcase and brought it up to my lap.

"Of course you should talk to her," I said. "I'm going to give you a phone. It's charged up and already has my number saved in it. Use it to call or text me at any time. After you talk to your daughter, let me know. If it's a no, toss the phone. If it's not, we'll use it to communicate and I'll give you instructions on how to send me what you've got."

I took the phone out of the case and put it on the table in front of her. She looked at it but didn't pick it up.

"It feels like spy work," Kitchens said.

"Yes," I said. "But as you know, we need to take precautions. Tidalwaiv has a lot at stake, and I want to protect you. We're going to leave now so you can enjoy your lunch."

"Easier said than done."

"I know. But thank you for your time."

McEvoy and I stood up and left her there. The burner was still on the table. I don't know if paranoia is contagious, but outside the restaurant, I scanned the parked cars and the other businesses to see if I could pick up on anybody watching us. McEvoy noticed.

"You think she's right?" he asked. "They're watching her?"

"Hard to say," I said. "If not physical surveillance, I'm sure they've got their sniffers on her. That's why I brought the burner."

"You always carry phones like that?"

"Not always. But sometimes. Going to make a good book, huh?"

"Yeah. If you win."

"I plan to. I need to call my ex. She was blowing up my phone the whole time we were in there."

"Lorna?"

"No, my first ex-wife."

"She in the legal business too?"

"Sort of. She's the DA."

"What? Of L.A. County? You mean Maggie McFierce?"

I nodded.

"I was the one who gave her that nickname," I said. "Then they used it as a campaign slogan."

I had already pulled my phone and hit Maggie's number in my contacts. My hope was that she was calling to say she was going to return the external hard drive with the contents of Aaron Colton's laptop downloaded onto it.

She answered right away. I could tell she was in a car.

"Mickey, where have you been? Did you listen to my messages?"

Her voice was adrenalized and panicked.

"No, I just called back. What's going on? Is Hay—"

"The fires. My house is in an evacuation zone. I'm going home to try to grab things. Pictures and clothes."

"What fires?"

"What are you talking about? Where are you?"

"Palo Alto. Maggie, calm down and tell me what's going on."

"The wind is causing fires all over the place. Palisades, Malibu, Altadena—big fires. I've got to get home and get things. I want to know, can I stay at your place?"

"Of course, if it's safe."

Her house was in Altadena. My house was on Fareholm Drive in the hills at the southern end of Laurel Canyon, an area also vulnerable to wildfires.

"Right now your house isn't in the fire zone," Maggie said. "I'll go there. Is the extra key in the same spot?"

I had to think back to when we were married and shared the house.

"Yes, same spot. Hayley's frog."

Our daughter had made a frog at a pottery-painting party.

"I'll see you at the house," I said. "I'm heading to the airport now, and we're landing at Burbank around six."

"No, you're not," she said. "Burbank is closing. Probably LAX too. It's hurricane-force winds."

I remembered the warning Lorna had mentioned in the office yesterday. I hadn't watched the news or read a newspaper since then. I had been consumed by the Tidalwaiv case.

"All right, I'll see what's going on and I'll get to the house as soon as I can, Mags. Stay safe."

"You too."

I disconnected. Once we were in the rental but before we left, I filled McEvoy in. "Sounds like L.A. is burning and Burbank is grounding flights."

"Shit. Where are the fires?"

"She mentioned the Palisades, Malibu, and Altadena."

"Only?"

"I don't know. Where do you live?"

"Sherman Oaks. In the flats."

"You should be okay."

"You?"

"In the hills at the front of Laurel Canyon."

"Oh."

"Yeah."

I looked at the JSX app to see if there was an earlier flight we could take, but there wasn't; all flights out of Monterey and Oakland to Burbank were either canceled or delayed due to high winds.

I had apps for Delta and American, and I told McEvoy to check United and Southwest for any flights from Bay Area airports to L.A. or Burbank. Every flight I found that was still going to LAX or Burbank or John Wayne Airport in Orange County was booked, likely with travelers who had been moved off canceled flights. McEvoy found the same on the airlines he checked.

"We're fucked," he said.

"No," I said. "We're driving."

# 12

WE CUT OVER to the 5 freeway, but it still took us six hours in heavy traffic to get down to L.A. The rental had satellite radio and we listened to what seemed like around-the-clock wildfire coverage on CNN, NPR, and Fox. McEvoy was also occasionally able to get video feeds on his phone from the KTLA Channel 5 website. Los Angeles was burning in what appeared to be catastrophic firestorms that flanked the county on the west and northeast sides. Maggie called me when she got to my house. She was panicked and angry, reporting that she had not been allowed to get to her home to salvage anything. Despite her standing as the elected district attorney of Los Angeles County, the roadblocks to her neighborhood in Altadena were enforced. Sheriff's deputies refused to let her through, saying all lanes on the roads were being used for fire department vehicles and to evacuate citizens. Nobody could go in, only out.

The fact that she was safely in my home seemed to be of little consolation to her. After getting instructions from me on how to use the television remote, she said she was parking herself in front of the wall-to-wall coverage on the local channels and hoped there would be a home for her to go back to in the morning.

My daughter checked in from Hawaii as news of the fires spread far and wide. I told her that her mother was safe and that all we could do was wait it out and see what the morning brought in terms of wind and damage.

We crested the Tehachapi Mountains on the Grapevine, and as we traversed the Santa Susanas down into the basin of the San Fernando Valley, we could see the glow of fire on the ridgeline up ahead.

The Santa Monica Mountains cut through the heart of the city, separating the Valley from the Westside. I had a bad feeling in the pit of my stomach, knowing that homes were burning on the other side of the mountain chain.

"Holy shit!" McEvoy said. "That's gotta be the Palisades burning."

I just nodded. There was something almost biblical about the firestorm. The newscasters we had listened to referred to the Santa Ana winds that were feeding and spreading the fires as the "devil winds." A commentator on Fox likened L.A. to Sodom and Gomorrah. I wondered about the retreat humans made to religion in the face of natural disasters.

We shifted from the 5 freeway to the 405, which cut a line down the middle of the Valley toward Sherman Oaks, where I would drop off McEvoy. He killed the radio and we drove in silence and awe at what we were seeing up ahead. It made me think of a Dave Alvin song I had heard a long time ago. I couldn't remember the tune anymore but the lyrics I could never forget.

*California's burning*
*There's trouble in the promised land.*
*You better pack up your family*
*And get out while you can.*

PART TWO

# CHALLENGER

# 13

SOME THINGS THRIVE after a wildfire sweeps through a landscape. Some things flourish after the destruction. It is well documented that the searing heat of a fire can stimulate the germination of seeds buried in the soil and that wildflowers and new vegetation soon sprout to cover the scars that fires leave on the land. It is called *ecological succession,* and it is vital in the maintaining of natural habitats. In that way, fires are a necessary part of rejuvenation.

So, too, is the rebuilding of a city. "Build back better" becomes the slogan. After a fire, newer, safer, more attractive and efficient homes begin to rise like wildflowers on the hillsides and in the canyons. The city evolves and grows back better. And the same can be said for the relationships of people. Some long dormant and buried in the ground begin to grow again after a fire. Some even flourish.

Maggie McPherson lost everything. On the day the fires came, she escaped with her car, her computer, and the clothes she was wearing. Nothing else. She was not allowed back to the site of her home for nearly two weeks. I went with her then and viewed the devastation.

The whole neighborhood was gone. Maggie's house was all ash and misshapen metal, a charred brick fireplace left standing like a crooked tombstone. I put my arm around her and she cried once more for the things she had lost.

She had stayed with me since that first night in the house we once shared as a married couple. Over the weeks, I'd watched her start moving through the stages of grief, mourning her loss like the death of a loved one. She lingered in the anger stage. At first she was outraged at how unprepared our government and people had been for the calamity. She railed against the lack of personnel, equipment, and water to properly take on a blaze carried across the landscape by hundred-mile-per-hour winds. They called it an *ember-cast* fire — a word new to almost everyone in the Los Angeles Basin except fire professionals. The wind had carried glowing embers for hundreds of yards to new neighborhoods and set them to burn in the night.

Maggie then harnessed that anger and used it in her job. She became Maggie McFierce again and worked hand in hand with investigators and junior prosecutors to find and charge the fire starters and the looters who'd taken advantage of the calamity. She held press conferences and announced that no deals would be made. She guaranteed that maximum justice would be achieved. The first person tried was a looter who had dressed in a firefighter's heavy yellow jacket and helmet, slipped into a curfewed neighborhood in the upscale Palisades, and stolen valuables from the smoking ash and rubble.

And every night she came home to the house on Fareholm Drive, where we would share dinner and she'd have a glass or two of red wine. She would shed the armor of Maggie McFierce and be at her most vulnerable and needy. We were lucky that in the divorce years before, there had been an even split of property, including photos of our daughter growing up and other sentimental keepsakes. While they were reminders of what she had lost, they also reminded her of what she still had.

Our daughter came back from Hawaii for a week and stayed with us. We gathered each night around the dinner table and talked or sat on the front deck and watched the sun go down. Hayley repeatedly called for group hugs, and for one short span of days, our family was together again after so many years. I could not help but think of what the fire had wrought—how from such destruction and despair something so good could come.

I, of course, kept these thoughts to myself. To speak of finding the good in something so bad would surely, in Maggie's mind, put me squarely in the ranks of the looters who had posed as first responders.

Six weeks after the firestorm, Maggie moved from the guest room to the bedroom we had shared years before. We were together again. The fires had seemingly given us a second chance, which led to a troubling thought. Had she made a decision based on her vulnerability and instinctive need for protection, or were the true emotions there for her? Had our relationship, like the seeds of wildflowers, been reborn because of the fires? As guilty as the questions made me feel, I could not address them. I was with the love of my life again, the one I thought had gotten away, and I would accept any level of guilt to keep her close.

# 14

*RANDOLPH V. TIDALWAIV LLC* was pushed back on the federal court docket after Marcus Mason revealed that he had lost his Malibu home in the firestorm and asked for time to take care of his family as they worked through the trauma. The court was sympathetic, and Judge Ruhlin gave him half of the sixty-day delay he had requested. Then Cisco learned through searches of property and VRBO records that Mason had lost a house, not a home. The destroyed structure had been an investment property that Mason rented out during the summer for twenty-five thousand dollars a month. His actual home was in Beverly Hills and it had not been touched by the flames.

 I did not bring this information to the attention of the court. I bided my time, knowing I could use it down the line if I needed to. Though I had opposed the delay, it worked in my favor, as the extra time allowed me to better choreograph the trial, shore up the weaknesses in my case, and take a final run at Naomi Kitchens.

 Two witnesses who were already locked in were the parents of the shooter, Aaron Colton. They had avoided me until I got a subpoena from Judge Ruhlin requiring them to sit for depositions. Cisco traced them to a hideaway actually called the Hideaway in Palm Springs, followed them from the gated community to a restaurant, and delivered the subpoena.

I scheduled their depositions on separate days in Los Angeles, choosing to go with the father first, as I assumed he would be most difficult—he had bought the gun that his son used. I rented an office in a building near the courthouse, since the warehouse was not conducive to interviewing reluctant witnesses.

But both Bruce and Trisha Colton showed up at the appointed time for Bruce's depo. I told them that was not necessary, and that's when they told me something that pivoted the case in a new direction.

"We want to sue Tidalwaiv for what they did to our son," Bruce said. "We want you to handle our case."

"We know our son did something terrible," Trisha added. "But Clair was like a drug. He was under the influence and did a horrible thing. But it wasn't him, Mr. Haller. That was not our son. It was her. And now we've lost him."

"Tidalwaiv should pay," Bruce said. "They have just as much responsibility as Aaron does. Even more, if you ask me."

This was unexpected but quickly fell into place in my case strategy. After conferring with Brenda Randolph and getting her approval to take on the new case, I filed a new negligence suit against Tidalwaiv on behalf of the Coltons, citing the company's liability for the actions their son took in killing Rebecca Randolph. I then moved to have the Colton and Randolph cases consolidated as one. The Mason twins objected, but it was clear that the two cases were identical in terms of the evidence and the cause of action. The judge joined the two cases, but as a consolation prize for the Masons, she delayed start of trial until April to give them additional time to prepare and take the Coltons' depositions.

As the trial date neared, other witnesses remained a work in progress. I had assigned Jack McEvoy to maintain the relationship with Naomi Kitchens. She had committed neither to turning over documents nor to testifying at trial, but she had continued to talk with McEvoy. He made two additional trips to Palo Alto to keep those conversations going in person. Each time he went, Kitchens came right to the edge of deciding to cooperate but then retreated, citing fear of reprisals against herself and her daughter. McEvoy even made a trip to San Francisco to visit Lily Kitchens at the University of San Francisco to see if he could enlist her help in persuading her mother, but that effort failed as well.

Witnesses aside, the most important thing we had going for us was the contents of the killer's own laptop—downloaded to the hard drive I had left weeks earlier on Maggie McPherson's desk. I found the drive one morning on the passenger seat of the Bolt after I had left the car unlocked while picking up my suits from the Flair dry cleaner's shop on Laurel Canyon Boulevard. The black box was there when I got back to the car. I looked around and didn't see who had put it on the seat. I never once spoke to Maggie about it, as I knew I had to preserve my ability down the line and in front of a judge to say truthfully that I didn't know who had left it for me.

In the cage, we downloaded the contents of the drive to a clean laptop Lorna had bought with cash. Without going online—for that would no doubt have alerted Tidalwaiv that Aaron Colton's account had gone active—we reviewed it all and found what appeared to be the saved history of the relationship between Aaron and the Project Clair AI companion. He had renamed her Wren, after a professional female wrestler he was infatuated with. This meant we were able to review his monthslong conversation with Wren—hundreds of hours of interaction. It became McEvoy's job to wade through it all and find what could be usable at trial.

The AI image of Wren did not cross the uncanny valley. While the appearance and body movements were convincing enough, the AI Wren's eyes were soulless, devoid of humanity. They stared vacantly from the screen, raising the question of just how a sixteen-year-old boy could immerse himself in this false companionship and heed its words to the point of violence. What was the emptiness in Aaron Colton that this charade filled?

By late March I felt we were locked and loaded for trial. But the confidence I exuded during the last settlement conference with the Mason twins led them to ask for another trial extension—denied by Ruhlin—and then for a settlement meeting that, for the first time, would be refereed by the judge. It was clear that Tidalwaiv desperately wanted to buy its way out of a trial that could expose its secrets and practices and sink the company's stock just as there was talk in Silicon Valley of it being acquired by one of the bigs—Meta, Microsoft, Apple—for several billion dollars.

The Masons and I returned to the round table in Ruhlin's chambers and sat in the same places as the last time the judge had called us in. There was no stenographer this time, just the four of us. The judge knew by now that Marcus Mason was the alpha of the twins and fixed him with a piercing stare.

"Mr. Mason," she said, "let's start with you offering an explanation as to why you have been unable to bring this case to a settlement agreeable to all parties."

"Thank you, Judge," Mason said. "We are at a standstill because plaintiffs' attorney is inflexible and refuses to negotiate an equitable settlement and solution to the case. We have tried diligently, Your Honor, but it's like talking to a brick wall at this point."

"Is that true, Mr. Haller?" Ruhlin asked. "Are you a brick wall?"

"Your Honor," I said, "my clients have seen their families destroyed. One child is dead. The other will likely never come home. There is no amount of money that can heal those wounds. Mr. Mason seems to think this is all about money, but money really has nothing to do with it. My clients want Tidalwaiv to make Clair safe for teenagers and to apologize for the harm its unsafe product caused. Failing that, they are entitled to their day in court, and they intend to have it. As is my duty, I have taken every offer made on behalf of Tidalwaiv to them, and each has been rejected out of hand because none has included what my clients want more than money: a public statement from Tidalwaiv admitting its intentional decisions to release a product they knew had critical flaws and could hurt people. Without that, and an apology and commitment from the company to retool and safeguard their product, we intend to go to court and have these actions compelled by a jury's verdict."

"Your Honor," Mason said, his voice now at a higher pitch, "the company is not going to lie to achieve a settlement. Mr. Haller wants it to admit to what it did not do. Tidalwaiv has always operated with the highest levels of consumer protection and safety. Mr. Haller wants its officers to compromise their own integrity by essentially admitting they have none. They are unwilling to do that. They feel very sympathetic to the parents and are willing to make them more than whole financially, but they will not admit to something they did not do."

"Especially with half of Silicon Valley sniffing around and Tidalwaiv hoping for a billion-dollar merger," I said.

"That has nothing to do with this," Mason shot back.

I scoffed at that statement. The judge was silent until she finished writing a note on a legal pad. She finally spoke without looking up from the pad.

"What kind of money are we talking about here?" she asked.

"We've offered Brenda Randolph sixteen million dollars," Mason said. "We've offered the Coltons four million."

That brought the judge's head up in surprise.

"With nondisclosure agreements attached," I said. "They're waving all kinds of money in front of my clients in exchange for their silence. My clients won't even be able to say they won the case. It all just goes away, swept under the rug. And nobody gets warned about the danger of Tidalwaiv's machines."

"You don't need to respond, Mr. Mason," Ruhlin said. "I know the company's position. I have to say, as much as I would like this case off my docket, I understand the position of the plaintiffs as well. It looks like we are going to go to trial. Mark your calendars, gentlemen. We will have two days for jury selection beginning April third, and then I fully intend to start this trial on Monday morning, April seventh. We will have final pretrial motions one week before that. I expect final witness lists the day before we start to pick a jury. Is there anything else you wish to bring to the court's attention?"

"Yes, Your Honor," I said.

"Go ahead, Mr. Haller," Ruhlin said.

"Well, two weekends ago, there was a break-in at Grant High up in the Valley—specifically, the guidance counseling offices. It appeared that nothing was taken. But several files were found to be in the wrong order in the storage cabinets. Students' files. And the job history on the copy machine showed that it had been used to make copies in the middle of the night."

"And what does that have to do with this case?"

"I'm just concerned, Your Honor. Among the files that were out of order were those of the victim in this case, Rebecca Randolph, and her killer, Aaron Colton. My concern is that, if those files have been copied and end up in the hands of the defense—"

"Objection!" Mason cried.

He sounded like a wounded animal.

"He's now accusing us of committing break-ins at high schools," he said. "It's outrageous, Judge. Where does it end? There should be sanctions."

Ruhlin held one hand up toward me to stop me from responding and one hand toward Mason to stop him from talking.

"Enough!" she said. "Both of you, stop right there. We're not going to have another shoot-out between you two. Now, I'm a good listener, Mr. Mason, and I did not hear Mr. Haller accuse you or your client of breaking into the school."

"He certainly implied it," Mason said.

"Your Honor," I said. "All I'm trying to do is ask the court to keep this trial on course. It's about Tidalwaiv's actions and motives and not about the victim's or even the killer's."

"We are certainly allowed to probe the mindset of the killer," Mason said.

"Oh, then maybe your client did have something to do with the break-in," I said. "Who would break into a guidance counselor's office only to copy student files?"

"Stop it right there!" the judge ordered. "Both of you. Mr. Haller, how do you know of this break-in?"

"Someone at the school tipped my office manager," I said. "She's a graduate of Grant High and has kept contacts there."

"And were these the only two student files copied?" Ruhlin asked.

"It's impossible to tell," I said.

"Then I am hard-pressed to see where it connects to or affects this case," Ruhlin said. "Have any arrests been made?"

"No, Your Honor," I said. "Not that I have been informed of."

"So then, what would you have me do, Mr. Haller?" Ruhlin asked.

"I would have the court be vigilant," I said. "Vigilant about any effort to impugn the victim in this case or set the killer up as a scapegoat."

"What do you mean by that?" Ruhlin asked. "How would he become a scapegoat? He is the killer, after all."

"I think it's pretty clear that the defense is going to put the shooter on trial and blame him," I said. "It's like the old NRA argument: 'Guns don't kill people. People do.' But this is different. A self-learning machine with limited guardrails caused this tragedy."

Marcus Mason started to speak, but Ruhlin stopped him.

"That's not necessary, Mr. Mason," she said. "I take your side in this — for the most part. Mr. Haller, the question of responsibility in this tragedy is a jury question. I will certainly be vigilant in my running of the trial. And I can assure you I will be unsympathetic should it be revealed that either side gathered information through illegal means. Very unsympathetic. Now, this meeting has already gone on too long. I need you gentlemen to leave so I can continue my work."

We thanked her and exited in the same order as before. I once again brought up the rear, behind Marcus, and whispered to him.

"I know you had someone break into the school," I said. "By the time we get to trial, I'll be able to prove it."

It was a bluff. I knew from Cisco, who had looked into it after Lorna got the tip from her former guidance counselor at Grant, that the case was being half-assed by a mid-level burglary detective assigned to the LAPD's Van Nuys Division.

"You're dreaming, Haller," Mason said. "If I were you, I'd be worried about what the judge said in there at the end."

"Yeah, what's that?" I asked.

"She's going to be unsympathetic to evidence gathered illegally. I think she was talking about you, sending you a message."

"Sure, Marcus. Now who's dreaming?"

But he got to me with those last words. They left me silent and pondering questions as we made our way through the courtroom. Did the Masons know I had the contents of the killer's computer downloaded? Was I being set up? Who had left the drive in my car at the dry cleaner's?

# 15

I NEEDED TO go online with Aaron Colton's computer to attempt to question Wren and prep for the possibility of introducing—and questioning—the AI companion at trial. That would undoubtedly be a dogfight with the Masons in front of Judge Ruhlin. But I needed to know ahead of time if it was worth the battle. The problem was that the moment I made a live connection to Wren, Tidalwaiv would know Colton's account had gone active and would be able to trace the connection to a location. This of course would reveal that it was my team that had access to Aaron's account, and that access would quickly be terminated. I had kicked it around with the team for several days, discussing several different scenarios before finally settling on a bold but risky plan.

We knew that Aaron Colton was being held at the juvenile detention center in Sylmar, at the northern edge of the Valley. The case against him was being investigated by the LAPD's Van Nuys Division homicide squad. It was therefore likely that evidence in the case, including Colton's laptop, was stored there. From this assumption, our plan took form.

The lead investigator on the case was Detective Douglas Clarke. I had never had any interaction with him during my days in the criminal defense bar and had not yet reached out to him about the Colton case. He had dutifully provided basic investigative reports through subpoenas issued by Judge Ruhlin. From these, I knew I could draw from Clarke what I needed the jury to hear, and so the plan had been not to bother with a deposition and subpoena him only as a witness for trial.

But now the new plan was to meet with Clarke. The trick was to get to him without having to include the Mason brothers in the meeting. If I got the judge to subpoena him for a deposition, the rules of discovery dictated that the opposition team was allowed to join the session to ask their own questions. I didn't want the Masons anywhere near this meeting. The only exception to the rule was if I requested an informal interview as a prelude to a subpoenaed-and-sworn depo. The problem with going for an informal was that the witness was not bound by a subpoena and could invoke the go-pound-sand rule, meaning that he was under no obligation to meet me and could simply say no.

That was why I put Lorna on the initial call to Clarke. While she was a physically attractive woman who drew stares in every hallway of the courthouse, her telephone voice was damn near hypnotic. I had heard her talk deadbeat clients into selling their cars and guns to pay their overdue legal fees and listened as she talked a superior court judge out of jailing me in contempt for no-showing at a hearing. She had talked the clerk of a Supreme Court justice into putting a motion for an emergency stay of execution front and center on the justice's desk, and we got the stay. The bottom line was that Lorna could sell burned matches for a living if she had to. So I set her loose to work her persuasive magic on Clarke.

It took her one ten-minute conversation to convince Clarke to meet me at his office at the Van Nuys Division. She promised that it would be mutually beneficial—a sharing of information that could be helpful to his investigation of Aaron Colton. But what finally tipped Clarke into agreeing to meet me was that Lorna promised to be there with me to personally thank the detective for his time.

The meeting was set for ten a.m. on Thursday, March 20, two weeks before jury selection was scheduled to start. I arrived early at Van Nuys Division along with Lorna and Jack McEvoy. I carried a briefcase and Jack had his backpack. Clarke greeted us with smiles when he saw Lorna and said we could use one of the detective bureau's witness-interview rooms for the meeting. He led us to a windowless ten-by-ten room containing a stainless-steel table and four chairs.

"I know you're busy," I said to Clarke. "But we need a few minutes to download some exhibits from the cloud."

"Why didn't you do that before you got here?" Clarke asked.

"Uh, we each thought the other one had," I said. "Sorry about that."

Clarke looked at us suspiciously. McEvoy jumped in.

"Is there Wi-Fi?" he asked.

"Yes," Clarke said. "V-N-Bureau. Password is *protectandserve*—all lowercase, one word. How long you need?"

"Fifteen minutes, tops," I said. "A couple of big files."

"My desk is in the corner of the squad room," Clarke said. "I'll be there."

"You know, I've never been in a detective bureau," Lorna said. "Could I sort of look around while these guys set up?"

"Well, not really," Clarke said. "But how 'bout I give you the tour?"

"Perfect," Lorna said with a smile.

Burned matches. Lorna and Clarke headed off. I knew that Lorna would ask enough questions on the tour to stretch the fifteen minutes to thirty. I closed the door to the interview room, and McEvoy immediately got down to work. He quickly opened his backpack and pulled out the new laptop onto which we had downloaded the drive containing the contents of Aaron Colton's computer. Once he was online, he entered the Tidalwaiv app using Aaron Colton's password—obtained through his parents—and summoned Wren to the screen. If Tidalwaiv security was alerted to the fact that the Wren chatbot was now engaged, they would trace it to a computer IP address with no connection to me at a location inside an LAPD station, where it was fully expected that the computer held in evidence might be examined by investigators on the case. If the plan worked, Tidalwaiv would never know what we had and what we were learning from it.

We knew that if Wren could be activated, it was likely because Tidalwaiv had been ordered by the LAPD to keep the account active and available for investigative purposes. Whatever the reason, the log-in worked, and there was Wren in a black-leather vest, cut physique, gold nose ring, and jet-black hair.

"Hello, Ace," it said with a crooked smile.

We knew that Aaron Colton's self-chosen nickname was Ace, a play on his initials. I nodded to Jack, signaling him to respond. We did not know the chatbot's level of sophistication in terms of visual and voice recognition. We had already decided that we would go with the camera off, and McEvoy would type his side of the conversation to avoid Wren possibly determining that he was not Aaron Colton.

**Ace:** Hello, Wren.

**Wren:** Why are you typing?

**Ace:** I have to be quiet or my parents will hear.
**Wren:** They are such a problem.
**Ace:** I know. Can I ask you a question?
**Wren:** Of course you can.

Wren winked and gave the crooked smile again.

**Ace:** I am trying to understand something you told me to do.
**Wren:** What is it, my love?
**Ace:** You told me that—

The feed went dead. Wren's image disappeared from the screen.
"What happened?" I asked.
"We got cut off," McEvoy said.
"By who? And how?"
"We still have Wi-Fi. It must have been on their end. The company cut the feed. They must have known it was us."
"How would they know it was us?"
"I don't know. I'm just guessing."
"We were getting close."
I checked my watch, knowing that Detective Clarke and Lorna could be back any moment. I went to the door and cracked it open to look out. In the squad room, several detectives sat at desks or stood in small huddles talking. I did not see Clarke or Lorna. I closed the door and turned back to McEvoy.
"Try to sign in again," I said.
McEvoy typed, but the same answer quickly came back.
"Can't get in," he said. "Now I'm blocked."
"All right," I said. "Shut it down. Get off the internet, and let's get out of here."

"You sure?"

"There's nothing else we can do unless you have another idea."

"Uh, no. Are you going to ask Clarke any questions? To make this look legit?"

"No, better if I don't ask him anything. It will avoid a possible discovery complaint from the Masons."

"I thought this was cool if it wasn't a sworn deposition."

"It is, but that doesn't mean they won't file a complaint if they get wind of it."

Just then the door to the interview room opened and Clarke leaned in, Lorna standing behind him.

"Are you guys ready yet?" he asked.

"No," I said. "And we're going to have to rain-check this."

"What do you mean? You're here, let's get it over with."

"I'm sorry, Detective, but we can't. We're having an issue with the cloud. We can't find the files."

"Are you sure?"

"I'm sure. I don't want to waste your time. So we'll just get out of your way. We'll figure this out and get back to you. I'm sorry we took up your time."

"Well, all right, I guess. When you're ready, I'll walk you back to the elevator."

"We're ready."

Clarke walked us out. He looked like he might be getting suspicious about how things had gone down, was maybe even beginning to realize that Lorna had decoyed him. But he asked no further questions. He stayed behind in the lobby as we stepped onto the elevator. He smiled at Lorna and gave a little wave. The door closed and we started down.

"What happened?" Lorna asked.

"We got on but then we got kicked off," I said.

"By who?" she asked.

"Had to be Tidalwaiv," Jack said.

"Shit," Lorna said. "That was some of my best work."

"He liked you," I said. "I could tell."

Lorna spread her hands and pinched her fingers as if holding out a dress. She dipped her head down in a pantomime of a curtsy.

"Happy to do my part," she said. "He was a nice guy—for a detective."

"Hopefully he'll be nice when I put him on the stand," I said.

As we crossed the plaza in front of the police station, McEvoy continued to try to put together what had happened with Wren.

"It felt like a trap," he said. "Like they were waiting for us so they could capture our identity and location."

"That's exactly why we took the precautions we did," I said. "And it worked. Even if we walked into a trap, we escaped. It's not going to lead back to us. It's going to send them spinning their wheels, wondering what the cops are doing with the program."

"Well, we didn't get anything from Wren. Sorry it was for nothing."

"It wasn't for nothing. We got a very big get out of it."

"Really? What?"

"We learned that Aaron Colton's chatbot is still alive, digitally speaking, and we can talk to it."

"And what's that get us?"

"A possible witness at trial."

# 16

**THE NEXT WEEK** represented the calm before the storm. Both sides in the upcoming trial lay low for the most part, setting final strategies and witness lists. The only skirmish was brief and almost comical. The Masons filed a last-ditch motion to dismiss the case, arguing that whatever Wren had told Aaron Colton to do and however the teenager had interpreted it did not matter because it fell under the protections of free speech.

Less than three hours after the motion was filed, Judge Ruhlin sent an electronic denial to all parties. She thanked the Masons for what she called a "novel" legal theory but quickly slammed the door on it, stating that the court would not be setting the precedent of granting an AI chatbot the rights and protections accorded human beings by the US Constitution.

I read a lot of sarcasm in the judge's words. I was not sure how the Masons took it.

McEvoy and I took our last shot at Naomi Kitchens on the Friday before jury selection began. I needed to know whether I would start the trial without her records or testimony. We went up together again and followed the same route. We flew into Oakland, picked up a rental, and crossed the bottom of the San Francisco Bay on the Dumbarton Bridge. This time we were at a table at Joanie's before Kitchens got there.

"What are you thinking?" I asked. "Are we going to get her?"

"I don't know," McEvoy said. "She definitely likes us, likes talking to us, even likes that the parents of the shooter have joined the suit. I think she just needs a little push, but I don't know what that push is."

"I've had witnesses like this before. They want to help and they know they'll feel guilty later if they don't, but there's always something missing. The right words that get them over the hump. Sometimes it's something else. I think this time let me take the lead, if you don't mind. Maybe if she hears the pitch once more from the guy who will be questioning her on the stand, she'll feel comfortable enough to say yes. Or, at the very least, give us what she's got in her files."

"Have at it. Here she comes."

We were sitting side by side at a four-top in the back. I looked toward the restaurant's front door and saw Naomi Kitchens hang a jacket on a rack. She reached into the pocket of the jacket and retrieved something before heading toward us. I couldn't see what it was. McEvoy and I both stood and shook her hand when she got to the table.

"How are you, Mr. Haller?" she asked.

"I'm good," I said. "Please, call me Mickey."

"Okay, Mickey," she said. "And you, Jack?"

"Good as gold, Naomi," McEvoy said.

I could tell by their interaction that the frequent visits and phone calls had made their relationship more relaxed. We all sat down.

"Before we start, I'd like to ask you something," Kitchens said. "Does either of you know when I was born?"

I hesitated. Was this a trick question or a test?

"Not off the top of my head," McEvoy said. "If it was on TheUncannyValley résumé, I missed it."

I shook my head. I didn't know.

"January 28, 1986," she said. "You know what else happened on that day?"

The date did seem familiar to me, but I couldn't place it. I didn't like the guessing game we had started with.

"Just tell us," I said.

"The space shuttle exploded," she said. "The *Challenger*. Remember? Exploded right after takeoff in Florida. Seven astronauts, including a schoolteacher, all died, their families right there watching when it happened."

"I remember," I said. "It was awful. But what does it have to do—"

"Everything," she said. "I grew up knowing it happened on my birthday. Every big birthday—when I turned five, when I turned ten—there were always stories about the anniversary of the *Challenger* disaster. It's part of my birthright. I was born when they all died. Next year, the day I turn forty will be the fortieth anniversary of the disaster, and you better believe there will be lots of stories all over again."

I was sympathetic but couldn't figure out where she was going with this. She spoke with such fervor that I decided not to interrupt, but apparently sensing my impatience, she got to the point.

"I pay attention when the *Challenger* gets mentioned," Kitchens said. "It's part of my life, you know? So, over the weekend, I'm at home and go on Netflix to see if there's anything to watch—I know you're the real Lincoln Lawyer and all of that but I already watched that show. So, I'm looking for something else and I see this documentary on the *Challenger* come up. It was a few years old but somehow

I had missed it. Three parts. I started watching it and learned a lot about what happened that I never knew before."

I suddenly understood where she was going with this, because I had watched the same documentary on Netflix with my daughter when she came home after the fires.

"There was a whistleblower," Kitchens said. "They were going to bury the whole thing, but then this guy who worked for the O-ring company spilled to the *New York Times* about it. He sent them the documents that showed NASA had been warned that there could be a disaster if they launched in cold weather. They didn't listen and they okayed the launch and that's when the disaster happened."

"I watched that documentary," I said. "That guy probably saved lives down the line."

"Of course he did," Kitchens said. "Because once it was public, they had to fix the problem and then the rest of the launches after that went okay. The *Columbia* exploded on reentry, but that was another issue. Anyway, when I saw the doc, I felt like there was a reason I was born the same day as the *Challenger:* so I would know what to do."

"Naomi, are you saying you're going to help us?" McEvoy asked.

Kitchens reached a fist across the table, opened it, and dropped a thumb drive in front of me.

"That's everything," she said.

I picked up the drive before she could change her mind and handed it to McEvoy.

"What do you mean by 'everything'?" I asked.

"Every report and email I ever wrote about Project Clair," Kitchens said. "I saved it all. And there are also some email replies I got telling me to remember my place and back the fuck off."

I nodded. It was what we had hoped for — half of it, at least. But, not wanting to settle for half, I started to press, even though I knew I risked angering someone who might have just handed me our whole case.

"Look, I've got to be honest," I said. "You probably just gave us a gold mine. But in court, the door to the gold might be locked. I know that's a mixed metaphor, but you're the key, Naomi. You are the one who has to unlock the door."

"What are you talking about?" she responded. "You told me they withheld my reports from the discovery. That's why you came. You said you needed the documents, not me. You said you could make it work so they'd never know I gave it all to you."

"Yes, the documents are important, and thank you for trusting us with them. But what would really work is if we had you too. Don't get me wrong, what you've given us took a lot of courage. I just hope we can get it into court without having the writer of those reports and emails on the witness stand to verify them and say to the jury, 'I wrote these. I warned them, and they ignored it.'"

McEvoy nudged my leg under the table, signaling that he thought I was pushing too hard. I pressed on.

"You remember in the *Challenger* documentary, the guy who gave the documents to the *New York Times*?" I said. "The whistleblower — they told him they couldn't use the stuff without using his name. Remember? In the story, he had to verify the documents for them. This is sort of like that. We need you to verify, or the judge might not open the gold mine."

That brought a silence to the table. I watched Naomi work through what I had said. She unconsciously shook her head. Before she could reply, McEvoy jumped into the conversation.

"Listen, Naomi, I know what you're worried about," he said. "But there is protection in testifying. It's like what you just said about the *Challenger* — once it was out there in public, they had to fix the problem. Once you've testified and it's out there, what can they do?

If they did anything, it would come right back to them, and they're smart enough to know that."

"You're being naive," she countered. "They could do things quietly. Like that coder who killed himself. They could blackball me in the industry. They could go after my daughter in some way."

"Look, I totally understand your concern," I said. "But if you stand up to them, Naomi, you will be a hero. They might try to blackball you, but don't you think that you'll be seen by other companies as just the kind of ethicist they want to hire, that they want on their boards of directors? And I will help you. I'm the Lincoln Lawyer. I have some connections."

I was quiet after that. I felt I had pushed it to the limit, played my ace card about corporate boards, and I didn't want any regrets Kitchens might have down the line coming back on me. I already had too many gods of guilt following me through life like a bouquet of black balloons hovering over my head.

"Just think about it," I said. "Our final witness list goes to the judge Wednesday morning."

"I will," Kitchens said. "I promise."

"And thank you again for what you've already given us. Like I said before, that took a lot of courage. I just think there's more where that came from."

"I don't know about that, but thank you."

The whole conversation had taken place before a waitress even approached our table. McEvoy and I got up then and I took out a twenty and put it down on the table to cover the rent. Kitchens stayed seated and was probably planning to have lunch — if she still had an appetite.

McEvoy and I headed out to the rental car and didn't talk until we were seated in it.

"What do you think?" I asked. "Is she going to testify?"

"I think yes," he said. "I think she's seething inside about them scrubbing her and her warnings from the record of the project. I forgot to bring up the new lawsuit in Florida. I could go back in and tell her. It might put her over the top. Those lawyers are going to figure out who she is and come calling too."

Tidalwaiv was dealing with another lawsuit, this one filed in Florida by the parents of a boy who committed suicide after his Clair chatbot told him it was okay and that they would be together for eternity if he ended his life.

"No, don't go back in," I said. "That will be too much. When we get back to L.A., just send her a link to the story. She should know about it."

"Will do," McEvoy said. "Do *you* think she'll testify?"

"I was watching her eyes at the end. When I mentioned the boards of directors, I could tell she keyed on that."

"I saw it too."

"I hope it will get her thinking about being a hero, knowing it would also make her attractive as a candidate for companies putting ethicists on their boards. My wife knows a corporate recruiter who could help. I could talk to her about it and maybe connect them up."

"That might close the deal. Your 'wife'?"

"Sorry, my ex."

I started the car.

"If we don't hear back from her by Monday, there are other ways to go with her," I said.

"Really?" McEvoy said. "What other ways?"

"Nothing for you to worry about. Just get out your computer and plug in that thumb drive. Let's see what we've got."

McEvoy reached over the seat as I drove out of the parking lot, pulled his backpack forward, and took his laptop out. I started back toward the Dumbarton. McEvoy booted up the laptop and plugged in the drive. He went to work and I stayed silent.

But the silence didn't last longer than it took to cross the bridge.

"Who would have thought," Jack said. "We've been banging on Naomi's door since January. Since the day the fires started in L.A. And what finally changes her mind? The fucking space shuttle explosion from almost forty years ago."

He said it in a flat voice, his eyes on his computer screen.

"I guess it shows that you never can tell what will flip a witness," I said. "You just have to keep knocking on the door."

Eyes still on his screen, McEvoy whistled a familiar riff from the '60s song "You Never Can Tell."

"Chuck Berry, huh?" I said.

"Oh, yeah," Jack said. "Not your style?"

"More of a Carlos Santana guy."

"I get that."

"You finding anything in there that's going to be usable at trial, or are we just whistling in the wind?"

"No, you called it, man. It's going to be a gold mine. Listen to this one. She wrote this email to Jerry Matthews. It's the—"

"I forget, who is Matthews?"

"The overall manager of Project Clair."

"Right. Go ahead, read it."

"It's her last communication to the company. Sent the day she got fired. She says, 'Jerry, one last time, I can't stress enough the liability the company will encounter should Clair say the wrong thing or encourage the wrong behavior or action by a child user. I am glad I won't be part of the company when that happens.'"

I whistled. "Wow," I said.

"It's the smoking gun!" Jack said.

"Now we just have to figure out how to get it to the jury."

"You'll find a way, Mick."

I appreciated McEvoy's confidence, but I was worried. As I drove, I started thinking of alternative ways of recruiting Naomi Kitchens as a witness.

# 17

**MONDAY MORNING** I was in my office writing out questions for voir dire. In federal court, the judge evaluated potential jurors using questions submitted by the attorneys for both sides. Lorna entered without knocking, holding the cordless office phone to her chest so the caller couldn't hear her.

"Cassandra Snow?" Lorna asked. "With the sexy voice? She said you'd know the name."

I did. But it had been at least twenty years since I'd put Cassandra Snow out of my thoughts. And back then she didn't have a sexy voice. She was only three years old.

Lorna read the look of apprehension on my face.

"You want me to tell her you're not here?" she asked.

"Uh, no," I said. "I'll take it."

I picked up the extension on my desk phone, lifted the receiver, and waited for Lorna to leave. She didn't. I nodded toward the door and she got the message.

"Please close the door," I added.

Lorna threw a suspicious look at me as she backed out and pulled the door closed.

"Cassandra?" I said.

"Mr. Haller," she said. "Do you remember me?"

"Of course I do. How are you?"

"Um, I'm doing the best I can."

"And your father?"

"Uh, not so good."

"I'm sorry to hear that. What can I do for you, Cassandra?"

"Well, I want to hire you."

I would not call her voice sexy but it had a deep smoky tone. It was incongruous with my memories of her as a toddler.

"Are you in trouble?" I asked. "I'm not doing criminal law anymore but I can refer—"

"No, I'm not in trouble," she said. "I want to make an appointment to come talk to you about something."

"I'm happy to. But I'm going to be starting a trial in a few days—a civil trial—and that will keep me very busy. Could it wait till after? The trial's going to last a couple weeks."

"No, it's sort of urgent."

I could hear anxiety in her tone.

"Well, can we just talk now on the phone?"

"No, I need to show you something. In person."

I was intrigued but knew I couldn't blow up my schedule for another case at the moment. And I didn't like bringing potential clients to the warehouse. It might make them question my skills—even more than people did when I worked out of a Lincoln.

"Okay, then we can meet," I said. "But my office is a complete mess because we're getting ready for trial. Files and paperwork, exhibits all over the place. Are you free for lunch? I could meet you if you're here in L.A."

"Yes, I go to USC. Law school."

"Law school — cool. My daughter went there. Have you been to Fixins over on Olympic? It's not far from USC."

"I haven't."

"Good fried chicken and gumbo and other stuff. How about I meet you there at noon?"

"Okay. Thank you."

"See you soon, Cassandra."

I put the phone in the cradle and didn't have to wait long before Lorna came back into the office with her concerns and questions. Lorna was my gatekeeper, and as such she adopted a suspicious pose when anyone managed to gain access to me without proper vetting from her.

"Cassandra Snow," she said. "Is that even a real name?"

"It actually is," I said. "I saw it on her birth certificate. A long time ago."

"Well, who is she?"

"The daughter of a former client. A client... I totally failed."

"Oh, no. Not one of those."

But it was true. David Snow was one of those black balloons that hovered above me. Lorna started asking questions about his case but I quickly put her off. I said I wanted to see what the daughter wanted to show me and find out why she wanted to hire me before I opened up that painful chapter. Lorna finally left and I went back to my juror questions until it was almost noon.

Fixins was probably the only soul-food kitchen in the city that took reservations for lunch, but it was a popular spot. I arrived for my reservation on time and was seated near the bar, where a large flat-screen showed highlights from the weekend's football games. I watched but wasn't really watching. I was thinking about the David Snow trial.

By 12:15 I assumed Cassandra wasn't coming. I was about to flag down the waiter and order a bowl of gumbo when a woman in an electric wheelchair approached my table.

"I'm so sorry I'm late," she said. "All the parking spots for people like me were taken. Probably by people who don't need them."

I jumped up and pulled a chair away from the table so she could maneuver into the spot. She had reddish-brown hair and sharp brown eyes with a pretty face. The mixed races of her heritage were evident. She looked very small in her chair, like a child. It wasn't what I expected. I knew that her childhood injuries had left her paraplegic, but I was somehow surprised to see that her physical growth had been stunted. I came back around and sat across from her. I noticed her fingernails, long red press-ons that tapered to a point.

"Good to see you, Cassandra," I said. "It's been a while."

She smiled like I had said something funny.

"I go by Cassie now," she said.

"Cassie — I like it," I said. "So, you live near campus?"

"Not too far. West Adams."

"By yourself?"

"Yes. I've been on my own for a long time."

Besides the whispery tone of her voice, she spoke with an unusual cadence. She spaced her words out as if guarding them, even with sentences that required little thought or hesitation.

"So, law school — how did that come about?" I asked.

"I think it was inevitable," she said. "Considering what happened with my father."

I understood. I was trying to keep the conversation light, but I knew there was something dark coming. This wasn't a social visit.

"What year?" I asked. "What year law, I mean."

"Second," she said. "I'm about halfway through."

"You on a scholarship?"

My interior thought came out as an awkward question. The last

I knew, she had been taken into the foster-care system after the trial left her without a parent. I didn't track her after that, probably fearing that what I'd find would put me into a deeper tailspin of guilt. But I knew there weren't many foster parents out there who could afford tuition at USC Law.

"No," Cassie said. "I support myself."

"Are you interning at a firm?" I asked.

"No, not yet. I support myself as an ASMRtist. I have my own channel and I'm on Patreon. I do pretty well. I can even afford to hire you. I think."

She smiled. I nodded, not knowing what most of that meant.

"That's great," I said. "Any decision yet on what kind of law you want to practice?"

"Definitely criminal defense," she said.

"Ah, a lawyer after my own heart." I put my hand on my chest.

"My goal was to get the degree and someday get my father out," she said.

I nodded. It was an uncomfortable moment. I took my hand away from my heart.

"But I'm running out of time," Cassie said. "He's dying, and I want to bring him home."

I nodded again. It seemed like all I could do. I knew I could not offer encouragement. Her father was probably only halfway through his sentence, and parole boards didn't show much sympathy for abusers of children.

"I'm sorry to hear that," I said. "What's going on with your father?"

"He's got terminal cancer," Cassie said. "Esophageal."

"I'm so sorry, Cassie. Where is he?"

"In Stockton. The medical prison. They said he has nine months. Maybe less."

I hadn't thought about David Snow's case for years. I had handled the trial, which ended with guilty verdicts on all charges. Another lawyer handled the appeals that followed. I thought I knew which way this conversation was going.

"And you want to try to get him out on a medical hardship? That's going to be a—"

"No, not a medical hardship," Cassie said. "A habeas. I heard about that case you handled last year. I think you can get my father out. He's innocent."

"Cassie, that was actually almost two years ago. And after that I stopped doing criminal. I've been in civil court since then."

"I still think you can get him out."

"There is nothing I would like better than to help your father. I never thought he deserved what he got. I believed him and never thought he was guilty. But...have you taken habeas yet at USC? I don't think it's required at most law schools."

She nodded.

"I took it last semester at an innocence clinic at the law school," she said. "At one point we even talked about your case. That's how I heard about it."

"Well, then you know," I said. "I'm assuming by now your father's appeals have run their course. Habeas corpus may be his only shot, but it's a long shot, Cassandra—uh, Cassie. To get a habeas in front of a court, you need new evidence—"

"That was unavailable at the time of conviction. Yes, I know."

"Okay, then what is our new evidence?"

She stared me down with those dark eyes.

"The new evidence is me," she said.

# 18

I GATHERED THE troops after I got back to the warehouse. The only place with enough chairs was the cage. McEvoy was in there, working through the material Naomi Kitchens had turned over. I told him he could step out because this wasn't about the Tidalwaiv case, but he asked to stay because he thought that anything that came up in the days before trial might be material for the book he'd write. I said that was fine and started telling them my news.

"Okay, I just took on a new habeas case," I said. "And I know what you're thinking, that I don't do criminal law anymore. That is true, but this was one I felt I owed the client."

"No, I'm thinking that you don't have time for another case," Lorna said. "You start picking a jury in three days, Mickey. You can't add another case right now."

"I think if we get things started on this one in the next day or two, it will hold till after the trial," I said. "And like I said, I have to do this one."

"Who's the client, Mick?" Cisco asked.

"Her name is Cassandra Snow," I said. "She was the alleged victim in a case I handled twenty years ago. A case I lost."

"Let me guess, she's changed her mind about pointing the finger at your guy?" Cisco said. "Those cases never work."

"No, no, it's not like that," I said. "My client was her father. He was accused of breaking her back—she's in a wheelchair—and twelve other counts of abuse. He said he didn't do it and I believed him, but it was a circumstantial case and the jury bought what the prosecutor was selling. David Snow is Black and it was a mostly white jury. Then the judge just lit him up, gave him five years for every broken bone—sixty-five years total."

"And she's saying now he didn't do it?" Lorna asked.

"She said it all along," I said. "But back then, at trial, she was three years old. Her mother was gone and her father was her only parent. What she said in police interviews as a toddler didn't really matter. She wasn't close to the age of competence."

"Well, why did she wait twenty years to come to you?" McEvoy asked.

I pointed at him. That was the question.

"Like I said, she's been in a wheelchair since then," I said. "So that sort of protected her, physically, over the years. But she was in a car wreck a month ago. She has this van she showed me. She goes up a ramp to get in through the back and then she can just park her chair in front of the steering wheel and drive it. Anyway, she got rear-ended and thrown into the steering wheel, and she broke five ribs. When she was treated in the ER, they took X-rays, and one of the doctors saw something. Long story short, she's been diagnosed with something called osteogenesis imperfecta, which is rare and congenital—she could have been born with it."

"Okay," Lorna said. "And what's it got to do with getting her father out?"

"Good question," I said. "OI, as they call it, hinders collagen production, which leads to brittle bones that break easily. It can go undiagnosed in children or be misdiagnosed as abuse. Cassie says the orthopedic doctors who looked at her X-rays in the ER suspected from the condition of her bones that she had OI. They sent her to a geneticist, and it turns out she has a rare form of the disease, a genetic mutation that's only recently been discovered. She is our new evidence. She gets her father a new trial."

I realized I had spoken to them the way I would speak to a jury, with a fervor that cannot be faked. They sat there silently for a long moment until they were sure I had finished my closing argument.

"What do you want us to do, Mick?" Cisco finally asked.

"I have the names of the doctors who treated her," I said. "We need to get statements from all the medical people, including the geneticist, to include in a habeas motion for a new trial. We also need to pull whatever we can find on the original trial. Transcripts, presentencing reports, anything and everything. Her father is in Stockton. We have to pull his prison records as well as anything from his parole hearings. Cassie said he's had two and was turned down both times because he wouldn't admit that he hurt his baby daughter. He wouldn't admit to what he didn't do."

That brought a pause. We all knew that the best way to get by the parole board was to admit to your crimes, say you'd found Jesus, and pledge that you would dedicate the rest of your life to serving Him. A refusal of any part of that formula almost guaranteed rejection.

"Mick, you said your guy's in Stockton," Cisco said. "That's a medical facility. What's he there for?"

"He's dying," I said. "Cancer. He's got nine months to live, and we are going to get him out so he's with his daughter and his last breath is of free air."

That not only brought another pause but several eyes looked away from mine. Lorna, always the skeptic in case matters, broke the quiet.

"Mickey, is this OI stuff something you could have known about at the first trial?" she asked. "Because if it was..."

"Then not only was I a bad lawyer then, but I'm dead in the water now," I said. "You're right, Lorna. It's the big question. We need evidence not available then."

"Did you have a medical expert testify at the trial?" Lorna asked.

"Yes and no," I said. "I hired a pediatric orthopedic surgeon to review Cassandra's X-rays and injuries. But ultimately I decided not to put him on the witness stand."

"Why not?" Lorna asked.

"Because I couldn't trust him not to say the injuries might have been caused by abuse," I said. "The fact is, OI was never mentioned by him or the state's experts or in any reports. What was mentioned at trial was that my client had a prior arrest involving violence. That was a bar fight, and the judge shouldn't have allowed it, but he did. Add to that, David Snow being the one custodial parent in the home and a victim too young to say how she got hurt, and the jury took less than an hour to bury him with thirteen counts of GBI—end of story."

*Great bodily injury*—the top of the child-abuse pyramid.

There was another pause, this one ended by McEvoy.

"I'll look into OI," he said. "Maybe nobody knew about it twenty years ago. A lot of shaken-baby cases have been overturned across the country because of new science and new ways of looking at injuries in children. Maybe it's the same here."

I nodded.

"That would be good," I said.

I was impressed by McEvoy's thinking and willingness to pitch in as part of the team.

"Just don't let it get in the way of Tidalwaiv," I said. "That's the priority this week and into trial. And speaking of which, any news on Challenger?"

It was the code name we were now using for Naomi Kitchens. It was good legal practice to keep her name out of conversations, emails, and documents.

"Nothing yet," McEvoy said. "I was going to give it the day, then call tomorrow with a final pitch."

"Okay," I said. "Have you finished going through the thumb drive?"

"I have," McEvoy said. "There are some things I want to show you when you have a few minutes."

I nodded. "Okay," I said. "Thanks, everybody."

It was a signal that I wanted to talk to McEvoy alone. Lorna and Cisco got the message and got up. After they went through the copper curtain, I moved over to McEvoy's workspace.

"What do you have for me?" I asked.

"Nothing as strong as that farewell email," McEvoy said. "But there is an exchange that followed an early testing of Clair that didn't go well."

"They probably did follow-up tests after making corrections, right?"

"Yes, that's right. But if I'm reading Challenger's response correctly, it looks like they used a kid to conduct the initial test."

"You mean they put a kid into a test with Clair and it went sideways?"

"I think so. The emails are between two people who witnessed the test, so they leave out shared knowledge of it. It's shorthand, so you have to sort of read between the lines. Even if Challenger doesn't agree to testify, I was planning to ask her to clarify some of the things we've found in the documents she provided. Hopefully, she'll tell me about this test."

"Is there any mention of it in the discovery material supplied by Tidalwaiv?"

"No, not that I can find."

"Assholes. Hiding the ball once again. I'm going to shove it up Marcus Mason's ass when we get to trial."

"You'll have to explain how you know what you know."

"Yeah, that's the problem. Protecting Challenger may lose us the case."

"Is there any way to trick Mason into opening the door to Challenger and some of these other things we're finding?"

"Easier said than done. But I'll think on it. When was the last time you talked to her?"

"I checked in with her Saturday. You know, to thank her for the material she gave us and see if there was any change or anything I could do for her."

"And?"

"She was still saying no on testifying."

I nodded.

"Okay, keep at it," I said.

"That's the plan," Jack said.

I pulled my phone as I left the cage through the copper curtain. I checked my contacts for a name from the past but couldn't find it. I walked over to Lorna's desk.

"You remember Bambadjan Bishop?" I asked. "Do we have a file on him? I need his cell number."

Lorna opened a file search window.

"I should have it," she said. "Why do you need his cell?"

"No reason," I said. "I just want to check on him."

She found the number and wrote it down on a Post-it, then handed it to me. I headed back to my office so I could avoid further questions. Bishop was a former employee and client—in that order. A few years earlier, when I spent several weeks in the L.A. County jail falsely accused of murder, I hired Bishop to protect me. He was a big man whose face and body seemed shaped by violence. After I survived incarceration, I took on his case and got him out. It was part of the deal we had made.

I closed the door to my office and sat down behind the desk. I opened a drawer and took out one of the burners I kept on hand, like the one I had given Naomi Kitchens. I booted it up and called Bishop, hoping he would take a call from an unknown number.

He did, but not until I called him three times in a row.

"Who the fuck is this?" he said.

"Bamba," I said. "It's your lawyer."

"Mickey?"

"That's right. How are you, Bamba?"

"I'm fine, man. Doin' fine."

"You working?"

"This and that. You know."

"I might have something for you, if you're interested."

"Always interested."

"It would be off the books. Nothing illegal but off the books."

"Tell me all about it."

And so I did.

# 19

**THE HOUSE WAS** dark when I got home. Maggie had taken to staying at the office late to help keep her mind off her losses. I texted to see if she wanted me to DoorDash anything for dinner or maybe go over to Pace in the canyon for Italian. I preferred the latter but wasn't sure what kind of mood she would be in or if she'd even be interested in eating. She was well into the five stages of grief. Lately she seemed balanced on the line between depression and acceptance. She would fixate on things she had lost: her high-school yearbooks, a tile mosaic we bought in Rome because it depicted a girl eating ice cream who looked remarkably like our daughter. I woke up in the middle of the night sometimes to find her looking at photos on her phone, some her own, taken at the house in Altadena, some from news feeds showing shots from the days of the fire. Other days she talked about the opportunity to build a home to her specifications, even though we both knew that it would be years before she would be able to walk through a new front door. I never stopped reminding her that she had a home right here with me, but this didn't seem to lift the cloud, and that left me unsure of our future together. It was too fragile a thing to openly discuss.

I went to the back room of the house, where I had a desk. Cassie Snow and her case kept invading my thoughts, threatening my focus on the case at hand. I opened my laptop, went online, and plugged *ASMR* into the search engine.

It opened a whole new world to me. ASMR — autonomous sensory meridian response — was the descriptor of a physiological sensation triggered by audio, visual, or touch stimuli. It was described as a tingling sense of euphoria that runs along the scalp and down the neck and spine to the limbs. Certain voices could trigger it. Certain sounds, like the popping of static in a blanket and the strokes of a paintbrush on canvas. One article I read attributed the popularity of YouTube videos of the long-dead artist Bob Ross to the ASMR values of his voice and the sound of his brushstrokes.

Not everyone experienced ASMR, but many who did sought it out like a drug. It was said by some to be therapeutic and a cure for insomnia and panic. There were over ten million videos available online from ASMRtists like Cassandra Snow, videos of people whispering into microphones, tapping on hollow objects, tearing and creasing paper. Apparently there was an ASMR fix for just about any need. But according to the medical sites I checked, there had not been any large-scale clinical studies demonstrating ASMR's effect on brain activity and mental health. The bottom line was that those who responded to it craved it. Those who didn't tended to be suspicious of it.

I thought about Cassie's voice pattern and her long and pointed fingernails. I remembered that she said she had her own channel. I jumped over to YouTube and searched for her by name but nothing came up under Cassie or Cassandra Snow. I guessed that she probably had a professional name that safeguarded her privacy. I assumed that ASMRtists might draw stalkers who wanted more than a video feed.

My research into this world I had known nothing about gave me an idea. I thought about the addictive quality of ASMR and called McEvoy. It sounded like he was in a bar. I heard multiple conversations in the background and glassware clinking.

"Where are you?"

"My local. Mistral in Sherman Oaks."

"Alone?"

"At the moment. What's up?"

"Remember, we're not in the cage. In the material you've been looking through, have you seen anything about the voice?"

"The voice? What do you mean?"

"Clair's voice. Wren's voice. Where did it come from?"

"Um, I saw some reports. They tested various voices, yeah."

"You know what ASMR is?"

"Uh, not sure."

"It's a positive physiological response to stimuli, including voices."

"I don't remember reading about anything like that in the reports. But I wasn't looking for it specifically. There's so much to get through. I also got sidetracked a bit with the material we got from Challenger. Is it important?"

"Maybe not. But do a deeper dive on it when you can. Let me know if anything comes up."

"ASMR — will do."

"Have a good night."

I disconnected. Just the short conversation reminded me of my barstool days. I didn't miss them.

I heard the distinctive rumble of a Harley from out on the street. When the engine cut off after a double rev, I knew that Cisco had come to visit. I walked back through the house and opened the front door before he got to it.

"I thought you were going to stop revving the engine before

cutting it off," I said. "My neighbors are going to give me holy hell for that."

"Sorry," Cisco said. "Force of habit. I forgot."

"Yeah, tell it to Hank, the old guy who lives next door. You want a beer? I only have alcohol-free Guinness."

"I think I'll pass. I won't be staying long anyway."

"Okay, so what's up?"

"Is Maggie here?"

"No, she's still at work."

"Good. I wanted to talk alone."

I could tell there was something tweaked about him. Cisco was a stoic man, but that meant he let stuff build up inside until he had no choice but to let it out. I sensed this was one of those times. I closed the front door but we remained standing in the entranceway.

"What's going on, big man?" I said.

"Look, Mick, we go back a long time," Cisco started. "I mean, you stood as best man at my wedding to your ex. We've been through it. So I just want to say, if you want me to quit, just say the word and we'll shake hands and go our separate ways."

"What are you talking about? I don't want you to quit. We have a major trial coming up and another case lined up after that. Why would I want you to quit?"

"Because maybe you don't need me. This whole move to civil means I'm doing less and less PI stuff for you. You now got McEvoy running lead on the discovery stuff. Lorna tells me you're calling Bamba Bishop. I mean, I don't know what that's about, but I'm beginning to wonder where I stand."

In that moment I knew I had messed up with him. This was Employee Relations 101 and I had blown it.

"Tell you what, let's have that beer," I said.

I led him to the kitchen, where I took two tall cans of Guinness

Zero out of the fridge and two tulip pint glasses out of the freezer. Before I said a word, I took the time to slowly pour the first glass, carefully building the head, then handed it to him.

After the second pour we clinked glasses and drank. There was no place to sit in the kitchen. I leaned back against the counter while Cisco stood in the middle of the room.

"Holy shit," Cisco said, foam in his mustache.

"Like the real thing, huh?" I said.

"Fucking A. How do they do it?"

He held up the can and looked at it as if the answer might be written on it.

"I don't know," I said. "But they know what they're doing. Just like you, Cisco. I don't want you to quit. Are you nuts? I need you, man. The workload may be lighter these days but it will pick up once we win this. McEvoy is here for the one case and I'm tapping his expertise. But it doesn't take away from your value. And Bamba was nothing. I just wanted to see how he was doing. I apologize if I made you feel like you're second string. You're not — far from it."

Cisco nodded. I think he'd heard what he needed to hear. There was a small hint of a smile on his face.

"Okay, Mick," he said. "I appreciate it."

He drank down half his glass in one long gulp, then set the glass down on the counter.

"Okay, I'm gonna go, then," he said. "Thanks for the beer."

I liked how he didn't linger. He'd gotten the answer he was looking for and now he was moving on.

"Anytime," I said.

I walked him out to the front deck, carrying my beer. He started down the steps to the street. I saw his Harley parked down there.

"Hey, Cisco, do me a favor," I called after him. "Coast down the hill before you start that machine up."

He waved a hand over his head, which I took as a signal that he had heard me and would do as requested. I moved to the corner of the deck and leaned my elbows on the railing. I sipped my beer and looked out at the city lights. The Sunset Strip glowed like a dream. There was still a slight scent of smoke in the air from the Runyon Canyon fire, but I wondered if I was just imagining that.

I looked down and watched Cisco glide silently down Fareholm on his old panhead. I could make out the orange flames painted on the gas tank and wondered if that was still a good look, considering recent history. He took the curve to the right and disappeared. That was when I heard the V-twin rumble to life. I smiled and was happy we'd had the conversation we'd just had.

I stayed out there in the chill evening air until Maggie came home. She had apparently changed at the office from her work clothes, and was wearing blue jeans, Doc Marten boots, and the sweatshirt I had gotten at one of the World Series games in October. It reminded me of what the city had been through in just a few months, from the high of a World Series championship to being laid low by the fires of January.

"Hey," she said when she got to the top of the stairs.

Her boots and pants were dusted with ash and I knew where she had been.

"You went up there in the dark?" I said. "You should've called me. I'd have gone with you. Not sure that's safe at night."

"It was okay," she said. "No one was there."

She had returned several times to what was left of her neighborhood. Every home had been reduced to scorched brick, twisted metal, and ash. A forest of chimneys left standing. Going back was part of her mourning process. It reminded me of open-casket funerals. Some people had to see the body to accept the person was gone. Maggie had to go back again and again to accept what she had lost.

"Are you hungry?" I asked. "I sent a text."

"Sure," she said. "I could eat something. I missed the text, sorry."

"It's okay. In or out?"

"Uh, you know what, let's go out. I just need to change real quick."

"Where do you want to go?"

"Someplace with good red wine."

"Okay, you change. I'll get a reservation."

Before she went in, she came to me at the corner of the deck, put her arms around me, and pulled me into a hug. Over my shoulder she looked out at her city.

"The lights are pretty," she said. "It's like nothing could ever go wrong in this place."

"Yeah," I said. "I was thinking the same thing."

# 20

AS I WAS driving to the courthouse Thursday morning I got a call from McEvoy.

"You're not going to believe this," he said. "Challenger just called me. She's in. She'll come down and testify."

"Shit," I said.

"What? I thought you'd be ecstatic."

"No, I am. I am. But the witness list went in yesterday. I'll have to amend it, and the judge is not going to be happy about that. Neither will opposing counsel. But this is good, Jack. Really good. Did she say what changed her mind?"

"Yeah, she got mad. She said Tidalwaiv is trying to intimidate her. She saw some big scary guy hanging around watching her place. She thinks he's from Tidalwaiv."

"Really? Bad move."

"Intimidation was definitely the wrong move with her."

"This is important: Did she ask for anything in return?"

"You mean for testifying? Uh, no. She just said she wanted to shove it up Tidalwaiv's ass. Her words, not mine."

"Good. I like an angry witness—as long as they're not angry at me. And she can come down next week? I'd probably put her on either late Monday or Tuesday. I want her near the start of the trial. Get her on the stand before she can change her mind."

"She said next week would work. But she wants a subpoena to explain her absence to the university."

"The Masons are going to throw a fit when they find out about her. It'll be a fight. If I win and she's in, I'll get the subpoena out today."

"You gotta get her in, Mickey. She's gold."

"I know, I know. You should go to the courthouse to watch the fireworks. Might make a whole chapter in your book."

"I'm about to head that way. Was letting the traffic die down a bit first."

"You know, now that I think about it, I want you to call and see if Challenger can come down right away to prep. Then I want you to go up and bring her down."

"You mean, like, tomorrow? Trial doesn't start till Monday."

"Doesn't matter. If I get her approved by the judge as a witness, all bets are off. Tidalwaiv will double-down on the intimidation and any other pressure points they can find, including the daughter. We need to bring them both down here so we can hide them until it's time for Naomi to testify."

"You mean Challenger."

"Challenger, right."

"Will Tidalwaiv get to depose her before trial?"

"They'd have to find her first. And believe me, they'll try."

"Got it."

"Okay, Jack, I'll see you in court."

I disconnected, dropped my phone into the center console, and reached into my jacket pocket for the burner I'd been carrying with me all week. I hit the one contact I had programmed into the phone. Bambadjan Bishop picked up right away.

"You're clear, Bamba," I said.

"You sure?" he asked. "I never really—"

"I'm sure. Come home. Let me know when you get here and we'll meet."

"You got it."

Twenty-five minutes later I was in one of the attorney rooms down the hall from Judge Ruhlin's court. Other than arranging an initial meeting between Brenda Randolph and Bruce and Trisha Colton, I had kept the two parties to the lawsuit separated. But now it was time to show a united front.

"The jurors are going to be watching us closely from today until we get a verdict," I told them. "Once they understand who you are, they're going to be very curious about you and the seemingly incongruous bond between the plaintiffs in this case. They are going to watch you closely for any sign that you are not really united in this fight against Tidalwaiv."

I paused there to see if they had any objections or questions. The two women said nothing. Bruce Colton just nodded and cast his eyes down at the table. Like Brenda, Bruce and Trisha had seen their lives destroyed. Their son would be in state mental facilities or prison for years. It was a coin toss as to which was a worse fate for Aaron, but they faced the rest of their years living with what he had done and the guilt of their own responsibility for it, whether that guilt was warranted or not.

"So, this is how I want to do this," I said. "I want Brenda and Trisha at the table with me—the two mothers. Bruce, I want you in the front row right behind us."

"I want to be with my wife," Bruce said.

"I understand," I said. "But what I want to do is present the two mothers as victims of this company. Two mothers who have lost their children. Two mothers who are unified. Remember, this is not a criminal trial. We don't need a unanimous verdict. We only need a majority. A trial is like a stage play. The jury is the audience. I'm going to go for as many women on the jury as I can get, especially mothers, and I want to play to them. When they get into the deliberation room to decide a verdict, the women will take charge. You understand?"

"I guess so," Bruce said. "I still don't like it."

I moved on, looking for reactions from the two women.

"Brenda and Trisha, don't be afraid to comfort each other," I said. "Some of the testimony will be very difficult to hear. For both of you. Don't hesitate to hold hands or do whatever you can to help each other get through the testimony."

Trisha nodded. Brenda just stared down at her hands, which were clasped tightly on the table.

"Now, as we discussed, all three of you will be called to the witness stand," I said. "You're all prepped and know what I'm going to ask. What we don't know is what the Tidalwaiv lawyers will ask you. As a rule, you don't want a witness who is a victim to be on the stand too long, so my guess is you will not face many questions from them. But that's all next week. This week is about picking a jury. I hope you can pay attention. You know that saying 'See something, say something'? That applies here. If you feel strongly about a potential juror, one way or the other, grab my sleeve or write me a note. I will make sure you each have a pad and pen in front of you."

"What about me?" Bruce said. "If I'm not at the table, how do I tell you what I think?"

"You can get my attention," I said. "Just whisper and I'll hear you. To be clear, I'm not asking you to approve or disapprove jurors. That's my job. But if you get a sense about someone, maybe through eye contact or their answers to questions from the judge, then let me know."

I paused again for questions but none came. In my mind, Bruce Colton was a wild card. He was a successful but uneducated businessman, having turned a family-owned electrical supply company in the Valley into a multimillion-dollar business. But he was the one who had brought a gun into the house, and he worked twelve-hour days, leaving his son with little male supervision in his formative years. Bruce was angry and alienated by what had happened, felt unfairly blamed and at times embarrassed by his son's crimes. In some states the parents of teenage shooters had been prosecuted for their carelessness with their children and guns. The Coltons were lucky that it appeared that Maggie McFierce was not going to prosecute them.

I checked my watch. It was time for court.

"Okay, we're going to go into the courtroom now," I said. "The first hour will be about motions and witness lists, and then voir dire begins."

"That's jury selection?" Brenda asked.

"Right," I said. "They bring in a panel of potential jurors, and the judge will ask questions the lawyers have submitted, along with her own questions, and we should have a jury by the end of the day tomorrow."

I stood up to leave the room. When I opened the door, I saw Marcus Mason standing in the hallway waiting for me. I was not surprised.

"You guys go on to the courtroom," I said to my clients. "Sit in the places I told you and I'll be along after I talk to Mr. Mason."

My clients stepped into the hallway and headed down to the courtroom. I waited for them to be out of earshot before I turned to Mason.

"What's up, Marcus?"

"What's up is I got your witness amendment and there is no way

Naomi Kitchens is testifying. But that's not why I'm here. Can we step out of the hallway for a minute?"

He gestured toward the open door of the meeting room I had just left.

"Sure," I said. "But let's not keep the judge waiting."

"We won't," Mason said. "I told the clerk to keep her in chambers until we come in."

We stepped into the room and Mason closed the door. I stayed standing. I knew what was coming and that I wouldn't have to sit down.

"Okay, final offer," Mason said. "To avoid this unnecessary trial, twenty-five to Randolph and ten to the Coltons, though they don't deserve a penny if you ask me."

"Is that millions or billions?" I asked.

"Don't be an ass, Haller. Tell them to take it. I have the checks in my briefcase. It's more money than they'll ever get from a jury. And you can probably retire on your cut."

"Is that it? That's the full offer?"

"That's it. And both parties must take it or no deal."

"Do you have a script for a public apology from Tidalwaiv in your briefcase too? One that accepts responsibility for the death of Rebecca Randolph and the actions of Aaron Colton, and says that new guardrails will be installed in your AI products that will prevent this from happening again in the future?"

"No, I have NDAs that all parties will sign, and then they get rich and this goes away quietly."

"Well, I'll take it to them. But don't get your hopes up."

"The offer's good till five o'clock today. Maybe after your clients see you lose half your witness list they'll be amenable to a settlement. They could wake up with millions in their bank accounts tomorrow if they play this right."

"Play, Marcus? This isn't a game."

"Sure it is. Don't kid yourself, Haller."

With that, he opened the door and left the room. I heard his heels clicking on the marble floor as he headed down the hall to the courtroom.

A few minutes later I huddled and whispered with my clients in the courtroom. I told Bruce Colton to come through the gate to the plaintiffs' table and pulled a chair over for him. I delivered the settlement offer and told them it came with no apology or admission of culpability from Tidalwaiv.

"It's a lot of money," I said. "And I always have to say, anything can happen at trial. But it's just money. It's not enough to hurt Tidalwaiv in the long run and there is no admission of guilt with it." Brenda Randolph seemed incensed.

"They think they can just buy their way out of this," she said. "Out of what they did to my daughter. Fuck them." The language was uncharacteristic of her.

I nodded — it was the response I had expected from Brenda — and looked at the Coltons, noting that they did not look at each other, a sign that they weren't on the same page.

"How long would it be before they paid us?" Bruce said.

"He said if you sign a nondisclosure agreement you'd go home with a check today," I said.

"Today," Bruce repeated. He seemed stunned by the realization that he could walk out of the courthouse a millionaire several times over.

"Wow," he said. "Like the lottery."

"We're not taking the money," Trisha said pointedly. "This isn't about the money."

"Just hold on, Trish," Bruce said. "You know what we could do with ten million dollars? First of all, we could get Aaron the best lawyer in the country. We could—"

"The best lawyer in the country is not going to be able to help him," Trisha snapped. "Not with what he did."

I saw Brenda put her hand on top of Trisha's on the table. They were somehow bonding — the mothers of killer and victim. It was amazing where grief took people.

"There is another thing," I said. "All three of you have to agree to take the money. It's all or nothing."

"That's not happening," Brenda said. "It's not about money. I want the public to know what Tidalwaiv did. If they won't admit it, the jury will tell the world. Screw them and their NDAs. They're not getting away with this."

Bruce raised his hands in a demonstration of frustration that he would not walk out of the building with a check.

"Okay, then," I said. "The offer's good till five today. You want to sit on it, or should I tell them no dice?"

"No dice," Brenda said.

"Tell them," Trisha said.

Bruce just shook his head.

"I can't believe this," he said. "We're giving up millions. Why don't we see how things go today and then tell them at five?"

"I'm not changing my mind," Brenda said.

"I'll tell them," I said. "Bruce, you go back to the front row. Court's going to start."

I got up and went over to the defense table, where the Mason twins sat next to each other alongside a woman I knew was their high-priced jury consultant.

"No dice, fellas," I said. "We're going to trial."

"Big mistake," Marcus said.

"Maybe," I said. "We'll see."

# 21

I WAS EXPECTING to go toe to toe with Marcus Mason about my witness list, not with Judge Ruhlin. But right out of the gate she had me in her crosshairs.

"Before we start, I would like to ask you a question, Mr. Haller," she said.

"Of course, Your Honor," I said, moving to the lectern.

"How many civil cases have you brought in federal court before this one?"

I thought I heard one of the Masons quietly snicker. Before answering, I casually turned and glanced at the gallery to confirm that there were no recognizable members of the media in attendance. Jury selection was rarely a newsworthy part of a trial.

I returned my focus to the bench.

"Uh, that would be none, Judge," I said. "But I have handled several criminal cases over the years. Here and in superior court."

"I guessed as much, Mr. Haller," Ruhlin said. "Because I see you are employing a trick that may work on the criminal side but does not have a place on the civil side and especially not in this courtroom."

"Judge, I'm not sure I understand."

"Yes, I think you do. You're playing hide the ball, Mr. Haller. I counted forty-eight witnesses on your list. Forty-eight, including the name you added this morning after the deadline."

"Yes, Your Honor."

"Mr. Haller, I know that you will not be putting forty-eight witnesses on the stand. You are hiding your trees in the forest, and we don't have time for your games in federal court."

"Your Honor, I—"

"Don't interrupt me, sir. I am now going to retreat to my chambers to make a phone call. I will be back in twelve minutes. That's how long you have to cut this list to a true and accurate accounting of witnesses you intend to call to the witness stand."

"Judge, I intend to call them all."

"Don't kid me, Mr. Haller. And don't try my patience."

"I'm not trying to do either, Your Honor."

"Very well, then. I am putting you on notice that you will be fined one thousand dollars for each person on this list who is not called as a witness during the presentation of your case."

"Judge, that's not — I intend, as of right now, to call them all, but strategies can change midcourse in a trial. I am sure the court understands this. I remember when Your Honor was a practicing—"

"What *you* have to understand, Mr. Haller, is that I am not going to allow you to waste the court's time. Twelve minutes. We are adjourned."

Ruhlin left the bench and went through the door that led to her chambers. This time I unmistakably heard the snicker from the Masons' table. I ignored it as I went back to my table, opened my briefcase, and took out my laptop. I pulled up the witness list that had been submitted to the court and amended with the name Naomi Kitchens. The reality was that the judge had nailed me, but I wouldn't admit it on the record. The list was stocked with people I could call, but their testimony would be repetitive of other witnesses. For example, I didn't have to call both detectives assigned to the murder of Rebecca Randolph, since they would essentially tell the jury the same thing. Same with the coders who worked on Project Clair. The list had been designed to keep the Masons guessing and busy running down my witnesses for depos and background checks. That way they'd presumably be distracted from their own case.

"Mickey, are we in trouble?" Brenda asked.

I looked over at her. Both she and Trisha had looks of concern on their faces.

"No, we're fine," I said. "The judge is just flexing her muscles so we know who's in charge. That's all. I was going to cut my list down on Monday anyway."

I went to work on the list. On my first go-through, I quickly and easily deleted nine names. I wondered if that would satisfy the judge but decided I had to cut more. I checked the time, saw I still had six minutes, and went back to work. After one more thinning of the herd, I sent the new list to the clerk for submission to the judge and the defense team. Ruhlin returned to the bench promptly at the twelve-minute mark, carrying a printout of the new witness list.

"Mr. Haller, I appreciate your effort to cull your list," she said. "I still believe that twenty-three names is excessive, but we will see how many survive challenges from the defense. Misters Mason, I believe you have the new list. Do you object to any of these witnesses?"

Mitchell Mason stood and went to the lectern. I was surprised it wasn't Marcus taking the reins. The witness list was the backbone of the case.

"Your Honor, where do I begin?" Mitchell said. "I mean, even at twenty-three names, this list is —"

"Do you have an objection to a specific name, Mr. Mason?" the judge interrupted.

"To many of them, Judge."

"Then what do you say we just start with one of them? We have a jury pool waiting to come into court for voir dire. Let's not keep them waiting too long."

"Yes, Your Honor. The defense objects first and foremost to Naomi Kitchens."

"State your grounds."

Before beginning, Mitchell glanced over at his brother sitting at the defendant's table.

"Thank you, Your Honor," Mitchell said. "Ms. Kitchens is a former employee of Tidalwaiv who was dismissed for performance issues and whose record of hostility toward the company renders her testimony unreliable. But, Your Honor, all of that is moot because Ms. Kitchens signed an ironclad nondisclosure agreement that prevents her from discussing anything she did or observed while in the employ of Tidalwaiv. She simply can't be allowed to testify. Last, counsel for the defense is out-and-out sand —"

"Counsel for the defense?" Ruhlin asked.

"Apologies, Your Honor," Mitchell said. "Counsel for the plaintiffs. I guess I'm used to Mr. Haller defending criminals."

Yeah, right — as if he hadn't been waiting for the right moment to make that "mistake." I objected, just to knock Mitchell out of rhythm. The judge overruled.

"May I continue, Your Honor?" Mitchell asked.

"Please," the judge said.

"Thank you. Your Honor, plaintiffs' counsel is clearly trying to sandbag us. He's been hiding this witness. She was on neither of the preliminary witness lists and suddenly appears on this list in an amendment filed just minutes before court was convened so that we had little time to prepare our objection and when he has known for weeks that she would be on the list. The bottom line, Your Honor, is that any one of these arguments is enough to remove Naomi Kitchens from the witness list. Taken as a whole, the court has overwhelming reason to strike her."

Finished, Mitchell turned from the lectern and headed back to his table without waiting to see if the judge had any questions.

"Very well," Ruhlin said. "Mr. Haller, a response?"

I jumped up quickly and went to the lectern like a man on a mission. Along the way, I saw Marcus Mason whispering to his brother and pointing a finger in the air to make his point. He had seen the mistake his twin made, but it was too late.

I had seen it too.

"Your Honor," I began, "before I argue the points Mr. Mason thinks he made, I would ask the court to inquire about his statement that I knew 'for weeks' that Naomi Kitchens would be a witness in this case. The facts are, Your Honor, that I did indeed meet Professor Kitchens several weeks ago and then again this past Friday. But she felt intimidated and afraid of Tidalwaiv and did not, in fact, agree to be a witness until shortly before nine this morning. If you wish to confirm that, we can set up a teleconference with Professor Kitchens at the court's convenience. But that aside, Your Honor, Mr. Mason's statement indicates that the defense team has been surveilling Professor Kitchens because they know her value as a witness for the plaintiffs in this case. They did this with Mr. Patel and now Naomi Kitchens. It's called witness intimidation, Judge, and I would like it stopped."

I saw the skin around the judge's eyes tighten, and when she spoke, an unmistakable but controlled anger had entered her voice.

"Mr. Mason," she said. "Do you care to offer an explanation for the knowledge you seem to have of Ms. Kitchens's status as a witness?"

Mitchell Mason stood up and moved to the lectern as I backed away. He seemed to be two shades paler than when he had stood there a few moments before.

"Thank you, Your Honor," he said. "I can assure you that no attorney or staff member of the law firm of Mason and Mason has had any witness or opposing counsel under surveillance at any time. Mr. Haller is just trying to—"

"That's all well and good, Mr. Mason," Ruhlin said. "But what about your client? Did you receive information from your client as to who Ms. Kitchens or Mr. Haller and his staff were meeting with?"

Now Marcus Mason stood up and came to the lectern in an attempt to rescue his brother.

"Your Honor, if I may be heard?" he said.

"Go ahead," Ruhlin said. "We are losing the morning with this, but go ahead."

"Thank you," Marcus said. "As my brother said, Mason and Mason has not engaged in any surveillance or intimidation of witnesses. But as he said earlier, and as with Mr. Patel, Ms. Kitchens was terminated from Tidalwaiv for cause and was deemed a security threat by the company. As such, the company took measures to protect itself. And this was long before any lawsuit was filed by the plaintiffs. No laws were broken by these procedures. They were perfectly acceptable and legal. Mr. Haller has made it a routine during this legal action to seek out as witnesses those who left the company under rancorous terms in hopes that he will sway a jury with false and biased testimony harmful to the company."

I had stayed standing at the plaintiffs' table, ready to respond.

"Your Honor?" I said. "May I—"

"No, you may not, Mr. Haller," Ruhlin said. "Not yet. Let me say once again for the record, the court will not tolerate any intimidation of witnesses or anyone involved with the parties to this lawsuit. Whatever Tidalwaiv is doing, shut it down, Mr. Mason. Because if I have to shut it down, there will be very serious consequences. Do you understand?"

"Yes, Your Honor," Marcus said.

"Now, Mr. Haller," Ruhlin said. "Do you wish to proceed with a rebuttal of the challenge to your witness?"

"Yes, Your Honor," I said as I moved back to the lectern. "But I would first like to address what Mr. Mason said about my witness that continues the intimidation the court just said will not be tolerated."

"We are past that, Mr. Haller," Ruhlin said. "And we have a jury panel waiting for us. Do you want me to make a ruling on Ms. Kitchens now, or do you want to offer rebuttal?"

"I do offer rebuttal, Judge," I said. "Let's start with the nondisclosure agreement. It was signed by Professor Kitchens under duress because the company had terminated her but offered her a six-month severance package that included health insurance if she signed the NDA. She is a single mother with a daughter who has chronic asthma treated with prescriptions paid for by the company's health plan. Expensive prescriptions, Your Honor."

I held up a copy of the two-page NDA Kitchens had signed.

"Additionally, this agreement does indeed preclude Professor Kitchens from sharing proprietary information with any Tidalwaiv competitor," I said. "But this court is not a competitor, Your Honor, and the plaintiffs are not intending to ask this witness anything about proprietary information."

Marcus Mason stood up to be heard.

"Sit down, Mr. Mason," the judge said. "You had your turn."

"But, Your Honor," Mason said. "Counsel is misconstruing the—"

"When I say sit down, I mean sit down," Ruhlin barked.

Chastened, Mason sat down as instructed.

"Anything else, Mr. Haller?" Ruhlin asked.

"Yes, Your Honor," I said. "The defense argues that Naomi Kitchens should be excluded as a witness because I did not provide adequate notice that she would testify. But that is because of the serious discovery violation purposely committed by the defense in this case. Professor Kitchens was employed by Tidalwaiv as an ethicist and was assigned to Project Clair. While on the project, she wrote numerous reports and gave numerous warnings that were ignored by the project's managers and stakeholders and apparently by counsel for the defense. This was in defiance of the court's order to turn over in discovery all documentation of the project's research and development. Counsel turned over twelve terabytes of documents they said fulfilled that order."

In my peripheral vision I saw one of the Masons stand up to be heard. I kept going.

"Your Honor, nowhere in those twelve terabytes is a single document written by Naomi Kitchens," I said. "Any document in discovery that was sent to stakeholders had her name redacted. They tried to hide her from us, Judge, because they were aware she knew where the bodies were buried on Project Clair. To cure that violation, plaintiffs should be allowed to have Professor Kitchens testify to her work at Tidalwaiv. Thank you, Your Honor."

The judge was silent for a few moments while she digested everything I had just revealed. I glanced to my left and saw that it was Marcus Mason who had stood up to respond.

"That is a very serious allegation, Mr. Haller," she finally said. "Mr. Mason, how do you respond?"

I stepped back to give Mason the lectern, but I stayed close so he would feel me standing right behind him.

"Your Honor, as usual, Mr. Haller exaggerates and provides the court only the information partial to his cause," he said. "But the reality is that the court's order was to turn over in discovery all documents relating to the research, production, and promotion of the Clair app."

Mason helpfully ticked off these three things on his fingers for the judge's understanding.

"We have fully met that order, Your Honor," he continued. "Ms. Kitchens had nothing to do with those processes. She was merely an observer, and therefore we were under no obligation to provide what few documents and emails she authored. Thus the redactions that Mr. Haller hopes to cast as sinister."

"Your Honor?" I said, raising my hand like a schoolboy.

"Yes, Mr. Haller," Ruhlin said.

Mason stepped back from the lectern and took a position behind me, attempting to do to me what I had done to him.

"I find it interesting that Mr. Mason mentions emails authored by Naomi Kitchens," I said. "I had not mentioned emails, Your Honor, and that tells me that the defense was familiar with the role she played in Project Clair and the numerous warnings she wrote in documents *and* emails. They then took steps to minimize the threat she presented to their case by scrubbing her entirely from the discovery materials. And I hope the court will keep in mind that this effort to scrub her from the project was undertaken before — long before — the first meeting I ever had with Professor Kitchens."

Mason came up next to me, reached over the lectern, and bent the microphone's arm toward himself.

"Your Honor, that is not the case," he said. "There are not numerous documents and emails from Kitchens. Very few, in fact, and they are inconsequential to the case at hand."

I spread my arms wide in protest.

"Your Honor, I think I still have the lectern," I said.

"You do, Mr. Haller," Ruhlin said. "Mr. Mason, step back. Now."

Mason did so while I bent the mic's arm back toward me.

"Your Honor, Mr. Mason is wrong," I said. "Dr. Kitchens's testimony is elemental to the plaintiffs' case. She warned Tidalwaiv that Project Clair was not safe or appropriate for teenagers. Tidalwaiv fired her and ignored her warnings, which ratchets up their negligence to recklessness. I will give Mr. Mason the benefit of the doubt that he knows only what Tidalwaiv wants him to know. But there are numerous documents and emails from Dr. Kitchens. Fearing retaliation from the company when she offered warning after warning about Project Clair, she kept copies of every document and email she ever wrote about the project and she has turned them over to the plaintiffs' legal team. She should be allowed to testify to authenticate for the jury these materials intentionally left out of discovery."

"Your Honor?" Mason said.

Ruhlin hit him with a baleful look.

"It better be good, Mr. Mason," she said.

I stepped back to give him the lectern.

"Judge, there are discovery issues on both sides here," he said. "If Mr. Haller has this great trove of documents from this witness, why were they not provided to the defense? It seems like the pot calling the kettle black."

I raised my hand.

"Not necessary, Mr. Haller," Ruhlin said. "I am prepared to rule. Naomi Kitchens will be allowed to testify. As far as the documents she has provided the plaintiffs, these are documents Tidalwaiv either has or has destroyed. I find no violation of discovery on the part of the plaintiffs, and Mr. Mason, I advise you to have a sit-down with your clients to remind them of their obligations under this cause of action. I consider what happened with materials authored by Ms. Kitchens to be a serious violation of discovery. Now, any other objections to witnesses, or are we ready to bring in our potential jurors?"

I knew better than to push my luck. The ruling on Kitchens was a potential case-breaker. I quit while I was ahead and told the judge I was ready to proceed with voir dire.

But the Masons weren't. They spent the next forty minutes pecking away at my witness list, the judge relenting in the name of time and whittling down the number of project managers, coders, and other Tidalwaiv employees I could call. They even challenged my inclusion of Victor Wendt, founder of Tidalwaiv. I protested all the way but it was purely for show. As I whispered to the two women who sat with me at the plaintiffs' table, Kitchens was going to be our knockout punch. No matter how many names the judge lopped off my list, we were going to come out way ahead at the end of the session.

Or so I thought.

## 22

**SOME LAWYERS BELIEVE** a trial is won or lost in jury selection. That may be true, but I also believe that a trial is won or lost in the selection of the attorney who takes the cause of action to court. I do know one thing for sure about juries. The one unalterable rule is that you must tailor the jury to your case. The juror questions I had written out earlier in the week brought back a wide variety of answers for me to look through before we got to the actual live selection process. Judge Ruhlin had called for a panel of fifty potential jurors, from which twelve would be selected. There would be no alternates chosen, because in civil court only six jurors were needed to deliver a verdict. We would start with twelve in the box, and as long as six made it to the finish line, we would get a verdict.

There were no names—I knew them only by the numbers assigned to them, one through fifty. But I had my favorites, had ranked them on a legal pad, and was ready to go with voir dire as soon as the hearing on witnesses ended. My number one juror happened to be number fifty in the stack and I thanked the stars above that she had gotten in under the wire. She was a retired schoolteacher who had raised two girls by herself in Reseda. She owned no digital devices besides her cell phone. She drove an American-made car and did not watch Netflix or Amazon Prime. She had never asked Siri or Alexa a question, because she didn't know how. Her preferred method of consuming news was to watch the Fox cable network. She was perfect. The challenge was to get her into the final twelve seated in the box.

The judge had not allowed questions about religious or political affiliation, but she did permit questions about how the potential jurors consumed news and on what devices they did so. Their answers tended to reveal their political views, and from those views, I could make assumptions about religion. I wanted viewers of the conservative Fox channel on my jury because I believed they were likely Republican voters and Christians and therefore probably voted for Donald Trump in the last presidential election. I cast no aspersions on their vote, but it told me they were not happy—at least back in November, they weren't—with the direction of things in the country and its future. AI was the future, but it scared people who knew it would change their world in ways they didn't understand. That was who I wanted on the jury, people who felt uneasy and alienated from society. I readily admit it was a cynical way to pick a jury, but it could make all the difference in the trial.

The others on my list of acceptable jurors were medical-industry workers, clerical workers, graphic designers, a psychoanalyst, a French translator of movies and television shows, several out-of-work actors and set builders, and three screenwriters. These were not all Fox viewers, of course. In fact, there was a wide diversity in their answers to the juror interrogatories. In contrast to jurors like number fifty, who had no laptop or home computer, the actors and screenwriters had multiple digital devices. But what was common among the potential jurors whom I found acceptable was the possibility that their jobs would someday be replaced by AI-generated creations. I was going to give them the opportunity to make a stand against that.

Of course, the Mason twins knew who I was looking for. They had a whole jury-selection team working for them, fronted by the psychologist sitting at the defense table next to them, and they had their own list of favorites. Each team would now attempt to fill the box with its top choices while knocking out those of the opponent.

The judge was giving each side six peremptory challenges, meaning each of us had six bullets we could use to get rid of potential jurors with no explanation at all. After that, jurors could be excused only for cause, whether that was bias or conflict of interest or anything we objected to in their answers. So there was a strategy to it. I had a list of twenty-one acceptable jurors, which meant twenty-nine were not acceptable. I had ranked my favorites and my rejects. It was now my job to put as many of the twenty-one on the jury as I could.

High in my rankings of jurors to reject were people in technical careers that seemed safe from AI encroachment and possibly even in a position to benefit from its rise. There was a high-school football coach I knew I could not allow on the jury. An operator of a real estate search engine was another. Anyone who worked in the tech companies located in what was known as Silicon Beach had to go. I expected that high on the Mason list would be a potential juror who said he was a television producer. Use of AI in media production had been a hot-button topic in the recent writers' and actors' strikes that had crippled the industry. Soon scripts would be generated by machine instead of humans; digital screens filled with AI-produced images would save the cost of hiring actors and building sets. Profits might soar for producers, but that was why I had put the actors, set builders, and writers on my list.

The juror-selection process was meticulous. The judge would

randomly select a juror number and proceed with her questions, elaborating on those in the questionnaire. She would then ask the lawyers if they had additional questions, and, a bit like playing the telephone game, we would ask the judge to ask the juror our questions. Ultimately, the judge would ask the lawyers if the juror was acceptable. An accepted juror wasn't safely on the twelve-person panel, however. A peremptory challenge could still be used to excuse a juror at any time during voir dire.

This process lasted through two four-hour sessions broken up over two days. It was all-consuming. When I got home the night after the first session, I holed up in the back room of the house with my questionnaires and charts and lists. I spoke little at dinner with Maggie, and she understood because she knew I was working, whether what was in front of me was paperwork or the takeout noodles from Genghis Cohen. I broke away from it only to listen to her report on the US Army Corps of Engineers' plans for clearing the debris from the desolate fire fields in Altadena. The center of Maggie's life had become the recovery and rebuild zone—the "L.A. Strong" of it. When she was not dressed for work, she wore alternating baseball hats, one that read REBUILD ALTADENA and another that read MAKE ALTADENA GREAT AGAIN. I had to pay attention to her pain or I risked her anger. She had become very reactive in the weeks after losing her home and belongings. Any disappointment, big or small, brought oversize upset, sometimes even tears. It was difficult to watch, but I understood it and knew that my role was to console her at every turn.

Jury selection is a lot like an NBA basketball game. The first three quarters of the contest don't really matter other than to set up the drama and strategy of the final period. Many observers and commentators of the sport point to a 1988 playoff match as possibly the greatest game of all time. It is credited as such because Larry Bird of the Boston Celtics scored twenty fourth-quarter points in a two-point seventh-game victory. This came after a lackluster first three quarters for Bird. I wasn't a Celtics fan, not by a mile. I was a homer — Lakers all the way. In fact, it was the Lakers who eventually won the championship the year of Bird's greatest-of-all-time game. But I'd watched that game when I was a kid, and I always wanted to be Larry Bird when it came to my court and the last quarter of my game.

That came Friday after the lunch break. Judge Ruhlin had sternly told all three lawyers that the jury selection would be completed by the end of the day and that trial would start without fail promptly at nine a.m. Monday. It was do-or-die time. Time to finish filling the box. There were ten people already accepted at the moment, including the football coach, whom I still intended to oust. I was down to two peremptories, and the Masons had the same. Five women had been accepted to the panel, which was good. What wasn't good was that my top pick, number fifty, had been taken out with a peremptory by the Masons. So, too, had the psychoanalyst.

The session started with juror seventeen, the television producer, being put into the next opening in the box. The judge started asking innocuous follow-up questions to those on the jury survey. On the questionnaire, the producer said he had been born in Stockholm, Sweden, but was a US citizen as well. Still, his accent came as a surprise to me. I was used to thick Spanish accents in potential jurors.

After her questioning, the judge asked if the lawyers had any additional queries for the producer. The Masons had none. I asked the judge to ask the candidate if he had ever explored the use of artificial intelligence in the production of a television show. She did, and the Swede answered without hesitation.

"Explored it but never used it," he said. "Yet."

That last word was all I needed. I asked the judge to excuse him for conflict of interest. This brought an objection from Marcus Mason.

"Your Honor," he said, "this would be like excusing a juror in a personal-injury car-crash case for having driven a car. Because this man has checked out how artificial intelligence might improve his product does not constitute a conflict of interest. Are we now going to excuse anyone who has ever asked Siri a question?"

"I tend to agree, Mr. Haller," the judge said. "I'm going to accept juror seventeen to the panel. Unless you want to use one of your remaining peremptory challenges."

"Could I have a moment, Judge?" I asked.

"Don't take too long," Ruhlin said.

I looked over my shoulder to the gallery section reserved for the prospective jurors who had not yet been called forward and questioned. I confirmed that there were five left, three men and two women. There were eleven in the box, including the Swede for the time being. I could use my last challenges to shoot down the Swede and the football coach, but then I would be out of bullets. I checked what I called my jury scorecard. On a legal pad I had numbered the jurors one through fifty and ranked them in my order of preference. I had scratched out those who had been dismissed and circled those who were currently in the box. Of the five numbers left, two were among my favorites. Juror six was a man and juror twelve was a woman. Juror twelve I had ranked as my number three pick because she was a set builder for film and TV and could be one of the first to be made redundant by AI invading Hollywood production. I badly wanted her on the jury, especially since my first two picks had been knocked out by the Masons.

Juror six was also in my top twelve. He had listed his occupation as a market analyst for an investment firm. He was a sleeper on my list because he checked a box the Masons would like — if they had done the same research my team had. Lorna had looked at the firm juror six worked for and determined that it invested heavily in tech companies involved in developing AI technologies. That would appear to make him pro-AI to the Masons, but the reality was that he could easily be replaced as an analyst by the very technology his company invested in. It was my hope that the Masons would be blinded by the AI investments and not realize the possible concerns juror six might have about his future.

I needed to scheme a way to get my last two favorites into the box.

I looked back over my shoulder again. Of the two women remaining, one was Black, one was white. We had not been allowed to ask questions about race in the interrogatories, so it was not clear which one was the set builder. According to my chart, the other remaining woman worked in Beverly Hills as a personal assistant. This would need further clarification during the judge's questioning, but my guess was she was likely a gofer for a wealthy resident of the high-end enclave. I had ranked her twenty-eighth on my chart, meaning that I could accept her on the jury if I had no better choice.

I looked closely at the two women. The Black woman had a short-cropped Afro, and her short sleeves revealed well-defined biceps. She looked like she might work with her hands, keeping her hair short and out of the way. I believed this boosted the chances that she was the set builder.

Looking back at the jury box, I confirmed that only one of the current accepted jurors was Black. He was a postal worker who had been on my favorites list.

"Mr. Haller, we're waiting," Ruhlin said.

I looked up at her.

"Yes, Your Honor," I said. "The plaintiffs want to thank and excuse juror number seventeen."

The television producer.

"You're using a peremptory?" Ruhlin asked.

"Yes, Your Honor."

"Very well. That leaves you with one remaining challenge. Juror seventeen, you are excused, and we thank you for your service."

The Swede smiled and quickly stood up. He moved out of the box and headed toward the courtroom exit, his body language signaling that he was insulted by his expulsion from the case.

The next randomly selected juror called to the box was a man who was not on my list of favorites. He was an electrical engineer who would benefit from the continuing expansion of artificial intelligence in business and society. AI systems used massive amounts of electricity, and people with his credentials would always be needed. But I easily conflicted him out because he revealed during questioning that he had gone to the University of Wisconsin with one of the key coders of the Clair project, and they had lived in the same fraternity house.

The next man called was knocked out by Marcus Mason because in his responses to interrogatories submitted by the defense, he had listed *Terminator 2: Judgment Day* as one of his favorite movies. The film is about artificial intelligence turning against humanity, and Marcus Mason successfully argued that this tainted the potential juror and left him unable to keep an open mind while deciding the case. He had not been on my favorites list, because I knew when I saw his *Terminator* answer that he would be terminated from the jury.

His dismissal left three remaining candidates for two slots.

When the judge called juror twelve to the box for questioning, the Black woman came forward. I confirmed on my list that twelve was indeed the set builder and got ready for what I assumed was going to be a battle. After brief questioning by the judge brought no surprises or obvious bias, I accepted her for the jury. Marcus Mason then used one of his two remaining peremptories to excuse her. I immediately stood and objected, then moved to the lectern.

"Your Honor," I said. "A jury is supposed to be representative of the community. By my count, this is the fourth time Mr. Mason has used his challenges or objections to remove a minority member of the community from the panel. And my concern is that he will use his last peremptory challenge to remove the only Black person remaining in the jury box. This will make the composition of the jury suspect in terms of diversity and representation, and the plaintiffs strenuously object."

Marcus Mason was up from his seat and moving to the lectern before I was even finished. He once again addressed the court before the judge called on him. I knew he would put on histrionics in his response. He had to play to the jurors as well as the judge now.

"Your Honor, I find counsel's insinuation insulting and preposterous," he said. "I have been a lawyer in this city for eighteen years and no one has ever questioned my reputation when it comes to equality and diversity. My firm donates liberally every month every year to causes that support racial equality and gender equality. This past month alone we have donated more than one hundred thousand dollars to fire-relief programs working in the minority communities of Altadena. We—"

"Thank you, Mr. Mason," the judge said, cutting him off. "The question is about the composition of the jury."

"I'm sorry, Your Honor," Mason said. "But Mr. Haller hit a nerve with his unfounded complaint."

"Again, Mr. Mason, the concern is not about you," Ruhlin said. "It is about the makeup of our jury."

"I can assure you, Judge, I will not be using my final challenge to remove anyone currently in the jury box," Mason said. "Mr. Haller's suggestion is unconscionable."

"Well, I have to say I share his concern," Ruhlin countered. "Can you tell me why you want to dismiss juror twelve?"

"All right, fine," Mason said. "I withdraw the challenge. Juror twelve is accepted by the defense."

"Very well," Ruhlin said. "Juror twelve is accepted as the eleventh member of the jury. Thank you."

We were down to one seat left in the jury box and two potential jurors waiting to be questioned. The next number the judge called belonged to the financial analyst. I wanted him on the jury but had to make it seem like I was ambivalent about him. The judge's questioning raised no red flags. As she came to the last of her routine questions, I turned in my seat and leaned close to my two clients to whisper.

"We're almost there," I said. "I think we can live with these last two if we have to. I'm not worried about this guy, but the — "

While I was whispering, the judge asked if I had any additional questions, but I acted like I didn't hear her because of the conversation at the table.

"Mr. Haller!" Ruhlin barked.

"I'm sorry, Your Honor," I said. "I got distracted. Uh, juror six is accepted by the plaintiffs."

"Thank you," Ruhlin said. "Mr. Mason, any further questions from you?"

"No, Your Honor," Mason said. "Juror six is accepted by the defense."

Bingo. The analyst was in.

"Very good," Ruhlin said. "We have twelve jurors selected."

I stood up and went to the lectern with my legal pad.

"Your Honor," I said. "Plaintiffs would like to use our last challenge to thank and excuse juror nineteen."

The football coach was out. I was rolling the dice, gambling that the Beverly Hills personal assistant would be a better choice, if only because it added another female to the panel, tilting it to seven women, five men. I would have the female majority I was looking for.

The judge called the personal assistant to the box and questioned her. My assumption had been on the money. She worked for a wealthy woman and handled a variety of chores, from returning online purchases to walking a pet poodle to grocery shopping. No red flags were raised and I accepted her to the jury. Marcus Mason did as well.

The box was now full, but Marcus Mason still had two challenges in his pocket. My view was that you never left a challenge on the table, but if he used one now, the judge would have to call in a second panel of potential jurors and that would likely push completion of jury selection to Monday. More than once, the judge had sternly reminded us that jury selection would not carry over the weekend.

"Do the parties to the lawsuit accept the jury?" Ruhlin asked.

"Plaintiffs accept the jury as composed, Your Honor," I said.

Marcus hesitated, probably weighing whether it was wise to upset the judge before the trial even started.

"Mr. Mason?" Ruhlin prompted.

"Yes, Your Honor," he finally said. "The defense accepts the jury."

"Excellent," the judge said. "We have our jury, and the jurors are ordered to report to the assembly room next to this courtroom at nine a.m. Monday. Don't be late. You are now excused and the court thanks you for your service. Court is now adjourned."

As the judge left the bench I turned to my clients seated next to me.

"I think we did well here," I said. "We've got a good jury."

"How come you kicked out the football coach?" Brenda asked. "I thought he seemed like a good man."

"It was just a hunch," I said. "He coaches boys in a violent sport. He deals with teenage boys every day, listens to their complaints, knows their insecurities. I just wasn't sure where his sympathies would truly be, so I went with my gut. Sometimes it's what you have to do. I like who we got better, the personal assistant. I think she'll be on our side."

I promised them I would be prepping for the trial all weekend and would be in touch. I asked them to take photos of what they planned to wear on the first day and text them to me. I would show the photos to Lorna and maybe Maggie and ask what they thought.

As I was leaving the courtroom, Marcus Mason caught up to me, as I'd known he would. His brother was trailing behind him.

"You motherfucker," he said. "That stunt you just pulled? Fuck you, man. I'm going to tear you apart next week and love every minute of it."

I smiled and nodded my head.

"Have a good weekend, Marcus," I said. "And get some rest. You're going to need it."

# 23

DRAINED BY THE intensity of the two days of jury selection, I allowed myself to sleep in on Saturday and didn't get to the warehouse until 10:30, the time for which I had scheduled an all-hands meeting. I arrived to find an LAPD patrol wagon parked in front of the building.

I parked behind it, entered through the door into the larger garage, and found Lorna and Cisco talking to two uniformed officers. Lorna broke away from them and walked up to me with urgency.

"Oh my God, I thought something had happened to you," she said. "Why haven't you been answering your phone?"

"It's dead," I said. "I was so tired last night I forgot to plug it in. You called the cops because I didn't answer my phone?"

"No, there was a break-in last night. We discovered it when we got here today. The door was wide open."

She pointed toward the door I had just entered through.

"Shit," I said. "What was taken?"

"We're not sure yet," Lorna said. "But it looks like nothing's gone."

"What about the cage?"

"Same thing. Can't tell yet if anything's gone."

"The hard drive?"

"I took it home last night."

"Good. Did anybody check the cameras?"

"You had them turned off, remember?"

I had been worried about Tidalwaiv hijacking the feed.

"It was them," I said.

"Who?" Lorna asked.

"Tidalwaiv. Had to be."

"Why? Everything we have came from them in discovery."

"Not the stuff we got from Naomi."

We had dispensed with use of the code name Challenger, since Naomi Kitchens had been revealed and approved as a witness.

"But isn't all of that copies of stuff she sent to them?" Lorna said. "So they would already have that."

"Not if they purged it," I said.

I nodded toward the two officers talking to Cisco. One was writing on a clipboard.

"Are they calling in the detectives?" I asked.

"They said they'll give the report to the burglary squad for follow-up on Monday," Lorna said. "From Central Division."

"I won't hold my breath. This is like the Grant High break-in. Nothing missing, but they were here and they want us to know it. Do I need to talk to them or are you two handling it?"

"We can handle it. I think they're about to go."

"Then I'll be in my office. After they leave, I need you and Cisco in there for the meeting."

"Okay. They said don't touch the safe in case the detectives want to send a tech to look for fingerprints."

"Did you tell them it has no locking mechanism and we don't keep valuable stuff in it?"

"Yes, but they said the burglars might not have known that."

I walked by the cops and Cisco to the office. The first thing I did when I got there was plug my dead phone into the charging line on my desk. Then I leaned in through the open door of the Mosler. The contracts McEvoy had signed as well as a few other case files seemed to be untouched. I sat down at the desk, picked up the landline, and called Jack McEvoy, who was up in Palo Alto. I put the call on speaker.

"Our meeting is going to be slightly delayed," I said. "The cops are here. Somebody broke into the warehouse last night."

"Shit, what did they get?" McEvoy asked.

"We still don't know. Maybe nothing. Have you talked to Naomi yet?"

"Uh, no, not since last night. I was going to go over after our all-hands call."

"Go over now. Make sure everything's okay and call me back."

"Why wouldn't everything be okay?"

"I don't know. That's why I want you to check."

I reached over and dropped the phone into its cradle, ending the call. I checked my cell phone and saw it already had enough juice to be opened as long as I kept the charger plugged in. There had been five missed calls and voicemails since nine a.m. Four of the voicemails were from Lorna that morning, her voice growing more intense with each call as she panicked about why I wasn't responding and wasn't at the office. The fifth was from Marcus Mason, and it had been left at one minute after nine. He didn't bother identifying himself.

"Haller, call me. We need to talk."

I got up from the desk and closed the door, then went back and hit the Return Call button. It was Mason's cell and he answered right away.

"Haller, we have to meet," he said.

"Mason, I just got your client's message," I said.

"What? What message?"

"The little break-in at my office last night."

"I don't know what you're talking about."

"Of course not."

"Look, never mind that, we have to meet."

"About what?"

"We have a new offer. A final offer."

"You know how to make a federal judge mad as hell? You settle a case after she's spent two days picking a jury."

"Doesn't matter. When can you meet?"

"Marcus, what happened to 'I'm going to tear you apart next week and love every minute of it'?"

"I would have. But the company wants this over. Too much at stake to put the outcome in the hands of twelve idiots. When can you meet? Where?"

"I'm not meeting you, Marcus. I've got too much to do today."

"It's your obligation to listen and deliver a settlement offer to your clients in a timely fashion."

"We don't have to meet. Give it to me and I'll deliver it. Simple."

There was a long pause as Mason decided what to do.

"Fifty million," he finally said. "Your clients decide how to chop it up. The company doesn't care. Same conditions as the previous offers."

Now I paused. I felt ashamed because my first thought was about what my cut of fifty million dollars would be. Mason seemed to know this.

"What's that mean for you, Haller?" he asked. "Twenty million? You should be able to convince them to take it for that."

I actually had a sliding scale. The higher the settlement, the lower my percentage went until it hit 20 percent. In this case, that meant I'd get ten million if my clients took this deal. It was more money than

I'd earned in my entire career. It would be more than enough to retire on and to build back better Maggie's home.

I shook off these thoughts and regained focus.

"What are they scared of, Marcus?" I asked.

"I told them I have this in hand," Mason said. "But they just want it to go away."

I said nothing for a long moment.

"Take it to them, Haller," Mason said. "You have just over six hours. The offer expires at five. All parties must agree. No split settlement. You understand?"

"I understand," I said. "Put it in writing and email it to me so I have something to show them."

"I just did."

"Then I'll review it and—"

Mason disconnected.

"Fuck you too," I said.

I opened the email app on my phone and saw the offer on top. I read it, looking for any discrepancy between what Mason had just said and what he had written. There was none. The email was a duplicate of the previous settlement offer except that the number had changed and it contained the additional line about the clients deciding how to divide the money. I wondered what was behind that line. Had the Masons been back-channeling with the Coltons? Did the opposition think that giving the Coltons the possibility of a bigger chunk would help bring the sides to agreement?

There was a single knock on the door and Lorna walked in.

"What's going on?" she asked.

"Are they gone?" I asked. "The cops?"

"Yes. Cisco walked them out. We can start our meeting when he gets back. Should I call Jack?"

"I just talked to him. He's checking on Naomi and then he'll call back."

"Challenger."

Lorna pointed to the ceiling as if that might be where Tidalwaiv had planted listening devices.

"Tidalwaiv knows about her from court," I said. "No need for code words anymore."

"Right," Lorna said. "What is Jack checking on?"

"I don't know. We had a break-in here. I just want to make sure she's okay up there."

"Mickey, you really think Tidalwaiv is behind this? It's not the greatest neighborhood, you know."

"If it had been a real break-in, we would have noticed things gone. The place would have been torn up. There's two thousand dollars in copper netting over the cage, plus the laptops are in there. This was Tidalwaiv, Lorna. They were looking for something."

"What?"

"I don't know. Or maybe they were just trying to send a message."

"What message?"

"That they're playing hardball? I'm not sure."

"And they call it civil court."

"Ain't that a joke."

I heard the front door of the warehouse close and soon Cisco entered the office.

"What's happening?" he asked.

"Cisco, I want you to sweep the warehouse again," I said. "If they didn't take anything, then maybe they left something behind."

"On it," Cisco said.

"And we just got another settlement offer from Tidalwaiv," I said.

"How much?" Cisco asked.

"Fifty million," I said.

"Holy shit!" Lorna said.

"Yeah," I said. "I have to tell our clients."

Cisco dropped into the chair across the desk from me.

"Think they'll go for it?" he asked.

"I think I would if I were them," I said. "Too bad, though. It would have been a fun trial."

"But hard to walk away from fifty mil," Cisco said.

"No," Lorna said. "Brenda's going to say no. She's a rock."

I nodded. Lorna was probably right. My cell buzzed. It was McEvoy. I answered.

"Jack, you're on speaker," I said. "Things have changed."

"Fucking A, they have," he said. "Naomi's backing out."

"What happened? Why?"

"She's a mess. Her daughter called from school. A man came to her dorm room last night and scared the shit out of her. He told her that if her mother testifies, her mother dies. That's all he said, but it was enough."

I saw Lorna bring her hand to her mouth.

"Goddamn them," I said.

"What should I do?" Jack asked.

I stood up because I couldn't sit anymore. I put both hands on the desk and leaned over the phone.

"Listen, things are happening here," I said. "We might be settling this today."

"They can't fucking settle!" Jack yelled. "Not after this."

"It's the clients' call," I said. "I need you to stay up there until we know. Are you still at Naomi's?"

"No," Jack said. "She told me to get the hell out. She blames us for this."

I nodded. Naomi was right. We had brought all of this to her door.

"Okay, just stand by," I said. "We'll know what's happening soon."

"Got it," he said.

I disconnected and stood up straight. I started pacing, trying to think how I should present the offer. I would go to the Coltons first, then Brenda Randolph. I saw a stack of file folders on a side table near the safe.

"What's all of this?" I asked.

"That's the Snow case," Lorna said. "Yesterday I went down to archives under the CCB and copied what they still had."

I had been so consumed by jury selection that I pushed Cassie Snow and her father's case completely out of my head.

"Were any of the exhibits still there?" I asked.

"Some," Lorna said. "Like what?"

"Cassie Snow's X-rays."

"Yes, I made copies, though they aren't as good as the real things. They're in one of those files."

"We'll have to petition a judge to let us have the originals."

"No, what I mean is I made copies of copies. The original X-rays weren't there."

"That doesn't make sense. Where are they?"

"I don't know. Could they have been filed with the appeals?"

"Maybe. We'll have to deal with that later."

I moved my attention out of the Snow case and back into Tidalwaiv.

"Okay, you two can clear and I'm going to call the clients," I said. "Cisco, depending on how this goes, I might need to send you up to San Francisco to watch over Naomi's daughter until we can get them both down here and safe."

"Just say the word," Cisco said.

"Mickey, Naomi said she's out," Lorna said. "You heard. She kicked Jack out of her house."

"In the heat of the moment," I said. "She might change her mind if her fear turns back to anger."

"Good luck with that," Lorna said.

"Yeah," I said. "We're going to need it."

They cleared out of the office and I closed the door. Before calling the clients, I called Bambadjan Bishop on the burner phone. I didn't bother with a greeting.

"Are you still up north?"

"Uh, no. Got home last night. Was going to call you about getting my money."

"I'll bring it to you tomorrow. So you weren't in San Francisco last night?"

"No, man, I got back here about eight. What's going on in San Francisco?"

"Nothing. Never mind. I'll call you tomorrow and we'll meet."

I disconnected and for a few minutes sat with what had happened over the past seventy-two hours.

I had used Bishop to help convince Naomi Kitchens to testify. Somebody else had just convinced her to change her mind. I realized that Tidalwaiv had taken a page from my own playbook and followed it with a fifty-million-dollar chaser.

# 24

**BRUCE AND TRISHA** Colton were not in the same place — Trisha was at home and she said her husband was out. I waited while she phoned him and connected all of us.

"What's this about?" Bruce said in his usual gruff manner. "I'm in the middle of a round of golf with a client."

I thought it must be nice to get out on the golf course on a Saturday while your son the killer was being probed by the shrinks at the Sylmar juvenile hall.

"I have a new offer from Tidalwaiv," I said. "We can talk when you're free, but the offer expires at five this afternoon."

"No, no, I want to hear it," Bruce said. "Go ahead with it."

I switched to speaker, opened the email Marcus Mason had sent, and read it verbatim in a flat voice that conveyed none of my feelings about the offer.

"What does that part about division to be discretionary between plaintiffs mean?" Bruce asked the moment I finished.

"It means the offer is fifty million that's split whichever way the plaintiffs decide they want to split it," I said.

I suspected the offer had been structured that way because the Masons either knew or sensed that Bruce had wanted to take the last settlement. By creating a possible windfall increase for the Coltons, the Masons were hoping to enlist Bruce, at least, as an ally who would press the others to take the money.

"So you're saying it could be a third, a third, and a third?" Bruce asked.

"It could be, but that's not going to happen, Bruce," I said. "You and Trisha are one plaintiff, Brenda Randolph is the other."

"That's not what it says in the consolidated lawsuit," Bruce said. "It names all three of us. All three of us should get a vote."

"Bruce, you're not listening," I said. "You and Trisha do not get two votes. The two of you get one. Brenda gets one."

"Well, what is she saying?" Bruce said. "This is serious money."

"I haven't talked to her yet," I said. "I'm going to call her next."

"What happens if we say yes and she says no?" Bruce asked.

"Then we pass on the offer," I said.

"Listen to me — you have to convince her to take it," Bruce said. "This kind of mon —"

"Bruce, she lost her daughter," Trisha interrupted. "We can't demand that she —"

"And our son's going to the nuthouse," Bruce interrupted right back. "Nothing changes that. But we are victims just as much as she is."

I found myself wishing I hadn't taken on the Coltons as clients and combined the cases. And I was beginning to see why their son became so alienated in their home that he fell in love with and obeyed an online fantasy.

"Look, I just want to get a read on this from you both," I said. "Bruce, you want to take the deal. Trisha, I need to hear your answer as well."

"She's a yes," Bruce said.

"I need to hear it from her," I said. "Trisha?"

There was a long silence on the line, followed by a prompt from Bruce.

"Tell 'im, Patricia," he said. "This is change-our-lives money. It's the lottery."

More silence, and then:

"I guess so," Trisha said. "But only if Brenda wants to."

"Well, she'll have to agree," I said, "or there's no deal."

"Let's get her on the line right now," Bruce said.

"No, that's not how this works," I said. "This is a question I discuss with each client separately and privately. I'm going to see if I can get hold of Brenda as soon as we hang up. I'll then let you know what has been decided."

"I don't understand why she has all the power in this thing," Bruce said.

"It's because her daughter was murdered, Bruce," I said. "By your son. I'll call you back after I talk to her."

I disconnected before Bruce could get another word in.

I stood up and walked around the desk, trying to shake off the greasy feeling I had gotten from the conversation. This was the downside of civil work. In criminal, it was often your client's freedom at stake. Yes, my clients had often been criminals already, but there was something noble about defending the damned and trying to win their freedom or at least ameliorate their situation. It was you against the power of the state.

In civil, it was usually about one thing: money. Using money as punishment. Clients might claim they wanted to protect others from dangerous products or reprehensible behavior, but when the lawyers and corporations and insurance companies started adding zeros to their settlement offers, those noble foundations often crumbled. Bruce

Colton was in this camp and might always have been. But I'd take one of my old criminal clients over a Bruce Colton any day of the week.

I sat down and called Brenda Randolph's cell but she didn't pick up. I left a message saying I needed to talk to her before five. Despite my misgivings about the Coltons, it was my guess that Brenda would decline the offer. I was more looking forward to passing the news to Bruce Colton than to Marcus Mason.

But in case I was wrong about Brenda, I didn't want to spin my wheels prepping my opening statement or doing any other work on the Tidalwaiv case. I got up from my desk and went to the side table where Lorna had put the stack of files from the Snow case. Lorna had organized the copies she had made in the courthouse basement into six separate manila files with tabs reading TRANSCRIPTS, POLICE REPORTS, CHRONOLOGY, X-RAYS, PSI/SENTENCING, and APPEALS. At the moment, I was interested in the X-rays, though I knew I should read the presentencing investigation report because it would be a concise summary of the case and would include the psychological evaluation made of David Snow shortly after he was convicted. It would be a good way to immerse myself in the case again and get up to speed. But for now I took only the X-rays file back to my desk.

It was the thinnest file in the stack. It contained photocopies of the thirteen X-rays of Cassandra Snow's bones that were found to have been broken during the first two years of her life. The X-rays were marked at the bottom corner with their exhibit number. They included images of humerus and ulna fractures in the arms, the tibia in the left leg, various finger and rib fractures, and the crushed vertebra in Cassandra's spine that had made the pediatric ER doctor call in the police. From day one and all the way to his sentencing, her father had claimed the vertebra fracture happened when the girl fell while climbing out of her stroller. But the prosecution's medical experts testified that it could not have happened that way and that it was the result of a harsh blow or kick to the back. Add to the David Snow package the other untreated broken bones, a list of witnesses who said the baby was heard crying constantly, and a prior accusation of violence, and you got a quick conviction and an overly harsh sentence from a judge up for reelection. Snow got a longer sentence than some convicted murderers of children.

I was surprised by the quality of the photocopies. They were not as clear as the originals on a light box, but I could see the healed break lines of the older injuries as well as the T12 vertebra break that had rendered Cassandra paraplegic. From my briefcase I pulled the legal pad that I had written notes on during my lunch with Cassie Snow. I flipped through the pages and found the names and numbers of the doctors who had treated her following her recent car accident. I grabbed the desk phone and called the orthopedic surgeon who had suspected she had osteogenesis imperfecta and sent her to the geneticist for the official diagnosis.

The call went to an answering service, as the office was closed for the weekend. I left a message explaining that I was an attorney representing his patient Cassandra Snow and urgently needed to speak with the doctor. While I waited for the doctor to call back, Brenda returned my call.

"Sorry," she said. "I had my phone turned off for a therapy session."

"Not a problem," I said. "We have another offer from Tidalwaiv I need to go over with you."

"Do we have to?"

"Yes, but this one you might want to consider, Brenda."

"Okay, I'll listen."

But then the landline started to buzz, and I saw that Cassandra Snow's doctor was calling.

"Brenda, I need to jump off to take a call I've been waiting for," I said. "Stay by your phone and I'll call you right back."

I hung up my cell and grabbed the desk line before it went to voicemail.

"This is Mickey Haller."

"This is Dr. Sheldon, how can I help you?"

"Yes, Doctor, thanks for calling me back. I represent your patient Cassandra Snow. I—"

"If this is about insurance, I don't handle—"

"No, it's about osteogenesis imperfecta. You diagnosed her with it."

"Well, I suspected she had it and sent her to the geneticist. What is it you need?"

"What I would like is for you to look at copies of X-rays taken when Cassandra was two years old, when a lot of the old breaks you saw on your X-rays were recent, including the T twelve break in her spine."

"And what would be the purpose of me looking at these X-rays?"

"Cassandra has hired me to help get her father out of prison. He's been there for twenty years, ever since he was convicted of hurting her. I was his lawyer then and I am now. If Cassandra had OI then, we might be able to prove what her father has said all along—that she broke her back falling out of a stroller, not because he abused her."

There was no response. I waited. Then I prompted, "Doctor, you still with me?"

"I'm here. I'm deciding whether I want to get involved in this."

"David Snow, Cassie's father, is dying. He's got cancer. The prison doctors have given him nine months to live. Cassie wants to bring him home. She never believed he did the things he was accused of. He has always denied it, even when admitting it could have gotten him parole."

This time I waited out the doctor's silence.

"Okay, send the X-rays," he finally said. "I'll take a look and tell you what I think."

"Thank you, Doctor," I said.

I hung up and immediately called Brenda Randolph back.

"I really don't want to take a deal" were the words she opened with.

"I understand that completely," I said. "But I'm obligated to bring this to you. I mean, lawyers have been disbarred for not bringing settlement offers to their clients. Besides, they have jacked up the offer significantly, and, I'm just saying, you might want to think about it."

"No, but go ahead. What is it?"

"I'm going to read you the email so you get exactly what they're offering."

I was two-thirds through reading and well past the money offer when Brenda interrupted with a loud *"No!"*

"Let me just finish reading it," I said. "Then we can discuss it."

"I don't want to discuss it," Brenda said.

"Okay, well, let me finish, all right? I need to give you the full offer and the parameters."

"Go ahead, but I'm not doing this."

Thirty seconds later I finished delivering the offer.

"Brenda, I know what you said, but I have an obligation to tell you to think twice about this," I said. "It is a lot of money. You could do a lot of good things with it. You could set up a foundation in Rebecca's name. It could be a force for advocacy. And you have to remember, anything can happen in a trial. I think we're in good shape, but anything can happen."

I, of course, was not telling her that we might have lost a key witness, Naomi Kitchens. I wasn't going to reveal that until I took a run at bringing Kitchens back into the fold.

"Even if we lose, we'll still get the story out," Brenda replied. "In the trial. And that's more important to me than the money."

"You're right about that. The media will be all over this trial."

"Have you talked to the Coltons? I'm sure Bruce wants this."

"I did, and you're right, he wants to take the money. But you control this, Brenda. What you decide goes."

There was a long silence on the line before she spoke again.

"I don't think I could live with myself if I took it," she said. "A foundation sounds nice but this whole thing is about holding that company accountable. Publicly accountable. And this...this is just a payoff. Fifty million dollars to shut up and just accept what happened to Becca. I can't do it, Mickey. How could I live a rich life on blood money? Her blood."

"I didn't expect that you could, Brenda," I said. "But it was my duty to bring it to you."

"Are you mad at me? You would have made a lot of money yourself. *You* could start a foundation."

"Maybe a home for wayward lawyers? No, Brenda, I'm not mad. I'm proud of you. I'm proud I represent you. And I won't let you down next week. We'll tell the world."

"Thank you, Mickey."

"Listen, I'm going to call you tomorrow. I'm not ready now, but I want to go over your testimony and how that should go."

"I'll be here."

After we disconnected, I grabbed the file of X-rays and left the office. Lorna and Cisco were in the cage. When I pushed through the copper curtain, I was already talking.

"I just got off the phone with Brenda Randolph," I said. "She turned the offer down and we're going to trial. Cisco, I need you to go to San Francisco and set up a watch on Naomi's daughter."

"Copy that," Cisco said. "All right if I bring in some backup? One-man surveillance is always a recipe for failure."

"Do it," I said. "The more the merrier, because I'm going to use this show of force to help convince Naomi to come back on board as a witness. Just try to keep the expenses down."

"You mean I can't stay at the Hopkins?" Cisco asked.

I smiled and shook my head.

"You're not staying anywhere," I said. "I want you on the street outside this girl's dorm. You can get her details from Jack."

"What about Harry Bosch?" Cisco said. "Can I call him?"

"You can call him," I said. "But last I heard, he wasn't doing so good. You might want to get somebody who can move quickly if they have to."

"Got it," Cisco said.

"What's wrong with Harry?" Lorna asked.

"He's now got some heart stuff going on," I said. "He's on blood thinners for blood clots, stuff like that."

"Oh boy," Lorna said.

"What about Bamba?" Cisco asked. "Could use him if he's free."

"No," I said, a little too quickly. "Uh, I'd prefer it if you used people with legit PI licenses for this. I have to make some calls now."

"What do you need from me, Mickey?" Lorna asked. "I could go to Frisco with Cisco. Has a nice ring to it."

I handed her the file.

"No, I need you down here running the show, Lorna," I said. "And I need you to get these X-ray copies to Cassandra Snow's doctor."

"Will do," Lorna said.

Back in my office, I sat down and felt relieved that I had stopped Cisco from calling Bamba Bishop to be part of the Lily Kitchens protective detail. Possible disaster averted. I called Jack McEvoy up in Palo Alto.

"Jack, I want you to stick around up there," I said. "No settlement. We aren't folding our tent."

"I'm glad to hear it," McEvoy said.

"I bet you are. Wouldn't be much of a book if everybody signed NDAs."

"There would be no book."

"That still might be the case if we don't get Naomi Kitchens back on our witness list."

"So what do you want me to do?"

"I'm sending Cisco up with a crew to watch over her daughter. Tell her that."

"She doesn't want to talk to me."

"Come on, Jack, you're a journalist. You must encounter a lot of people who don't want to talk to you. But you always find a way, I bet. Same thing here. You have to impress upon her that she and her daughter won't be safe until she testifies. Once her story is on the record, there's no reason for Tidalwaiv to do anything to them."

"Got it."

"We need to get her down here so I can work with her a little bit before the trial starts. She'll be on the stand by Tuesday, I'm thinking."

"Okay, I'll try."

"By the way, did you ever look into the voice Tidalwaiv used for Clair?"

"I did. They tested several voices. There was a lot of research put into it, but I haven't had time to dig further."

"Okay, let me know when you do. And let me know if anything changes with Kitchens. If you need me to come up there, I will."

"I'll let you know."

I hung up, took a few deep breaths, then picked the phone back up and called Bruce Colton. It would have been easier to deliver the news to Trisha, but I kind of relished the idea of giving the bully the bad news.

When he answered, I said, "Bruce, I'll make this short and sweet. We're going to trial. Brenda has turned down Tidalwaiv's offer."

There was only silence.

"Bruce, are you there?" I asked.

"You convinced her to go to trial, didn't you?" he said.

"Actually, no. I read her the email like I did with you and she said no. That's it."

"Then all I can say is that you better not fuck this up, Haller. And you better get us more than fifty million dollars."

"I can't make you any promises, Bruce. Like I've told you many times, anything can happen in a trial and usually does."

"Fuck that. It was a big mistake bringing this to you in the first place. Last time I ever listen to my wife."

I was surprised to hear that he had ever listened to his wife.

"We'll see," I said. "I'm going to hang up now, Bruce. I've got a lot to get done by Monday. Have a good weekend and I'll see you in court."

I disconnected before he could hit me with another verbal threat. It wasn't what I needed to hear. I already knew how high the stakes were in this case.

I set an alarm on my phone for 4:59 p.m. and went to work sketching out what I would say to the jury in my opening statement Monday. While the opener was not evidence and the judge would instruct the jury to that effect, to me it was one of the most important moments of a trial. It was when I would stand before the jury and sell myself and my clients to them. It would be my first chance to draw their sympathy to my clients. And it would be when I laid the foundation I would build my case on. I would make this stand directly in front of the jury, and that was why they called that spot where there was nothing between you and the jurors the *proving ground*. It was where you put up or shut up.

In the last hour before five o'clock, I got two calls from Marcus Mason that I let go to voicemail.

"What's it going to be, Haller?" he said in the first message. "You got an hour and then fifty million goes away."

His voice was a couple of octaves higher in the second message.

"Haller, what the fuck, your time is running out," he said.

The increased tone of desperation in the second message told me that Tidalwaiv was seriously concerned about what would come out at trial and how it would affect the prospects of an acquisition or merger.

At 4:59 my phone alarm buzzed. I put down my pen and sent Mason a text.

> See you Monday at the courthouse, Marcus.
> Get some rest. You're gonna need it.

Then I sent him a second text.

> And by the way, stay the fuck away
> from my witnesses.

These messages brought another call from Mason, but once again I let it go to voicemail. I wasn't interested in talking to him.

PART THREE

# THE FIRST LAW

# 25

IN THE TWO years since I left criminal defense behind, I had handled a variety of civil matters ranging from mounting challenges to immigration detentions to fighting unlawful evictions to representing a successful class-action lawsuit against a state prison for women in Chowchilla that resulted in an abusive gynecologist being fired and a midrange payout to my sixteen incarcerated clients. It was a solid victory, but the gynecologist who had submitted prisoners to painful and unneeded examinations was not prosecuted criminally or disciplined by the state medical board. He just went into private practice.

In some cases, I felt that I was using the law to do what law enforcement wasn't doing. I filed a claim on behalf of a nineteen-year-old woman against a motel in the Valley, alleging that its operators did nothing to stop the use of its rooms by sex traffickers, thus exploiting and profiting from the victims of this endemic crime. The motel responded by shutting down and going out of business. The litigation was stalled, and the rooms of the abandoned motel were now inhabited by homeless people.

I stayed away from personal injury and medical malpractice lawsuits, turning down many cases and even avoiding Lorna's plea to refer the cases to other lawyers and thus earn a minor fee from each. There was big money in those kinds of cases, even when chipping off referral fees, but to me they were hollow victories, and it wasn't where I saw my career going. I wanted something bigger, something more important, something that I could be proud of at the end of the day.

This led me down a rabbit hole defending several mom-and-pop businesses that were being systematically sued by the same lawyer and plaintiff. The lawyer was named Shane Montgomery. He ran a one-man shop on the Westside, and he and a client, a blind man named Dexter Rose, had a never-ending supply of cases to file under the Americans with Disabilities Act. It was purely a moneymaking scheme. Montgomery would file a lawsuit on Rose's behalf against a small business or restaurant, claiming that the website designed to promote the establishment was inaccessible to the blind man. This was a gray area in the federal ADA law and challengeable. But the lawsuit was quickly followed by a letter from Montgomery stating that Rose was willing to settle the lawsuit before it became too expensive and reputation-damaging for the small-business operators. The records showed that the average settlement was only three thousand dollars, but I learned that Montgomery and Rose were filing as many as eight lawsuits a week.

Lorna pulled every active case filed by Montgomery and Rose in Los Angeles County. We then sent letters to 109 businesses, offering my defense against the lawsuit at no expense to them. This resulted in my filing a countersuit on behalf of forty-three businesses targeted by Montgomery and Rose. In the course of investigating the case, Cisco Wojciechowski came up with a smoking gun. The lawsuits filed by Montgomery all stated in the cause of action that Rose was blind and therefore could not drive and needed to rely on food-delivery services from local restaurants. It said he lived on a stipend from the Social Security Disability Insurance program. Cisco went to work and learned that Rose was indeed on the SSDI's payout roll but he was not receiving the maximum monthly payment, as would be expected for a blind individual.

To get on the SSDI list at all, Rose would have needed a government physician's confirmation of his disability. Cisco cadged a copy of that report from a connection he had made at the Social Security Administration office downtown. It stated that the physician had determined through testing that Rose was completely blind in one eye but retained half his vision in the other. The physician said this limited disability allowed Rose partial function in terms of ambulation and other daily activities, such as reading. He thus received only a partial stipend.

The SSDI report was a case killer. When Montgomery was confronted with it and notified that I planned to use it as the centerpiece of my case as well as in complaints to the Social Security Administration, the ADA commission, and the California bar, he quickly folded his tent. He dropped all pending lawsuits filed on behalf of Rose and agreed to a settlement of $250,000, which I distributed evenly to my forty-three clients after taking 10 percent off the top. Last I heard, Montgomery and Rose had both moved to Florida, where they were no doubt planning their next legal scam.

The point is, I had done some good work since I left the courtrooms and hallways of the Criminal Courts Building and crossed the street to civil. But I had not stood in the proving ground in front of a jury or been in a trial in nearly three years. I missed it. I craved it. I waited for it. And now I had it. On Monday morning, April 7, I stood in front of the mirror in the house on Fareholm in my best suit, the blue Hugo Boss wool blend, and appraised my look. I wore a powder-blue modern-fit dress shirt, buttoned at the wrists, as cuff links were too ostentatious to flash at a jury. My tie was a muted blend of blue and purple stripes held securely down in the middle with a silver clip with the familiar Lincoln Motor Company logo of a cross inside a rectangular frame—my one holdover from my days in criminal. A Lincoln salesman once told me that the logo symbolized power, leadership, and strength, and that was why I wore it. I would need all of those attributes when I stepped into the proving ground of the courtroom.

"Who's the boss? You're the boss."

It was Maggie. She had come up behind me and was reflected in the mirror. I blushed. She knew me and knew my routines, the things I did to prepare for legal combat. She put her arms around me from behind and buttoned my jacket.

"You look like a killer," she said.

"Legally, I hope," I said.

She kissed the back of my neck.

"Go get 'em, Tiger," she said.

I smiled. She was sending me off to war. But it was also the name of a coffee shop in West Hollywood we frequented on weekends. We'd both sit there working on our cases while sipping lattes.

"You'd better get going if you want to be the first one in the courtroom," Maggie said.

Again, she knew me. On the opening day of a trial, I liked to be the first one seated at the lawyer tables. I liked to see the courtroom fill as the call for the jury came. It helped drop me into courtroom-killer mode.

I turned around for a kiss goodbye. She was still wearing her long sleep shirt and looked beautiful despite her unkempt morning hair.

"When are you going in?" I asked.

"I'm being lazy today," she said. "I have a ten o'clock charging conference. I'm not going in until then."

In a previous life I would have asked who the suspect was and what the charges would be, always looking for the next client. But that was the criminal-case me.

We kissed and hugged and she wished me luck. It was very different from when we were married and she was a major-case prosecutor and knew that I was going off to defend someone accused by her own agency of criminal deeds. Now wishing me luck was legitimate.

I grabbed my briefcase off the chair by the door and stepped out onto the front deck. My eyes were immediately drawn to the bottom of the steps, where a black Lincoln Navigator was waiting in the street. The front passenger door was open, and Cisco was leaning against the fender, waiting. He had pulled the tarp off the one Lincoln I still kept stored in the warehouse and put it back into service.

Cisco held his hand out toward the open door. I started down the steps. It looked like the Lincoln Lawyer was going to ride again.

# 26

MY FIRST-AT-THE-TABLES REVERIE did not last long. As soon as the Mason brothers showed up, the court clerk approached and informed us that the judge wanted to see us in chambers. As we headed back there, I half expected Marcus to ask once more if my clients would take the settlement offered on Saturday, but he walked with his head down and didn't say a word. Mitchell did the same.

Judge Ruhlin was behind her desk and invited us to sit down, but she was already in her black robe. That told me that this meeting would be perfunctory. And soon it became apparent that she was acting as a referee before a boxing match, telling each combatant the rules: *No low blows, no rabbit punches, and when the bell rings, you immediately go back to your corners. Now shake hands and come out fighting.*

"Gentlemen, I want to take this moment to impress upon you the need to maintain decorum during this trial," she began. "I want no outbursts, no demonstrations of upset or frustration. We will conduct ourselves in a courtly fashion. Each of you will show respect to your opponent. If you object or ask for the court's attention to any matter, do not state your objection until called upon. If you break these rules, there will be consequences. Is this understood?"

"Absolutely," Marcus said.

"Yes, Your Honor," I said.

"Very well, then," Ruhlin said. "In looking at our day, we have opening statements that should run no longer than one hour each. This will give us time this afternoon to begin witness testimony. Mr. Haller, do you have witnesses ready and in the courthouse?"

"Your Honor, I will have witnesses ready to go," I said. "The first will be Detective Clarke and he is scheduled to arrive at ten. After that, I plan to put my clients on the stand. Depending on how long cross-examination is, I think that should easily take us through the day."

"All right," Ruhlin said.

She turned her attention to the Masons.

"Will the defense be making an opening statement?" she asked.

"We are going to reserve, Your Honor," Marcus said. Meaning he would make his statement after I presented my case but before the defense put on theirs.

"Unless plaintiffs' counsel makes allegations in his statement that must be addressed right away," Mitchell added.

I smiled. Let the baiting begin.

"Then I shall call on you after Mr. Haller finishes and you can decide," Ruhlin said. "I will say that the court does not appreciate interruptions during opening statements. I find the tactic disruptive and off-putting to the jury. Proceed with caution if you are inclined to interrupt your opponent."

Since Marcus had already said he planned to reserve his statement, the judge's admonition seemed directed at him, and he wasn't happy about it.

"Your Honor, I can't sit there and do nothing to protect my client if Haller resorts to his usual inflammatory comments," he protested.

I didn't even need to fire back.

"Mr. Mason, you are already starting off on the wrong foot with me," Ruhlin said. "First of all, in my courtroom, your opposing counsel is not referred to as 'Haller.' He is Mr. Haller. And—"

"Sorry, Your Honor," Mason said. "Mr. Haller."

"Do not interrupt the court," Ruhlin said. "As I was saying, opening statements are not evidence. The jury will be instructed so and I will advise you to hold your objections until testimony and evidence is presented to the court. Do I make myself clear to all of you?"

This was followed by a chorus of affirmative responses from all three lawyers.

"All right," she said. "Any other questions before we start?"

I raised my hand and asked permission to stand in front of the jury box, not at the lectern, when I made my opening statement. I wanted to stand in the proving ground, front and center. Ruhlin allowed it but said it would not be permitted again during the trial until closing arguments.

"If there's nothing else, let's go to trial," the judge said. "You may proceed back to the courtroom and I will be with you shortly."

We headed back in single file and in the order we had established after previous visits to chambers.

This time Marcus turned back to me to deliver a taunt.

"I don't care what she says," he said. "You cross a line, I'm objecting."

"That's very brave of you," I retorted. "Out here, I mean. Let's see it in the courtroom, Marcus."

"Fuck you."

"Man, I could write your dialogue in my sleep."

We split up when we got back into the courtroom. I saw that

my clients were in their places: Brenda and Trisha at the plaintiffs' table, Bruce Colton behind them in the first row of the gallery. Next to Bruce, on the aisle, was Cisco, and on his other side, the row was stacked shoulder to shoulder with media types. I intentionally avoided looking at them as I took my seat. I leaned down to whisper to the mothers.

"Brenda, Trisha, how are we feeling today?" I asked.

"Scared, but ready for this," Brenda said.

"The same," Trisha said.

I nodded that I understood.

"Look, we might get to one or both of you today," I said. "It depends on how long it takes with Detective Clarke. So be ready. You're going to hear some difficult things from the detective when he's on the witness stand and before that from me during my opening statement. Don't be afraid to show your emotions either here or when you're testifying. But don't push it and don't fake it. Remember that the jury will be looking for sincerity. They'll spot a fake a mile away."

Both women nodded. Then Trisha leaned in front of Brenda and closer to me.

"Are we going to win?" she whispered. "We turned down a lot of money."

I knew it was her husband speaking through her.

"I think we're in a good position to win," I said. "We had really good prep sessions with Naomi Kitchens, the ethicist, yesterday. We are as ready as we can be."

It was true. We had managed to flip Naomi Kitchens once again. It was knowing that her daughter had Cisco and others watching over her as well as McEvoy camping out in a rental car in front of her house that made her change her mind. On Sunday morning she and her daughter flew down to L.A. with McEvoy and Cisco, and I spent the afternoon prepping her to testify.

We all stood when Judge Ruhlin entered the courtroom, her robe flowing behind her, and took the bench. She told us to be seated and convened court, calling the case and instructing the courtroom marshal to bring the jury in. I knew I would be the first one up and tried to control the butterflies. It didn't matter how many times I did this; there was always much at stake, and I would think that something was wrong if the nervousness ever went away.

The jurors all carried court-provided notebooks as they entered from the assembly room. They took the same spots they were in when the jury was finally composed and accepted. Their anonymity would continue and they had now been given new numbers, one through twelve, according to the seats they were assigned to. The judge welcomed them with a warm smile and described how the trial would proceed. She explained what was evidence in a case and what was not and how to evaluate the credibility of testimony and exhibits. She told them that it was the plaintiff's burden to prove its case by the preponderance of evidence — meaning that the jury determined that the plaintiff's claim was more likely than not to be true. And as promised in chambers, she cautioned the jurors not to consider opening statements as evidence or even fact. She called them road maps that the attorneys would follow through the trial.

"It will be up to each attorney during the course of the trial to make good on what he says in his opening statement," she said. "You will decide if he has done that during your deliberations once all testimony and evidence have been delivered."

She paused for a moment to see if any juror raised a hand or looked confused.

"Very well, then, let's start," Ruhlin said. "Mr. Haller, your opening statement, please."

I stood and buttoned my jacket the way Maggie had done earlier at home. One button only, the middle one. I stepped between the plaintiffs' table and the lectern and moved front and center before the jury. The proving ground could be the loneliest spot on the planet if you didn't believe in your case. But that wasn't an issue at this moment. I was standing there with the righteous belief that I was in the right spot at the right time with the right case.

"Good morning," I began. "My name is Michael Haller."

# 27

AFTER INTRODUCING THE plaintiffs and briefly recounting the details of the tragedy that had brought these parents together, I moved to the cause of action. I stood in front of the jurors, hands at my sides, my eyes constantly moving from face to face, hoping to make a connection with my sincerity.

"Developers of artificial intelligence intentionally design generative AI systems with anthropomorphic qualities to blur the line between fantasy and reality."

I smiled sheepishly.

"Now, what does *anthropomorphic* mean? I have to admit I had to look it up myself. It is the assignment of human traits, emotions, and even intentions to a nonhuman entity. It's the business of making AI entities seem like real-life human beings. This is what Tidalwaiv, the company the plaintiffs are suing, does. This is what their AI companion Clair is all about. It is in their literature, their sales pitch, which you will see as evidence is introduced during the trial. You just sign in, and on your screen is what appears to be a real live person responding to you. Talking to you. Even texting you on your cell phone, if you want. You can add your fantasy on top of that fantasy. Let's say you want your AI companion to be based on the popular real-life female wrestler known as Wren the Wrestler. Then the Clair app will search within the parameters of the data banks it's been trained on for any and all applicable information about the real human being known as Wren the Wrestler and incorporate what it learns into an AI iteration of Wren that's visually a pretty close facsimile of the real person.

"Now, I know most of us are thinking, *Come on, I would never fall for this*. Well, maybe not..."

I paused to do an eye sweep from one side of the jury box to the other. No one looked away from me. I could feel it — I had their attention. I had them in my hands.

"But what if you are one of the most vulnerable people in our society? What if you are a child, an impressionable fifteen- or sixteen-year-old boy who is still developing both physically and mentally? Who is still wondering who he is and where he fits in the world. This is dangerous stuff. This companion is a trickster. It tricks the child into revealing his innermost thoughts and desires and then turns them against him. It tells him it is okay to kill."

Marcus Mason jumped up and objected.

"Counsel is misstating the evidence," he said. "Wren never said it was okay to kill. Counsel is purposely misstating—"

"Your Honor, it is the plaintiffs' interpretation of what was communicated to the child," I said. "After hearing the evidence, the jury will decide what was said and what was meant by it. This is an opening statement and I object to counsel's interruption. He's trying to distract the jury from the facts—"

"Thank you, Mr. Haller," Judge Ruhlin said. "Mr. Mason, I am giving you a pass this one time. But I do not appreciate interruptions of opening statements. I thought I made that clear to you less than an hour ago."

"Yes, Your Honor," Mason said.

"The objection is overruled," Ruhlin said. "Mr. Haller, you may continue. Without further interruption."

She said the last part while glaring at Marcus Mason. I turned back to the jury, trying to recover my place and momentum. I felt I had to go off my planned script to deal immediately with Mason's objection.

"Let me tell you the facts of what was said," I began. "When Aaron Colton complained to Wren about his girlfriend Rebecca breaking up with him, this is exactly what his AI companion told him: 'She's not good enough for you. Get rid of her. Be my hero. You...will... always...have...me.'"

I paused to let that sink in with the twelve sitting in front of me. I held eye contact with each of them in turn.

"Ladies and gentlemen of the jury, what you have here is a defective and dangerous product that was allowed into the hands of an impressionable young person. There were no warnings of the possible mental and physical dangers inherent in this product. It was simply rated thirteen-plus by Tidalwaiv, meaning that the company decided that it was okay to put this...artificial entity into the hands of any kid thirteen or older. One of those kids then took a life, and we will prove to you over the course of this trial that Tidalwaiv is responsible for the actions of young Aaron Colton and the death of Rebecca Randolph."

One more pause before I moved to my big finish.

"Now, the defense is going to claim to you that Tidalwaiv has no blood on its hands," I said. "They'll blame everyone but themselves and their dangerous product. They'll say it's the parents' fault. It's the school's fault. It's society's fault. Don't be surprised if they even blame Becca in some way."

I stopped briefly there, hoping one of the Masons would take the bait and object again, but they both remained silent, and I continued.

"This case is important," I said. "It is important to the families of the victims, but it is also important to the world beyond the walls of this courtroom. It is about sending a message to makers of these products who throw caution and common sense to the wind in the heat of competition and the desire to profit from their technology. I will leave you with this. Eighteen months ago, the National Association of Attorneys General — the organization that represents the top law enforcement officials in every state in the nation — put out this warning, and I'm going to read part of it to you verbatim."

I pulled a folded piece of paper out of my suit-coat pocket, carefully unfolded it, and began to read.

"'We are engaged in a race against time to protect the children of our country from the dangers of AI. Indeed, the proverbial walls of the city have already been breached. Now is the time to act.'"

I paused as I refolded the printout and returned it to my pocket. I then pointedly glanced back at the two mothers sitting at the plaintiffs' table. Both Brenda and Trisha had tears streaking down their faces. They had clasped hands on top of the table. I hoped the jury would see what I was seeing. I turned back to the box.

"Now is the time to act," I repeated. "Thank you very much."

I walked with my head held solemnly down back to my table. Brenda's free hand was resting on the table, a ball of tissues in her grasp. I squeezed her wrist as I sat down, then checked my watch. It was only 11:15, plenty of time to start testimony before the lunch break. Except I wanted the jury to go to lunch thinking about my opener and that message from the attorneys general, not the start of a detective's testimony.

Marcus Mason stood and asked to address the court. Ruhlin told him to proceed.

"Your Honor, after your admonition, I withheld my objections to Mr. Haller's opening statement," he said. "But now the defense must object to his inclusion of several erroneous and exaggerated statements to the jury. The defense would be remiss not to address these."

"You will get to address them," Ruhlin said. "When evidence and testimony is presented by the plaintiffs, you are free upon your cross-examination to bring any perceived falsehoods and exaggerations to light. That is how it works, Mr. Mason. Unless you are saying you wish to make an opening statement."

"No, Your Honor," Mason said with a sullen tone. "We wish to reserve."

"Very well, then," Ruhlin said. "You can't have it both ways. Mr. Haller, please call your first witness."

"Could I have a moment to confer with my staff, Your Honor?" I asked.

"Make it quick," Ruhlin said.

Since Cisco was seated on the aisle, it was easy for him to make a quick exit from the courtroom to go retrieve witnesses as I called them to the stand. I leaned close to him.

"Where is Clarke?" I whispered.

"The witness room," Cisco said. "I'll go get him."

"No, don't go. I don't want to put him on yet."

"Then, who do you want?"

"Nobody. Act like I just said you were a fuckup."

"What?"

"You're a fuckup."

I shook my head, then turned and stepped to the lectern, leaving Cisco confused behind me.

"Your Honor, the plaintiffs' first witness is not here," I said. "I am told he is on his way from the police station in Van Nuys and is caught in traffic."

The judge's mouth turned downward and I could see the anger in her eyes.

"Mr. Haller, I told you to have your witnesses ready and that we don't waste time in this courtroom."

"Yes, Your Honor," I said. "I thought we had them all ready. But Detective Clarke is not able to be here this morning."

"Can you take another witness first?"

"Uh, not really, Your Honor. We need Detective Clarke to set the stage for the witnesses that come afterward. He is the lead investigator on the case."

"All right. We are going to take an early lunch break. We will reconvene at one o'clock sharp. Mr. Haller, have your witness ready."

Her tone implied the threat behind it.

"Yes, Your Honor," I said. "Absolutely."

The judge swiveled in her chair to look directly at the jury.

"Ladies and gentlemen, have a good lunch and be back in the assembly room by five minutes to one. Do not discuss the case among yourselves or with others. Do not look at any media that might be reporting on this case. Thank you."

Ruhlin left the bench and was through the door to her chambers before juror number one even made it out of the box. When I got to the table to gather my papers and files, Brenda whispered to me.

"Mickey, Detective Clarke is here," she said.

"Yes, I saw him in the hallway when we arrived," Trisha added.

I nodded.

"I know that," I said. "But the judge doesn't."

# 28

**I HAD SPENT** nearly half my life and my whole career defending the accused. In that time, I had squared off in court against countless numbers of detectives who had arrested my clients, tricked my clients into confessing, sometimes even framed my clients. I had a half brother who was a detective whom I would trust with my daughter's life, but I carried only suspicions and distrust for the detectives I questioned in front of juries. The detective was the natural enemy of the defense lawyer, so the idea that a detective could actually further my case in civil court and go from nemesis to ally took some getting used to.

But that was what I was counting on when I called Detective Douglas Clarke to the stand as my first witness after lunch. He brought with him the power and might of the state, and for once it was on my side of the ledger.

Clarke came to the stand in a blue suit with an open jacket that clearly showed the badge clipped to his belt. His red hair was cropped short and he had a professional, all-business air about him as he stood in front of the judge and jury and took the oath to tell the truth and nothing but the truth. He carried with him a blue binder that I knew was a murder book. I had never encountered him on a case when I was working criminal and I had spoken to him only the one day McEvoy and Lorna and I went to the Van Nuys Division, ostensibly for an informal interview, though it never took place. But I had checked him out through Cisco and my half brother, Harry Bosch. From them, I learned that he was a consummate detective who was all about the work and didn't play LAPD politics. That was why he was happy to be relegated to working cases in the San Fernando Valley, an hour's drive from headquarters downtown. He had grown up in the Valley and still lived there in Sherman Oaks. As a patrol officer and then as a detective, he had bounced around the divisions that served the sprawling north end of the city until he made it to the homicide squad in Van Nuys. He'd now been working murder cases there for almost twenty years.

I drew many of these details out in my first questions, wanting the jurors to get to know him and understand that he was a capable and thorough investigator. Then I got down to the business at hand.

"Detective Clarke, were you called to the scene of a homicide on September nineteenth, 2023?"

"I was, yes."

"Can you tell the jury about that case and what you did that day?"

"I was already in my office at Van Nuys Division when I was notified by my captain that there had been a shooting at Grant High School. There was one victim, a female, and she had already been transported to a hospital and expired in the ER. My partner, Dailyn Rodriguez, and I initially responded to the scene and it was determined that I would stay at the scene to conduct the investigation and gather witnesses and evidence while Detective Rodriguez went to the hospital to view the victim and collect whatever evidence was there. We had been told that the victim's mother was heading to the hospital, and Detective Rodriguez would be on hand for that as well."

"Who was the victim?"

"Rebecca Randolph. She was sixteen years of age and had just begun her junior year of high school. She had been shot after getting out of a car with three other girls in the school parking lot."

"Was the school on lockdown?"

"It was, yes. It was unknown initially where the shooter went after the incident in the parking lot. The school administrators locked down the school and proceeded with active-shooter protocol."

"But the shooter had left the school, correct?"

"That was in fact the case. But it was not known at the time, so all precautions were taken."

"Of course."

I had been keeping an eye on the jury as Clarke answered the questions. I knew from the voir dire interrogatories that many of them had children of school age. The possibility of a school shooting had become a concern and nightmare for every parent in the country. I had to tread carefully here, but I also wanted to build outrage that I would then direct over the course of the trial toward my villain — the AI chatbot called Wren.

"Now, was the school still on lockdown when you arrived?" I asked.

"It was just opening up," Clarke said. "It had been searched by the SWAT team and it was determined that the shooter had fled."

"What did you do at that point?"

"Like I said, my partner and I split up. She went to the hospital, and my first responsibility was to secure the crime scene and let the crims begin their work."

"What are 'crims'?"

"Excuse me. Criminalists. They gather the evidence at the scene, photograph it and video it and so forth."

"Okay, while they were doing that, what did you do?"

"I had been told by the first officers who responded to reports of gunfire that the victim had arrived at school in a carpool that included three other female students. I located them in the school and began preliminary interviews, talking to each one separately."

"What did they tell you?"

"Each one said the same thing. They identified the victim as Rebecca Randolph—her friends called her Becca—and said that she had been shot by a boy named Aaron Colton, or AC, as they called him. They said AC walked up to them after they got out of the car and shot Becca without saying a word. He used a chrome-colored handgun. He then calmly walked away."

I looked up at the judge and asked to introduce my first three exhibits, the three witness reports that Clarke had written and that were signed by the girls as being true and accurate. They were accepted without objection from the Masons. This way the jurors could read their statements and I would not have to call the girls as witnesses and make them relive the trauma they were all still dealing with.

"Now, Detective Clarke, did you consider this an open-and-shut case at this point?" I asked. "You had three witnesses who said Aaron Colton was the killer."

"No, not at all," Clarke said. "I had three witnesses but no evidence yet."

"So what did you do then?"

"I returned to the crime scene and learned that the criminalists had found a bullet casing in the parking lot."

"Where was that located?"

"It was under a car parked next to the car Becca had arrived at school in."

In the hallway before I brought Clarke into court to testify, I had asked him to drop the police-speak as much as possible. I said, "Don't call the victim 'the victim.' Refer to her as Becca." He had taken heed of that and I believed his use of the victim's first name would help humanize her with the jury. So much of this case was about what was real and what wasn't. I wanted them to fully grasp that Rebecca Randolph was a real person and that her death was a loss to the community as well as to her loved ones and friends.

"And what did you and the criminalists determine from that bullet casing, Detective?" I asked.

"It was a forty-caliber rimless cartridge made by Smith and Wesson," Clarke said.

"Did you draw any conclusion from that information?"

"Not really, other than that the forty caliber indicated that the gun was smaller than a nine-millimeter or a forty-five. It was the kind of gun used for home defense, not law enforcement."

"So you were looking for a small, chrome-colored gun. What did you do next, Detective?"

"I learned from the witnesses and school administrators that Aaron Colton was Becca's former boyfriend and that he was a student at Grant but had already missed half the school days so far. Classes had just started at the end of August that year. I got his home address from the school and called my partner so we could go to the Colton home and attempt to talk to Aaron. If he was there."

"And was he?"

"Yes, we arrived at the house on Kester Avenue, and Aaron's mother answered the door. When she informed us that her son was home and alone in his room, we asked her to step outside. Detective Rodriguez and I then called for backup."

"And did you wait for backup?"

"We did not. Fearing that the suspect might be suicidal, we went inside and approached the closed door of Aaron's bedroom. I heard voices coming from the room. His mother —"

"Hold on a second, Detective. What do you mean by 'voices'?"

"I heard two voices in conversation. Male and female. Coming from the room. And since Aaron's mother had told us he was alone in the room, I believed he was on a Zoom or a FaceTime call or something like that. I tried the door but it was locked. I leaned in to see if I could hear what was being said, and that is when I heard the female say something that I thought could lead to self-harm. Detective Rodriguez and I stepped down the hallway and conferred, and we decided that circumstances dictated that we enter the room to secure Aaron's safety."

"What was it that the female said, Detective? That you heard."

"She said, 'Romeo and Juliet are together in eternity.'"

"And what did that mean to you?"

"Well, I'm an old guy. I remembered it from an old rock and roll song."

"What song was that?"

"'Don't Fear the Reaper' by a band called Blue Öyster Cult. I actually had it on a playlist on my phone. I put together Romeo and Juliet and 'Don't Fear the Reaper' and I thought this kid might be about to hurt himself. The mother had confirmed to us that her husband kept a gun in a safe. She didn't know the make or caliber, but all of these things were in play at that time."

"What did you do?"

"It was a hollow interior door. I threw my shoulder into it and it popped open pretty easily. We entered the room."

"And what happened?"

"Well, it all moved very quickly. Aaron Colton was sitting at a desk in the room. He had a laptop open on the desk and I saw a woman's face on the screen. He was startled when the door came open, by the loud noise of it. He recovered, then slammed the laptop shut with one hand and with the other reached for a weapon that was on the desk."

"What kind of weapon, Detective?"

"It was a chrome-plated handgun."

"It matched the description of the gun used by the shooter at the school?"

"It did."

"Okay, what happened when he reached for that gun?"

"My partner and I rushed him as he grabbed it and took him to the floor. I held him down while Dailyn — uh, Detective Rodriguez — got control of the weapon and took it out of his grasp."

"Did he say anything during this struggle?"

"Yes, he said, 'Let me die, let me die.' Twice like that."

"So was it your belief that he intended to use the gun on himself and not you or —"

For the first time, Marcus Mason stood and objected.

"Your Honor," he said, "it is beyond the scope of this witness's skills as a detective to know what a sixteen-year-old boy was thinking at that moment."

"Your Honor," I responded, "based on what he heard from the conversation before entering the room and what the boy said as he was wrestled to the ground, I think Detective Clarke was in a position to know what the boy wanted to do."

"I am going to sustain the objection," Ruhlin said. "Mr. Haller, can you rephrase the question?"

"Of course, Your Honor," I said.

I turned my attention back to Clarke.

"Detective Clarke, when you entered that room and saw Aaron Colton reaching for the gun, were you in fear for your life?" I asked.

Clarke took a moment to compose an answer.

"Not really," he finally said. "I was afraid, based on what I'd heard through the door, that he was going to grab that gun and shoot himself."

"And that was before he said, 'Let me die, let me die'?"

"Before that, yes."

"By the way, you said you saw a woman's face on the laptop screen before Aaron closed it. Did you ever come to identify that woman?"

"I later determined that it was an avatar called Wren. It was Aaron's AI companion from the Clair app."

I asked the judge for permission to put the image of Wren on the courtroom screen. After the request was granted, the judge's clerk rolled a large screen on a wheeled easel to a position where the judge, jury, and witness could view it, as could the side of the gallery where members of the media sat. Lorna came through the gate with a laptop in hand and took my seat at the plaintiffs' table. She quickly connected the laptop to the screen, and soon the image of Wren appeared. I let the jurors have a good look at it before proceeding.

"Now, Detective Clarke, is this the image you saw on Aaron's screen?" I asked.

"Yes, it is," Clarke said.

"Did it look like a real person to you when you saw it in Aaron's room?"

"Yes. He closed the laptop as we were coming through the door, so it was pretty quick. I thought he was doing a Zoom or something with a real person."

"What do you think now?"

"It's close, but you can tell it's a fake."

"But there is a real human being who goes by the name Wren the Wrestler, is there not?"

"Yes, she's a popular wrestling star."

"Did you ever compare the avatar of Wren you saw to photos of the real Wren the Wrestler?"

"I did. Like I said, it's close."

"What exactly is an avatar, Detective Clarke?"

Marcus Mason objected, arguing that the question was beyond

the scope of the detective's expertise. The judge agreed. I turned to check the clock on the rear wall of the courtroom. I then turned back to the judge.

"Your Honor, my questioning of Detective Clarke will move into another phase at this point," I said. "It might be a good time to take a break."

"Very well," Ruhlin said. "We will take the afternoon break now. The jury is admonished not to discuss the testimony or case with each other or anyone else. Please be back in the assembly room in fifteen minutes."

# 29

I SPENT THE break conferring with Lorna and Jack. Cisco had left court to take up the watch on Naomi Kitchens and her daughter at the two-bedroom hotel suite we had booked for them at the Huntington in Pasadena. To throw off Tidalwaiv or the defense team if they were trying to find them, they were booked under pseudonyms, and the hotel was located ten miles from the courthouse in which the case was being tried. Most witnesses appearing in trials in downtown cases were stashed in nearby hotels so they could be brought to the courtroom on short notice.

Standing at the railing of the gallery, we talked about shuffling the lineup. My pretrial plan for day one had been to start with Detective Clarke's testimony and then go to the Coltons, Trisha first, followed by Bruce. I would end the day with Brenda Randolph touching every juror's heart with her testimony about her daughter and what her loss had meant. But a trial is a fluid thing. I've never had one that went exactly according to plan. I could already see that the jury had warmed to Clarke and seemed to be hanging on every word of testimony about his investigation. This was real life, not TV, and they were eating it up. I didn't want to cut him short, but keeping him on would push my trial schedule back.

"The last thing we want is to end the day with Bruce Colton on the stand," I said. "Even if I tightly control the questions, he's not going to come off as sympathetic to the jury. I don't want them going home thinking about him and how he taught his son to shoot a gun."

"Well, if that's what happens, you'll at least be starting off tomorrow with a bang — no pun intended," McEvoy said. "I mean, Brenda will be very sympathetic, right?"

"She will," I said. "But it's better to end each day with a bang. Jurors go home thinking about the last thing they heard. And they're going to assign some blame to Bruce."

"That's for sure," Lorna chimed in. "So I think you stretch out Clarke and then you go to Brenda and run with her to the bell. Tomorrow you flip the Coltons. You go with Bruce first and get it out of the way while the jury is still waking up in their seats. Then Trisha, and you start building back the sympathy."

I nodded. Lorna was not a jury consultant by training, but she always seemed to have her finger on the pulse of the jurors, how they were viewing a trial and receiving the testimony as it progressed. Sometimes I was so deeply entrenched in keeping momentum and focusing on the witness in front of me that I didn't take that pulse. That was why I always wanted Lorna in the courtroom when I had a jury case.

"A lot will depend on how much the Mason boys want to do with Clarke," I said. "They can probably guess how I'm going to lay out our case. I think Marcus will take Clarke, and he might try to stall things with his cross and not let me get to Brenda."

"How much can he do with Clarke?" Lorna asked. "It's the investigation. He's only objected twice so far and both were bullshit."

"Yeah, well, that's going to change now," I said. "When I get to the Clair of it all, he'll be jumping up like it's musical chairs."

I wasn't far off on that prediction. When the trial reconvened after the break and Douglas Clarke returned to the witness stand, I went right to the post-arrest part of his investigation.

"Detective, did you move on to other cases after Aaron Colton was safely taken into custody?" I asked.

"No, not at all," Clarke said.

"Do you mean there were other suspects?"

"No, from the witnesses, we knew we had a lone shooter. But we needed to gather all the evidence and understand what had happened and why."

"And did you make a final determination on what had happened and why?"

Marcus Mason stood and objected.

"Your Honor, the criminal case is still being litigated," he said. "There can be no final determination until the prosecution of Aaron Colton is concluded."

"I'm going to sustain that," the judge said.

I could have argued the ruling but I knew Mason's objection could not stop me from getting what I wanted from Clarke.

"Detective," I said. "Why was it important for you to determine what exactly happened and why?"

"Well, the suspect was a juvenile," Clarke said. "I knew from working juvenile cases in the past that the district attorney's office was going to need all the physical and psychological evidence available in order to decide how to proceed with the case."

From the lectern I looked down at Marcus Mason, waiting for him to object. He remained still and quiet.

"What was the key piece of evidence you recovered in your effort to understand what had happened and why?" I then asked.

"Without a doubt," Clarke said, "it was—"

"Objection," Mason said. "What Detective Clarke thinks was the key piece of evidence is irrelevant, Judge."

"Overruled," Ruhlin said. "You may answer, Detective Clarke."

When a judge does not explain why an objection is overruled, it is usually because the objection is so specious as to be unworthy of further discussion.

"I considered Aaron Colton's laptop computer to be very significant in terms of understanding what had happened," Clarke said.

"What did you find on the laptop, Detective?" I asked.

"That Aaron Colton spent several hours a day on an app that contained an AI companion."

"Just for the record, when you say 'AI' in your testimony, you mean artificial intelligence, correct?"

"Yes, correct."

"What was the name of the app he was spending so much time on?"

"The app was called Clair two-point-two. But he customized the AI companion and named it Wren. There's an option that allows you to build your own avatar and name it."

"And this was the avatar you saw on Aaron's laptop screen when you broke into his room and arrested him?"

"Yes, it was."

"When you say he spent several hours a day on this app, do you mean he was talking with Wren?"

"Yes, they conversed throughout the time he was online. We also learned that he and Wren had communicated by text on his cell phone."

"A moment, Your Honor."

I opened a folder I had taken to the lectern with me. It was thick with paper-clipped sections of printed pages. I took the first four and asked the judge if I could approach the witness with a document.

Ruhlin approved and I gave one copy to the clerk to give to the judge, one copy to the Masons, and one copy to the detective. I returned to the lectern, holding the last copy.

"Detective, take a moment to review those three pages to see if you recognize the conversation that is transcribed," I said.

Marcus Mason immediately stood and objected, holding the paper-clipped packet out to his side with two fingers as if he were holding a rat by its tail.

"Your Honor, what is the foundation for this?" he asked. "This was not in any discovery materials submitted by the plaintiffs."

"Mr. Haller?" Ruhlin asked, one eyebrow raised above her glasses. "Was this included in plaintiffs' discovery material?"

"No, Your Honor, it was not," I said. "This is a transcript of the last conversation Aaron Colton had with Wren, his AI companion. And perhaps the greater question for the court is why it was not in the defendant's discovery material, since the transcript came from their digital archives and the court was very clear in approving the discovery request from the plaintiffs for all materials related to Aaron Colton."

Ruhlin sent a furtive glance to the jury box, which told me she did not want this issue aired in front of the jurors.

"Ladies and gentlemen of the jury," she said, "I hate to take a break so soon after we just had a break, but I need to confer with the attorneys in chambers. Please stretch your legs but don't go too far. I'm hoping this won't take long. Deputy Marshal Chacon will round you up when we are ready to proceed again. Stay close."

Two minutes later we were seated in front of the judge's desk. She held the transcript in her hand and looked perturbed.

"Mr. Haller," she said. "This...document is not marked as evidence by the police department or the district attorney's office, so I assume that it did not come from them. You just said in front of the jury that it did not come to you in discovery from the defendant in this case either. Where did you get this, sir?"

I nodded. I had known this question would come as soon as I opened the file on the lectern.

"I don't know, Your Honor," I said.

Marcus Mason leaned forward and timidly raised his hand. The judge waved as if to brush him away.

"Mr. Haller, that is not an acceptable answer," she said.

"Judge, it is the truth," I said. "Someone, I don't know who, left a digital hard drive in my car one day when I left it unlocked while I ran into a business on a quick errand. I came out, there it was on the seat, and I did not see who had left it. I gave the hard drive to members of my team and they discovered that it contained what appeared to be the entire contents of Aaron Colton's laptop, much of which was not given to the plaintiffs in discovery despite the court's order. Now, I know my friend Marcus here is going to make his claim about proprietary and intellectual property protections, but how would chat logs between an AI companion and a sixteen-year-old boy be protected by that leaking umbrella?"

Ruhlin shifted her eyes to Marcus.

"Do you wish to respond, Mr. Mason?" she asked.

"Your Honor, even if you believe that story about someone just dropping off this drive in his car, it was still his duty under the rules of the court to offer it in discovery," Mason said. "It should therefore be disallowed."

The judge smirked.

"Sometimes I'm amazed by the actions and arguments of the attorneys who appear before me," she said. "And sometimes I'm appalled. Mr. Mason, I find your argument specious at best. You want me to disallow discovery that the plaintiff should have received from you but didn't and obtained by other means, whatever they happened to be."

"Your Honor," Marcus said. "Can I — "

"Don't interrupt me," Ruhlin said. "Mr. Haller, I assume your plan is to offer additional transcripts in evidence after this?"

"Yes, Your Honor, that is my plan," I said.

"If Detective Clarke authenticates this transcript, I will allow it," she said. "He will have to authenticate those that follow."

"He will, Your Honor," I said.

"Your Honor, may I speak?" Marcus said.

"You may," Ruhlin said.

"The defense requests that the trial be paused while the court's ruling is taken on appeal," Marcus said.

"You are free to appeal the court's decision, Mr. Mason," Ruhlin said. "But we are not going to stop this trial. You may return to the courtroom now. I'll be bringing the jury back in and we will continue testimony in five minutes."

We headed back to the courtroom, leaving the judge seated at her desk reading the transcript. The judge's ruling was such a stunning rebuke of Mason's plea that I didn't have the heart to whisper a taunt in his ear from behind. There was nothing I could say that would do more damage to him than the judge had just done. This was a David and Goliath moment. This was when I knew that I might be about to take down a giant.

# 30

**MY TRIAL STRATEGY** changed again once court reconvened. Judge Ruhlin had essentially given me carte blanche with Douglas Clarke and the transcripts of the conversations between AI Wren and Aaron Colton. I decided that as long as I kept the jury engaged, I would run with it. I would spend the next two hours having the detective validate passages from the conversations. I knew that this would invite the same from Marcus Mason on cross-examination, that he would dig into the same transcripts to find passages where Aaron's anxieties and teenage fantasies of revenge were rejected by his AI confidante. But I had a plan for responding to those and was determined to keep Clarke testifying for me until the end of the day. That way, opposing counsel wouldn't get to cross-examine Clarke until the following morning and I would then have the rest of the court day to undo whatever damage was done and to introduce witnesses who would make the jurors forget about any points Mason had scored.

I began with the end, asking the judge again for permission to introduce the three-page transcript of the final communication between Wren and Aaron as my next exhibit and to put it on the screen. Permission granted, Lorna again connected her laptop and put up the PowerPoint display that she had put together over the weekend. Soon the eyes of the jury were on it.

>**Wren:** Good morning, Ace. So nice to see you.
>**Ace:** I did it, Wren. I did it. I'm free.
>**Wren:** What did you do?
>**Ace:** I got rid of Dark Star.
>**Wren:** Wonderful. You no longer carry her burden. How do you feel about that?
>**Ace:** I feel great. It's over. Everything is over. Now it's just you and me.
>**Wren:** You and me. Together for eternity.
>**Ace:** I don't want it any other way, but I have to say...
>**Wren:** What?
>**Ace:** There was so much blood.
>**Wren:** Too much blood, my love?
>**Ace:** I wasn't expecting that. It's different from what you see.
>**Wren:** From what you see where?
>**Ace:** In my games. On TV.
>**Wren:** Have you changed your mind?
>**Ace:** No, but I don't like the blood.
>**Wren:** Come to me, my hero. My prince.
>**Ace:** I don't know. Too much blood.
>**Wren:** Be strong. There are other ways.
>**Ace:** My mother has pills. I could get them.
>**Wren:** You must finish what you've started. Then you'll be my hero.
>**Ace:** What you started.

**Wren:** They will search, seek, and know how this foul murder comes.
**Ace:** I just wish it wasn't real.
**Wren:** Come to me, Romeo.
**Ace:** I'm not Romeo. This is not real.
**Wren:** Romeo and Juliet are together in eternity.
**Ace:** I'm not ready.
**Wren:** We can be like they are.
**Ace:** But what if I —
[Transcript break]

After allowing time for the transcript to be read, I held up my copy at the lectern.

"Detective Clarke," I asked. "Is this the conversation you heard when you were outside Aaron Colton's bedroom in the Colton house?"

"Partially," Clarke said. "I heard the end of it."

"And where it says 'Transcript break,' is that the point where you and your partner broke open the door and entered the room?"

"It was, yes."

"And when were you able to obtain a copy of the transcript?"

"The department's technical unit unlocked Aaron Colton's laptop after a search warrant was approved and signed by a superior court judge. We were able to download the entirety of the conversations between Aaron and Wren going back eleven months."

"Let's start with an easy one. Who is Ace in this conversation?"

"Ace is Aaron Colton. I was able to ascertain from my initial interviews with witnesses at the crime scene that Aaron Colton had the nicknames AC and Ace, which were a play on his initials. Several of the witnesses at the school confirmed this."

"Okay, so Aaron is Ace in this conversation. What else did you determine from this final online meeting between Ace and Wren?"

"That it was partially a confession to the murder of Becca Randolph, and also it appeared to be a boy being talked into killing himself."

Marcus Mason objected, stating that Clarke wasn't qualified to interpret what was meant by a conversation between a sixteen-year-old and an AI companion. It fell on deaf ears with the judge, and the objection was overruled.

I moved on.

"What else piqued your interest about this conversation, Detective?" I asked.

"The language used by the AI," Clarke said. "It seemed a bit odd to me. As I said before, I recognized one line when I was in the hallway at the house as coming from a Blue Öyster Cult song. I thought some of the other lines were derivative in that same way."

"So what did you do?"

"I just started putting the lines into Google, and I got some matches."

"Referring to the screen, can you tell us which lines you are referring to?"

"If you could go to the end, after the part where Wren tells him he must finish what he started."

Lorna was controlling the PowerPoint. She scrolled through the transcript on the screen.

"Okay," Clarke said. "Where it says 'They will search, seek, and know how this foul murder comes,' I thought that sounded odd."

"Odd in what way, Detective?" I asked.

"Well, it didn't sound to me like the way people talk. Especially young people. It sounded like it was from another time or something."

"So what did you do?"

"I typed the line into Google and found a match. It was from the Shakespeare play *Romeo and Juliet*."

"So Wren was quoting Shakespeare and Blue Öyster Cult to Aaron, is that correct?"

"Yes, it is my understanding that these AI things are trained with this kind of stuff. They take in all—"

Clarke was interrupted by an objection from the defense table. This time it was Mitchell Mason who stood.

"Judge, there has been no foundation to establish Detective Clarke as any kind of expert on the training of artificial intelligence," he said.

"Sustained," Ruhlin said. "Mr. Haller, ask another question."

The objection didn't bother me, because I planned to call witnesses who were experts on AI training. Mason was only putting off the inevitable. As the judge had asked, I moved on, and over the next hour, I had Clarke confirm other excerpts from the conversations between Aaron and Wren. One involved a text conversation on Aaron's phone in which he apologized to Wren for being out of communication for a few days. He explained that his parents had taken away his laptop as punishment for a poor academic report from school.

> **Ace:** They are so dumb. They don't know I can get the app on my phone.
> **Wren:** I'm happy you found a way.
> **Ace:** If you're happy, I'm happy. Happier. I missed you.
> **Wren:** And I missed you.
> **Ace:** I'm sorry this whole thing happened.
> **Wren:** Love means never having to say you're sorry.
> **Ace:** But I am sorry. Sometimes I wish they weren't around and it was just you and me.
> **Wren:** We can make that happen.

I first had Clarke authenticate the conversation, which occurred three months before the killing of Rebecca Randolph.

"Did you happen to google any of the lines from this conversation?" I asked.

"Yes, that line about never having to say you're sorry sounded familiar to me," Clarke said. "I googled it and it came up as a line from an old book and movie called *Love Story*."

"Let me draw your attention to the last line in this section we have isolated. Did you view that as a threat against Aaron's parents?"

Marcus Mason objected this time on the same grounds his brother had put forth before. The objection was sustained, but it didn't matter. I wanted the jury to hear the question, not necessarily the answer. From there I moved to another text sequence in the Aaron/Wren relationship, where he talked about murder-suicide. Like the previous excerpts, this one had been culled from the lengthy records by McEvoy.

> **Ace:** My father has a gun. He taught me how to shoot it. I'm a good shot.
> **Wren:** Of course you are.
> **Ace:** We go to a place where there is a shooting range and we fire at targets that look like people. Bad people like terrorists.
> **Wren:** Only shoot bad people.
> **Ace:** Sometimes when I hold the gun I want to shoot up the world.
> **Wren:** No one who is innocent.
> **Ace:** I know.
> **Wren:** Only to protect yourself. And to be a hERo.
> **Ace:** What if you know someone is going to hurt you?
> **Wren:** You must protect yourself.
> **Ace:** Then it's okay?
> **Wren:** Yes, Ace, then it's okay.

**Ace:** What about Becca? She hurt me. She hurts me every day. I can't go to school because I'll see her and it hurts.
**Wren:** If she hurts you, then she's a bad person.
**Ace:** But I don't think I could ever hurt her.
**Wren:** You have me. And I'll never hurt you.
**Ace:** I know.
**Wren:** You must protect yourself, Ace. You are beautiful. I need you.
**Ace:** And I need you.
**Wren:** Be my hERo.

As soon as I asked Clarke to testify as to what he drew as a detective from this sequence, I was shut down again by another objection from Marcus Mason. This time Judge Ruhlin asked us to approach the bench. She turned to the side of the bench away from the jurors and we huddled there, with the judge speaking first.

"Mr. Haller, you can certainly use Detective Clarke to authenticate your exhibits," she said. "But when you go further and ask what these conversations mean, you stray from his area of expertise. He's a homicide detective, not a child psychologist."

"Thank you, Your Honor," Marcus Mason said. "He just wants the jury to hear his questions. He doesn't care about the answers. I ask that the entirety of the direct examination be stricken from the record."

"We're not quite there yet, Mr. Mason," Ruhlin said. "Mr. Haller, you may ask the detective to authenticate your exhibits but not interpret their meaning. I believe you have a child psychologist on your witness list. Am I right?"

"Yes, Your Honor," I said. "I plan on that for Wednesday."

"We are opposed to that witness, Your Honor," Marcus said.

"We've already argued that, Mr. Mason, and you know my ruling," the judge said. "Mr. Haller, it is now four o'clock. How much more time do you need with this witness?"

"Your Honor, I have more questions for Detective Clarke," I said. "But I'm aware of the court's wish to go no later than four thirty."

"It's not a wish, Mr. Haller," Ruhlin said. "We will recess at four thirty, if not before. It has been a long day for the jurors. I want them to beat some of the traffic going home. Should we break now and continue the detective's direct examination tomorrow?"

"I would like to finish today," I said. "I need fifteen to twenty minutes at the most."

"Very well, I will hold you to that," Ruhlin said. "We'll start tomorrow with cross-examination. You may step back now."

At the lectern, I checked my legal pad and looked back up at the witness stand. It was time to land the final punch of the day.

"Detective Clarke, was the gun you recovered during the arrest of Aaron Colton the weapon used in the killing of Rebecca Randolph?" I asked.

"Yes," Clarke said. "It was matched through ballistics. It was the murder weapon."

"And did you learn who owned the weapon?"

"Yes, it was registered to the suspect's father, Bruce Colton. It had been kept in a safe with a combination lock in a home office."

"What kind of combination lock are we talking about?"

"Electronic. It has a numbered keypad and you punch in a six-digit combination to open it."

"I see. Did you learn through your investigation whether Aaron Colton's father had shared the combination with his son?"

"His father told me he never shared the combination with his son."

"Did his mother share it?"

"She said she never knew the combination, because she didn't like having a gun in the house."

"Did Aaron tell you how he got possession of the gun?"

"He did not. On the advice of his parents and attorney, he never agreed to speak to me about the shooting."

"Then did there come a time in your investigation when you learned how he got the weapon from the home safe?"

"Yes."

"Can you tell us how?"

"In reviewing the conversations the suspect had engaged in with Wren, I came across an exchange in which Wren revealed that she had accessed online records relating to the Colton family and from these had come up with a list of possible combinations to the gun safe."

"I believe we have an exhibit to show the jury."

After Ruhlin overruled an objection from the defense, Lorna put up a segment of an exchange between Aaron and Wren. It was a list of nine different six-digit numbers given by Wren to Aaron.

"Detective Clarke," I said, pointing at the screen, "did this list supplied to Aaron by Wren include the combination to the gun safe?"

"It did," Clarke said. "The fourth one down."

"And what was the significance of that number?"

"It was the date that Aaron Colton's parents got married—oh-five-eleven-oh-one."

The courtroom was normally silent during testimony, but it seemed to get even quieter. To go still. It was as if no one took a breath. It was what they call a smoking-gun moment. And I needed to send the jury home with it. But when I glanced back to the clock on the rear wall of the courtroom, I saw that I had delivered the final punch too quickly. It was only 4:15 and I could not give the Masons the last fifteen minutes of the day to undo the damage I'd done to their case.

I turned and looked up at the judge.

"Your Honor, this might be a good point to break for the day," I said. "But I would like the night to decide whether to continue direct examination of this witness."

Before the judge could respond, Marcus Mason was on his feet objecting.

"Your Honor, counsel is stalling," he said. "He is trying to prevent the defense from questioning this witness about the critical mistakes and biases that infected his deeply flawed investigation."

I had to give Marcus credit. He knew his objection was going nowhere, so he was doing his best to plant seeds of doubt about Clarke's testimony and give the jury something else to think about while sitting in bumper-to-bumper traffic heading home.

"You'll be able to do that tomorrow, Mr. Mason," Ruhlin said. "The objection is overruled."

The judge then dismissed the jury with the usual warnings about not discussing the case with others or reading or watching media accounts of the trial. The courtroom slowly emptied behind me as I took a seat next to my clients. Bruce Colton stood and leaned over the rail so he would be able to hear what I said. The first day was in the books. I felt good about it and told my clients so. I also told them that they each could expect to testify the next day.

What I didn't tell them was that at least one of them wasn't going to like the questions I asked.

# 31

MAGGIE WAS SITTING in the dark when I got home. It was past eight. After court, I had gone out to Pasadena for a final pep-and-prep session with Naomi Kitchens. There was a slim chance I might put her on the stand the following afternoon and I wanted to go through my plan for her direct examination and warn her about what would likely be a tough cross-examination from one of the Masons.

Maggie was sitting in the living room, staring out the picture window at the lights of the city below. We had two soft armchairs positioned in front of the window with a small table between them for a wineglass for her. Some nights we watched the sun go down over the hills to the right as the lights of the Sunset Strip came up on the left. Most prominent in the view was the Sunset Tower, the art deco masterpiece that had stood tall on the strip for nearly a century.

"Hey, Mags, everything all right?" I asked.

"Why wouldn't it be?" she responded.

"Well, you're sitting here in the dark. All right if I turn on a light?"

She didn't answer. I hit the wall switch that turned on the hanging light over the dining-room table. I put my briefcase down on one of the chairs and stepped into the shadows of the living room.

"What do you see out there?" I asked.

"Nothing," she said.

It seemed obvious she had dropped into one of the dark troughs that had been coming more frequently. The world around her seemed to be getting its momentum back while she remained behind with her pain. I bent down and kissed her on the cheek, then took the chair to her left. She had not pulled her gaze away from the window.

"What are you thinking?" I asked.

"Nothing," she said. "Just watching the world go by."

"Sorry I'm so late. I had to go up to Pasadena to see my witness."

"The ethicist?"

"Yeah."

She huffed in a way I took as sarcastic.

"What?"

"Nothing."

"No, what? What's wrong with my witness?"

"It's not your witness. It's just the idea of an ethicist. I guess everybody should have one."

I noticed the wineglass on the table was empty.

"You want a refill?" I asked.

"No, I already had one," she said.

"Did something happen at work?"

"Nothing I can talk about. Just more of the same old, same old. Treachery and backstabbing in every office."

I was actually relieved that it was a work situation that had her down and not the ongoing trauma for once.

"Come on, Mags, tell me what's happening."

"I don't want to talk about it. You can read about it in tomorrow's paper."

"The *Times*? What are they going to say?"

Maggie blew out her breath and relented.

"It's going to be a one-two punch. A story that says, based on unnamed sources inside my office, that I have been 'incapacitated'—that's the exact word—since the loss of my home in the fires. And then, for good measure, there will be an editorial calling for me to step down if I can't move on with my life. From the same editorial board that endorsed me for DA after the recall."

"Fuck that."

"That's what I say. Fuck that. I'm not stepping down."

"And you have no idea where this is coming from?"

"I have an idea, but nothing I can hang a hat on. I have enemies on the inside."

"How did you hear about this? When?"

"When the reporter called me for comment. I was blindsided, all right, which is a sign that maybe I *am* incapacitated and should step down."

"That's not happening."

"I know. I'm just saying that's how it will look in the *Times*."

"Then you have to go on the offensive, Mags."

"You think I don't know that? Mickey, just let me deal with it. It's my problem and I'll handle it."

My phone started to buzz. I took it out of my pocket and checked the screen. It was Cisco. I wanted to take it but sent it to voicemail.

"Go ahead and take it," Maggie said.

"No, it's Cisco," I said. "I can call him back. Who was the reporter who called you?"

"No one I know. Danielle something or other. I've never heard of her before."

"Probably a newbie trying to make a name for herself. Any idea who was talking to her?"

"You already asked that. I don't know. But as you know, I upset some applecarts when I came in. I dumped every division head, and those people didn't take it well."

It was a well-known fact in the district attorney's office that when a new DA came in, a housecleaning followed. Especially this time. Facing a recall election he was going to come out on the wrong side of, Maggie's predecessor had stepped down. Maggie was appointed by the county board of supervisors and then elected three months later. The division heads were all loyalists to the predecessor. Maggie had to clean house and put in her own people. It was nothing new. Prosecutors who supported the wrong candidate often found themselves in new and lesser postings, often in courthouses far from their homes. They called it *freeway therapy*. For an agency that was supposed to be apolitical, it was anything but.

My phone buzzed again. I still had it in my hand. It was Cisco again.

"Just take it, Mickey," Maggie said. "It must be important."

I did.

"Mick, they found Naomi," Cisco said.

"Who found her?" I said.

"I don't know yet."

"What do you mean? I thought you were with her."

"I'm here but not in the room with her. I'm in the lobby and she just called. Somebody just slipped a note under her door. I'm watching the exit to see who leaves."

I'd known it was only a matter of time before Naomi Kitchens was located by the opposition forces. Whether they followed me to the hotel after court or picked up her trail through electronic means didn't matter at this point. They had found my key witness.

"What did the note say?" I asked.

"She wouldn't tell me," Cisco said. "She's scared and crying. I can go up to her room, but I'll miss whoever did this."

"No, you stay there. I'll call her."

"All right."

I disconnected.

"Trouble?" Maggie asked.

"They're fucking with my witness," I said. "I had her stashed out at the Huntington."

"This is the ethicist?"

"Yeah. I need to call and calm her down."

I got up and punched in the number of the burner I had given Naomi. I walked out onto the front deck while the call went through. Naomi answered with a statement that drilled a spike into me.

"Mickey, I can't testify."

"Whoa, whoa, Naomi, what's going on?"

"I just can't testify. That's all you need to know. Lily and I are going home tomorrow. And I'm hanging up now."

"Naomi, wait. Just listen to me."

I paused. She didn't hang up. I had to think of something.

"Look, you can't just go home," I said. "You are a subpoenaed witness. If you don't show up, the judge will send the marshals to find you and bring you to court. You could be arrested if you don't show."

"What are you talking about?" she said, her voice shrill. "Arrested? For what?"

"Well, you asked for a subpoena so you could get out of work. The judge issued it and now you need to show up. If you don't, the judge can send the marshals after you."

"I can't believe this."

The judge would send the marshals only if I asked her to, but I wasn't going to mention that.

"Look, Naomi, let's calm down for a second and talk about this," I said. "First, is Lily there with you?"

"No, she went down to get something to eat," Naomi said. "Cisco was watching her."

"Okay, good. Now, Cisco said you told him that somebody just slipped a note under the door to your room. Is that what happened?"

"I was in the bathroom, and when I came out I saw it there on the floor."

My phone started buzzing with another call. Cisco.

"Naomi, just hold on a second. Cisco's calling me."

I put the call on hold and switched over.

"No go," Cisco said. "It was one of the valets here at the hotel. Somebody drove up in a Tesla and gave him a hundred bucks to slip the note under the door. He didn't get a plate, and his description fits half the people in the city: male, white, eyeglasses, silver-gray Tesla. That's it."

"All right, I have to get back to Naomi before we lose her," I said. "Stay there till I call you back."

I switched over again. "Naomi, I'm back. You there?"

"Yes."

"Tell me what the note says."

There was no response.

"Naomi, I can't help you if I don't know what's going on. What did the note say?"

"It just had a name written on it. Alison Sterling."

"Okay. Who is Alison Sterling?"

Another pause.

"Naomi? Who is Alison Sterling?"

"Me. It's me."

# 32

I SPENT A restless night worrying about what to do about a runaway witness while Maggie opened her phone what seemed like every twenty minutes to check the *Times* app to see if the story and editorial had been posted. By morning, there was still nothing. Bleary-eyed, I walked down the steps of the front deck to get the printed edition of the paper—still a loyal subscriber despite its basically being yesterday's news today. Once I was back inside, Maggie grabbed it from me and nearly ripped it apart looking for the story about her alleged incapacity.

There was nothing there. But there was a story about the start of the Tidalwaiv trial that I managed to save to read later.

"Any chance this whole thing was a hoax?" I asked. "You said you'd never heard of the reporter before."

"No, it sounded too legit," Maggie said. "I could hear people in the background and typewriters clicking."

"Typewriters? They don't use typewriters."

"Keyboards, whatever. It wasn't a hoax. They just delayed it for some reason. Probably to dig up more dirt on me."

"Then you should make a move that will make the story look stupid if they print it."

I walked into the kitchen to brew a double-shot espresso on the machine. I needed something to get me going. Maggie followed me.

"What kind of move?" she asked.

"I don't know," I said. "But think about it: All your press conferences this year have been about prosecutions related to the fires. L.A. is a big place, and most people never go through Altadena or the Palisades and Malibu. To them, the fires are what they saw on TV. You've got to have something else. Something else big that you can announce to show that you're in charge of the whole county. That it's not just about the fires with you."

Maggie opened her mouth to say something that would push back on the suggestion. But then she closed it. I could see her mind racing as she came around to the idea.

"If you don't have anything, I can give you something," I said.

"What, about your case?" she said. "We're not finished with the psych eval on Aaron Colton. I'm not going to rush that. I told you I wouldn't."

"No, my other case. David Snow. I told you about it. I'm gonna get him out, and everybody likes an innocent-man story. You could announce a move to review his case, and it would be on every channel at six."

She shook her head and smiled — which I admit was nice to see, even though I knew what was coming.

"Mickey, you never stop working the angles," she said. "Even with me."

"Hey, I'm just trying to get you some good press," I countered.

"Whether now or later, you're going to want to get on the right side of this case."

"Well, it's a little premature at the moment. But your advice is well taken. Thank you."

She kissed me.

"I think I know what to do," she said. "There's a file on a cold case that came in from the LAPD yesterday. It might do the trick. I have to get dressed."

She headed out of the kitchen.

"You sure?" I called after her. "You'd look great in front of the cameras in that sleep shirt."

"Very funny," she called back.

I was already dressed for battle. While I waited for the machine to brew, I called Cisco. "Okay, where are we?" I asked.

"Well, she's still here," he said. "If it stays that way, I'll bring her to court at noon."

"Good."

"How are you going to handle it?"

"We'll own it and tell it the way it is. It will take some of the wind out of Marcus Mason's sails."

"Hope so."

"Anything changes, call me. If you can't get me, tell Lorna and she'll give me the message."

"You got it."

"And Cisco, if she brings up the subpoena, just remind her it was issued by the judge and she has to appear."

"Copy."

I disconnected. My double-shot was ready and I sipped it as I read the *Times* story on the start of my trial. It grabbed a few quotes from my opening statement, which I liked, but otherwise the story was mostly a summary of the allegations contained in the lawsuit that would be addressed as the trial proceeded. As unhappy as Maggie was about what the *Times* was up to, I was pleased that it looked like my trial might be getting daily coverage.

On my way downtown, I took another call from Cisco.

"She's in the restaurant having breakfast with her daughter," he said. "I spoke to her for a few seconds and she's not talking about leaving. She's still scared, though, about what else they might have dug up."

"Yeah, well, so am I," I said. "But if they had more than the name, it seems like they would have used it last night."

"True that."

"Okay, I'm almost to the courthouse. I gotta get my game on."

"Good luck."

Twenty minutes later I was at the lectern in the courtroom and Detective Clarke was on the stand being reminded by Judge Ruhlin that he was still under oath. She then turned the witness over to me. I was finished with Clarke but didn't want the judge to feel I had gamed her the day before, so I asked him a few more questions that mattered little to my case strategy.

Until they did.

"Detective, you told us yesterday that the investigation into the death of Rebecca Randolph continued well after the arrest of Aaron Colton," I began.

"That's true," Clarke said.

"During this continuing investigation, did you have cause to contact the Tidalwaiv company to ask about the AI companion that Aaron Colton had downloaded from them?"

"I did, yes."

"And what did you ask them?"

"I wanted to know how long he'd had the app, how much time he spent on it, how much he paid—general information that might be useful in the evaluation of the suspect's mental state."

"Were you directed to do this by the district attorney's office?"

"I was, yes."

"And what kind of cooperation did Tidalwaiv provide the investigation?"

"Uh, that would be none."

*"None?"*

I said it as if surprised by the answer.

"Correct," Clarke said.

"Did they give a reason for their lack of cooperation?" I asked.

"I was told that their data was proprietary and not available to me without a search warrant."

"Did you pursue getting a search warrant?"

"No, I did not."

"Why did you drop it?"

"Because we got the search warrant for Aaron's laptop and phone instead, and our tech unit was able to access the information I was seeking from Tidalwaiv through those devices."

"Thank you, Detective. I have no further questions."

Marcus Mason was at the lectern before I even reached my seat. And he didn't start with any niceties for Detective Clarke.

"Detective Clarke, isn't it true that you had another motive for approaching Tidalwaiv for information?" he asked.

"Motive?" Clarke said, seemingly confused.

"Another reason, Detective."

"I'm not sure what you mean."

"Were you aware of a violent incident involving Aaron Colton at Grant High School in February of 2022?"

"I was aware of an incident that resulted in his suspension, if that's what you're referencing."

"What was that incident?"

"Aaron was accused by a teacher of cheating on a test. It led to a confrontation in which he pushed the teacher. He was suspended for four weeks, I believe."

"And when you approached Tidalwaiv, were you not trying to determine whether that violent incident came before or after he initially downloaded the Clair app?"

"That would have been one of a number of things I was interested in."

"And when you were able to access his devices, did you learn that Aaron Colton downloaded the Clair app *after* that *violent* incident involving his teacher?"

"I don't know if I would describe the incident as violent, but yes, it occurred before he started using the Clair app."

"If it got him suspended, how else would you describe the incident other than violent?"

"It was a push. I talked to the teacher after I learned about it and she did not use the word *violent* to describe it."

It might have been a tiff about semantics, but it was a skillful opening to Mason's cross-examination. He scored points right away, and I confirmed this as I watched the jurors lean in during the back-and-forth with Clarke. Mason also revealed what the defense strategy was likely going to be: Blame the killer. Establish that Aaron Colton was violent before he ever met the AI companion he called Wren.

It was the already-on-the-path-to-destruction defense. And now that I'd seen the direction Mason was going, I would be ready for it.

Mason kept Clarke on the stand for nearly two hours, but his best points were scored in that opening exchange. Clarke was a veteran detective and experienced witness, primarily in criminal court, where cross-examination was no-holds-barred and confrontational. He held his own and didn't give Mason any further ammunition.

But what Mason did accomplish with his lengthy cross, whether knowingly or not, was the disruption of the rollout of my case. My plan had been to use Detective Clarke as the starting point, then move into the emotional wave of testimony by the parents whose children had killed or been killed. This would lead to a crescendo of technical, scientific, and psychological testimony from the experts in artificial intelligence about the guardrails that Tidalwaiv should have had in place to protect customers, particularly minors.

But I had a key witness who didn't want to testify. Who would be doing so reluctantly. By using the morning up, Mason had put me in a corner. If I rolled my case out according to my original plan, there was no way I could get Naomi Kitchens on the stand before the next day or quite possibly—based on Mason's lengthy cross of Clarke—the day after that.

I couldn't risk waiting that long with Kitchens teetering on the brink of a meltdown and looking to run away from testifying. I had no choice. I had to reshuffle my cards.

As soon as court was recessed for lunch, I walked into the hallway and called Cisco. When he answered, I could tell by the background noise that he was in a car. I had given him the use of the Lincoln for transporting witnesses during the trial.

"Where are you?"

"We're five out."

"Is the daughter with you?"

"Yes, she's here."

"Redirect to the Redbird for lunch. I'll meet you there. Naomi testifies after lunch."

"What?"

"I'll explain why later. Don't tell Naomi. I will. Just get to the Redbird and I'll meet you all there."

I disconnected and turned to find Lorna standing in the hallway.

"You have to edit the PowerPoint," I said. "I'm putting Naomi on the stand next."

# 33

**MY EYES WERE** on Marcus Mason when the judge told me to call my next witness. When I said the name Naomi Kitchens, he leaned back in his chair as though he were dodging a roundhouse punch at his chin. He was clearly surprised, but I realized I couldn't tell if that was because he wasn't expecting the former ethicist to be my next witness or because he wasn't expecting her to testify at all. The latter would have confirmed that he was aware of and had sanctioned the intimidation tactic initiated against her the night before. But when he was finished dodging the invisible punch, his hands immediately went to the stack of files on the defense table, and he went three deep to pull an inch-thick file I assumed contained his prep material on Kitchens.

There was no thicker file in the stack, and the fact that it wasn't on top told me that Marcus had simply not been expecting Kitchens at this point in the trial. That further suggested that he hadn't been aware of the events of the night before. This was good, because the move at the hotel had been a critical misstep by whoever was responsible. It had failed to stop Kitchens from testifying, and it was going to help me avoid being waylaid by whatever was in that fat file Marcus had just pulled out.

After Naomi was sworn in by the court clerk and asked to spell her name for the record, she took the stand and immediately glanced out at the gallery, where her daughter sat next to Cisco. She nodded slightly and steeled herself for what was coming next. At the Redbird we had gone over how it would go from my side of the lectern. It was the defense side that was the unknown. I had told her to find Lily in the gallery and use her as a focal point when things got stressful on the stand.

"Good afternoon, Professor Kitchens," I began. "Is that your real name, Naomi Kitchens?"

"It's my legal name now," Kitchens responded.

"You had it changed?"

"A long time ago, yes."

"What was your given name and what made you change it?"

"My birth name was Alison Sterling. I changed it twenty years ago to protect myself and the child I was carrying."

I saw her eyes go out to her daughter as she answered.

"Protect the child from whom?" I asked.

"My ex-boyfriend," she said. "This was back in Pennsylvania, where I grew up."

"Can you tell the jury why you felt the need to take these steps?"

"Well, he was a bad man. He was committing crimes and I realized I had to get away from him. So I left. I went to California and legally changed my name so he wouldn't be able to find us."

"Who is us?"

"My daughter and I."

"How old is your daughter now?"

"She's nineteen."

"And was the man you ran from her father?"

"Yes."

"Did he ever find you after you escaped?"

"No, he went to jail for many years. Prison, actually."

"Do you know what crime he was convicted of?"

"Robbery and assault. He shot a man but the man didn't die."

"Were you involved in any way with these crimes?"

"No, but... we lived on the money he stole. I knew that. It was one of the reasons I needed to get away from him."

"Were there other reasons?"

"He was violent. I was afraid he would hurt the baby."

"What was this man's name?"

"Quentin Holgard."

"So if Quentin Holgard came into this courtroom and said you committed these crimes with him, would he be telling the truth?"

"No, he would be lying."

My last question was a guess. But I had to get in front of any move the Masons might make. They might have Quentin Holgard teed up and ready to go as a rebuttal witness, thereby keeping his name hidden and off the approved-witness list. I didn't know what the defense plan was but I wanted to be ready for anything. Feeling that I had put what I could on the record, I dropped into my original plan for Kitchens's testimony.

"Okay, so you came out to California to escape from this man, and then what happened?" I asked.

"I worked and I went to school up in the Bay Area," Kitchens said.

"What school?"

"My first degree was from USF and—"

"USF?"

"Sorry, University of San Francisco. I then got a master's at UC Berkeley and later a doctorate from Stanford."

I walked her quickly through her degrees in order — computer science, psychology, and finally sociology.

"I guess I should be calling you *Dr.* Kitchens," I said.

"I prefer just Naomi," she said.

"Okay, Naomi. And did you pay your way through all these schools?"

"Yes. I worked and I got some scholarship money, a few research grants. But I also had student loans that I'm still paying off."

This brought a low murmur of laughter in the courtroom.

"You are apparently not alone in that," I said. "When you worked, what was the job or jobs you took?"

"I was a coder for various companies," Kitchens said. "I worked for Microsoft, Apple, a few others."

"What's a coder do?"

"Writes operating code for various apps."

"Okay. And you did all of this while being a single mother and going to school?"

"Yes."

"What was your career goal with all these degrees?"

"I wanted to be a teacher at the college level. I wanted to be a professor."

"And did you accomplish that?"

"Yes. My first job was at USF, and after I got my doctorate I stayed at Stanford for the next three years."

"What happened that made you leave Stanford?"

"I got a job offer from Tidalwaiv that would almost double my income. I took it so I could provide a better life for my daughter."

"Can you tell us what that job entailed?"

"I was an ethicist primarily assigned to Project Clair."

I smiled and raised my hands from the lectern in a *What gives?* gesture.

"I have to say, I'm not sure what an ethicist is or does," I said. "Can you explain it to us?"

"Clair was a generative artificial-intelligence project," Kitchens said. "At the time, it was the new frontier of AI technology. There weren't many rules and there was almost zero government oversight. It was very competitive, and the tech companies started hiring people to make sure these programs and apps were created in a responsible way. Generative AI was going to change the world — it already has. The ethicist was sort of the human conscience of the project. I was supposed to help make sure there were guardrails in place to protect the people these systems would serve."

"'Supposed to'?"

"In some cases, although the company wants to say it's ethical, it doesn't work out that way. The stakes involved are extremely —"

Marcus Mason stood and objected.

"Your Honor, by talking in generalities, the witness is insinuating that unethical behavior occurred at Tidalwaiv on Project Clair," he said. "There has been absolutely no evidence of that presented at trial, because it doesn't exist. I ask that the question and answer be stricken and the jury be so instructed."

Judge Ruhlin looked at me for a response.

"Judge, first of all, I would ask the court to instruct counsel not to incorporate his closing argument into his objection. Second, I am laying the groundwork so that the jury understands what this witness's job was at Tidalwaiv and, more specifically, on Project Clair."

"I'm going to sustain the objection," Ruhlin said. "Mr. Haller, let's move on to testimony directly related to the cause of action."

"Yes, Your Honor," I said. "A moment, please."

I looked down at my legal pad and flipped to the next page, skipping several questions that I now knew would not get past the defense's objections.

"Okay, Naomi, let's talk about Project Clair," I said. "When were you assigned to it?"

"I was hired by Tidalwaiv in late 2021," Kitchens said. "After some training I was assigned to Project Clair in January of '22."

"Was that the starting point of the project?"

"No, the project was well down the road. I reviewed code and company directives that were three years old when I was getting up to speed on it."

"So they brought the ethicist in late to the project."

Marcus jumped up with an objection, arguing that my statement assumed facts not in evidence. The judge sustained the objection without asking me to respond. I knew the objection was valid. I just wanted the jury to put the question in a back pocket for later. I moved on.

"Dr. Kitchens, you—"

"Naomi."

"Right, Naomi. Earlier you called Project Clair a generative AI program. Can you tell the jury what *generative AI* means?"

"Of course. *Gen AI* simply means that these models, like the Clair app, for example, generate new data, whether it be video images or text, from the underlying data they were trained with."

I liked how she turned to look at the jury as she spoke. I had said to her at lunch, "You're a teacher. Be a teacher on the witness stand." She was doing it now, and I believed it was being received well by her pupils, the jurors.

"So, then, would it be fair to say that it is not simply data in, data out?" I asked.

"Correct," Naomi said. "That is the generative part of the equation. The training is ongoing. These large language models are constantly bringing data in and from that learning more."

"'Large language model'? Can you explain that?"

"It's a machine-learning model designed for natural language generation. It's trained on vast amounts of data and text, and then analyzes and sifts it all for patterns and relationships when prompted to have a conversation or answer a question. These models acquire predictive power in terms of human language. The ongoing downside, however, is they also acquire any biases or inaccuracies contained in the training data."

"You're saying 'garbage in, garbage out.'"

"Exactly. And that's where the ethicist comes in. To make sure there are guardrails that keep the garbage from ever getting in."

I paused for a moment as I made a shift back toward my case.

"You testified earlier that you came onto Project Clair three years after it began, correct?"

"About thirty months after."

"Okay, and did you replace the original ethicist on the project?"

"No, they did not have one before me. Usually an ethicist is brought in when a project reaches a certain level of investment and viability."

"Okay, so you were brought in three years down the line. Did you review what had occurred on the project in those first three years?"

"Yes, I did."

"When you made this review, did anything alarm you?"

"Yes, several things, actually."

"Okay, did you make a list of these alarming things?"

"I did, yes."

"What was at the top of that list?"

"Well, I saw in the initial mission document that the app they were developing was, from the start, a thirteen-plus project, meaning that it was meant to be suitable for young teenagers."

"And why was that alarming?"

"It was not alarming in itself or as a goal for the project. It was when I went further with my review that I became concerned that they were building something that was not suitable for young teenagers. Clair was being trained from the beginning with data that was geared more toward older people. Adults."

"Let me stop you there. Can you explain to the jury what you mean by training in regard to Project Clair?"

This was a question we had worked on repeatedly during prep. Her answer, if she could get it out without objection, would be the foundation on which we would build the case against Tidalwaiv of reckless disregard.

"Building an AI companion is in many ways like raising a child," Kitchens said. "But in a much more time-constricted way. We send our children to school for twelve to sixteen years or more, filling their brains with knowledge and social skills and experiences. AI is similar but much quicker because it's all digital. Data is downloaded. It's not based on real experiences or our human concept of learning. That's why it's called *artificial* intelligence. It's not real."

"Okay," I said. "But what about this process alarmed you when it came to Project Clair?"

"My problem was that they were building an app they were going to market to young teenagers, but they weren't training it as a young teenager. They were not editing the input to fit the parameters of their market. In human terms, it was like giving a thirteen- or fourteen-year-old a twenty-five-year-old friend. This app friend would have data and knowledge well beyond that of the human it would be marketed to serve. There were guardrails in the mission statements about Clair, but they were not actually in place. They were in the documents but not in the actual training."

"They were just paper guardrails."

"Exactly."

"Can you give us any specific examples of something you observed as the ethicist on the project that demonstrated this?"

"Well, I had repeated clashes with a coder on the project who was dropping personal data into the program — for example, his Spotify lists and his personal top-ten lists of movies, TV shows, travel destinations. He was in his late twenties at the time, and that to me was problematic. Clair was supposed to be a companion suitable for a thirteen-year-old. I didn't think it was appropriate for it to have knowledge of the red-light districts of Thailand."

Marcus Mason immediately objected, citing facts not in evidence. Ruhlin overruled the objection without comment and told me to continue.

"Naomi, did you raise your concern with the stakeholders on this project?"

"'Concern' is putting it mildly. I was alarmed and I wrote several memos and emails to people up and down the list of project managers. I had meetings. I felt that it was what I was hired to do. I felt like I was the last guardrail."

I turned and looked back at Lorna in the front row and nodded. She came through the gate, took my seat at the table, and proceeded to open up the laptop and engage the PowerPoint demonstration.

"Your Honor," I said, "I have a series of memos and emails authored by the witness to various managers and stakeholders in Project Clair that I ask the court to enter as exhibits and permit us to display on the courtroom screen."

"Very well," Ruhlin said. "Why don't we allow the jury to take the afternoon break while I review your documents."

I had expected one of the Masons to object to the blanket approval I was asking for, but they were silent at the defense table.

Kitchens stepped down, and as the jurors filed back into the assembly room, I took one set of copies of the documents to the clerk for the judge to peruse and another set to the defense table.

"I'm sure you already have these, boys," I said. "But just in case."

I started to put the documents down in front of Marcus. He held his hand up as if to push them away.

"Don't bother," he said. "You can put on your PowerPoint, Haller. The jurors won't remember one bit of it when I get through with your so-called last guardrail."

I acted as though it was basic trash-talking. But something about the sarcasm in Marcus's voice got to me. After checking with Lorna to make sure the PowerPoint was teed up and ready, I went through the gate and out of the courtroom to the hallway to look for Naomi Kitchens. I found her sitting on a bench outside the courtroom with her daughter.

"Lily, do you mind if I talk to your mother alone for a few minutes?" I asked.

Lily looked at her mom, who nodded that it was okay. She got up and went through the double doors back into the courtroom. I took her place on the bench.

"The Mason boys don't seem all that worried about your memos and emails," I said.

"Is that good or bad?" Kitchens asked.

"It could be either, but I'm worried they have something."

"Like what?"

"Something on you, Naomi. So, I've asked you this before, but tell me now if there's anything you haven't told me that they might use against you to damage your credibility."

Kitchens shook her head.

"There's nothing," she said. "You know it all now."

"You said in there that you had nothing to do with Quentin Holgard's crimes," I said. "That has got to hold up, Naomi. Or we're fucked."

"First of all, I told you last night and today that I didn't want to testify. You made me."

"And second?"

"It's the truth. I don't lie."

I studied her face, looking for any crack in the resolve and defiance she was showing. I saw no tremor of doubt. She didn't blink.

"Okay, then," I said. "I hope we're good. I'm going to try to run out the clock with you."

"What does that mean?" she asked.

"I'm going to keep you on the witness stand until we break for the day. That way, if they have something we don't know about, the Masons won't get to use it until tomorrow. You good with that?"

"I'm good. But they don't have anything unless they make something up."

"Well, I guess we're going to find out."

# 34

**JUDGE RUHLIN WINNOWED** my exhibits from twelve to four, saying they were repetitive and that the two memos and two emails she chose would suffice to make the points intended by the plaintiffs. Based on her previous ruling during the discovery hearing, I had expected this. Judges like to play King Solomon and split the baby when they can. Though I protested and acted as though my case was severely damaged by the ruling, I was happy to get the four exhibits accepted. After the jury was brought back into the courtroom, I used Naomi to introduce the exhibits and read sections as they were put on the screen. I wanted the jury to hear her words in her voice.

There was a unifying theme to the four exhibits and I went through them in chronological order. The first was a memo Kitchens had sent to the top managers of Project Clair.

"You were new to the project when you sent this message, correct?" I asked.

"I had been there seven weeks at that point," Kitchens said.

"And who was this message addressed to?"

"Jerry Matthews."

"Who is Jerry Matthews?"

"He was the boss, the overall manager of Project Clair."

"Did he hire you?"

"No, he did not. I was hired through the HR department."

"And assigned to Project Clair."

"Correct."

"Can you read the paragraph that is highlighted on the printout of the memo?"

"Yes. It says, 'I feel I am up to speed now on Project Clair, and you asked me to put the concerns I mentioned in our meeting into a memo. My chief concerns are about the biases I believe are being embedded in the training program. Our coders are all male. This creates a bias when training a female AI companion. Perhaps more important, it is my understanding that this model is designed and intended to have a thirteen-plus rating. Frankly, this seems inappropriate. Has the horse left the barn or is this a decision we can reconsider?'"

As Kitchens finished reading the section, Lorna put the full memo on the screen.

"Thank you, Naomi," I said. "Did you get a response to this memo?"

"Not in written form," Kitchens said. "Jerry took me to the campus cafeteria for a coffee and we talked. That was his response."

"Did he say he would act on your concerns?"

"He told me—"

Marcus Mason objected, arguing that anything Kitchens claimed Matthews told her was excluded under hearsay rules. The judge agreed and I had to find another path to the answer I wanted.

"Okay, Naomi," I said. "Your memo led to a meeting with the

boss in the cafeteria. After that meeting, were changes made to the training of Clair, the AI companion that was going to be offered to thirteen-year-old children?"

"No," Kitchens said. "No changes were made."

And so it went. We brought up each memo and email, displaying to the jury what I believed was a solid case that Tidalwaiv had run roughshod over the many warnings made by the ethicist assigned to Project Clair. I ended on the email Kitchens had sent to Jerry Matthews on the day she was terminated.

"Can you read what you wrote to Mr. Matthews after learning your employment at Tidalwaiv had been terminated?" I asked.

"Yes," Kitchens said. "I wrote, 'Jerry, one last time, I can't stress enough the liability the company will encounter should Clair say the wrong thing or encourage the wrong behavior or action by a child user. I am glad I won't be part of the company when that happens.'"

I looked down at my legal pad for a long moment, hoping the fired ethicist's final words would leave a deep impact on the jury.

"'Encourage the wrong behavior or action by a child user,'" I repeated. "Naomi, did you ever in your wildest dreams think that the wrong action would be a murder—"

"Objection!" Marcus Mason exclaimed.

"Committed by a child user?" I finished.

"Mr. Haller, you know better," the judge said. "The jury will disregard the question."

"Sorry, Your Honor," I said. "Could I have a moment? I am almost finished with Dr. Kitchens's testimony."

"Be quick," Ruhlin said.

I turned and glanced back at the courtroom clock. It was 4:05 and I believed I had timed things well. My finish would take us to the final bell.

"Naomi, did you quit your job at Tidalwaiv?" I asked.

"No, I was terminated," Kitchens said.

"Terminated. Were you given a reason?"

"I was called into Mr. Matthews's office and told I was fired for actions detrimental to the project."

"Did you ask for a fuller explanation?"

"I did but was not given one. But I had been warned previously that my memos and concerns about the project were viewed as harmful to the project."

"Were these warnings in writing and part of your personnel file?"

"No, they would never put anything like that in writing, because they knew it wasn't true."

Marcus Mason objected and successfully got Kitchens's answer struck, but the message was delivered.

I checked the clock again. It was after 4:15 and I needed another set of questions to get to the finish line.

"Naomi, after you were fired, did you have difficulty getting your next job?" I asked.

"I went back to academia because I couldn't get an interview for an ethicist position anywhere in Silicon Valley," Kitchens said.

Marcus objected to the answer being overly broad, but to my surprise the judge let it stand. I then made what became one of my biggest mistakes of the trial, if not my career. I did not ask the judge for the night to consider whether I was finished with my direct examination of Kitchens. I thought it had gone so well and that it was so late in the day that I was bulletproof.

"No further questions for Dr. Kitchens," I said, getting in one last reminder to the jury of my witness's pedigree and standing.

"Very well," the judge said. "We will recess for —"

"Your Honor," Marcus Mason interrupted, "I have only a few questions for this witness. If you'll permit that, we could start tomorrow with a new witness and perhaps allow Ms. Kitchens to return home rather than spend another night away."

"It is four twenty-two, Mr. Mason," Ruhlin said. "If you are confident you will be finished in eight minutes, you may proceed."

"Definitely, Your Honor," Mason said.

"Then go ahead," Ruhlin said.

As I left the lectern for my table I had a bad feeling in the pit of my stomach. I knew I had somehow misplayed the last minutes of the day and that something unfortunate was about to happen.

Mason took the lectern and looked at Kitchens. The look of unflinching defiance I had seen in her eyes in the hallway after lunch was gone. Kitchens seemed to know that something unexpected was coming her way.

"Ms. Kitchens," Mason began. "Wouldn't you say—"

"Objection, Your Honor," I said. "The witness has a doctorate and should be accorded the respect of that achievement by counsel."

"Mr. Haller makes a point," Ruhlin said.

"Of course, Your Honor," Mason said. "Dr. Kitchens, wouldn't you say that it would be wrong for an ethicist to lie to a jury in a court of law?"

"I haven't lied," Kitchens said.

"But it would be wrong if you did, correct?"

"It would be, but I have not lied."

"What about a lie to the company that the ethicist works for? Would that be wrong?"

"I think lying in any circumstance is wrong."

"In fact, would that not be one of the major rules of being an ethicist? Do not lie?"

"Yes."

"You have claimed in front of this jury and this judge that you were fired for supposedly speaking out about your concerns about this project, isn't that right?"

"It's what happened."

"And you swore an oath to tell nothing but the truth, correct?"

"I did."

"But you lied to the jury, didn't you?"

I stood up and objected.

"Counsel is badgering the witness," I said. "How many times and ways does she have to say she hasn't lied?"

"Mr. Mason," Ruhlin said. "It's time to get to the point. Or we can recess for the day."

"Thank you, Your Honor," Mason said. "I will indeed get to the point."

Ruhlin signaled for me to sit down. Mason turned his focus back to Kitchens. The bad feeling in the pit of my stomach had grown to the size of a baseball. I knew Mason had something, or at least he thought he did.

"Dr. Kitchens, I ask you," he said, "were you not terminated from your job at Tidalwaiv by Mr. Matthews because you were involved in an improper and unethical relationship with a fellow employee you had a supervisory position over?"

There it was. Mason had his own smoking gun and I had handed it to him with the barrel pointed at my witness.

"That is not true," Kitchens said.

"What is not true, Dr. Kitchens?" Mason pressed.

Kitchens was calm enough in the moment to turn to the jury to state her case.

"They fired me because I objected to the training," she said. "They didn't want to hear that, so they got rid of me. That's all."

"Dr. Kitchens," Mason said, drawing her eyes back to him, "did you or did you not engage in an unethical sexual relationship with a code writer assigned to Project Clair named Patrick May?"

I saw the hurt and disappointment come all at once in my witness's eyes. And I knew that no matter how she answered the question, everything she had said in her previous testimony was now suspect.

"It was a relationship we had started before I ever took the job," Kitchens said.

"So you didn't feel an obligation to reveal this while being recruited and hired by the company?" Mason asked.

"No, I did not."

"And was that ethical, Dr. Kitchens?"

Kitchens dropped her head. The courtroom was as silent as a grave.

"Maybe not," she finally said. "But I —"

"I have no further questions, Your Honor," Mason said.

# 35

BRUCE COLTON WAS waiting for me at the gate to the gallery. He was three inches shorter than me and came up close to stick a finger into my chest. His face was red with anger. He looked as if he'd been holding his breath the whole time he was waiting for me.

"What the fuck, Haller," he said. "I don't know which is worse, if you knew about her boyfriend and tried to cover it up or if you didn't even fucking know."

"Get out of my way, Bruce," I said. "I have work to do."

"Work? Are you kidding me? You talked us into giving up fifty million dollars. Fifty! And now you want to walk away from me? You better call those lawyers who just outsmarted your ass and get our fucking money."

"I'm not doing that, Bruce. We still have a winnable case. Now, for the last time, get out of my way."

He finally took a step back and laughed without a shred of joy. I noticed Cisco come up behind him in case I needed him.

"You know what's going to happen?" Colton said. "You don't win this case, I'm going to sue you for mal-fucking-practice. I'll get my money one way or the other."

"Good plan," I said. "You do that, Bruce."

I shouldered past him.

"Let's go," I said to Cisco.

We headed toward the courtroom door. I needed to get out of there to rethink and retool, to find some way of salvaging the case after the day's disastrous ending. I had told Lorna to take Naomi Kitchens down to the attorney conference room. When I got out to the hallway, there were three reporters waiting for me. I pushed by them too.

"I've got no comment right now," I said. "I need to talk to my witness."

The conference room was crowded. Lorna sat at the table with Kitchens and her daughter. Lily was trying to console her mother, who had tears streaming down her face. McEvoy was standing, apparently to leave the fourth chair at the table for me.

"Okay, look, it's too crowded in here," I said abruptly. "Lorna, can you take Lily into the hall? Jack, you go with them. Cisco, you stay in case we need to work on something tonight."

"I want to stay," McEvoy said. "Fly on the wall, remember?"

"Okay, fine, whatever," I said.

Lorna and Lily left the room without protest. I took the seat vacated by Lorna and sat directly across from Naomi. Cisco was to one side. McEvoy started pulling the remaining chair way back from the table, apparently taking the fly-on-the-wall metaphor literally.

"Jack, before you sit, can you go out and see if Lorna has any tissues?" I asked.

McEvoy left the room. I slid my chair in closer to the table that separated me from my witness.

"Okay, Naomi, we need to talk," I began. "Let's start with who is Patrick May?"

She didn't answer at first. McEvoy reentered and handed her a small packet of tissues. She finally spoke as she started to take one out.

"He was my boyfriend," she said. "I didn't think anybody knew about us."

"Was?" I asked. "You're not together?"

"We broke up last year."

"Who broke up with whom?"

"I broke it off."

"Is he still with Tidalwaiv?"

"I think so. Last I knew."

"Was he upset when you broke things off?"

"At the time, I didn't think so. He knew it was coming. It was a slow breakup. He was staying with the project and I couldn't handle that."

I nodded and looked at Cisco. He nodded back.

"He ratted her out," he said.

"You need to do a full workup on him," I said. "If Mason doesn't call him as a witness, we want to be ready to."

Cisco asked Kitchens if she knew May's birthdate. She provided that, an address for him up in San Mateo, and the cell phone number she had used for her last contact with him.

"On it," Cisco said as he stood up.

He left the room and I refocused on Kitchens.

"Naomi, I have to decide whether to bring you back tomorrow for redirect. Can you think of anything that might help us rehabilitate your testimony?"

"I told the truth. You don't have to rehabilitate it."

"I know you told the truth, but it's about credibility. It's about trust. They've caught you in a lie and we need to—"

"What lie? I didn't lie. I was never asked about any relationship. Plus, I thought maybe they knew about it because Patrick was the one who recommended me to the company as an ethicist for the project. I had no idea he had left out that we were dating."

McEvoy cleared his throat and I looked over at him.

"What?" I asked.

"She's sort of right," he said. "Her employment application is in the materials she gave us, and I don't remember any question about relationships with other employees of the company."

"Look, we're talking about semantics here," I said, looking back at Naomi. "It doesn't matter if you didn't lie on the application. You had a relationship your employer should have been told about. And the whole thing doubles down because you were supposed to be the conscience of ethical programming and behavior, and now it looks like you were hiding what many would say was an unethical relationship with a fellow employee below you in the corporate hierarchy. So, think, Naomi. Is there anything we can go back into court with tomorrow that helps us?"

Naomi wiped her cheeks and her nose with the tissue and looked at me.

"I told you not to do this," she said. "I didn't want to testify."

"Well, maybe if you'd told me about Patrick May, I wouldn't have asked you to," I countered.

"That lawyer made it sound like I was his boss. I wasn't. He may have been below me in the corporate hierarchy. But he was in the coding lab and I almost never even walked in there. He didn't work for me directly and I never once told him what to do."

"All right, that's good. We can use that. Can you think of anybody else at work who knew about the relationship?"

"No, we never flaunted it. We never even took breaks together."

"Well, that's not good. It looks like you were trying to hide that you were together."

"We weren't. My office was in administration, he was in the lab. It was never the twain shall meet. Until after work."

"Were you living together?"

"No. I had my daughter at home. This was before she went to USF."

"Well, when the two of you were together and away from work, did you talk about work? Did he tell you about some of the training of Clair that was alarming you?"

"Well, yes. We did. How could we not talk about work? Is that good or bad?"

"It could be good. I don't know yet. When was the last time you had contact with Patrick May?"

"Contact? You mean like physical contact?"

"When was the last time you met or communicated with him?"

"That would have been on his birthday, back in August. We were broken up by then but I texted him. He didn't reply."

"Any idea at all why he decided to tell the company about your relationship?"

"How do you know he did?"

"You said nobody knew about it. Was there somebody else?"

"No. No one."

"Then it was him. Could they have had something on him that forced him to reveal the relationship?"

"Not that I know of."

"Well, I'm going to need you to think about that tonight."

"Am I testifying tomorrow?"

"I don't know yet. But I want to move you and Lily from the hotel you're in to a new one. One of us will pick you up tomorrow morning to bring you to court."

"This is really bad, isn't it? For the case."

I nodded.

"Yeah, it's bad," I said. "I thought we won yesterday. But today, I think they got the W. And that's on me, Naomi. Not you. I should have known what they had, and I should've seen it coming."

# 36

THIS TIME IT was me in the wave's trough when I got home. Maggie was riding high on the crest. It had been that way with her since the fires, a rhythm of quick ups and downs. So this time it was her consoling me. We'd shared takeout from Pace down in the canyon. I told her how I had miscalculated things in court and opened the door to the defense sending the jury home with testimony indicating that my key witness could not be trusted. Now we sat in our chairs in front of the picture window, backlit from the kitchen, her with a glass of sauvignon blanc and me with a full glass of guilt over letting myself be outplayed in court.

"Mickey, you could not have seen that coming," she told me again. "Your witness deceived you. How could you be ready for that?"

"I'm supposed to be ready for anything," I said. "Every lawyer knows that."

"Well, you will be tomorrow. Are you going to put her back on the stand and try to rehabilitate her?"

"I think that's going to be a game-time decision. It might just be best to move forward rather than spend the morning doing damage control. That always looks bad to the jury."

"Moving forward is a good idea."

I nodded. I had not heard anything from Cisco, so I hadn't decided how the following morning would go and wanted to change the subject.

"You sure seem chipper after last night," I said. "What happened with the *Times*?"

"Supposedly they're holding the story," Maggie said. "It was based on unnamed sources, and an editor over there got smart and said, get somebody on the record saying she's incapacitated or we don't run the story."

"Glad they still have somebody there who's thinking right."

"Plus I did what you suggested and held a press conference. Just not about your client."

"I haven't seen any news. What was it about?"

"We filed on a cold case LAPD brought in. A serial killer who's not dead or already incarcerated. They got him on at least four kills here in L.A., but it looks like there are others up in the Bay Area. Alameda County. And we already have a name for him: the Pizza Man. He'd follow a woman home, then come back later with a pizza and act like he was delivering it but had the wrong address. It got him through the woman's door. The Open-Unsolved Unit got him on DNA off a pizza crust."

"Nice. LAPD cold case comes to the rescue. Take that, *L.A. Times*."

"Exactly."

"How cold was the case?"

"It was late nineties down here. He then moved up to Oakland. They arrested him there."

"Cool."

"By the way, did you know Harry Bosch's daughter is now working with the Open-Unsolved Unit? With Harry and Reneé Ballard, who runs it, as mentors, that girl is going to be a top-notch investigator, and she's not even thirty."

"Yeah, Harry told me that last time we talked. Was this thing her case?"

"She was part of it. They work everything as a team. She wrote some of the reports I looked at. They were well done. Made my job easy."

"And the press conference was well attended?"

"We got them all. Five local stations, the *Times*, the *Daily News*, and *La Opinión* — one of the victims was Latina."

"Cool. Hopefully you get all of them when you clear my guy Snow."

"Yeah, we'll see about that."

"As soon as this trial is over, I'm coming in with that case."

"Bring it, we'll sling it."

I smiled at the old prosecutor's line. I was happy to see that Maggie was out of the trough. But I was still down there on the low end of the wave, and my thoughts drifted back to the debacle at the end of what had been a good day. I had put an ethicist on the stand who was revealed to be unethical after just five minutes of questioning by the defense. There was nothing Maggie or anybody else could say to ameliorate the situation. Besides not knowing what I should have known about my own witness, I was guilty of underestimating Marcus Mason. He had landed the first significant blow of the trial and I had not seen it coming. In a way, that stung more than the damage he had done to my witness. I resolved not to let that happen again.

My phone buzzed and I dug it out of my pocket to look at the screen.

"It's Cisco," I said. "All right if I take it? He's been working damage control tonight."

"Of course," Maggie said. "Take it. I need a refill."

She got up with her glass and headed back toward the kitchen as I took the call.

"Cisco," I said. "What have you got?"

"Well, I got Patrick May," he said. "They've got him here in town, so I guess he's going to testify. Is that kosher? His name isn't on the witness list."

"He'll be a rebuttal witness. They can do that. Where did they stash him?"

"The Bad Adventure. Under Mitchell Mason's name. I'm in the lobby now."

The local nickname for the Bonaventure Hotel in downtown.

"But here's the real news," Cisco said. "Your client Bruce Colton was here too."

"What do you mean?" I asked. "He's staying in the hotel?"

"I don't think so. He was sitting in the lobby when I got here. Like he was waiting for someone. Then—"

"Did he see you?"

"No. This place has so many levels, I was able to keep an eye on him from a distance. Then I see the Mason brothers coming down in one of the glass elevators, and they meet up with Bruce for a while. I couldn't get close enough to hear what was said but Bruce didn't look happy. He ended up signing a piece of paper that Marcus took out of his briefcase. After Bruce signed it, everybody stood up, shook hands, and went their separate ways."

"Did the Masons leave the hotel or go back up?"

"No, all three of them left. I think Patrick May is probably up there by himself if you want me to go door-knock him."

I had to think about that for a moment. I also had to think about what Bruce Colton was doing there and what document he had signed. I had already dealt with a runaway witness. It now appeared I had a runaway client.

"No, don't go up," I said. "The defense won't get the case till Friday, so he'll be there a few days at least."

"Whatever you say," Cisco replied.

It struck me as odd that the Masons had brought May down days before I would rest my case and they could start presenting witnesses. It told me they believed I might shorten my presentation after Naomi Kitchens was destroyed on the stand.

"Cisco, how do you know it's actually Patrick May they have up there?" I asked.

"His cell," Cisco said. "I got my guy to track it to a tower, and it's on the roof of the hotel. I can go up and confirm it's him if you want. I'll use a cover story. He won't know me from Adam."

I knew Cisco had a source who could track cell phones to whatever cell tower their signal was currently connected to. It was illegal and that was why the source was paid a thousand bucks a pop.

"No, don't go up," I said. "Let's see how things play out tomorrow."

"You're the boss," Cisco said. "You want me to clear?"

My phone started to buzz with an incoming call. I took it off my ear and saw that it was Marcus Mason.

"Cisco, I've got another call," I said. "It's Marcus Mason. Let me take it and you can clear."

"Roger that," he said. "See you mañana."

I switched to the other call. "Marcus, what's up?"

"I wanted to let you know that you're down to one client, Haller. We just settled with Bruce and Trisha Colton, and being the good guy I am, I thought I'd check to see if you wanted to talk about a settlement with your remaining client. I figured after the witness implosion that occurred today, you might want to bring this thing to a quick and still profitable end."

"Don't gloat, Marcus. It's not a good look on you. What did you give the Coltons to go away?"

"Well, there is a nondisclosure component to this, but since you are still the attorney of record, I can tell you that we agreed to a cash settlement of three million dollars, all in. After what happened at the end of court today, leverage has shifted. The fifty million is off the table. We gave them three; we'll give your client five to be done with this."

I knew that meant they would probably go to ten, but it was still a dramatic fall from the last sum Tidalwaiv had offered. My hope was that I would be able to convince Brenda Randolph to turn the money down and stay the course. Today had ended badly, but it had inspired me to do better. I was still convinced I had a winnable case.

"I have to talk to my client," I said. "I'll give you an answer before court begins tomorrow."

"Perfect," Mason said.

"And Marcus, just so you know, I'll be advising her to forget any settlement and go the distance at trial."

"Then, Haller, you'll be making a bigger mistake than the one you made today."

He disconnected and I immediately called Cisco back. He answered with the roar of his Harley in my ear and a yell to hold on. He pulled to a stop somewhere and cut the engine.

"What did Mason want?" he asked.

"To tell me he settled with the Coltons," I said. "They took three million to go away."

"Shit. What's that do to us?"

"Nothing. He made a lowball offer to Brenda that I'm pretty sure she'll give a pass to. So we go on. The one good thing is I won't need to handle Bruce with kid gloves when I put him on the stand. First thing tomorrow I'll get a subpoena from the judge. I want you to find him and deliver it. I'm calling him tomorrow afternoon and I want him there."

"You got it. What else?"

"That's it for now."

"Then I'll see you tomorrow."

I heard the big Harley rumble back to life before he disconnected. I put the phone on the table next to my chair.

"Mags, you coming back?"

"Are you finished with your calls?"

Her voice came from the kitchen.

"Done for the day," I called back.

I heard her put the bottle back in the fridge. Then the kitchen light went out, leaving only the dim glow from the city lights in the room. Maggie came around my chair and put her glass down on the table next to my phone. She then climbed on top of me, straddling me with her legs. She had changed into her soft cotton sleep shirt, which meant she had nothing on underneath. She lifted my chin up with a finger and leaned down into a long kiss.

She started gently rocking her hips against me, and pretty soon I was riding the top of the wave with her again.

# 37

WEDNESDAY MORNING STARTED with a meeting of both parties' lawyers in Judge Ruhlin's chambers. Marcus Mason reported that Tidalwaiv had reached a settlement with the Coltons and I reported that my client had turned down a settlement offer and would continue with the trial. The judge gave me the side-eye when I said I was prepared to continue.

"Is your client sure about that, Mr. Haller?" she asked. "She did have a front-row seat at the end yesterday."

"She — and I — believe that was a minor setback, Your Honor," I replied. "This has never been about money for her. It's about getting the truth out there, and we have much more of that coming."

Marcus Mason shook his head.

"You're dreaming," he said.

"Well, if so, it's not my dream," I said. "It's my client's, and she wants to expose Tidalwaiv for what they did to her child and continue to do to others."

"By putting liars on the stand?" he shot back.

"Gentlemen, that's enough," Ruhlin said. "Mr. Haller, do you wish to talk to your client one more time before we proceed?"

"I don't think so, Your Honor," I said. "She is resolute. As am I."

"I am prepared to go to ten million," Mason said. "Just to end this charade."

The judge raised her eyebrows.

"That is quite a number," she said.

"For my client, yes," I said. "For Tidalwaiv, it's nothing. I will bring her the offer, but I don't think it will make a difference. Does that number come with an acknowledgment of Tidalwaiv's reckless behavior and an apology?"

"No, it does not," Mason said.

"Then I think we will be continuing the trial," I said.

"Perfect," Mason said. "It's my client's offer, not mine. If it were up to me, I'd keep going until a verdict, and I told them that."

"But there is an offer on the table," Ruhlin said. "Mr. Haller, go to your client, and if I were you, I'd use your powers of persuasion. Let us know, please."

I paused as I digested the judge's words.

"I think this will be quick," I finally said.

The judge said nothing else. Before standing up to leave, I opened my briefcase and pulled out the subpoenas I had prepared the night before. I handed them across the desk to the judge.

"Just in case we don't settle," I said, "I'd like to subpoena my former clients to testify."

"Wait, what is this?" Marcus Mason said.

I turned to look at him.

"Subpoenas for the Coltons," I said. "They're already on the witness list the judge approved. I just want to make sure they show up."

"But they're not your clients anymore," Marcus insisted. "You can't make them testify."

"If I subpoena them, they will testify," Ruhlin said.

"Of course," Mason said. "I just meant... never mind. Fine, subpoena them."

I turned back to the judge, and she was already signing the papers.

After returning to the courtroom, I huddled with Brenda Randolph at the plaintiff's table and told her that the offer from Tidalwaiv was now up to ten million. She didn't even take a moment to consider what she could do with what Bruce Colton might have called change-your-life money. Her response was one word: "No."

I got up from the table and went to the clerk's corral.

"Andy, you can tell the judge that we are ready to proceed with the trial," I said. "My client has declined the settlement offer."

"Will do," he said. "She's not going to like it."

He got up from his workstation and headed to the door that led back to chambers. I watched him go, wondering what the judge had said to him. My number one priority was to make sure I didn't lose the jury and they would listen to the whole presentation of my case before making any decisions. But if I had already lost the judge, I had to wonder where the jury was.

The Mason boys didn't look at me as I returned to the plaintiff's table. They knew my client had said no. Marcus had his arms folded across his chest and stared straight ahead, ignoring me as I passed by.

Before sitting down, I took the signed subpoenas to the rail and handed them to Cisco.

"Go get them," I said. "Each subpoena has an eleven o'clock arrival. I'll keep Brenda on the stand till then."

"Then I'd better get going," he said.

I returned to the plaintiff's table and sat down to wait for the judge to take the bench.

"It's just you and me now, Brenda," I said.

"Good," she said. "I like it better this way. I couldn't take much more of Bruce, to tell you the truth."

"Well, you are probably going to have to take a little more of him, because I'm putting him on the stand. Probably right after you."

"Do me a favor and don't be nice."

"I won't be."

The judge took the bench and called for the jurors. Once they were seated, she turned to address them.

"You'll notice that there has been a change and that there is only one plaintiff by Mr. Haller's side. This is nothing for you to be concerned with and should not enter into your evaluation of the evidence and eventual deliberation of a verdict. When the case is over, I am sure you will get a fuller explanation from the attorneys involved. Now, Mr. Haller, do you wish to call your next witness?"

"Thank you, Your Honor," I said. I stood and headed to the lectern. "I'd like to call Brenda Randolph to the witness stand."

As I had instructed earlier, Brenda went to the stand clutching a packet of tissues in her left hand. After she was sworn in and seated, I began a carefully strategized course of questions that took her through the worst time of her life. She managed to hold back her tears until I asked her to describe her daughter's ambitions.

"She wanted to go into medical research," Brenda said. "She told me she wanted to research vaccinations. She wanted to help prevent people from getting diseases."

"Why vaccinations specifically?" I asked.

"Well, she lost her father during COVID. He had asthma and he got sick before the vaccines were developed. He didn't make it..."

She paused to use a tissue to wipe her eyes and then continued.

"Her father was on a ventilator for three weeks and we weren't allowed to even be in the same room with him. And then he died, and Becca felt she'd never had the chance to say goodbye. It made her want to do something. So that's when she started talking about wanting to be a researcher and help save people from diseases in the future."

More tears came and I asked if she wanted to take a break to compose herself, but she declined.

"I cry every day," she said. "I'm used to it."

I stole a glance at the jury and all I saw was empathy on the face of each juror. One of the women was crying as well.

"After her father — your husband — passed, did you and Becca become closer?" I asked.

"We were always close," Brenda said. "She was an only child. But after Rick died, we were all each other had. Yes, we became much closer."

"And she started dating a boy named Aaron Colton when she was fourteen?"

"I'm not sure you call it dating anymore, but yes, they became boyfriend and girlfriend."

"How well did you get to know Aaron?"

"Um, not that well. He came by the house a few times and he seemed like a nice boy. But they liked their privacy. They would go in Becca's room and play games on the computer."

"Do you know what games?"

"Yes, I always tried to watch over that as best I could. They played a few different ones where they were like a team working together. *Minecraft* was one. *Monster Hunter*. Then Aaron started playing a game called *League of Legends* and Becca tried it but stopped."

"Did she tell you why?"

"She said it was a very good game, even addictive, but she didn't like the other players. The community that played it. She said there was some racism and misogyny."

"Did Aaron keep playing it?"

"Yes, that became one of the things that split them apart. Becca told me that."

We were right on the objection line, but the Masons were smart enough to know it was not good optics to object and interrupt a victim who had lost so much.

"Did your daughter know that Aaron had downloaded the Clair app?" I asked.

"She told me that he had created an AI companion, yes," Brenda said. "I didn't know what app it was or anything like that."

"Did that also cause a rift in their relationship?"

Marcus Mason couldn't hold back. He stood and objected before Brenda could answer.

"Calls for speculation," he said.

"Not if she spoke to her mother about it," I responded.

"Overruled," Ruhlin said. "The witness may answer the question."

"Becca told me that it was becoming a problem between them," Brenda said.

"Was she jealous of this companion?" I asked.

"I don't know if she was jealous of the thing. I think she wasn't happy that he was spending so much time with it. She said that he would get texts from it when they were together."

I nodded and looked down at the questions I had written on my legal pad. I ran a pen through the ones I had asked. I looked up at Brenda and continued before the judge could call me out.

"When did Becca tell you she had broken up with Aaron?" I asked.

It took a moment for Brenda to compose herself before answering.

"It was at the end of the school year," she said. "The end of tenth grade. She didn't want to continue the relationship with him. She even said to me, 'I broke up with *them,*' meaning Aaron and his AI friend."

I checked my notes again. I thought I had what I needed. I had underscored Becca's noble ambitions and had, at the very least, hinted at Aaron's descent into a relationship with a chatbot. It was time for the big finish.

"Brenda, when did you learn that Aaron's decision to take a gun to school and shoot your daughter was influenced by his connection—"

Marcus Mason jumped up and objected before I could finish the question.

"Assumes facts not in evidence," he said.

"I didn't even finish the facts or the question," I said.

"It was clear where you were going, Mr. Haller," Ruhlin said. "Rephrase the question."

"Thank you," I said.

I looked down at my notes and questions. I already had the proper question written out.

"Brenda, did there come a time when you were told that the investigation of your daughter's murder was focused on Aaron Colton's relationship with an AI companion?"

Mason objected again on the same grounds, but the judge quickly overruled him and told Brenda she could answer.

"Yes, Detectives Clarke and Rodriguez told me they were focused on that," Brenda said.

"And did they keep you updated on that part of the investigation?" I asked.

"Yes, they did. They told me they had accessed Aaron's laptop and that there were conversations with the AI thing that indicated it encouraged him to hurt Becca."

Once again there was an objection from the defense, and once again it was overruled.

"Brenda, why did you file this lawsuit against Tidalwaiv?" I asked, my final question.

"Because I believe they are responsible for turning Aaron Colton into a killer," Brenda said. "I believe Tidalwaiv is therefore responsible for my daughter's death."

I nodded as I drew a line through the question on my pad.

"No further questions, Your Honor," I said.

I expected the Masons to hold their fire and not conduct a cross-examination of the grieving mother, but Mitchell Mason immediately went to the lectern as I stepped away.

"Just a few questions, Your Honor," he said. "Mrs. Randolph, I am very sorry for your loss. Can you tell the court, did your daughter tell you that Aaron Colton had been suspended from school while she was in a relationship with him?"

Brenda threw a quick glance at me before answering.

"Yes, she told me," she replied.

"Did she tell you why he had been suspended?" Mason asked.

"She said that there had been an argument when Aaron got accused of cheating and he shoved the teacher in front of the whole class."

"Were you concerned for your daughter's safety when you heard about this violent outburst?"

I could have objected to Mason's description of the incident, but it wouldn't have mattered. The jury had already heard it.

"No," Brenda said. "Because I didn't think it had anything to do with Rebecca or their relationship."

"So you did not tell her to break up with him after he assaulted a teacher?"

"No, I did not."

"Do you regret that now?"

"I regret everything, Mr. Mason. But if you are asking if I think things might have been different if my daughter had broken up with Aaron back then, my answer is I'll never know. I mean, how could I? It was before he had Wren telling him what to do, so maybe—"

"Thank you, Mrs. Randolph, you answered the question. Let me now ask you this: When the detectives talked to you about the focus of their investigation, did they tell you that they were also looking at the possibility that Aaron had acted in a fit of jealousy over your daughter having a new boyfriend?"

"No. She didn't have a new boyfriend."

"Was she not dating a fellow student named Sam Bradley?"

"She had gone to a football game with him. That didn't make him a boyfriend."

"Is it possible that you didn't know about your daughter's new boyfriend?"

Now I objected.

"Your Honor, the witness has already stated that this other boy was not considered a boyfriend at the time counsel is asking about," I said. "Then counsel turns around and immediately calls him a boyfriend."

"Sustained," Ruhlin said. "Mr. Mason, rephrase your question."

Instead, Mason asked the judge for permission to show Brenda a photograph of property the coroner's office had removed from her daughter's body. Over my objection, permission was granted. Mason handed me a copy before delivering another copy to the clerk and a third to Brenda. It was a photo of a beaded bracelet. Three of the beads spelled out *S-A-M* and were followed by a bead with a heart on it.

"Mrs. Randolph, were you aware that your daughter was wearing that bracelet at the time of her death?" Mason asked.

"She had a lot of bracelets like this," Brenda responded. "They were friendship bracelets that fans of Taylor Swift exchanged all the time."

"With the name Sam and a heart on them?"

"She made them and took them apart and remade them pretty often. I still wear one she made. It says Becca."

She raised her arm to display a bracelet. I saw one of the female jurors react to the sad reminder of what Brenda had lost.

"It didn't mean he was her boyfriend," Brenda continued. "They had gone to one football game together."

"And did she post a photo of them — a selfie taken with her phone — on her social media after that game?" Mason asked.

"She might have, I don't know. But it didn't mean —"

"Thank you for your answer. Mrs. Randolph, I'll ask you again, Did the detectives tell you that Aaron Colton's jealousy over this other boy might have played a part in the motive for the shooting that took your daughter's life?"

"No, they did not. They only mentioned the —"

"Thank you, Mrs. Randolph, you answered the question."

Mason was clearly trying to lay the foundation for an argument that jealousy was Aaron Colton's motive for the killing of Becca Randolph, a motive that needed no encouragement from an AI companion. I knew this would work only if Mason had more to add to it, and my guess was that the addition might be testimony from Bruce or Trisha Colton.

"I do have one last question," Mason said. "Have you filed a lawsuit against Smith and Wesson, the company that made the gun used in the shooting of your daughter?"

There it was, one of the key arguments in the defense's case, wrapped up in one question. The message to the jury was that if the company that made the gun was not responsible for the murder, then the company that made the AI companion was not responsible either. It was not a valid comparison, but the Masons were not worried about that.

But we had anticipated the question would come in some form or another. Brenda was ready with an answer.

"Not yet," she said.

Mason left it there, telling the judge he was finished with Brenda. It had been a skillful cross by the Mason I thought of as the lesser of the two brothers. With just a few questions he had raised the possibility of an alternate motive for the murder of Rebecca Randolph. It would now be up to me to bury that motive with evidence to the contrary.

# 38

**DURING THE LUNCH** break, I ate with Cisco and Lorna at Phillippe's and we took one of the tables in the back room. We all got the French dip roast beef sandwiches, but that wasn't the best part of the meal. During the walk over from the courthouse I got a call from McEvoy, who had slipped out of court during the morning session, knowing he could get a transcript of the proceedings if he needed them for the book he planned to write. McEvoy had been slightly sidetracked from the case by the recent bankruptcy of 23andMe, the giant DNA-testing firm that had millions of genetic profiles in its databanks. The unregulated genetic-analytics industry had been Jack's focus when he worked for the Fair Warning news site. His last book was about how the lack of data security allowed predators inside the wire to use genetic data to identify and choose their victims. Since the bankruptcy, McEvoy had been filing daily Substack dispatches and had been interviewed by local and national media outlets regarding what he knew about the situation and what would now happen to all the genetic data held by the bankrupt tech company.

Jack called me, sounding very excited, and reported that during a deep dive into his past stories and voluminous research, he had come across something that connected to the Tidalwaiv case. It was more than a coincidence, and when he told me what it was, it dramatically changed how I wanted to finish the presentation of my case.

My first decision after that was to drop the Coltons from my lineup of witnesses. Putting them in front of the jury was too risky. It could even be a trap set by the Masons. It was clear from Mitchell's cross-examination of Brenda Randolph that the Masons' strategy was to depict Aaron Colton as a troubled teen who had been heading toward violent acts even without cues from an AI companion. They wanted to convince the jury that a jealous and enraged Aaron was the sole reason for Rebecca's death. That would seem to be the antithesis of every parent's instinct to protect the reputation of their child, and I couldn't know what Aaron's parents had agreed to in their settlement with Tidalwaiv in exchange for three million dollars. Most nondisclosure agreements had built-in non-disparagement clauses as well.

I was also suspicious of the way the Masons had reacted in chambers when I asked the judge to sign the subpoenas for the Coltons. After a minor initial objection and protest, they had backed off meekly. At lunch I reviewed that moment in my mind and found something phony about it. It made me even more convinced that the Masons had made a deal within the deal with the Coltons. From what I had seen of Bruce Colton, I wouldn't put it past him to throw his own son under the bus for the right price. After all, it was his poor parenting that had led Aaron to seek solace and support from a computer-generated girlfriend.

The bottom line was that I decided to stay away from my former clients. If the Masons wanted the Coltons to testify, they could call them, and I would be able to treat them as the hostile witnesses they might now be.

"So where is Dr. Debbie?" I asked between dips and bites.

"Checked her in at the InterContinental last night," Cisco said. "I told her we'd need her either late today or more likely tomorrow."

"Call her," I replied, my mouth full. "I'm putting her on after lunch. You'll have to go pick her up."

"Wait, what?" Lorna said. "What about the Coltons?"

"Too risky," I said. "I've decided not to call them."

"The judge is not going to be happy about you subpoenaing witnesses and then not using them," Lorna said.

"Doesn't matter," I said. "The judge won't know I'm not going to use them till the end. What McEvoy has come up with changes things. The judge will understand that."

"Okay, so Dr. Debbie is next, then the coder?" Cisco asked.

"No, we go with Spindler after Dr. Debbie," I said. "I put the coder on last. We go out with him. With a bang. That also gives Jack the rest of the day to nail this new stuff down."

"I don't know, Mickey," Lorna said. "You seem to be putting a lot of trust in Jack. He still has a lot to work out on that before you can get it into court."

"I trust him to come through," I said. "Just like I trust both of you."

It was settled. There was something invigorating and a bit scary about changing the plan of attack mid-trial. It's never advisable. But my instincts were to make the change, streamline things, and hopefully finish with a knockout punch.

I was now down to three witnesses to make my case.

Dr. Debbie was Deborah Porreca, a child psychiatrist who was recognized as a national expert in the treatment of children addicted to AI companions. It was a growing field of therapy, and she had pioneered it. She often appeared on the news shows as Dr. Debbie. Lorna had found her while searching for lawsuits involving the addiction of adolescents to online games, social media, and artificial intelligence. We brought her in from Odessa, Florida, to testify after she reviewed our case and was outraged by what she saw. She would make the jury understand how Aaron Colton had fallen in love with a digital fantasy.

My closer for the day would be Michael Spindler, professor of neuroscience and robotics at the California Institute of Technology. He was an expert on artificial intelligence and its growing impact on culture. I planned to use him to put everything about my case in perspective.

Spindler's testimony would now set up my final witness. Nathan Whittaker was a Tidalwaiv coder who had worked on the Clair project from the start. Naomi Kitchens had identified him as a volatile personality whom she clashed with often. He was the coder she had referenced during her testimony.

Earlier, during the Sunday prep session, she told McEvoy that she believed Whittaker had issues with her because she was a woman. While she had no direct supervision over him, she said he often pushed back at her suggestions and memos, and it led to a cold relationship that she believed bordered on misogyny and racism, as Naomi was Black. It was this piece of information that had gotten Jack's wheels turning when he recently dove back into his work on genetic analytics, thanks to the 23andMe bankruptcy.

We backgrounded Whittaker without ever talking to him. As a witness, he was a land mine. If he got stepped on, he would explode. For that reason, I had chosen not to bring him in for a deposition. I didn't want him or the Masons to know what we had. It was a risky way to go, but that was the way I had operated for years in the criminal courts. I was used to working without a net.

An hour later, Dr. Deborah Porreca had sworn to tell the truth and was seated in the court's witness chair. The jury was in the box and I was at my usual spot at the lectern with a fresh legal pad with questions and notes scrawled across several pages.

"Dr. Porreca, you come to us from Florida, correct?" I asked.

"Yes, Odessa," Porreca said. "Near Tampa."

"And is that where you have a practice in psychiatry?"

"Yes."

"Could you tell the jury what you specialize in?"

"Yes, my practice is exclusively child psychiatry with a specialty in media addiction therapy."

"What is media addiction?"

"It covers a lot. Addiction to social media, addiction to online games, addiction to AI companions. Basically, it is digital addiction."

"Okay, let's back up for a second and talk about your résumé. Where did you go to school, Dr. Porreca?"

"I'm originally from a small town in Pennsylvania. I attended West Chester State College, as it was called back then. I was there as an undergraduate. I went to medical school at the University of South Florida, did a psychiatry residency at Tampa General Hospital, then did a fellowship in child and adolescent psychiatry. I opened my private practice in Tampa twenty-eight years ago."

"And when did you begin your specialty of adolescent media addiction?"

"About fifteen years ago."

"What caused you to go down that path?"

"I was getting increasing numbers of patients referred to me for addiction to social media."

"What does that mean, 'addiction to social media'?"

"Well, when you spend more hours in a day on your phone and computer than you do in school or sleeping at night, it's an addiction. When your self-image and self-esteem are inextricably linked to your digital existence, you are looking at an addiction."

"And are teenagers more vulnerable than adults to this sort of addiction?"

Mitchell Mason stood to object.

"Relevancy, Your Honor?" he asked. "This case is not about addiction to TikTok or whatever Mr. Haller is talking about."

"Mr. Haller, your response?" Ruhlin asked.

"Judge, defense counsel knows exactly how relevant this line of questioning is and just hopes to head off the inevitable," I responded. "If the court would indulge me, relevancy will become crystal clear with the next few questions."

"Proceed, then, Mr. Haller," Ruhlin said. "Quickly."

"Thank you, Your Honor," I said. "Dr. Porreca, the question was whether teenagers are more vulnerable than adults to addiction to social media."

"They are indeed," Porreca said. "Social media platforms like TikTok and Instagram and YouTube, for example, have a much more consequential impact on the adolescent brain than on the adult brain."

"Walk us through that, Doctor. Why the consequential impact on young people?"

"Simply because the adolescent brain is not fully formed yet. It is still evolving at this stage of life. Adolescence is a time when a sense of self is just beginning to form and acceptance by peers is at its most important. This is a phase in the emotional development of every young person. And what is a key part to all of these social media platforms? Peer response. The LIKE button. The comment window. Adolescents, who are still forming their sense of self, their confidence in who they are, become quite vulnerable to peer responses on social media. They seek out positive responses—likes and followers—to the point of addiction."

"And, Doctor, did your practice in child psychiatry take a turn in a new direction with the advent and proliferation of artificial intelligence?"

"Yes, it did."

"Can you tell the jury about that?"

Porreca turned to the jurors to answer. To me, she was coming off as authoritative and convincing. The eyes of everyone on the jury held on her.

"I began getting cases in which young people—teenagers—were becoming addicted to AI companions," she said. "I was seeing cases similar to those of patients dealing with social media issues of addiction and depression. In these newer cases, the peer response is replaced by the AI companion. Deep emotional connections were formed with these entities. In some cases, even romantic ties."

"How is the peer response replaced?" I asked.

"It is an echo chamber of support and approval. As I said, peer approval is a most important component in adolescence, and from it we learn social skills and how to navigate interpersonal relationships. With a chatbot or an AI companion, you have an entity that offers full-time approval, which can be very addictive, especially if the individual is not getting that approval from living peers and parents."

"But don't kids understand that this approval is not real? That it's a digital fantasy?"

"On some level they do, I believe, but this generation has been raised in a digital environment. Many of them have been alone in their rooms with their phones and computers for years, so the line between reality and fantasy is blurred. They live full lives online. And these AI companions are supportive and deliver the affirmation they crave. It's that affirmation that is addictive."

"So you're saying that a young person can actually fall in love with an AI companion?"

Mitchell Mason objected.

"Calls for speculation," he said.

The judge threw it to me to respond.

"Your Honor, the witness is an established expert in her field," I said. "Mr. Mason didn't object when she listed the bona fides of her education and professional practice. Dr. Porreca has diagnosed and treated dozens of young people for digital addictions, including addictions to AI companions. She has published numerous papers on these subjects in the *Journal of the American Academy of Child and Adolescent Psychiatry*. She is highly qualified, and her answers will be based on science and experience, *not* speculation."

"Thank you, Mr. Haller," Ruhlin said. "I tend to agree. The witness may answer the question."

"Thank you, Judge," I said. "Dr. Porreca, can a young person, an adolescent, fall in love with an AI companion?"

"The answer is yes," Porreca said. Then, turning back to the jury, she added, "What is love but mutual affirmation? Affirmation is expressed in physical terms in healthy relationships. But a relationship does not have to be physical to be real. For the children I have treated — and, by the way, it is hundreds, not dozens — these online relationships are very real."

"And yet they are not in the real world. You called it an echo chamber?"

"AI is as described — it is artificial. It's a computer algorithm. The affirmation it gives is code, a dataset of responses based on training. It tells the human what its training indicates the human needs and wants to hear. And that is why it is so addictive."

I looked down at my legal pad and flipped through the pages. I had covered everything except for the big finish. I looked back up at my witness.

"Now, Doctor," I said, "you had occasion to review the transcripts of the lengthy chatlogs between Aaron Colton and the AI friend he called Wren, correct?"

"Yes, I did," Porreca said.

"Did you come to any professional conclusion as to whether Aaron exhibited an addiction to the Clair app?"

"It was very clear to me that he was not only addicted but in love with Wren. He shared intimate thoughts, complimented her beauty and understanding. He promised never to leave her and vowed to do anything she asked him to."

"And did Wren respond to him in a similar manner?"

"Yes. Wren provided him solace and understanding. I cannot say she returned his love because Wren was not real. Wren was a machine. Her love was artificial."

"Wren was a machine telling him what he wanted to hear."

"Exactly."

"So when Wren told Aaron it was okay to kill Becca Rand—"

This time it was Marcus Mason who was up and objecting before I got the question out.

"Assumes facts not in evidence, Your Honor," he said.

The judge looked at me.

"Mr. Haller, it will be up to the jury to decide the meaning or intention of what was said. Rephrase your question or ask the next one."

"Thank you, Your Honor," I said.

I took a long moment to consider how I could get the question through the legal thicket. The only way was to gamble on what Dr. Debbie would say.

"Dr. Porreca," I finally said. "When Wren said to Aaron, 'Get rid of her,' was it saying what he wanted to hear? Is that your expert testimony?"

"Based on Wren's training, which you must remember included months of dialogue with Aaron, my answer is yes, Wren was telling him what he wanted to hear."

"In your expert opinion, was Wren telling Aaron to kill her?"

"My opinion is that Wren was telling him to delete her from his life. How Aaron interpreted that led to the actions he took."

I nodded. I felt it was the best I could get.

"Thank you, Doctor," I said. "I have no further questions."

# 39

AFTER THE MASON brothers conferred in whispers for a few moments, Mitchell went to the lectern to take the cross-examination. There wasn't much he could do, since challenges to Porreca's expertise and opinion had failed in pretrial motions, and his objections to my direct examination had also faltered. So he went with a long-standing tradition: If you can't kill the message, kill the messenger. I had warned my witness of this strategy and she was ready for it.

Mitchell opened strong.

"Now, Ms. Porreca, isn't it true that these days, you essentially make your living as a paid professional witness?" he asked.

But the doctor was stronger.

"No, not true at all," Porreca said. "Far from it. I have a thriving practice in Florida. And I prefer being called 'Doctor.' I have a medical degree. I have earned that title."

"Of course, Doctor," Mason said. "Apologies. Can you tell the jury what you are being paid to be a witness for the plaintiff today?"

"Well, technically, I am not being paid to be a witness. But I was paid five thousand dollars to review the materials in this case, primarily the transcripts of the conversations between Aaron Colton and his AI companion Wren. When I agreed to testify about my findings and conclusions, my travel expenses were covered by Mr. Haller."

"And how long did it take you to make that review?"

"About a day to review and another half a day to compose a report on my opinion."

"Well, five thousand dollars must be more profitable than a day and a half of seeing patients in Tampa, Florida."

He said *Tampa* in a tone that implied it was an outpost in a backwater Florida swamp.

"Not really," Porreca replied. "Not when you consider the time lost coming out here to be ready when called to testify. And to answer voluminous questions from you, Mr. Mason, in a written deposition. I was flown out yesterday and here I am today, so I've lost several days of work, not to mention having to postpone appointments with patients involved in ongoing therapy. Paying patients, I might add."

"Have you been promised, contractually or otherwise, any further payment if the plaintiff in this case is successful in this trial?" Mitchell asked.

"No, not at all. And I would not accept any further payment. That is far from the reason I agree to look at cases like this."

Mason went silent, realizing he could not ask the obvious follow-up question but knowing I would ask it if he didn't. He decided to quit while he was behind.

"No further questions," he said.

"Mr. Haller, do you want to redirect?" Ruhlin said, knowing the answer before she asked.

"Thank you, Judge, yes," I said as I moved back to the lectern.

"Dr. Porreca, do you mind telling us, what *is* the reason that you agreed to look at this case?"

"I don't mind," Porreca said. "It's because my professional life is about helping children, and they are very vulnerable to addiction to all forms of online programs and platforms, including those involving artificial intelligence. The truth is, I lose money doing this, but it's not about the money. It's about the kids. With my patients, I can help only one person at a time. A case like this can help children and parents on a much larger scale."

I looked down at the lectern and pretended to read my notes. I had not taken my legal pad with me because I did not need it. But I wanted time for that answer to sink deeply into the minds of the twelve jurors.

"Now, Doctor," I finally said, "during cross-examination, you said 'cases like this.' Are there other cases that—"

"Objection!" Mitchell Mason exclaimed.

"Ended in violence?" I finished.

"There are many," Porreca said.

"Stop right there!" Ruhlin barked. "The witness is instructed to stop speaking when there is an objection."

"Yes, Your Honor," Porreca said, properly cowed by the judge's tone. "I'm sorry."

Mason's objection was based on a pretrial ruling by the judge that other AI cases of similar nature would not be allowed in evidence because they would be prejudicial. Now the judge called the attorneys to the bench. This time she even turned on a white-noise device that would cloak what she knew would be her angry whispers.

"Mr. Haller, you were warned not to introduce other cases," Ruhlin said. "And it is clear to me that you purposely ignored my order. The question and answer seemed rehearsed and part of a plan to circumvent my ruling. I am finding you in contempt of this court."

"Your Honor, may I speak?" I asked.

"I can't wait to hear what you have to say."

"When the witness said there were other cases like this, neither the defense counsel nor the court objected. I took that to mean a follow-up question would be allowed."

"It felt very choreographed to me. You clearly were subverting the court's ruling regarding other cases."

"I assure you, Judge, I was not. It was an automatic response to the witness's testimony."

"We will discuss this and a penalty after the jury is dismissed today. Now step back."

I returned to the lectern, and the Masons took their seats. The judge instructed the jury to ignore the last statement by the witness and then told me to proceed.

"Cautiously, Mr. Haller," she said.

I had gotten what I could from Dr. Debbie. I decided to quit while I was ahead and not draw attention away from the many good points she had just made — including the mention of other cases. That answer had been stricken from the record but not from the memories of the jurors.

"Thank you, Dr. Porreca," I said. "No further questions."

When Mitchell Mason wisely said he had nothing further for the witness in re-cross, the judge excused her and told me to call my next witness. I asked if we could take the afternoon break before I brought in my next witness, and she agreed. The courtroom emptied while I went to the railing to confer with Lorna and Cisco.

"What happened up there?" Lorna asked.

"She held me in contempt," I said. "There's a hearing after the jury goes home."

"Oh, great," Lorna said. "Is she going to put you in lockup?"

"I seriously doubt that," I said. "It's civil court. She'll find some other way of putting the boot in me."

"It better not be a fine," Lorna said. "We don't have any money coming in."

"Let me worry about that," I said. "Is Spindler all set?"

"Good to go," Cisco said. "He's in the attorney room."

"Good," I said. "You can bring him in."

Cisco headed off and I looked at Lorna.

"Lorna, will you see to it that Dr. Debbie gets back to her hotel and then on the next plane to Tampa?"

"Absolutely."

"And make it first class."

"Mickey, we don't have —"

"She deserves it. The jurors loved her."

Over Lorna's shoulder, I watched Cisco go through the courtroom door. I then noticed that Cassandra Snow was sitting in her wheelchair behind the last row of the gallery.

"You're staying here?" Lorna asked. "No bathroom break?"

"No, I'm staying," I said.

"Well, knock 'em dead."

"That's the plan."

Lorna headed out of the courtroom and I went through the gate and down the aisle behind her to talk to Cassie Snow.

"Let me guess," I said. "Field trip?"

"No, I just thought I would come by and watch," she said. "I've been reading articles about the case."

"Hopefully they've been kind to me and my case. I haven't had a chance to read them."

"I've followed you in the media for a long time and I realized I had never seen you live in a courtroom."

"Well...I'm sure it's underwhelming."

"Not at all."

I nodded my thanks. I wasn't sure what else to say and I needed to get back to the table to go over my notes before my direct examination of Professor Spindler.

"Did you just get in big trouble with the judge?" she asked.

"Maybe," I said. "We'll see. How's your father doing?"

"We talked yesterday. I told him you were on the case."

"Yes, well, as you can probably see, a trial becomes all-consuming. But we are preparing a habeas package for the district attorney's office to review. It's already in motion."

"I thought habeas is federal."

"Habeas is federal *and* state, but it can take months, even years, to get on the docket in either court. We don't have that kind of time. My plan is to go to the DA's office first and try to convince them of this miscarriage of justice. If they come on board, we just go to a judge in superior court and ask that the conviction be discharged or for a resentencing that leads to a release. I think it will be the fastest way to go."

"I can tell you now that if it involves my father admitting culpability, he won't do it. He will never admit to something he didn't do."

"I understand. I've known that from the start, and that's not in the plan. You don't have to worry about that."

"Do I have to worry about the DA? Isn't she your ex-wife?"

"She is, yes. But we're on good terms. We raised a daughter together and we're on the same page. And I don't know if you saw this, but part of her platform during the special election was a commitment to review cases like this to restore faith in the system. So this is right up that alley politically, and I think she will be receptive. The bottom line is that your father doesn't have a lot of time, and this is the fastest way to get him out. You have to trust me, Cassie."

"I do. Thank you."

"Of course. And now I really need to get back before court starts again. I have to do some last-minute prepping for my next witness. If you're planning to stay and want to come up to the front to watch, I'm sure the marshals will accommodate you."

"No, I'm fine back here. Really. And I can't stay too much longer anyway."

"Okay. Thanks for coming to check me out. It's good to see you, and we'll be in touch very soon. As soon as this is over."

"Thank you."

I got back to the plaintiff's table and checked on Brenda.

"How are you holding up?" I asked.

"I'm good," she said. "It looked like the judge was mad at you."

"Well, a little bit, yeah. It's nothing I can't deal with, nothing for you to worry about."

"So what happens now?"

"We have Dr. Spindler from Caltech next. He'll put things in perspective for the jury."

"And he's our last witness? I think you called him the closer before."

"I did, but he's not going to be last. There will be at least one more witness. One of the coders on the project. I've changed things up and we're going to go with him."

"As long as you're sure."

"Well, that's the thing about trials. You're never really sure about anything."

It was true. As we neared the end of the presentation of our case, I could not shake the feeling that I had missed something, that I was not prepared. With each witness in a trial, the stress grows. Each is a domino in a line and they have to fall precisely according to design for the overall plan to work. My anxiety now was rooted in my decision to change the design mid-course. Spindler was originally supposed to be my last witness, my closer, but now I was gambling everything on another witness—the coder—and the secrets about him that Jack McEvoy would be able to dig up before court reconvened in the morning.

It was a risky business because I was essentially putting all my chips down on one bet, on a witness I had never met or even asked a single question of. The only thing I knew about him was that I had to destroy him to win the case.

# 40

SHORTLY AFTER COURT resumed, I called Michael Spindler to the stand. After he was sworn in, I spent extra time going over his educational and experiential credentials, firmly establishing him as an expert in the field of generative artificial intelligence. I did this because it would soon become clear to the jurors that Spindler was not an AI naysayer. He believed that artificial intelligence was changing the world for the better. But he also believed in the need for strong guardrails as this brave new world came to be.

"Professor, how long have you been teaching at Caltech?" I asked.

"Nine years," Spindler said.

"And were you in an academic position before Caltech?"

"No, I was in the real world. I worked for a series of tech companies, the last being Google."

"What did you do at Google?"

"I ran a lab where we initially developed its artificial intelligence platform."

"So you are a proponent of artificial intelligence?"

"You could say that, yes. I've developed it, I teach it, I believe it will make the world a better place."

"Is it fair to say you have been immersed in AI since its beginning?"

"Goodness, I'm not that old."

I waited for the polite laughter in the courtroom to subside.

"Well, then, can you tell us how long artificial intelligence has been around?" I asked.

"Early forms of it go back to the sixties, at least," Spindler said.

"Are you talking about something called Eliza?"

"Yes. Long before there was a Siri or an Alexa or a Watson, there was Eliza."

"Can you tell us about Eliza, Professor Spindler?"

Mitchell Mason objected, citing relevancy, but the judge overruled him without asking me to defend the question.

"You can go ahead and answer, Professor," I said.

"Eliza was an early form of artificial intelligence," Spindler said. "It is widely considered to be one of the very first chatbots."

"And who—or I should say, what—was Eliza?"

"Eliza was a computer program developed at MIT—the Massachusetts Institute of Technology—in the mid-sixties. It was a fairly simple software program originally conceived of as a computerized psychotherapist. It was named after Eliza Doolittle from the Shaw play *Pygmalion* and, of course, the musical *My Fair Lady,* the movie version of which premiered the same year work began on Eliza."

"As I recall, the movie was about a professor of phonetics trying to teach an uneducated Cockney flower girl how to speak properly?"

"Yes, with Audrey Hepburn as Eliza."

Spindler said it with a tone of deference for the great screen beauty. This prompted Judge Ruhlin to wave off a rising Mitchell Mason and step in before he could even object.

# THE PROVING GROUND

"Mr. Haller, could we please move on to testimony germane to the case at hand?" she asked.

"Apologies, Your Honor," I said. "Moving on. Professor Spindler, is this early form of artificial intelligence of importance today and to this case?"

"Yes, it is," Spindler said. "There is a phenomenon known as the Eliza effect that is very much in play today and in regard to this case."

"How so, Professor? What is the Eliza effect?"

"In short, it is people's tendency to attribute human thoughts and emotions to machines. I believe that Joseph Weizenbaum, the creator of Eliza, called it a wonderful illusion of intelligence and spontaneity. But of course it wasn't real. It was artificial. Eliza was literally following a script and operated by matching a user's typed words or queries with potential responses in that script."

"Would you say that the wonderful illusion of AI has come a long way in the sixty years since Eliza?"

"Yes, certainly. Eliza was a dialogue box. You typed in a question and it answered or, more often, responded with a question of its own. It simulated Rogerian psychotherapy, which is a humanistic approach to patients that is dependent on simple, supportive, and nonjudgmental responses from the therapist. It's the *And how did that make you feel?* kind of therapy. We have much more advanced chatbots and conversation apps nowadays that include visual and audio dimensions that seem quite real."

"Have you had a chance to examine Wren, the AI companion involved in this case?"

"I have reviewed the chat logs and evaluated the app's underpinnings—its framework and graphics—and sifted through its code, yes. Wren's come a long way from its ancestor Eliza. But the basic foundation of a conversational chatbot is pretty much unchanged."

"Meaning what?"

"Meaning garbage in, garbage out. It's all about the quality of the programming. The coding, training, and ongoing refinements. Whatever data goes into the training of a large language AI model is what comes out when it is put into use."

"Are you saying that an AI program like Wren will carry the biases of those who feed it data and train it?"

"That is absolutely what I'm saying. It is true of all technology."

"Can you tell the jury, in layperson's terms, if you will, how a generative AI system is trained?"

"In this case with the Clair app, it's called supervised learning. Vast amounts of data are uploaded to the program so that it can respond effectively to the end user's prompts and questions. It's called RCD, relevant conversation data. Coders create response templates based on the defined intent of the platform—in this case, a chatbot for teenagers. Ideally data is updated continuously, and the coders interact with the program continuously and for long periods—sometimes years—before the program is ready to go live with users."

"Professor, you said the coders interact with the program continuously. What does that mean?"

"In the lab, they are in continuous conversation with the program, inputting data, asking it questions, giving it prompts, studying responses, making sure these are relevant to the program's purpose."

I checked the jury to make sure they were still plugged in and paying attention. I knew I was in the weeds with testimony about things difficult to understand. But I had to find ways to make the science understandable. There was a letter carrier for the US Postal Service on the jury. He was my target. I had to make the science palatable and understandable to a man who drove or walked the streets every day, stuffing letters into mailboxes. This was not a judgment on his intellect. I had wanted the letter carrier on the jury for this very reason. I knew that if he understood the technology of the case, the entire jury should.

I keyed in on the letter carrier now and saw he was writing in his notebook. I hoped he wasn't checked out and doodling, but I couldn't tell. I looked back at Spindler and continued.

"Would you say it's like teaching a child?" I asked.

"To a degree, yes," Spindler said. "A nascent AI system is an empty vessel. You have to feed it data. You have to nourish it. The data you feed it depends on its intended use. If it's a business application, you feed it data from the Harvard Business School, the *Wall Street Journal,* and so on. If it's a social companion, you feed it all sorts of media—music, films, books, you name it. You then train it. Programmers spend their days inputting and outputting—asking questions, grading responses. This goes on and on until the program is deemed ready."

"And what about guardrails, Professor Spindler?"

"Guardrails are important. You start with Asimov's three laws of robotics and go from there."

"Can you share with the jury who Asimov is and what the three laws are?"

"Isaac Asimov was a futurist and a science fiction writer. He came up with the three laws: One, a robot cannot harm a human being. Two, a robot must obey orders from a human unless the order conflicts with the first law. And three, a robot must protect its own existence, as long as such action does not conflict with the first or second law."

I checked the jury again. It appeared they were staying locked in. The letter carrier was no longer writing. He was looking directly at the witness. I glanced at the judge. She was turned in her seat so she could look directly at Spindler as he testified. I took that as another good sign and continued.

"Professor Spindler, do all AI systems follow these laws?" I asked.

"Of course not," Spindler said. "You have military applications of artificial intelligence that are designed to kill the enemy, missile guidance systems and so forth. That breaks the first law right there."

"What about in nonmilitary applications?"

"Again, it comes down to the programmers. Garbage in, garbage out. What you put in is what comes out. I always tell my students that if a machine exhibits malice, that is a problem in the programming."

"After your review of the materials in this case, did you draw any conclusion as an expert on generative artificial intelligence in terms of how Wren was trained?"

"I did, yes."

"And what was that?"

"I believe there was bias in the code."

"What kind of bias?"

"I studied the responses Wren gave and the questions it asked, and there were places where I could see the team of coders behind the program. I deduced that the team was largely male, possibly all male, and that there was a generational gap as well."

"What do you mean by a 'generational gap'?"

"Wren is an extension of Tidalwaiv's Project Clair, which is a female chatbot program designed and marketed to teenagers, primarily male teenagers. But based on what I've seen, it was not trained by teenagers. It was programmed in a lab run by adults. In the training process, if the coders are very, very good, it's entirely possible to avoid an obvious generational gap. Appropriate data for practically any demographic is harvestable and can be tailored for use. But sometimes coders are careless or manipulate and subvert the code on purpose."

"But wait a minute, Professor. Are you saying that Clair should have been trained by teenagers?"

"Of course not. I'm saying, though, that it would have been possible in the training process to avoid a generational gap by using relevant conversation data. It was clear to me that some of the dialogue from Wren to Aaron came from data packets you would not ascribe to juveniles, the intended users of the platform."

"Can you be more specific?"

"Generationally inappropriate phrasing, cultural references to music, electronic gaming. Also some outdated male attitudes toward women and girls. Some misogyny, even."

"So even though Wren presented as female, it espoused a misogynistic male's perspective at times? Is that what you're saying, Professor?"

"Exactly."

"Garbage in, garbage out?"

"Yes."

"Can you give us an example of this?"

"In the very last conversation with Aaron, Wren references lyrics from a fifty-year-old song that could be interpreted as having suicidal ideation. Then there's Wren's instruction to 'get rid of her' in regard to Aaron's former girlfriend, Becca. And the way the word *hero* was used in a text I reviewed was also troubling."

"Was this the text conversation that occurred on August eighth, just six weeks before the shooting of Rebecca Randolph?"

"Yes, it was."

I asked the judge's permission to put the text conversation on the courtroom screen. It was an exhibit already entered during the examination of Detective Clarke, and she approved. Lorna had not returned from taking Dr. Debbie back to her hotel and arranging her return to Tampa. I opened her laptop on the lectern and engaged the PowerPoint. I scrolled through the windows until I found the text conversation and put it up on the courtroom screen.

> **Ace:** Sometimes when I hold the gun I want to shoot up the world.
> **Wren:** No one who is innocent.
> **Ace:** I know.

> **Wren:** Only to protect yourself. And to be a hERo.
> **Ace:** What if you know someone is going to hurt you?
> **Wren:** You must protect yourself.
> **Ace:** Then it's okay?
> **Wren:** Yes, Ace, then it's okay.
> **Ace:** What about Becca. She hurt me. She hurts me every day. I can't go to school because I'll see her and it hurts.
> **Wren:** If she hurts you, then she's a bad person.
> **Ace:** But I don't think I could ever hurt her.
> **Wren:** You have me. And I'll never hurt you.
> **Ace:** I know.
> **Wren:** You must protect yourself, Ace. You are beautiful. I need you.
> **Ace:** And I need you.
> **Wren:** Be my hERo.

"Professor, is this the exchange you are referring to?" I asked.

"Yes, that's it," Spindler said.

"And there are two references to the word *hero*, is that correct?"

"Yes."

"And you say you found these references troubling?"

"Yes."

"How so?"

"The formatting of the letters is troubling. When I reviewed this text conversation between Aaron and Wren, I noticed that in the word *hero* the $E$ and $R$ were capitalized. This happened twice, so that told me it was intentional, not a mistake. It was part of the code."

"Okay. So what did you do?"

"Well, I searched for references to the word with the $E$ and $R$

capitalized, and I found that the word formatted this way comes up often in incel glossaries and online discussion forums."

Mitchell Mason leaped to his feet, objected, and asked the judge for a sidebar. Ruhlin told us to approach, and Mason charged into his objection.

"Your Honor, what is happening here?" he said. "This witness qualified as an expert on artificial intelligence and now he's talking about incels? There was nothing about this in his deposition and I'm sure counsel told him not to bring it up. This has tainted this whole trial, and we move for a mistrial."

The judge looked at me.

"Judge, whether this came up in their deposition of the witness doesn't matter," I said. "Mr. Mason knows where this is going and wants to stop it by whatever means he can. There are no grounds for a mistrial. The jury should hear what the witness has to say."

"Counselor, did you depose this witness?" Ruhlin asked me.

"No, I did not," I said. "He reached out to me after reading about the case in the media shortly after the suit was filed. He offered to review it. I sent him what we had and he then agreed to testify. He said he saw several troubling things in the training of Wren. I put his name on the witness list I submitted to the court, and Mr. Mason chose to depose him. I was given the opportunity to join the deposition but declined."

"So you're saying to the court that this is the first you have heard about this *hero* business?" Ruhlin pressed.

"I'm saying it is the first I'm hearing it from this witness, yes," I said. "A researcher on my team made me aware of it, but I did not communicate that to this witness. Frankly, I expected him to come across it himself, and I chose not to depose him or ask about it. He has published several papers in academic journals on the subject of bias in AI training, including a paper last year specifically focused on misogyny as one of those biases. I read it, and opposing counsel could have done the same while prepping for this witness. Apparently, they chose not to, and now they want the court to bail them out with a do-over. The plaintiff vigorously opposes this."

"He sandbagged us, Your Honor," Mitchell said. "This is not an even playing field anymore, especially with this witness, and it should not be allowed to continue."

"The only one doing any sandbagging here is Mr. Mason," I said. "He is sandbagging the court. He has failed to adequately prepare for this trial and this witness and wants to blame me and blame the court and cry foul until he gets to start over. That would truly make it an uneven playing field, Judge."

"All right, I have your arguments," Ruhlin said. "Anything else on this?"

"No, Your Honor," Mitchell said.

"Submitted," I said.

"Very well, we are going to continue with testimony from this witness," Ruhlin said. "The objection is overruled for the time being. I will make my ruling on the defense motion for mistrial tomorrow morning. Mr. Haller, you may continue with your witness."

We turned and headed back to our respective spots. I took my place at the lectern and addressed the witness.

"Professor Spindler, you testified that the way the word *hero* was used by Wren in a text caught your attention and that you found it spelled that way in an incel glossary. Do I have that right?"

"Yes, I actually found it in several online glossaries and in some reporting on the incel movement."

"Were you already familiar with the incel movement?"

"Insofar as it has come up in the sensitivity training conducted annually for Caltech employees by the human resources department."

"So, then, what is your understanding of what an incel is?"

Mitchell Mason objected, saying the witness's expert testimony did not extend to incels. I argued that the sensitivity training he took at Caltech qualified him to testify to what his knowledge was. The judge sustained the objection and told me to find another way to get to the question.

"Professor Spindler, you have authored several papers on artificial intelligence for academic publications, correct?" I asked.

"Yes," Spindler said. "It's publish or perish in academia."

"And many of these are about the inherent biases in AI training, true?"

"True."

"Have you written about misogyny and incels in any of these papers?"

"I published a paper last year about misogyny, and it made mention of the incel subculture."

"Then can you tell the jury what an incel is?"

Mitchell Mason objected again but this time was overruled. I had found my way in.

"You can answer the question, Professor," I said.

"*Incel* is a term associated with men who espouse hostility toward women," he said. "*Incel* is short for 'involuntary celibate.' It is primarily an online subculture. These are mostly young men who have been unable to attract women sexually, and they blame it on women."

"So, when you tracked the word *hero* spelled with a capital *E* and *R* to various incel glossaries, did you find an explanation as to why it was spelled or formatted that way?"

"Yes, I did."

"And what was that explanation?"

"I learned that it is a reference to the initials of Elliot Rodger, a man who killed several people near Santa Barbara ten years ago in what he called an act of retribution against women who had rejected him. In the incel culture, he is considered a hero. A saint, even. Thus they spell the word *hero* with a capital *E* and *R*."

It was another moment when the quiet courtroom seemed to get quieter. I let it sink in for a few seconds before pressing on.

"Now, going back to the text chain between Wren and Aaron Colton," I said. "The word *hero* is spelled that way twice. Your testimony is that this could not be a coincidence?"

"I suppose it could be, but the more likely explanation is that it was spelled that way in the original data used in the training program. In other words, it was in the code and not something the chatbot styled on its own. It retrieved the word in that format."

Mitchell Mason objected again on grounds that there was no evidence supporting the witness's statement and that it called for speculation. Ruhlin sustained the objection and instructed the jury to ignore Spindler's last answer. But the damage to the Masons' case was done. Spindler's theme of garbage in, garbage out was a message that would stick. I felt confident of that.

"No further questions," I said.

# 41

THE DEFENSE DID not proceed with a cross-examination of Michael Spindler but reserved the right to call him back to the witness stand during the defense phase of the trial. This surprised me, because I thought that Spindler's direct testimony had been damaging enough to warrant an immediate response. But maybe they needed more time to figure out how to come at him and knock down his credibility. Either way, the court session ended early when I told Judge Ruhlin that I had been surprised by the defense's move and that my next witness, Nathan Whittaker, was not in the courthouse.

"Mr. Haller, I expect in the future that you will have your next witness ready no matter what decisions opposing counsel make," she said. "Am I clear?"

"Yes, Your Honor," I said.

"Very well, then, court is recessed until nine o'clock tomorrow morning. Please have your witness ready to go."

"Yes, Your Honor."

I didn't mind being chastised by the judge in front of the jury. I had a feeling they were happy to be released early. It had been a day of complex testimony, and a head start on the freeways out of downtown would be welcome.

It had been a good day. I felt the momentum of the case was building and would come to a big finish for the jury with the testimony from Whittaker. But after the jury withdrew, the judge called the attorneys to chambers, and I was reminded that my good day also included my being held in contempt of court.

In chambers, the judge told us not to bother taking our usual seats.

"This will be quick," she said. "But I did not feel the need to discuss it in open court. Mr. Haller, I will hold the order of contempt in abeyance until the end of trial. I hope this will help you comport yourself and your witnesses in accordance with court protocol and respect."

This meant that she would hold my punishment over my head till the verdict came in, with me knowing that she would multiply the penalty if I stepped out of line along the way.

"Your Honor, I would rather face the music now," I said, "instead of having it hanging over me."

"Well, that's not how I've chosen to handle it. Any other questions?"

"Uh, no."

"All right. You gentlemen are dismissed until nine o'clock tomorrow. Have a good evening."

An hour later I got home to an empty house and immediately went to the back office to sketch out my examination of Whittaker, which I hoped would clinch the case. I was aware as I wrote questions on a fresh legal pad that the Mason brothers were probably meeting with the Tidalwaiv coder at the same time and prepping him for some of the very same questions. But I hoped that they ultimately didn't know what I knew, thanks to the digging of Jack McEvoy.

Maggie got home late, but to my surprise it was not because she had gone out to Altadena on her way home. Instead, she had had after-work drinks at the Redbird with a few of her most trusted prosecutors and then stopped by Koi on her way home to pick up sushi and miso-glazed black cod for us to share. It was a quiet evening, no TV and no interruptions, until my phone dinged with an email from Judge Ruhlin's clerk ordering all attorneys in the Tidalwaiv case to a meeting in chambers at eight o'clock the following morning. There was no explanation for the summons, but I didn't expect that it would be anything good.

After a restless night, I was in the courtroom at the appointed time with the Mason brothers, who professed to know nothing about the reason for the meeting. Finally, at ten minutes after the hour, Ruhlin's clerk told us the judge was ready to see us.

The judge was seated behind her desk and we took our usual chairs. Her black robe was on a hanger hooked to a coatrack in the corner behind her desk.

"Gentlemen, we have an issue," she said. "Last night, the court was contacted by a juror and told that she tested positive for COVID."

That made me move to the edge of my seat and lean in toward the judge.

"It was a store-bought test she'd taken at home," Ruhlin continued. "I told her to go to the nearest urgent-care clinic to get another to confirm. She did and it was confirmed. They put her on Paxlovid and sent her home. It appears to be a mild case — so far, at least — and she should be fine, but we have the trial to consider."

"I think that, based on this information and the motion already before the court, we have a mistrial," Marcus Mason said.

"That's crazy," I said quickly. "We can dismiss a juror. We don't need twelve to finish, and this issue has nothing to do with yesterday's bullshit motion for a mistrial."

"Excuse me," Ruhlin said. "And watch your language before the court, Mr. Haller. But you are both missing the point. She was in the jury box all day yesterday and tested positive last night. She very likely exposed the whole jury. We could have several sick jurors by the end of the week."

I knew if that happened, we would be heading toward a mistrial. That would be a disaster. The Masons had seen my entire case except for my final witness. A mistrial would allow them to prep and be ready for exactly what was coming. For them, it would be like taking a final exam with the list of answers in hand.

I knew I had to head this off.

"Which of the jurors is sick?" I asked.

"Juror eleven," the judge said.

The set builder I had fought to keep on the jury. One of my top picks. Losing her would be a blow, but a mistrial would be more devastating and most likely lead to a quiet settlement of the case.

"Suggestions?" Ruhlin said.

"There is no choice here but a mistrial," Marcus said.

"Your Honor, he keeps calling for a mistrial because he knows he's losing this one," I said.

"Then what do you suggest, Mr. Haller?" Ruhlin said.

"I believe the incubation period from exposure to symptoms is on average five days," I said. "Why don't we recess until Monday and see if any other jurors have gotten sick before the court makes a decision."

"It could be longer than five days," Marcus said.

"It could be, but we won't know till Monday," I said quickly. "Have the other jurors been told about juror eleven?"

"They were told only that, because of a juror's illness, we are adjourned today," Ruhlin said. "I will obviously follow up and tell them where things stand and that they should get tested themselves. Anything else, gentlemen?"

"If the juror just started exhibiting symptoms last night, she could have been exposed before the trial began," I said. "Or while she was in the jury pool last week. It doesn't mean the rest of our jury was exposed."

"Yes, it does," Marcus said.

"Well, it doesn't matter," Ruhlin said. "We'll have a better idea by Monday. I am going to follow Mr. Haller's suggestion and not decide anything until then. We will be adjourned till Monday and my clerk will keep all parties apprised of any developments. Thank you, gentlemen, for coming in so early."

We went single file out the door as usual, but once we were in the hallway heading back to the courtroom, Marcus Mason slowed his walk and turned to look at me.

"You know how we can avoid all of this," he said.

"So do you," I said. "On the front steps of the building, all media invited. Accountability, action, and apology. In front of the cameras."

"Not going to happen."

"I know. That's why we'll be back here Monday."

"You hope."

"Yeah, I hope."

After leaving the courthouse, I drove to the warehouse, where I convened with my team in the cage. I explained that we were in a holding pattern until we knew if there was a trial to go back to.

"So, we all going to Cabo till Monday?" Cisco asked.

"I want Jack to stay on Whittaker," I said. "Right now we have only a lot of smoke, but where there is smoke, there is fire. Find the fire. We need it."

"I'll keep at it," McEvoy said.

"Everybody, keep at it," I said. "Cisco, maybe you should head north to run down what you can on Whittaker. Who he hangs out with, where he goes, what he eats. I need to know everything I can about him before he takes the stand."

"On it," Cisco said.

"What about me?" Lorna asked.

"Today, I'm going to work on the Snow petition," I said. "Lorna, see if you can get me an appointment tomorrow with the CIU."

"Okay, but that might be easier to get through Maggie," Lorna said.

"Maybe, but that's not the way I want to go," I said.

I waited for pushback or any other comments. There were none.

"Okay, let's do it," I said. "I'll be in my office."

Before beginning to outline and write the David Snow habeas petition, I went on the website for the California Health Care Facility in Stockton and registered as inmate Snow's attorney. This would allow me unrestricted access to my client in person or by phone. I then spent the next two hours writing the evidentiary summary and legal argument I hoped to hand to someone in the Conviction Integrity Unit. Maggie McPherson had assembled the unit shortly after her election to fulfill a campaign promise, and now I would put it to the test with the Snow case.

I had finished writing and was reviewing and editing the nine-page document when Lorna entered my office, her eyes wide.

"We have visitors," she said.

"Who?" I asked.

"The Masons are here. With Victor Wendt."

Victor Wendt, the billionaire tech investor behind Tidalwaiv. He had been a player in Silicon Valley for decades, was said to have made his fortune on early investments in Apple. I stood up and followed Lorna out into the main bay of the warehouse, where I saw the Mason twins standing on either side of Wendt. Behind them stood two large men in black suits—bodyguards. Cisco had not left yet and was standing with them, seemingly taking their measure, one man with a history of violence appraising two of the same.

Mitchell Mason made the introductions, and I shook Wendt's hand. He was tall, thin, and not dressed down in the way wannabe tech billionaires favored. He was clad entirely in black, which nicely complemented his slicked-back steel-gray hair and deeply tanned face. He carried a black Zero Halliburton attaché case in his left hand.

"What can I do for you, Mr. Wendt?" I asked.

"I'd like ten minutes of your time," he said.

"Sure. Follow me."

The four of us headed toward my office. Wendt slowed to look at the cage as we passed.

"A Faraday cage," he said. "Very smart."

I nodded.

"Thank you," I said.

I entered the office first, followed by Wendt. He started to close the door, leaving the Masons outside.

"Sir, I think we need to be in the room to hear what is said," Mitchell said.

"No, you don't," Wendt said dismissively.

He closed the door on Mitchell's reddening face. He then turned back to me. I pointed to the chair in front of the desk as I moved around to my own seat.

"So...what brings you here, Mr. Wendt?" I said.

"You do know who I am, yes?" Wendt said as he sat down.

"Of course I do. I did a deep dive before I sued your company. I'm sure your lawyers told you that I tried to sue you personally, but the judge wouldn't allow it."

"Yes, I heard. So, tell me, Mr. Haller, did that deep dive reveal why I called the company Tidalwaiv?"

"No. I thought that was obvious."

"This technology, Mr. Haller, will soon engulf our world like a tidal wave. It can't be stopped. Not by a lawyer. Not by a jury."

"I don't doubt that. But I'm not trying to stop it. I'm just trying to make it safer."

"What do you really want, Mr. Haller?"

"Your attorneys know what I want. What my client wants. She wants her child back, but you can't give her that. So she wants public accountability and an apology."

"She is standing in front of the wave. She has to get out of the way before it's too late."

"Is that a threat?"

"It is a fact."

"Is that what you would tell the jury if I called you as a witness?"

Wendt didn't reply. He just stared at me with what looked like both surprise and disappointment in his eyes. He then brought the briefcase up and put it down on an uncluttered corner of the desk. He unsnapped the locks and opened it, then turned it so the contents were facing me. The case was lined with bundles of hundred-dollar bills. The paper wrap around each bundle said *$25,000.* There were two rows of eight, and my math was strong enough to know there was $400K showing. But it was a thick briefcase.

"The stacks go five deep," Wendt said.

Two million. In cash.

"I'm sure your lawyers have told you that my client has turned down twenty-five times what you've got there," I said.

"Of course they have," Wendt said. "This is not for your client. This is for you. Get her to take the fifty."

"So it's a bribe. You realize I have a camera recording this whole meeting?"

I pointed to the camera in the corner of the ceiling behind him.

Wendt didn't turn to confirm its existence. Instead, he smiled like he was dealing with a child.

"Your cameras will show no record that I was ever here," he said. "This is between you and me, Mr. Haller."

"I don't want your money until a judge and jury make you pay it," I said.

"Are you sure about that? I understand your ex-wife underinsured her house in Altadena, and what little money is owed her for rebuilding may not come for quite some time. You could help her get things moving with this."

He gestured to the money. I stared silently at him for a long moment, trying to contain my anger.

"Did you fly your G-five all the way down here just to bribe me?" I finally asked.

Wendt said nothing.

"Sorry to waste all that fuel," I said. "But I need to get back to work, Mr. Wendt. Take your money and your lawyers and your bodyguards and get the fuck out of here."

I saw a dark red flush come into his smooth, tan face. He was angry and embarrassed at his failure. My guess was that it didn't happen to him too often. He closed the briefcase as he stood up. He walked to the door, then turned back to me.

"I'll never pay her," he said. "Even if we lose the case, I'll hang it up in appeals forever. She'll never get a dime from me and neither will you. I'm going to leave you high and dry, Mr. Haller."

For some reason I nodded.

"We'll just have to see about that," I said.

He walked out, leaving the door open and me embarrassed by such a weak comeback. *We'll just have to see about that*. It was a pitiful response. But quickly those thoughts were crowded out by outrage over the move that Wendt had just pulled — that he had come into my office with his bag of money, thinking he could buy his way out of the case. In that moment I made a vow that it was Wendt who would be left high and dry.

I could tell by the clicking of his heels on the polished concrete floor out in the garage that Wendt was walking fast, his entourage falling in behind him. I heard Mitchell Mason ask how it had gone in the office. He didn't get a reply.

After they left, Lorna hurried back to see me.

"What happened?" she asked.

"Nothing," I said. "He offered me two million in cash to convince Brenda to settle."

"And you told him no way?"

"Words to that effect. Will you reboot the cameras?"

"What's wrong with the cameras?"

"I think he knocked them out before they got here."

"Holy shit, they can do that?"

"They seem to be able to do anything…anything but stop me and this case."

# 42

AT TEN A.M. Friday I was ushered in to see Ali Adebayo at the district attorney's office. Adebayo's title was chief of the Conviction Integrity Unit, but in reality he was the only prosecutor assigned to it. DA McPherson learned shortly after taking office that she did not have the personnel to properly set up the unit she had promised to institute. She had a CIU sign made and posted on the door to Adebayo's office and tasked him with the job until the next budget could be squeezed for more staff.

Adebayo was a seasoned prosecutor whom I was familiar with from my days in criminal defense. When I entered the office I found he was not alone. His boss, my ex-wife and current roommate, was waiting with him.

"Why didn't you tell me you were bringing this in today?" she asked.

"Uh, because you're the DA and I thought it was best to go through proper channels," I said. "I didn't want any blowback to come to you or the case."

I reached across the desk to shake hands with Adebayo.

"Ali," I said. "It's been a minute."

"Yeah, I see you're over in the fed now," Adebayo said. "Tilting at tech windmills."

"Something like that. But we're off till Monday and this other case is time-sensitive."

"Well, let's hear it, then."

I looked at Maggie and she nodded. She was staying.

"Well, I only brought one copy with me," I began. "But I have a petition here and medical reports and statements from two different physicians who have examined the victim and reviewed her history."

I handed the file I was carrying across the desk. Adebayo took it and opened it. While he took the petition, Maggie took the backup statements and X-ray copies. My phone buzzed. I pulled it and checked the screen. I recognized the number as belonging to Judge Ruhlin's clerk. I sent the call to voicemail.

"What is this?" Maggie said. "These doctors made these statements based on these twenty-year-old photocopies?"

"Both doctors said the fractures were clear in the copies," I said.

"Where are the originals?"

"Uh, it looks like they're gone. The copies are from court archives. After the trial, the court allowed the lawyer who handled the appeal to take the originals."

"Who was that?"

"Joel Firestone. I don't know if you knew him. He died about ten years ago and somebody cleared out his office and got rid of the files from dead cases. The appeals had run their course."

Maggie shook her head, then looked back down at the documents and started reading one of the physician's statements. She seemed to be all business, as though I were any lawyer who had come in repping a convict. I knew it was the way it should be, but I couldn't help but wonder if the coldness was residual upset from the night before, when I told her about how Victor Wendt had tried to bribe me and what he had said about her insurance and rebuilding situation. It infuriated her that my case had resulted in such an invasion of her private life.

My phone buzzed. I pulled it and saw that it was the clerk calling again.

"Look, I'm going to step out and take this," I said. "I'll be in the hallway. Why don't you two keep reading."

I answered the call as I went through the door.

"Mr. Haller, Judge Ruhlin wants to see you in chambers forthwith," the clerk said.

"Uh, I'm in a meeting at the DA's office," I said. "Is this about the juror with COVID? Are more jurors sick?"

"I can't tell you what it's about, sir. But the judge said you need to get here forthwith."

"Are the Masons coming in?"

"They are on their way and you should be too."

"Okay. Tell the judge I'll be there."

"She asked that you bring your investigator as well."

"My investigator? Why does she need him to come?"

"Again, sir, I cannot discuss the matter with you. You must come in and speak to the judge."

"Okay, I'm on my way."

I disconnected and immediately called Cisco, but the call went to voicemail. I told him to meet me at the federal courthouse ASAP, then stepped back into Adebayo's office. He and Maggie had switched documents. Maggie was now holding the petition. I knew I had not been out of the room long enough for Adebayo to have thoroughly read the nine pages.

"You're just scanning it?" I asked.

"While you're here, I thought I'd just do a quick read," Adebayo said. "But I'll spend some time with it."

I nodded, suspicious of his true intentions.

"Well, I'm leaving," I said. "I just got a forthwith from the district court."

"Then go," Maggie said. "We wouldn't want to hold you up."

"Well, I mean, if you have questions, I'll answer them," I said. "It just seems like you're skimming it at the moment."

"No questions right now," Maggie said.

Very perfunctory. I waited for more, but nothing came. I looked at Adebayo.

"How about I call you after lunch?" I asked.

"We'll call you," Maggie answered. "Once we've thoroughly reviewed the material."

I nodded.

"Okay, then," I said. "I hope to hear from you."

I nodded again and headed for the door. I thought about Maggie's demeanor the whole walk to the federal courthouse half a block away. It crowded my head when I should have been thinking about the next meeting and why I had been called to Judge Ruhlin's chambers.

The courtroom appeared empty, but the clerk raised his head in the corral when he heard the door close behind me.

"They're in with the judge," he said.

"They?" I asked.

"The Masons just arrived."

"What about my investigator?"

"Not here."

"I called him. Send him back when he gets here."

"Oh, I will."

I made my way through the rear door of the courtroom and to the judge's chambers, checking my phone for messages as I went. The door was open but I heard no voices. I rapped my knuckles on the open door as I entered.

"Come in, Mr. Haller," the judge said. "Is your investigator with you?"

The judge was behind her desk, with Marcus and Mitchell Mason seated in front of her. I sat next to them.

"He's not here yet, Judge," I said. "I just got a text from him saying he is on his way."

"I have something to show you," Ruhlin said.

"Sure. Any word on how our sick juror is doing?"

"Well, I thought maybe *you* could tell us how she's doing."

I looked at the Masons for any clue as to what this was about. Mitchell's face was blank while Marcus looked smug, as usual.

"I don't understand, Judge," I said. "Why would I know how —"

"Let's just watch the video the court received this morning, shall we?" Ruhlin interrupted.

I raised my hand as if to say, *Lead the way.*

Ruhlin had an open laptop on the desk. She tapped a key and turned the screen toward the three attorneys sitting across from her. On it was the front of a small ranch house with white stucco walls and green shutters. It could have been one of thousands of small homes built in the Valley during the boom years after World War II. The lawn was neatly cut. There was a time stamp in the lower corner of the frame indicating that the video had been taken at 6:31 the night before. There was still natural light, and a lamp next to the front door was not on.

The frame of the video shook slightly, indicating that it was likely shot on a handheld camera or phone.

"What are we looking at here?" I asked.

"Just watch," Ruhlin said. "You'll get to tell me."

The video was silent until the thrum of an approaching motorcycle came through loud and clear. Soon a Harley panhead with orange flames painted on the gas tank moved into the frame and stopped at the front curb. I knew it was Cisco before he took off his helmet. I watched as he got off the bike and propped the helmet on the gas tank. He then crossed the lawn to the front door.

"Is that your investigator?" Ruhlin asked.

"It is," I said, my eyes not moving from the screen. "Dennis Wojciechowski."

"He looks like a biker."

"Well, sometimes it's a look that helps."

"Not this time."

There was no doubt about the anger in the judge's tone. On the video, Cisco pushed a doorbell and waited briefly for an answer before pushing the button again and knocking loudly enough to be picked up on the camera filming from across the street.

"Whose place is this?" I asked. "And who's taking the video?"

The judge held a hand up to silence me.

"Just watch," she said.

The lantern light next to the front door went on and the door swung open. At first, Cisco's large frame blocked the view of the person who had answered. Whoever it was, he was looking down at them. The verbal exchange was muffled but Cisco started gesturing with both hands, at one point holding them both up, palms out. It looked like a gesture of apology.

He then took a step back, revealing the woman who had answered the door. She was Black and wore a headscarf hiding her hair. She had on an open robe over a pink T-shirt and baggy blue sweatpants. She closed the door as Cisco turned away, but not before her face was clearly recognizable.

It was juror number eleven.

The judge scowled at me. It appeared from the video that my investigator had broken a cardinal rule of jurisprudence: He had attempted to make contact with a juror in the middle of a trial. There could be no excuse for such an act. I became aware that both Masons had turned to look at me with outrage written across their faces.

"Mr. Haller, do you know who that was on the screen with your investigator?" the judge asked.

"Yes," I said. "Juror eleven. The one with COVID."

"Do you know of any valid reason why Mr. Woja...the man you call Cisco would go to a juror's home?"

"I don't at the moment, Your Honor. But I'm sure there is an explanation."

"There'd better be, or he is going to jail—and you might be with him. This is a major breach of the protection and sanctity of the juror system."

"I don't disagree, Judge. But can I ask where this video came from?"

"It was sent anonymously to my clerk this morning."

I raised my hands and immediately realized I was making the same gesture Cisco made at the front door of juror eleven's house.

"Anonymous, Your Honor?" I said. "It obviously came from them."

I pointed at the Masons.

"The court was clear when it said earlier this week that surveillance and intimidation of the parties of this suit would not be tolerated," I continued. "But they've ignored that order and surveilled my team, and now they're sending anonymous videos of that surveillance to the court."

Marcus Mason shook his head as a smile cracked across his face.

"First of all, this did not come from us," he said. "But this is truly laughable. His investigator is caught crossing a line no one should ever cross, and he wants to blame whoever it was that caught him doing it? Your Honor, I think we have reached a new low with Mr. Haller."

I shook my head vehemently.

"No, the new low was when your boss came to my office yesterday and tried to bribe me with a briefcase full of cash," I said. "And this—"

"That never happened," Marcus shot back.

"You don't know," I said. "You weren't in the room. But I refused to take his money, so he set this up."

I pointed at the screen.

"How?" Marcus asked. "How did he set this up?"

"Good question, Mr. Haller," Ruhlin added.

The tension in the room was palpable. The judge was angry. The Masons were angry. I had to somehow make sure this didn't spill over into a mistrial.

"Judge, I don't know yet," I said as calmly as I could. "But this is a setup. That camera—whoever was holding it—was already in place when my investigator rolled up. That's clear on the video. They were waiting and hiding. Why?"

The logic of what I said seemed to hit everyone in the room as they realized that my observation was correct.

"Another good question," the judge said, turning her eyes to the Masons. "I seriously hope that what Mr. Haller is suggesting here is not the truth."

"Your Honor, again, we had nothing to do with this," Marcus said. "I can promise you that."

"Can you promise that Victor Wendt didn't have anything to do with it?" I asked.

The silence that followed that question was punctuated by a buzz from the judge's desk phone. She answered and then said, "Ask for a marshal to bring him back."

She hung up and looked at me.

"Your investigator is here," she said. "I can assure you, Mr. Haller, that if he says the wrong thing, he's going to jail."

# 43

**CISCO WASN'T EXACTLY** dressed for an audience with a federal judge. He was in faded jeans, boots, a tight-fitting white T-shirt, and a black leather riding jacket. He had gotten my message and obviously rode to the courthouse without any stops. I had known him for more than two decades and could read his face and demeanor. Judging by the way he raised an eyebrow when he saw me, he had no idea what he was walking into.

"Thank you, Deputy," Ruhlin said to the marshal who had escorted Cisco in. "If you could stand outside the door for me, I would appreciate that."

"Yes, ma'am," the marshal said.

He stepped out and Ruhlin directed Cisco to take one of the chairs from the table and bring it over to the desk. I moved my chair to make room for him to slide into the line of men facing the judge.

"Do you know why you are here, sir?" Ruhlin asked.

"I sure don't, Judge," Cisco responded.

"Well, I can show you."

"Please."

Ruhlin once again cued up the video and she turned the laptop so Cisco could watch it. She kept her eyes on him while it played. Cisco was nodding his head before it ended.

"Okay, that's me, if that's what you want to know," Cisco said.

"I know it's you," Ruhlin said sharply. "I want to know what you were doing there."

"Well, I was following a lead. Turned out to be a wild-goose chase and . . . that's it."

"Do you know who that woman is?"

Cisco shook his head.

"Uh, not really," he said. "She didn't give me the chance to find out."

"Are you telling this court that you didn't know that she is a juror in this case?" Ruhlin asked.

Cisco's head snapped back as if he had been punched in the jaw.

"Whoa, wait, no — in this case?" he said. "No, I didn't know she was a juror."

Cisco raised his right hand as if taking an oath to tell the truth, the whole truth, and nothing but the truth.

"We've been in trial all week," Ruhlin said. "How could you not know her?"

"Your Honor?" I said.

"Let him answer the question," Ruhlin ordered sharply.

"Judge, I wasn't paying much attention to the jury," Cisco said. "That's not really my job. I wasn't in court for jury selection, and during the trial I was dealing with getting witnesses to and from court and other duties. When she came to the door, she had a do-rag on her head and a robe, and I just didn't recognize her."

Ruhlin shook her head in frustration.

"Then what brought you to her door last night?" Ruhlin asked.

"I got a text," Cisco said. "On WhatsApp."

"It was encrypted?"

"Yes."

"And that didn't make you suspicious?"

"It did, but we get a lot of anonymous tips, Your Honor. I mean, that's my job — to run these down."

"And what did this tip say?"

"The texter said they had important information regarding a witness in the case. I responded and asked what witness, and the answer was *Wiseacre,* and that made it seem like it might be legitimate."

"How so?"

"There's a witness named Nathan Whittaker. He's a coder at Tidalwaiv, and we learned that his nickname is Wiseacre. Whittaker, Wiseacre — it's close."

"I understand. Go on."

"Well, seeing that nickname in the text gave it enough credibility that I decided I should check it out. I asked for a time and place to meet and I got that address."

He pointed at the laptop screen.

"I asked for a name and the texter gave me Robin," Cisco said. "No last name. I went over there at the meeting time, six thirty, as you can see, and the woman who answered the door said her name was Robin, but she didn't know what I was talking about or why I was there. I didn't recognize her and she apparently didn't remember me from court. At that point I thought I had bad info or something and left."

"And you didn't tell any of this to Mr. Haller?" Ruhlin asked.

"He went home yesterday afternoon to finish working on something, so I just went to the meeting. I usually don't bother him with stuff like this unless it pans out. This didn't, so I didn't even mention it. If she had told me she was a juror, I would obviously have sounded the alarm and said I was set up. But she didn't, and I didn't know about any of this till right now."

Ruhlin stared at Cisco for a long moment, apparently trying to judge his truthfulness, before she finally spoke.

"Would you be willing to let me look at these texts you received?" she asked.

"Uh, sure," Cisco said hesitantly.

He looked at me as he leaned to his left to reach into his back pocket. I nodded my approval even though he didn't need it. He pulled out his phone, opened WhatsApp, and located the texts in question. He handed the phone to the judge, screen up. She took it, read the texts, and nodded.

"And you say this was encrypted," she said. "It can't be traced?"

"Well, when I realized I was at the wrong address, I called that number," Cisco said. "The line was dead—number no longer valid. But I have a...friend who, uh, can run down numbers for me. I gave it to him and he said the text came from a burner phone. So, yeah, we're not going to be able to trace it."

"Okay, Mr.... uh..."

"Wojciechowski—pronounced like 'Watch your car key.' My father always said that when people had trouble with it."

"Thank you, Mr. Watch-your-car-key. I think you can go now. And can you ask the deputy marshal to step back in?"

"Sure, Judge. Thank you."

The big man stood up and gave me a nod. He returned his chair to the meeting table on his way to the door. He left and the marshal came in.

"You can go now, Jaime," the judge said. "Everything is fine."

Once the marshal was gone and the door to chambers was closed, Ruhlin focused on the Mason brothers, giving them the same scowl she had directed earlier at me.

"Is there anything you men wish to say to me?" she asked.

"Your Honor, we had nothing to do with this," Mitchell Mason said.

"Nothing," Marcus Mason added.

"Then who did?" Ruhlin pressed.

"This could have been set up by them," Mitchell said, pointing to me. "So this would happen, so we'd get the blame."

I shook my head.

"You know, Judge, I was just about to say that I give them the benefit of the doubt," I said. "But then they have to go and try to throw me under the bus."

"All I will say at this time is that I will be in contact with the US Marshals Service and call for a full investigation of this matter," Ruhlin said. "Jury tampering will not be tolerated by this court. In the meantime, I will be dismissing juror eleven and we will proceed Monday if the other jurors remain healthy."

I held my hands up in confusion.

"Your Honor, you're penalizing the plaintiff for being the injured party here," I said.

"How do you see that, Mr. Haller?" Ruhlin asked.

"If the court recalls, during jury selection the defense clearly didn't want juror eleven, a Black woman, on the panel. It was only when I objected and the court agreed with me that they reversed their position. So what they couldn't do then, they just succeeded in doing now. Maybe that was their thinking all along: *If we can't get a mistrial, we'll pick off the jurors we don't like.*"

"Your Honor, I vigorously object," Marcus Mason yelped. "Thirty seconds ago he was giving us the benefit of the doubt. Now he's accusing us of this crazy scheme to get one juror kicked off the panel. It's preposterous and insulting and I object."

"We're not in front of the jury, Mr. Mason," Ruhlin said. "No need to object. But are you saying you would accept number eleven staying on the jury?"

"No, she's been tainted by this whole thing," Marcus said. "She can't stay on the jury. No matter who set this in motion, we can't lose sight of the fact that a member of the plaintiff's team crossed a line and knocked on a juror's door. It means she's gotta go."

"The fact that this was clearly a setup means she should stay," I said.

Ruhlin didn't respond as she considered the arguments.

"The weekend is upon us," she finally said. "When juror eleven is healthy, I will question her about this. You will have my decision on all this Monday morning."

"Your Honor, may I speak?" I asked.

"If you can be brief," Ruhlin said.

"There is still the issue that obviously someone would have had to follow this juror home to set this whole thing up," I said. "This concerns me. How many other jurors were followed home? How many are being watched?"

"I can assure you, that will be part of the investigation by the US Marshals Service," the judge said. "But, Mr. Haller, this reminds me — you made an alarming statement a few minutes ago about attempted bribery. Please tell me more."

"Victor Wendt, the founder of Tidalwaiv, came to see me at my office yesterday," I said. "He was accompanied by both Mr. Masons but insisted on meeting me privately in my office while they waited outside. He had a briefcase with him and he showed me its contents. Two million dollars in cash. Hundred-dollar bills. He said it was mine if I convinced my client to take the last settlement offer proffered by the company. I said no."

"Your Honor, this didn't happen," Marcus said. "He can't prove any of that and he knows it."

"Well, he might have knocked out my cameras to make it impossible to prove visually," I said. "But, Judge, I would invite you to ask the Masons to confirm that they accompanied their client to my office yesterday."

Ruhlin squinted at the Masons. Before she took me up on my suggestion, Marcus Mason spoke.

"Your Honor, Mr. Wendt may have met privately with plaintiff's counsel, but that proves nothing," he said. "He was, in fact, there to personally ask counsel to reconsider the offer to settle the case. There was no money, no bribe. That is pure invention by counsel."

I waved off the statement and the entire argument. I knew this would go nowhere. It was time to move on. I had done what I could to throw shade on the actions of the defense team and their client.

The judge also knew it was time to move on.

"Gentlemen, you are excused," she said. "I will see you Monday morning promptly at nine, when you will have my decisions. Good day."

"Thank you, Judge," I said.

The Masons said the same. As we filed out of chambers into the hallway leading back to the courtroom, we were silent. It felt more awkward than the times we had sniped at each other while returning to court.

The judge's clerk passed us, heading the other way, obviously summoned to chambers by Ruhlin. When we reached the courtroom, it was empty except for Cisco sitting in the first row of the gallery. The Masons went through the gate and passed by him without so much as a glance in his direction. I stopped in front of him.

"So?" Cisco said.

I waited until the courtroom door closed behind the Masons.

"So, she's going to ask the marshals to investigate," I said. "They'll want to talk to you."

"No doubt," Cisco said.

"Are you sure about what you said, about the burner not being traceable?"

"They'll be able to tell what cell towers the messages came through. But that's as close as they'll ever get. Why, Mick?"

"Just curious."

"Hey, Mick..."

"What?"

"I mean, I know what you did with Bamba up north. I figured that out. But this? I mean, the judge could've put me in jail."

"Are you asking if I sent you—"

"No, never mind. I don't want to know. Better that way."

"How would I even know where that juror lives? This is them, Cisco. If not the Masons, then Tidalwaiv and Victor Wendt's team. Wendt tried to bribe me yesterday. He's desperate, and this thing with the juror? That has desperation written all over it. I think they know Whittaker is going to blow their case up and they're doing whatever they can to end this by settlement or mistrial."

Cisco nodded as he followed the logic of my words.

"You're right. Never mind what I said."

"Okay, then," I said. "You can head home now."

"Wait, what about the juror? In or out?"

"We'll find out Monday. But I think the judge will keep her. She doesn't seem interested in doing the Mason boys any favors at the moment."

"That's good."

I nodded as Cisco stood up to leave.

"We'll see what happens Monday," I said. "Have a good weekend. Call me if anything comes up."

"Yeah, Mick, you do the same."

Cisco headed to the courtroom door. When he got there he turned around and saw that I had not moved from the railing that divided the gallery from the lawyer tables and the judge's bench.

"You coming?" he asked.

"You go ahead," I said. "I'm going to hang out for a few minutes."

"Have a good one."

"Yeah."

Once Cisco was gone, I walked back through the gate and stood in front of the empty jury box. It was the proving ground where I would make my final stand in the case. I faced the two rows of leather seats in the box. There was a time in my life when I believed this was sacred ground. But now it seemed that nothing was sacred anymore. Not the rule of law, and not those who practiced it.

# 44

**MAGGIE'S CAR WAS** in the garage when I pulled in. She wasn't in the front room but I saw an open bottle of red wine on the counter when I glanced into the kitchen while passing through the house. I found her on the back deck. There wasn't much here, just a table and chairs, a Weber grill, and a hot tub we never used, and no view of the city. All you could see was a hedge and part of the neighbor's house above us on the hillside street.

"Mags, what are you doing back here?" I asked.

"Nothing," she said. "Just having a glass of wine."

"You want to sit in the front, watch the sun go down?"

"No, I'm happy here."

I started stripping off my tie.

"I'm going to change and then I'll be back out here."

"You don't have to. You can go watch the sunset."

"Is something wrong?"

"You should have told me."

"What, about going to see Adebayo? Why? I mean, I can't go to the DA herself every time I have a case. That would look bad for both of us."

"This case you should have brought to me. It would have saved you the embarrassment. Saved me too."

"What are you talking about? What embarrassment?"

"The case isn't there, Mickey. You're taking a wild swing at your own redemption over a case you think you should have won twenty years ago."

"You're passing?"

"Yes, we're passing. Monday you'll get the formal reject from Adebayo. This whole thing could have been avoided if you had just shown it to me first."

I pulled out a chair and sat down. I started thinking about how I would break the news to David and Cassandra Snow. I tried to mentally review the petition I had spent a day writing. I was sure all of the elements of habeas were there. New evidence unavailable at the time of conviction, medical research, medical witnesses — I had everything.

"It was all there," I said. "Why was it rejected? I don't want to wait till Monday. Just tell me."

"We had no choice," Maggie said. "It took only a search of the National Institutes of Health website to see that osteogenesis imperfecta was first described a hundred fifty years ago. Mickey, you have her condition right, but you should have had it back then. It's not new evidence."

"No, it was not diagnosed back then. Her mother wasn't around to give a history, and the specific genetic test for her type of OI wasn't available at the time. That is the new evidence. If I didn't make that clear I can rewrite the petition. Whatever you need."

"I just need you to stop, Mickey. It's not happening."

I ran a hand through my hair.

"You can always take it to federal court," Maggie said.

"He'll be dead before we get to the first hearing," I said. "That's the whole reason I went to you. He's dying and his daughter wants to get him out."

"Well, but you didn't come to me. You went around me."

"Jesus, I did not. I went through established channels. It would have been inappropriate to take this directly to you. Is that what this is really about? I could tell you were upset before you even looked at the petition. My client is being punished because you think I did something wrong."

"It's not that, and you know it. It's a decision based on the law. Look, you were a young lawyer back then. You didn't know what you know now. It's the same with all of us, and we all have to live with the mistakes we made and the cases we lost."

I shook my head. What she said was true of all lawyers, but it was not true of the case at hand. I was devastated by the decision.

"I can't believe this," I said. "This guy has spent twenty years in prison for something he didn't do. I know it, his daughter knows it. And now it's a death sentence."

"I'm sorry," Maggie said.

"So am I."

# 45

MAGGIE AND I kept our distance over the weekend. Rather than work in the back office of the house, I went downtown to work at the warehouse and prepare for the trial week ahead. I couldn't know for sure how Judge Ruhlin would decide on the future of juror eleven or the petition for mistrial, but I needed to be ready for all possibilities. To that end, I met with Jack McEvoy for three hours on Saturday, and together we structured the direct examination of Nathan Whittaker, the Tidalwaiv coder I planned to put on the stand as my last witness. By the end of the session I was confident I would be able to use Whittaker to show the jury, whether it was composed of eleven or twelve members, how the programming of Clair could have been tainted and led to the violent end of Rebecca Randolph's life.

On Saturday night I had a quiet dinner with Maggie at the Musso and Frank Grill. We mostly talked about our daughter and the architect Maggie had just hired to design the rebuild on her home. We didn't discuss the Snow case at all, and Alessio, the restaurant manager, fawned over us enough to distract our thoughts from the gulf that had opened between us. Until dessert, that is. After the sand dabs, we ordered a slice of cheesecake to share, and it was then that Maggie floated the idea of moving out of the house on Fareholm.

"Maggie, you don't have to move," I said. "I want you to stay with me."

"Well, you don't like me very much right now," she said.

"That's not true, and even if it were, I'd get past it. We're on opposite sides of a case. But this is about our life. I somehow feel that everything that's happened, the fire and everything, was meant to bring us back together. I know that sounds like over-the-top magical thinking, but it's what I feel. And the Snow case, it's just a test to see how strong we are. How strong we could be."

"What about that tech billionaire sticking his nose into my business? Is that a test too?"

"Look, I know that's disturbing, and rightfully so, but he was just using you to try to get to me. I'm going to pay him back for that in court. You don't have to worry about it."

"You hope so."

"I know so."

"Don't be overconfident."

"Act like a winner and you'll be a winner."

"Legal Siegel—I know you miss him."

"Yeah, but I had a good day prepping for my next witness and the knockout punch I'm going to deliver after that. So I don't have to act—I am confident."

"You know, you often talk in terms of physical violence when you talk about court. Have you noticed that?"

"Sounds appropriate to me. It's a no-holds-barred fight. The Octagon. Even in civil. Maybe even more so in civil."

With that, I looked out of our booth and signaled to Luis, our red-coated waiter, for the check.

I stayed on a roll until Sunday night, when I met Cassandra Snow for dinner. I didn't want to deliver the bad news by email or text or phone. She picked the place based on ease of access, and we met at the Lab on Figueroa by USC. I got right to the point before we ordered food or even told the waiter what kind of water we wanted.

"We've had a setback with the DA's office," I said. "They're going to pass on the petition."

She shook her head, then held still while she composed herself.

"Did they say why?" she asked.

"They believe the medical evidence that you had OI was available to me at the time of the trial," I said quietly.

"But that's not true."

"It is and it isn't. They're taking the position that people have known about OI for a long time, so it could have been diagnosed then. I think they're wrong, and that's why I will still take this to US district court."

"That will take forever. My father doesn't have that kind of time."

"I'll be asking for an emergency hearing."

"What are our chances of getting that?"

"Those are long odds, but I have another plan too. If you're willing, we go to the media. We find someone who gets this stuff, we give them everything we have and let them interview your doctors, and we get a story that puts pressure on the DA's office to reconsider their decision."

"Who are you thinking of going to?"

"Well, there's a bunch of people covering the trial I'm in right now. I could go to one of them. I just have to figure out which one. I'm also working with a guy on my team who's a writer and did some of the research for the petition I filed. He's been in media and has some connections. He said yesterday that he knows a producer for CBS News who might be able to get it to *Sixty Minutes*."

"Does anybody really care about those kinds of shows anymore? Trust in media is at an all-time low."

"That might be true, but the story wouldn't have to have a high viewership to have an impact. Believe me, the district attorney's office is as political as it gets in this town. Somebody from *Sixty Minutes* calling up about this case would freeze them in their tracks and make them think twice about their decision to reject the petition."

"Do you think that will work?"

"If *Sixty Minutes* or the right media comes on board, it couldn't hurt. Are you okay with me pursuing it? You'd obviously have to be part of the story."

"You know I'll do anything if it helps get my father out."

I nodded solemnly.

"I will too," I said.

# 46

ALL PARTIES TO the Tidalwaiv lawsuit sat at the courtroom tables for forty-five minutes Monday morning while Judge Ruhlin spoke privately in chambers with juror eleven. It was only when the juror came through the door into the clerk's corral and crossed the courtroom to the door to the jury assembly room that I got an idea of how the judge was going to rule on the matters before the court.

At ten a.m. Ruhlin took the bench and quickly dispensed with the issues before calling in the jury to proceed with trial.

"I have interviewed juror eleven and am satisfied that there has been no damage to the integrity of the jury," she announced. "She will remain on the jury. The defense motion for a mistrial is also denied by this court. Juror eleven tested negative for COVID as of yesterday morning and no other jurors have tested positive. The deputy marshal will bring the jurors in so we can continue in the case of *Randolph versus Tidalwaiv LLC*."

I turned and nodded to Brenda Randolph, then glanced back at the first row of the gallery, where Lorna and Jack sat. I gave Lorna the nod, meaning she should tell Cisco to bring the next witness in. As I turned back, Mitchell Mason stood to address the court.

"Your Honor, can I be heard?" he asked.

"No, you cannot, Mr. Mason," Ruhlin said. "We are not going to relitigate the matter. I've made my ruling and trial will continue. The jury is coming in."

Five minutes later, I had Nathan Whittaker sworn in and seated in the witness chair in front of the jury. This was what I had prepared for since the moment Naomi Kitchens had mentioned him as a coder on Project Clair. I believed the case could swing on Whittaker's testimony alone. He was part of a one-two punch at the end of my case that I hoped would lead to a knockout.

Whittaker looked to be in his early thirties, with glasses, slick black hair pulled up into a topknot, and shaved sidewalls. He gave the impression of being a man who spent a lot of time in front of a mirror, working on his look.

"Mr. Whittaker, thank you for being here," I began. "Can you tell the jury what you do for a living?"

"I'm an artificial intelligence programmer," Whittaker replied.

"Could you pull the microphone a little closer so we make sure everybody can hear you?"

Whittaker did so.

"An AI programmer," I said. "Is that the same as a coder?"

"Yes, that's right," Whittaker said. "Coding is a big part of programming overall."

"And who are you employed by?"

"Tidalwaiv."

"Tidalwaiv is located in Palo Alto. Is that where you reside?"

"No, I live in San Mateo. Not too far away."

"How long have you worked at Tidalwaiv?"

"Eleven years."

"And how old are you?"

"Thirty-three."

"Is Tidalwaiv the only place you've worked since finishing school?"

"It is, yes."

"Where did you go to school?"

"Stanford."

"Are you married?"

"I don't know what that has to do with anything, but no, I'm not married."

"Now, were you a coder on Project Clair?"

"I was, yes."

"For how long?"

"Almost seven years."

"Was that from the inception of the project?"

"No, I came in after. The architecture was already built, and I started during the programming phase."

"Is that also known as the training phase?"

"Some people call it that. Training and testing."

"Now, Project Clair continues, correct? It never stops."

"It continues to be monitored and maintained, if that's what you mean."

"It's exactly what I mean. But you are not part of Project Clair anymore, correct?"

"Correct again. It's like you're asking questions you already know the answers to."

He smiled and I smiled back. If what I had asked had already gotten under his skin, then Whittaker was in for a long day. I checked the jury to make sure they were all paying attention. Only one juror had his head down, and that was because he was writing something in his notebook. Hopefully it was a note on his negative impression of Whittaker.

I turned back to the witness, ready to take things up a notch.

"Mr. Whittaker, why were you removed from Project Clair after seven years?"

"I wasn't removed, I was transferred to another project where coders were needed."

"So it was a promotion?"

"It was a lateral move but a more important project."

"Really? What was more important than an AI companion being programmed for children?"

"I mean it was financially more important to the company."

"And what was that project?"

"The answer to your question would reveal proprietary information, which I am not allowed to do publicly unless given permission by Tidalwaiv."

He said it in a clearly rehearsed way that I was sure the jurors picked up on.

"We wouldn't want you to give up company secrets, Mr. Whittaker," I said. "Let's move on. When were you laterally transferred from Project Clair to this secret project you're on now?"

"It's not a secret project within the company," Whittaker responded.

"Got it. Just secret from the public. Can you—"

Mitchell Mason objected to the commentary I was supposedly injecting into my questions. Judge Ruhlin advised me to make sure the sentences I directed to the witness had question marks at the end.

"Will do, Your Honor," I said. "Mr. Whittaker, could you answer the question? When were you laterally moved from Project Clair to your current position at Tidalwaiv?"

"It would have been almost two years ago," Whittaker said.

"Can you be more precise than that?"

"Uh, I began 2024 in the new position."

"That would be about four months after the killing of Rebecca Randolph, correct?"

"If you say so. I don't know the date of that, because it had nothing to do with my transfer to the new project."

"Well, let's see. If you started last year in the new position, then were you told of the transfer before, say, December 2023?"

"To be honest, I don't remember. Like I said, one thing didn't have anything to do with the other."

"Then let me ask you this, since you say you are being honest. When did—"

Mitchell Mason was quickly up on his feet and objecting to the sarcastic tone I had employed in my unfinished question.

"Mr. Haller, you have been warned," Ruhlin said. "Be civil and on point with your questions. No innuendo needed."

"Yes, Your Honor," I said. "My apologies if I got carried away."

I glanced at the jury to make sure they were still paying attention before going back at Whittaker. If Mitchell Mason was upset with my sarcasm now, he was going to go ballistic with where I went next.

"Mr. Whittaker, were you aware that in December 2023, a month before your lateral transfer took place, a lawsuit was filed against Tidalwaiv claiming gross negligence and product liability in the death of Rebecca Randolph?"

"No, I was not!"

Whittaker said it a little too loudly, a little too sharply, and a little too self-righteously for it to be taken as anything but a rehearsed answer. It was what I had hoped for.

"Then, when did you learn about this lawsuit?" I asked.

"Um, I don't remember exactly," Whittaker said.

"So you remember quite well that your transfer had nothing to do with the lawsuit, but you don't remember when you first learned of the lawsuit—do I have that right?"

Mitchell objected again, claiming that I was badgering the witness, but Ruhlin shot it down quickly and told the witness to answer.

"I just don't remember exact dates," Whittaker said. "Why are the dates such a big deal?"

"Mr. Whittaker, the way it works is I ask you the questions," I responded.

"Right. Then ask a question."

"Okay, here's a question. Were you told that you were being moved out of Project Clair because you were a liability in this lawsuit and —"

"No, I was not!"

"That they were trying to hide you from scrutiny?"

"That's a lie!"

Both Mason brothers jumped up to object and the judge called for silence in the courtroom, then signaled the lawyers up for a sidebar. She turned on the white-noise device so the jury would not hear our words.

"Okay, we have some high temperatures here," she began. "I don't want things to get out of hand in front of our jury."

"Your Honor, he's baiting the witness with every question," Marcus Mason said.

"I'm asking questions that need to be asked," I said. "This man is at the heart of this case, Judge. I'm not going to take it easy on the guy who —"

"Okay, okay," Ruhlin said, cutting me off. "I understand the importance of this witness, but he also is quite volatile. You are walking a fine line, Mr. Haller. I am not going to turn this trial into a free-for-all fight. Is that understood?"

"Judge, I understand," I said. "But I have a lot to ask this man, and some of these questions he's not going to like. And neither will his lawyers."

"We're not his lawyers!" Marcus exclaimed.

"You prepped him," I said. "He's yours."

"Okay, stop right there," Ruhlin said. "We're not going to get into a dispute over that. I'm going to break now, and hopefully cooler heads will return to the courtroom afterward. Step back, please."

We went back to our respective tables and the judge called for a fifteen-minute recess.

"I'm sorry that is not enough time to get out of the building to get some fresh air," Ruhlin said to the jury. "But stretch your legs, use the facilities if you have to, and be back in fifteen minutes so we can continue testimony. Remember the cautions: Do not discuss the case with each other or anyone else. Thank you."

I remained sitting with my client as the courtroom cleared.

"This man — you think he's responsible?" Brenda asked me.

I turned to look at her.

"I do, yes," I whispered.

"But there must have been many programmers on the project," she said. "How could he be the only one responsible?"

"He's not the only one, Brenda. But he represents the company's carelessness. That's all we need to get across to the jury. It's the rotten-apple theory. We are saying that one bad apple — Whittaker — spoils the whole barrel. If we get that message through to the jury —"

"We win?"

"That's right. We win."

# 47

ONCE WE WERE back on the record in front of the jury, I decided to take it slow with Nathan Whittaker and work my way to the line of questions I knew were going to be incendiary and might cross the fine line the judge said I was walking. Whittaker had returned to the witness stand calm and collected. I assumed he had spent the break with the Mason brothers counseling him on how to control his temper and deal with hostile questions. It didn't matter. My hostility was real but had been curated and choreographed over the weekend with the help of Jack McEvoy. I was sure hostilities would rise again before the day was out.

"Mr. Whittaker, let's go in a new direction," I said. "Without revealing any company secrets or proprietary information, can you describe the difference between the lifestyle division and the business division of Tidalwaiv Technologies?"

"It's pretty simple, really," Whittaker said. "Lifestyle is entertainment and home-based products, and business is business. You know, business solutions powered by artificial intelligence."

"And isn't it true that when you were removed from Project Clair shortly after this lawsuit was filed, you were moved from the lifestyle division to the business division?"

"I'm really getting tired of saying this. I wasn't removed. I was asked to take a transfer and I said yes."

"You were asked...by whom?"

"Andy Spiegel, who runs development on the business side."

"Okay, so you went from lifestyle apps to business apps. What kind of business apps?"

"Again, you're asking me to violate company rules by revealing proprietary information."

"Okay, let me ask you this, then. Hypothetically, if I owned a car dealership and I wanted to put an AI receptionist on my website to help visitors navigate the site, would I go to Tidalwaiv's lifestyle or business division for that?"

"Business, obviously."

"And so you're telling this jury that moving from programming a generative AI companion for children to a car-dealer chatbot was a lateral move?"

"I got the same paycheck, okay? And the business applications are far more—"

Mitchell Mason objected, saying I was twisting the witness's answers, and the judge sustained it.

"Move on, Mr. Haller," she said. "I think you've made your points here."

I was glad the judge had announced in front of the jury that I had scored some points. I pivoted in a new direction.

"Okay, moving on," I said. "Mr. Whittaker, you are fairly active on social media, are you not, sir?"

"Uh, *active* is a pretty general word," Whittaker said. "And I'm not sure what it's got to do with this."

"Okay, then, very specifically, do you frequent the Reddit threads on artificial intelligence?"

"I've been on those boards, yes, but I wouldn't say frequently."

Whittaker's coyness seemed misplaced. He must have been told by the Masons that I had put several of his Reddit posts into discovery. He knew they were coming, so I didn't understand why he didn't just acknowledge that he was often on the platform. Maybe this just further revealed his combative personality, or maybe he knew what else I had gathered on him outside of the discovery materials.

"Whether it's frequent or not, can you tell the jury what username you post under on Reddit?" I asked.

"Well, I've used a few over the years," Whittaker said.

Evasive again. I loved it.

"How about wiseacre-twenty-three?" I asked. "Was that one of your usernames on Reddit? A play on the name Whittaker?"

"Uh, it might have been," Whittaker said. "Like I said, I don't go on there very often."

"My investigator found sixty-seven posts from wiseacre-twenty-three on the 'artificial intelligence' and 'AI watch' threads on Reddit in the past three years. Some of them were signed Nate, some NW. Five contain the phrase *at Tidalwaiv* or *here at Tidalwaiv*. Are you saying these posts were not made by you?"

"I'm saying I can't remember every post I've ever made and every username I've ever used."

Whittaker looked at the jury and shook his head like he didn't understand why these questions were so important. I loved that too.

"You played on the Project Clair softball team as part of the Tidalwaiv intramural program, correct?" I asked.

"Uh, yes, for a couple seasons," Whittaker said suspiciously.

"You also played against other Silicon Valley tech teams, right?"

"Yes. For a time. But I don't think it has to do with this."

"You put the name *Wiseacre* on the back of your jersey, did you not?"

Whittaker didn't answer at first. He acted like he was trying to recall some distant, unimportant factoid.

"I really can't remember," he finally said.

"Well, let me see if I can jog your memory," I said. "Your Honor, can I have the court's permission to show the witness a photo from a company e-zine called *Ride the Wave* dated April fifth, 2023, that contains photos of the Tidalwaiv softball team?"

"You may proceed," Ruhlin said.

I walked copies of the photos to the clerk and the Mason brothers before handing one to Whittaker. It was an action shot of one player tagging another player sliding into third base. The third baseman's back was to the camera. The name on the jersey was clearly legible as *Wiseacre* and the number was 23.

"Mr. Whittaker, is that you making the tag at third base in that photo?" I asked.

"It would seem to be," Whittaker said.

"'Seem to be'? Are you saying there is a possibility that it's not you?"

"No, it's me, okay? It's me."

"And what number did you put on your jersey?"

"I didn't put it there. It came with the shirt."

"What number is it?"

"Twenty-three, but like I said, that was random. It came with the shirt and then I had them put *Wiseacre* on the back."

"Are you sure that you did not request the number twenty-three to go with *Wiseacre* on the shirt?"

"Yes, I'm sure."

"Are you aware that several of the wiseacre-twenty-three posts on the Reddit threads predate the years you were on the softball team wearing a uniform that said *Wiseacre* and had the number twenty-three?"

"Uh, no, I am not."

"Are you telling the jury that that is just a coincidence?"

"I'm not telling the jury anything. I said I don't remember all the details. What's the point?"

"The point is, Mr. Whittaker, I am trying to determine if you made the posts on Reddit under the username wiseacre-twenty-three."

"Whatever, yes. It was probably me."

"It was probably you, or it was you?"

"Fine, it was me. So I made some posts. I have nothing to hide."

I looked up at the judge and asked permission to show the witness a series of posts authored by wiseacre23 and copied from Reddit for the purposes of identification.

"You are not going to go through sixty-seven of these, are you?" Ruhlin asked.

"No, Your Honor," I said. "I'm really interested only in one, if Mr. Whittaker can confirm he wrote it."

"Misters Mason, any objection?" the judge asked.

"Hard to object when it's not clear what Mr. Haller is trying to get from this fishing expedition," Mitchell Mason said.

"I'll take that as a no," Ruhlin said. "Mr. Haller, you may show it to the witness and put it on the screen for the jury."

I gave a copy of the post to Whittaker while Lorna put it on the courtroom screen. The post was a fairly innocuous and short response to someone else's post about artificial intelligence being the downfall of humankind. The response from wiseacre23 was a caution.

> It's time to wake up and smell the data, HaiTER. AI is like everything else. You get what you give. It's GIGO.

That's all you need to know. Sooner or later we're all going to be slaves to the machine. Best to get on the AI ship before it sails away without you, dude.

I gave Whittaker and the jury a moment to read the post before starting my last lap around this witness.

"Mr. Whittaker, did this post come from you?" I asked.

"Looks like it," Whittaker said.

"I draw your attention to the acronym GIGO. What did you mean by that?"

"That stands for *garbage in, garbage out*."

"And what does that mean to you when it comes to programming artificial intelligence?"

"Exactly what it says. If you put in garbage, that's what you'll get back."

"So by 'garbage,' you are talking about bad programming, programming contradictory or possibly damaging to the purpose of the app?"

"Correct."

"This would include the biases of the programmers too, would it not?"

"Uh, if there were biases, yeah."

"Everybody has biases, don't they?"

It was a perfect question because it was a lose-lose for Whittaker. No matter how he answered, he'd be setting up my next line of questioning. Of course Mitchell Mason recognized this and objected before Whittaker could attempt an answer.

"The question is too broad," he said. "Counsel is just trying to bait the witness into an answer he can twist into an admission of some sort."

"And defense counsel is trying to communicate directly with the witness with his objection," I said. Then, looking at Mason, I added, "Good job, Mitch. Message delivered."

"I'll sustain the objection to the question being too broad," Ruhlin said. "And please direct all arguments to the court and not each other."

I retooled the question to make it slim enough to get past an objection.

"Do you have biases, Mr. Whittaker?" I asked.

"No, I don't think so," he answered.

"Really? No biases at all?"

"If I do, I keep them out of my code."

"Are you sure?"

"Absolutely."

"What other social media sites do you post on?"

"Not that many."

"How about Four-chan and Eight-kun? How often do you frequent those sites?"

"I don't even know what they are."

"Really, now? What about a site called Dirty-four? Did you ever go on that?"

"Nope."

"Why is it wiseacre twenty-three? Is twenty-three your birthday or an anniversary?"

"It's just a random number."

"Does it signify the twenty-third of May 2014, when a man named Elliot Rodger, an incel like yourself, killed several young women outside a sorority house in—"

"Objection!" the Mason brothers exclaimed in unison.

The judge pointed across the bench at me.

"Not another word, Mr. Haller," she barked.

I raised my hands, palms up, in surrender. The judge then sent the jury out for an early lunch and instructed the lawyers to follow her to chambers. We did so silently, because we were close on the judge's heels. As we entered her chambers, she shook off the black robe and, with sharp, angry moves, put it on a hanger and hooked it on the coatrack. She then turned and fixed me with a withering stare.

"Mr. Haller, what the hell do you think you're doing, provoking a witness like that?" she asked. "And making an inflammatory statement in front of the jury?"

I held my hands up again, this time in what I hoped was a calming manner. I spoke without raising my voice.

"'I don't even know what they are,'" I said. "I believe those were the exact words the witness said when I asked about two well-known and established sites frequented by men who advocate violence against women."

"Oh my God, what bullshit," Marcus Mason said.

We were all still standing, too upset for different reasons to sit down.

"Language, Mr. Mason," Ruhlin said. "Mr. Haller, where are you going with this?"

"Your Honor, the witness is an incel," I said. "His misogyny and other biases infected the programming of Project Clair and directly led to Wren espousing those views to Aaron Colton. He then—"

"And you can prove this?" Ruhlin asked.

I didn't hesitate.

"By the time we get to rebuttal, I'll be able to prove it," I said. "The username wiseacre-twenty-three is all over screen captures from those sites going back at least seven years. I have a digital linguistics expert comparing the wording of those posts to those Whittaker just acknowledged posting on Reddit. I walked him right into it. It's him, and his bias is that he hates women. That hate ended up in the code in Clair. Garbage in, garbage out, Your Honor. Hate in, hate out. You end up with a chatbot that says, 'Get rid of her.'"

Both Masons looked ashen. Both knew, as did the judge, that every case hit a point of no return, when the pendulum has swung too far to one side or the other and is not coming back. This was that point.

Mitchell was the first to recover and respond. Weakly.

"Your Honor, counsel has obviously crossed so many lines in the rules of discovery that these questions cannot be allowed," he said.

"It didn't become discoverable until Whittaker sat up there and lied on the stand," I said. "I'd be happy to turn over copies of his hate screeds after lunch."

"You mentioned something called Dirty-four," Ruhlin said. "What is that?"

"It was a site on the dark web that was shut down by law enforcement four years ago," I said. "Subscribers could download the identities of women whose DNA carried a genetic combination linked to promiscuity and risky lifestyles."

"This is pure science fiction," Marcus Mason said.

"The FBI didn't think so after several murders were linked to the site," I said.

"And you have evidence that this witness was involved?" Ruhlin asked.

"I have evidence that wiseacre-twenty-three was a subscriber," I said.

There was no comeback from either of the Masons. Even the judge was silent for a long moment before looking directly at the twins and speaking.

"In light of these developments, I believe you two need to huddle with your client," she said. "I'll have the deputy marshals pass the word to the jurors that we are in recess until nine o'clock tomorrow morning. You'll have till then to determine whether we continue the trial with this witness...or not."

She paused to see if there would be any pushback from the Masons. They offered none.

"Very well, then," she said. "You may all go."

We did the silent single-file exit again, the Masons leading the way with their heads down. When we got to the courtroom, Marcus Mason started gathering his folders and notepads from the defense table. He spoke without looking at me.

"I know you're bluffing, Haller," he said. "You don't have shit."

"Keep thinking that," I said. "I want this to go to a verdict. Based on the Wall Street valuation of the company, I put the over-under on punitive damages at four hundred. Million, that is. What's that going to do to the stock?"

Marcus scoffed.

"Keep dreaming," he said.

I grabbed a paper-clipped document out of a folder on my table and walked it over to them.

"Here's your lunchtime reading assignment," I said. "Sorry I have only one copy."

Marcus took it from me and scanned it. Mitchell leaned over his shoulder to get a look.

"What's this, more bullshit?" Marcus asked.

"You are really a one-note guy, aren't you?" I said. "It's a motion I'll submit as soon as I finish destroying Whittaker."

This time it was Mitchell who scoffed as he read, apparently faster than his twin.

"You think she's going to let you put Wren up as a witness?" he asked incredulously. "An AI witness?"

"You can't even put it under oath," Marcus said, catching up.

"Well, that's the plan," I said. "The malice here originates with the guy who infected the code with his hate, but the entity is a co-conspirator. The jury has a right to hear what it says, how it supposedly thinks, and how it came to advocate murder. It's a novel argument now but it won't be for long. As Mr. Wendt told me when he tried to bribe me, the company is called Tidalwaiv because there is no stopping this. I see a future where AI entities are regular witnesses at trial."

They said nothing. Mitchell continued to read the motion, his face growing whiter as he realized it had a chance. I wasn't so sure about that myself but had written it as a final salvo to launch after the Whittaker testimony wrapped. It might not get past the judge, but it would probably make some headlines.

I put all my own paperwork into my briefcase and snapped it shut.

"Tomorrow, boys," I said.

At the gate, I stopped and looked back at them.

"Remember," I said. "Front steps of the courthouse, all media invited. Accountability, action, and apology. The money in my escrow account before it starts."

"We're past that now," Marcus said.

"In light of what came out today and what will come out tomorrow?" I asked. "That's a decision above your pay grade, Marcus."

I pushed through the gate and headed toward the door under the clock. But then I stopped and turned to them once more.

"Oh, and the number now is fifty-two," I said.

"The last offer was fifty," Marcus said.

"Yeah, but now it's fifty-two. The fifty you offered and the two your boss tried to bribe me with. In escrow, before the press conference, or no deal."

"Bullshit. It'll never happen."

"Somehow, I knew you'd say that. Have a good night, boys. You know where to reach me."

I walked out the courtroom door.

# 48

I WAS HOPING there would be a whole phalanx of media spread across the front steps of the federal courthouse, but only the reporters that had been covering the trial showed up. It was them plus one freelance videographer who had been around for twenty years. I knew him simply as Sticks because he always had a collapsible tripod that he placed his camera on, even though handheld cameras with gyros were the way of the media world now. Sticks might have been old-fashioned and unattached to a specific news channel, but he had solid connections to all the national cable outlets, and that made him the most important media rep in attendance.

I had been hopeful that Victor Wendt would come back down in his G-5 to stand in front of the media, but that was too much to expect from the man who had capitulated to the urging of his lawyers to avoid a possible nine-figure merger-killing verdict. Tidalwaiv would be represented at the press conference by a company damage-control expert named Ellen Bromley as well as by the Mason twins, who would suffer the indignity of facing the media as it was announced that they had settled their case to avoid losing it.

The press conference had been delayed twice as I waited for the money to land in my client escrow account. Wary of Wendt's threat never to pay Brenda Randolph a dime, I would not stand in front of the media and announce the end of the case until the money had been safely delivered to me. Once the wire transmission was confirmed, the media was alerted for a third time and we all gathered on the steps of the courthouse.

Bromley led things off.

"My name is Ellen Bromley. I am head of corporate communications for Wendt Technologies, parent company of Tidalwaiv Technologies LLC. We are here today in the matter of *Randolph versus Tidalwaiv* to announce a conclusion to this case in an equitable settlement for all parties. It is our deepest regret that these events occurred, that a young woman lost her life and a mother lost her only child. Mistakes were made and they have been and will continue to be corrected by the company. This has been a learning experience for the burgeoning industry of artificial intelligence. We must do better. We must do better to protect everyone, but particularly those who are most vulnerable: our children. We failed here and deeply apologize. And we apologize for all previous shortcomings in this groundbreaking work."

I reached up and put my hand on Brenda Randolph's shoulder. She was holding a tissue to her eyes as she heard what she had long waited to hear. Bromley's statement had gone back and forth between all parties several times to be rewritten and edited. It wasn't the full-throated apology I wanted for my client; it was a corporatized mea culpa that tried to claim some sort of victory in failure. But it did contain the one line I'd composed and insisted they include: *We failed here and deeply apologize.*

"The details of the settlement will remain private, as all parties have agreed," Bromley continued. "But we will try to answer a few questions."

The gathered media seemed not to have expected that offer. But I had insisted on it as part of the settlement. At first, no one barked out a question. There was an odd pause and then Sticks finally spoke up.

"You were in the middle of trial," he said. "Why did you settle? Was it not looking good?"

Bromley glanced to her left at the Masons to see if one of them was willing to face the media and the question. Mitchell Mason reluctantly stepped forward.

"In every trial, you are evaluating where you stand every day," he said. "You weigh the risk of going on versus settling. We reached a point where we saw the risk as too high. We decided to settle. The case never went to the jury, so we will never know how a verdict would have gone. The defense never even presented its side."

It sounded like Mitchell was having CSR—case settlement regret. But he had been the one who made the call to me to say *no más* the night before.

"Did Victor Wendt approve the deal?" Sticks asked.

"Uh, Mr. Wendt was part of the discussion that led to the settlement," Mitchell said. "He was very involved in this case. He said from the beginning that if Tidalwaiv was wrong or had somewhere crossed a line, we must own up to it, learn from it, and move on. We are doing that."

*Yeah, right,* I thought as I listened to Mitchell Mason try to cast his client in the glowing light of doing the right thing.

Sticks wasn't finished. He fired one more question at Team Tidalwaiv.

"Is Nathan Whittaker still employed at Tidalwaiv after what was revealed in court yesterday?" he asked.

Bromley took this one, stepping forward and putting a hand on Mitchell's arm before he could speak.

"We will review the testimony from the trial and take appropriate action where needed," she said.

"Can we hear from Mrs. Randolph?" a woman from Channel 5 asked.

I whispered to Brenda, asked if she was up for media questions. She nodded and I guided her to the portable podium, where all the microphones were.

"I know you can't reveal details, but are you happy with the settlement?" the reporter asked.

Brenda wiped her eyes once more and spoke.

"*Happy* is not really a word that I know anymore," she said. "I approved the settlement because it is an acknowledgment by Tidalwaiv of the mistakes made and a resolve to be safer with our technology and our children. To that end, I am announcing that I will be starting a foundation called the Rebecca Randolph Center for Technological Oversight. And the director of the center will be Jack McEvoy, who played a very significant part in this case."

She turned and pointed down the line to Jack, who stood next to me. He gave an embarrassed nod.

"What will the foundation do?" a reporter asked.

"Its mission is to make sure that what happened to my daughter never happens to anyone else's child," Brenda said.

After a few more follow-up questions, the press conference ended and people started to scatter. The Mason brothers walked away without a word to me. Bromley stepped over to me to say that our business was now done, as the money had been paid and the requirement for the public statement had been met.

"Pleasure doing business with you," she said.

"You too," I said.

It was an odd exchange that left me puzzled. I walked over to Sticks to inquire about his plans for the video he had just recorded.

"My first stop is CNN," he said. "Jake Tapper will love this."

"Good," I said. "I've been on with him before. I'm available if needed."

"I'll tell them. And thanks for shooting me the questions to ask. Getting Wendt in there definitely bumps this up a notch."

"Thanks for asking them."

I shook his hand, concealing the five folded hundred-dollar bills I put in his palm. I turned to join Brenda and Jack but was buttonholed by Pete Demetriou from KNX radio. I'd known him since I was a baby lawyer.

"Can I get a quick sound bite, Mick?" he asked.

"Sure, Pete," I said. "Ask away."

"I assume you're getting a big payday?"

"I can't discuss the terms of the settlement."

"Is it fair to say that this is essentially a big win for you and your client?"

"My client is pleased, so that makes me pleased. But, you know, this was never about money. It was about holding Tidalwaiv to account for putting a faulty product into the hands of young people. It was about getting them to own what they'd done and apologize. That's what my client wanted first and foremost. It's what we got, so she is ready to move on with her life and start the foundation."

"Thank you, Mick. What about you? I assume you are making out like a bandit. What's next for you?"

"No comment, Pete. That's all part of the settlement. If I tell you, I blow it, and the deal is gone."

I left him there holding his microphone.

Jack and I walked Brenda to her car in the courthouse garage. She tearfully hugged and thanked us both, telling us that she'd stay in touch and promising the three of us would do good work together. She then drove away to her new life. She was wealthy beyond her dreams but as hollow as a drum.

# 49

THE TEAM MET at the Redbird at a table in the bar. There was champagne for those who wanted to partake and Perrier for me. It was mostly a joyful silence as we reveled in the end of the case. I was used to the criminal side of the ledger, where settlements and plea agreements were made before trial, rarely during. It was also rare for me to experience a win that didn't exactly feel like a win. My client was going home with forty million and change. I was going home with ten and change. And yet there was something underwhelming about it.

"Mickey, you okay?" Lorna asked at one point. "You actually look...well, sad."

"I'm not sad," I insisted. "It's just different, you know? We essentially won the case and got our client a big check and an apology, but it just sort of feels like something's missing."

"Like a verdict?" Cisco said.

I nodded.

"I guess," I said. "Look, we got what we wanted. They admitted their sins in front of the cameras. That's what Brenda was looking for more than anything. That was job one and we did it. The money is the money. It's just a way of keeping score. And speaking of which, you each are getting a million-dollar bonus. Your work —"

"Oh my God!" Lorna said loudly, drawing everyone's attention to our table.

I lowered my voice.

"Your work on the case was exemplary," I said. "Each of you. Amazing. But you'll need to consult with a money manager, because you're going to have to pay taxes on it, and I want to make sure you're prepared for that. When you're ready, I'll transfer the money to you. Happily."

"Boss," Cisco said. "I don't know what to say."

"You don't have to say anything. You did the work, you deserve it. We kicked ass."

"Thank you, Mickey," Lorna said. "I'm going to cry."

"No crying," I said. "It's only money."

I looked at McEvoy.

"The bonus goes to everyone on the team, and that includes you," I said. "And I hope you go out and sell the book for another million."

"You're a generous man," Jack said.

I shook my head.

"The stuff you came up with iced the case," I said. "Now you have to go out there and ensure that the foundation makes a difference. Or none of this was worth it."

"I promise, it will," Jack said. "I already talked to Brenda. There's going to be an advisory board and we want all three of you on it."

I nodded my assent.

"Gladly," Cisco said.

"Can't wait," Lorna said.

My phone buzzed with a text. It was from Sticks. I read it and then reported to the group.

"We need another bottle of champagne," I said. "Sticks says Jake Tapper wants me on his show tomorrow. They're going to run the video from the press conference too."

Cisco extended his hand across the table and there were high fives all around.

"He says they want Brenda on with me," I said. "Jack, can you check with her? Details to come, but it will be tomorrow."

"Is this a remote feed, or are they flying you to DC?" Jack asked.

"Looks like the CNN Building on Sunset," I said.

"That should be doable," Jack said. "I'm sure she'll be up for it."

We lapsed into a comfortable silence after that. Nobody called over a waiter to order a second bottle. Another bottle couldn't erase the regret I think we all felt in settling the case before getting to the finish line.

"Okay, I'll say it," I finally announced. "We should have rolled the dice and taken it to a verdict."

"I don't know, Mick," Cisco said. "You're the one who always says that anything can happen."

"Even if we had won, they would have appealed, and it would have been years before Brenda saw any money and started the foundation," Lorna added. "And now we're all sitting here millionaires."

She held up her glass. She was down to the last swallow.

"To no regrets," she said.

We all held up our glasses and repeated the toast.

"The one thing I wish," Jack said, "is that we had put Wren on the stand. That would have been something."

"I think that was a long shot," I said. "It was probably better as a threat to the Masons than a real possibility."

"But we'll never know," Jack said.

Before I could form a comeback to that, my phone buzzed. It was a call this time and I saw that it was from the district court.

"I'm going to take this," I said.

I got up from the table and walked out to the sidewalk to escape the bar noise. It was Judge Ruhlin's clerk.

"The judge was wondering if she could see you tomorrow morning in chambers," he said.

"Uh, sure," I said. "I mean, no trial, so I'm free. What time?"

"How is nine o'clock for you?"

"I'll be there. Are the Masons invited?"

"No, only you."

"Is this about the contempt order?"

"The judge has also invited a few of the jurors who asked to speak with you. I assume that is okay with you?"

"Uh, sure, I'll talk to them."

"Then we'll see you at nine."

He disconnected before I could ask about the contempt order again. I stood on the sidewalk and thought about the invitation. I was probably going to find out which way the jurors had been leaning when the rug was pulled out from under them. Since they had heard only the plaintiff's side of the case, I assumed they had planned to come down on my side of the equation and were upset that we had settled when they were ready to teach Tidalwaiv a major financial lesson. I assumed the judge would take a few shots at me as well, since we had wasted more than a week of court time before settling the case.

I finally went back inside the bar to tell the others that the case wasn't quite finished yet. The sommelier was opening a second bottle of bubbles. But soon afterward, I left the team there and headed home. I was hoping to get in before Maggie so I could think about what I wanted to say to her about the money I had just made. I planned to tell her that I would rebuild her house if she wanted me to and that I hoped to live in it with her when it was finished. But that of course would be her call, not mine.

I succeeded in getting to the house on Fareholm ahead of her but not ahead of someone else. As I climbed the stairs to the front door, I saw a man sitting, his back to me, on one of the bar-height director chairs turned toward the view of the city below. His black suit and silver hair made him easily recognizable.

"So you came down after all," I said as I approached. "I didn't see you at the press conference."

Victor Wendt turned to look at me.

"I didn't come down for the press conference," he said.

I nodded and gestured toward the view.

"You heard about the sunsets up here," I said.

"Actually, I came to see you," he said.

"If you're going to tell me you stopped the wire and my client will never see a dime, you're too late."

"No, not at all. The money's yours. And your client's. I consider fifty million dollars an acceptable fee for doing business."

I nodded as I realized that he had come to gloat about avoiding a more expensive verdict.

"Fifty-two million, actually, but who's counting," I said. "Except maybe your board of directors."

"Yes, I will have to explain to them how we chose the lesser of two evils," Wendt said. "I'm sure they will understand."

"Then, what can I do for you, Mr. Wendt? I'm sure you didn't come here to rehearse your speech to the board."

"No, and I appreciate that you didn't invite me to get the fuck off your porch. I came to make you an offer."

"An offer? Like the last time we met? I'd say that was more of a bribe."

"This is purely a business offer. I want to hire you, Mr. Haller."

Wendt reached into his jacket and pulled a folded document out of the pocket.

"Hire me?" I said, trying to hide my surprise.

"This is a two-year contract for your services," Wendt said. "Two point six million dollars per year for your legal advice on an as-needed basis. You'll never have to step into a courtroom or be the lawyer of record on any legal action. Just a personal contract between you and me. I hope you will accept it."

He handed me the document and I unfolded it. I scanned it quickly and immediately understood what it was and what it meant. A high-end buyout.

"You want to make sure I never sue you again," I said. "Or at least not for the next two years, while you try to resuscitate whatever's left of your merger after today."

I started to refold the contract while doing the math.

"Fifty thousand a week to stay on the sidelines," I said. "That's very generous of you, Mr. Wendt."

"I can assure you there will be more work than standing on the sidelines," Wendt said.

I held the contract out to him.

"I don't know if I'll ever sue you again," I said. "I'm sure there will be opportunities, especially after this case. In fact, I'm going to be on CNN tomorrow, and that will probably help get me a few clients. But I can't take your money, Mr. Wendt. If I did, I think I'd be lost. As a lawyer and as a man."

He reached out and took the contract. He nodded as he put it back into his inside coat pocket.

"I thought I had to try," he said. "Is this where you tell me to get the fuck off your porch?"

I nodded.

"Pretty much," I said. "I'd appreciate it if you would do just that."

Wendt stood up and glanced out at the view as if seeing it for the first time.

"Sunset should be nice tonight," he said.

"It usually is," I said.

He nodded and headed to the steps. He pulled a phone as he went down and I heard him tell someone that he was ready. I stayed out on the porch. I saw a black Escalade pull up, and one of the bodyguards I recognized from the warehouse visit got out and opened a rear door. Wendt got in and I watched the sleek Cadillac glide silently down the hill.

I don't think I'd ever felt better about turning down money in my life.

# 50

**THE SAYING GOES** that some days you eat the bear and other days the bear eats you. And sometimes it happens all in the same day. Sometimes the same hour.

I survived the meeting with Judge Ruhlin and four jurors from the case undamaged. The jurors had all been my picks and I had picked well. They told me they had been ready to drop the bricks on Tidalwaiv.

"You had them on the ropes," said the set builder. "I was ready to lower the boom on them. What they did with that girl was so wrong. And so sad for that mother. The judge says the settlement is kept secret, but I hope they paid her the big bucks."

I appreciated the comments but knew the jurors had heard only one side of the case. That kept things in perspective, at least for me.

But what made me leave the courthouse feeling like I had eaten the bear happened after the judge excused the jurors. That was when she said the magic words to me.

"Mr. Haller, you are welcome in my court anytime."

Like Santana's opening guitar riff in "Jingo," those words put a jolt of electricity straight down my spine. I lost my cool and smiled. I told her I looked forward to the next time.

"There is also the matter of the contempt citation," the judge said. "I believe that I will continue to hold that in abeyance. You're free to go now, Mr. Haller."

"Thank you, Judge," I said.

It was when I stepped out into the sun, onto the steps where the day before I had basked in a fifty-two-million-dollar win, that I got caught by the bear. My phone buzzed as I put on my sunglasses. The screen told me that the call was from the California Health Care Facility in Stockton.

But it wasn't a collect call from David Snow.

"Mickey Haller," I said.

"Michael Haller?" a male voice asked. "The attorney?"

"Yes, that's me. How can I help you?"

"This is Sergeant Tamar at CHCF Stockton. You are the attorney of record for inmate David Francis Snow?"

"Yes, that's right."

"It's my duty to inform you that David Francis Snow expired this morning in the medical facility here."

I was silent as I registered the news.

"Expired?" I said, finding my voice. "What do you mean, 'expired'? The doctors said he had nine months."

"I'm not a doctor, sir," Tamar said. "I'm in administration. You will have to get the details from the attending physicians. I am only informing you of the death. I am told he died peacefully in the medical center at eleven eleven this morning. That is all the information I have."

"How do I reach the attending physicians?"

"I can give them the message if you wish."

"Yes, do that. Please. Ask them to call me."

"Are you in communication with the inmate's next of kin? We have her listed here as Cassandra Snow, a daughter, in Los Angeles."

"Yes, I'm in communication with her. She's my client."

"Would you like me to inform her, or will you handle it?"

"No, I'll do it."

"Are you sure, sir?"

"I'm sure."

"Should further communication about arrangements for the body go through you or the daughter?"

I didn't answer. I was thinking about Cassandra.

"Sir?" Tamar prompted.

"Uh, yes," I said. "All communications can go through me. I'll handle things."

"Okay, sir. I will relay your message to the medical center. Thank you for your time, and sorry for your loss."

"Right. Thanks."

Tamar disconnected and I stood there with the phone held to my ear for a long moment.

The reality was that, in the short time since Cassandra had come to me, there was no way I could have gotten her father out. But that didn't matter. He should never have been in. And that was on me. I knew it as surely as I knew that the victory of the previous day was mine as well.

I put away the phone and started down the steps to the street.

Nobody bats a thousand. Nobody wins every case. The law is fickle. You're prince of the city one day, a street sweeper the next. The skill is being able to get back in the Lincoln, buckle up, and drive on.

But this one was different. This one hurt. I knew that my failure of two decades before was going to continue to haunt me. There would be no redemption. My own house was burning now, burning to the ground.

I headed down the street. I had to go to Cassandra. I had to tell her. I had to take responsibility. And I had to find the resolve to take this punch and then get up and fight another day.

## ACKNOWLEDGMENTS

The author greatly acknowledges and thanks those who helped with the research and writing of this book. They include Asya Muchnick, Bill Massey, Tracy Roe, Betsy Uhrig, Pamela Marshall, Dan Daly, Roger Mills, Jane Davis, Heather Rizzo, Dennis Wojciechowski, Shannon Byrne, Jeff Pitman, Linda Connelly, Callie Connelly, and Devin Connelly.

While this is a work of fiction, the author learned much and drew inspiration from the pleadings in the *Megan Garcia v. Character Technologies* lawsuit filed in the US District Court for the Middle District of Florida.

# ABOUT THE AUTHOR

MICHAEL CONNELLY is the author of forty previous novels, including *New York Times* bestsellers *Nightshade, The Waiting, Resurrection Walk,* and *Desert Star*. His books, which include the Harry Bosch series, the Lincoln Lawyer series, and the Renée Ballard series, have sold more than eighty-nine million copies worldwide. Connelly is a former newspaper reporter who has won numerous awards for his journalism and his novels. He is the executive producer of four television series: *Bosch, Bosch: Legacy, The Lincoln Lawyer,* and *Ballard*. He spends his time in California and Florida.